LADY OF ROSES & RUIN

AN EMPIRE OF WOLVES NOVEL

COURTNEY SHACK

Lady of Roses and Ruin

Published by Griffin Wing Press LLC

Cover Design by bestselling-covers.com by David Gardias

ISBN (paperback): 979-8-9893477-0-4

AISN: B0C1NY8Z5D

For my love.
Beyond darkness, beyond doubt, beyond death.
No Witch King would ever need to force me into marriage to you. I can't wait
to spend the rest of our lives together.

CONTENT WARNINGS

This book discusses the terminal illness of a parent, death, themes of grief and loss, contains violence (gore), and explicit sexual content. This is the first of a planned series. As ever, please take care when reading.

The Gods may set down the pieces, but They rely on the princesses, the villains, the blacksmiths, and the witches to move Their Will into play.

See then, O, Pious One, that you do as you're told.

-High Reaper Priest Xater of the Dead One's Order of the Seven

PART I
THE LINE OF FATE

If thy word be gold, may thy tongue be silver.
—Old Lumari Proverb

CHAPTER 1

BOY

oy snarls, leaping toward Father. The man ducks to the other side of the oaken desk. Boy pauses. Cocks his head like a wolf listening to what's on the wind. Another rake of agony slices through his body and he crouches. Whimpers.

Inside, two Beings battle for Boy's flesh. For his soul. A ripple slides across his chest. Boy wants to clutch his heart, but he doesn't. But, oh, it hurts, hurts. They hurt him.

Erebos, an ancient creature beyond description except for the hide like a pool of rippling midnight and a taste for blood. And the other. Ghost. A hateful, cursed wolf spirit—he prefers souls. Neither good and neither should win. But one of them will. One of them must.

The Beings inside of Boy leap to one another. Clawing. Erebos lands atop Ghost. Erebos crows a victory, a howl like a scream. A fang snags and rips down Ghost's fur. Pain. A world of pain.

On Boy's chest, a brutal mark slices the skin apart. Pomegranate red bursts from his flesh. Iron perfumes the air as bright rust stains his shirt. He smells his own blood. Saliva drips in his mouth. Boy screams. His stomach gurgles. The temptation of his own ichor fills his mind as much as the torturous spirits do.

"Which will win? Wolf or man?" Boy's father asks behind his desk. Fear shakes the older man's voice. Father never asks the right questions. He never has.

Rabid, animal agony contorts Boy's bones. Something cracks. Leaks.

Boy will not win, even if he survives long enough to call himself Man. It is a matter of which monster will be victorious. It always has been.

Father flinches when Boy's nose lifts to the air, just like a dog. Boy smells the stink of fear. It smells almost as good as the red pain at his ribs.

Boy falls to his knees and looks at Father, who simply stares in hopeless surrender. Boy knows Father loves him, but Boy also knows that the man's hand rests on the pommel of his sword. Just in case. Father's palm spasms against the weapon. Boy meets his gaze. Father doesn't move an inch except for the scared ticking of his hand on the sword and the jitter of the vein in his forehead.

Boy says nothing. Hunger, pain. His tongue snakes across the back of his knuckles again, licking a fleck of the redness from it. The taste reminds him of coins. Agony shivers through his flesh, scraping angry marks in ragged arcs. The wounds burn. He ignores their acute throb. The boy learns early to ignore the suffering in his heart and body. It is the only way to survive.

Instead, he turns. Father's breath huffs like a gale, high and loud. The terror stinking in the room makes Boy hungry. His stomach pinches. Wet drips down his chest in acidic torment.

Guided by the Beings, some primitive instinct, he pounces on the whisper of movement behind him. Blood soaks his tunic and he turns.

In his mouth, is a dead, bleeding rat.

When he looks at Father, Boy's eyes pool edge to edge in an inky abyss. Boy smiles and the dead thing drops out from his lips onto the floor. His teeth are stained red with blood.

He howls.

CHAPTER 2

onight, I'm here to die a little.

The moon bleeds overhead. It always does this time of year. The strange celestial light stains the ramparts, casting gray stone as scarlet as gore, as if yet another battle has taken place. *Skirmishes,* they call them. Like these disagreements haven't resulted in our people screaming until death frees them from the pain the Wolves bring.

I slip through shadows, silent as the black panther gliding ahead of me on the cobblestoned street. Nisha tosses a glance in my direction. Muscles ripple beneath her dark fur, soaking in the deep midnight. The cat's eyes glint like silver blades before they find a home in flesh. *Come on, Briar,* the look says. She slinks ahead. I follow. My cloak slides around me in a spill of dark ink.

Up and down the wall, soldiers trek a tight line. Banners flap overhead, their sound muffled by the wind. Leather bound swords hang in scabbards, creaking eerily. It's strange to think that our enemy worships the same gods that we do and that our sacred nights might align. It's not as if our values do.

It's the Red Season. A month where the world is painted scarlet, day and night. Only the first week of this uncanny light means anything, though—a supposed peace, a celebration during this holy week as we mark the favor of the gods. The smell of warmed sugar curls through the air, but underneath it the scent of old violence and stringent alcohol sours my palette. Fear skitters through my shaking hands and I clench them. The edges of my nails bite little half-moons into my skin. Tonight is not the festivity for me that it is for many others.

This night should be joyful, with no waiting soldiers on the wall, but all we do on the border is wait.

Tension winds my shoulders tight and my fingers spasm around the handle of my ax. The grain shifts against my palm —polished wood, from the vesperi tree. Many things the tree is known for, but the only one that matters is that it grows ever-stronger when fed blood. My ax is hungry.

A howl rises up from beyond the forest line on the southside of the wall. A chorus of six or seven follows in reply. It's hard to say if the call is from the Cursed men—the half human, half beastly enemies that call themselves Wolves—or the actual animal. They sound so similar in the deep night.

The far-off cry kills any easiness we might have had outside amongst the summer nights during the Saytr Feasts. I wonder if those partaking in the salacious festivities down by the square hear it. Doubtful. Restraint is something Berrat House is known for, except for when our gods turn their eyes from us. Then we make up for the days spent in pious prayer. The Red Season is a time the gods let us discard our righteousness for something more pleasurable.

The Satyr Feasts are weeklong parties full of summer spirits, sex, and risqué dancing. Not that I would have been allowed to be there, regardless of the rabid Wolves stalking the perimeter.

Near the border, the solemn air stills. The guards pause their pacing along the stoned ramparts and settle their palms to weapons. Jealousy burgeons on the wall, mutters of discontent slipping between companions. Everyone would rather be fucking and feasting, myself included. I swallow, a dribble of moisture slipping down my brow and sliding to my cheek. I don't feel resentment, though. No, terror beats a frantic tattoo under my breast bone and sweat slicks my back.

The wolf calls fade, but the tension doesn't. The sound comes again, this time more distant. Eerie light filters through the leaves of the titan-like trees on the other side of the wall. Little hairs on my arms rise in salute to the sound and I shiver. It's summer, but something about the air freezes the marrow in my bones.

Part of me clamors to go back, to go to bed. But I don't.

The dark scares me; it has ever since I can remember. And even the memories I don't have, something must have made me fear the deep blanket of night. Shadows hide wretched things, ugly monsters. All I want is light, but that will get me seen.

This is too important to let something as inconsequential as fear keep me from doing what is necessary. Papa needs me. The look of death across his wasted face earlier today—his sunken eyes like pits of despair—curdles my stomach. Pain visibly creases deep divots in his now-downturned mouth and splinters across his brow. The idea of seeing it tomorrow, again—it's too much to bear. I don't know how the world doesn't notice, but perhaps they assume it's the stress of keeping our southern border strong against the Wolves and sending our best men to the northern war effort.

The man who tended my skinned knees, taught me to wield an ax, and read me stories of maidens overcoming monsters is *dying*. What's more, it's a slow, painful demise that no one deserves.

Whatever has happened in the last decade, I can't let anything happen to Papa. An ache cracks my heart, but I shove the feeling away.

I move.

The moon hangs like a fat, rusted coin and the wind smells salty, as if tears ride it. But there's no time for weakness, and we are too far from the sea. Red season is a time to stay inside, except for the Satyr Feasts. The strange light touching one's skin directly promises misfortune. Almost as much as drawing someone else's blood on a night like tonight. Light catches the faces of two of the guards nearby, giving a demonic pall to their features.

Now *that* is ill luck.

I pull my hood higher over my face, partly out of superstition and partly out of practicality. The well-made cloth weighs as little as a feather and brushes my skin the way my mother's hand might have long ago—comforting and safe, barely there at all.

"Blood on the moon, blood in the wood." One of the guards sighs. The phrase sounds tired, as if it's been used over and over again. She crosses herself in a lazy X at her throat. I frown. Our morale is lower than I thought.

The gods decreed that there would be no violence during the Red Season.But then again, these folks have been ordered to guard the wall during nights of supposed peace.

The green uniform of a Bear Knight silhouettes in the distance, like an emerald smear that pops like a bright leaf in a pool of gore atop the wall. I'm not sure who it is, but I have no urge to find out. If they see my face or my stark, silvered hair, I'll be sent straight back to my rooms and locked away. This time, they'd probably place someone next to my bed to make sure I can't slip out, perhaps for the rest of my life.

I pause for a moment, the voices of the guards lulling over me, as my eyes track with cat-like precision the movement of the person half a mile away. An itch skritches across my skin, like they're staring directly at me.

Whoever it is, they slide away. The feeling of being watched doesn't.

"Aye," the guard's companion says, mirroring her gesture.

Another X. *I'm dead*, the gesture means. Dark-bearded and burly, the man reminds me of Barro, my only friend, and his twin, Valor.

Nisha protests, pressing something between a growl and a purr into my mind.

My only human *friend*, I amend.

The guard's fingers brush the hair on his neck as he makes the X again. Once, twice, thrice. My own throat itches, as if the skin begs me to mimic the killing gesture. It's superstitious nonsense. The itch increases, a near burn, but I push the impulse away.

This is not a time to be a little girl, waiting for a faerie tale to happen to her, scared of made up monsters. I'm a woman grown—ax in one hand and dagger at my hip. Little Briar might have waited in fear, but I am years past childhood. Red night or no, whatever blood wets my hands will be necessary and will feed both the appetite of my ax and my own.

I don't have time for folk tales. And certainly don't have time to get caught. But the gods love their games; even if they don't look tonight, and I can't help but wonder if fate tugs the air. A lone woman on a red night, trekking into the forest with her magical cat. It has the smack of an ancient tale and everyone knows that the gods love their stories.

Nisha sits somewhere ahead— a silent shadow, waiting.

"The Witch King Hisself will be here soon," the guard says casually, spitting out of the corner of his mouth. It lands in a wet plop at his feet. Along with it, a silver coin falls from his lips—thick and slick. He doesn't notice it. The silver drops, flipping over on its way down, and evaporates before impact.

I ignore it, like I usually do. Metal slips from their lips as they continue to talk. My gaze slides past the worthless money falling from their mouths. No one else knows of my illicit-magic, and I've never had anyone to confess my secrets to— besides Nisha and the ghost of my long-gone mother.

After a lifetime of this, though, it's easy to tell even from this far away the type of coin. Tin, silver, the rare gold. Often, inconsequential copper. But the guards believe they're saying important things— words about the movement of kings and nations and omens. Copper won't do.

The woman gives a nod. "Ain't a good sign it's during a blood moon. As if he ain't safe at another time." A flash of silver again. "Makes Lumar look weak."

"Not a good sign at all," I say under my breath. My stomach clenches. The war with Selva on the northern front steals all our good men and sends them back in boxes. If they're sent back at all. The Wolves of House Galibran choose to fight *my* people instead of our true enemy at the border. They keep their best fighters to themselves, the lumber from the war effort, and defy our king at every moment.

Worse, they kill those of my House in *our own territory* in an attempt to land-grab more for themselves. They are parasites. Evil, bloodsucking, flea-ridden vermin.

What's more, they're cursed.

I keep walking, sliding through the deep black that slips around me like water as a piping rage fills me. I have to get to the forest. Time is running out. It always is.

The guards' figures fade further away as they trek up the stairs leading to the top of the wall. It looms like a monster from beyond Ash Mountain. Tall, with vines spider webbing across its face, it protects us from the wood and from the wild wolves of both the canine and the ill-fated human variety. It keeps out supernatural tricksters, the last of the fae, and failed gods. The green uniform that watched from above is gone. I sigh in short-lived relief.

A migraine ticks in the back of my mind, the strain of incessant use of my magical sight pulling on my consciousness. I'll pay for this little adventure later, though the cost will come in too many ways to count.

I haven't been beyond the wall, at least not alone. First, I need to get up this giant thing, without being seen. Then the real danger starts.

Fear licks my insides and fills me up. What am I even doing? The muscles below my breastbone clench. This is stupid. Even if I make it out there and over the tree line, the wood might take me for prey and I'll be dead anyways.

But going back isn't an option.

I tighten my fist over the polished handle at my side. So many things ride on me succeeding here, so many lives. Whether my House knows it or not, everything we are—everything we have—balances on the edge of an ax's blade. And I'm holding it steady, trying to ease my father's pain and stalling his early death the only way I can think of.

If the Duke of House Galibran dies, the Wolves will feast on what is left of us. The border dispute will become a civil war, Wolf fighting Bear, and conscription to the northern border to fight the *real* war will halt from our provinces. Other duchies will be forced to choose sides, and the Ash Mountain territory will be lost. The temple of the Seven Orders, fallen. The gods enraged. The Bears will be left with not only blood-soaked land, if we're lucky, but a hated heir to preside over the shit show.

Me.

I'll make sure that doesn't happen. Even if the Bears never truly trusted me to begin with, it doesn't matter. Loyalty is loyalty, and being a Bear is bred into the bone.

I sidle up to the wall. The stairs disappear into the vine-ridden stone, and I disappear along with them, going as far as I can before an itch at my shoulders jerks me into paranoid movement. I hop the last few steps before swinging myself to the side. I pause. Waiting.

If I succeed, ultimately I am promised an early grave. Fear heightens my senses, and I wrangle in a gasping breath. Death isn't something most pray for, and I am no different. But if splicing my life into fractions guarantees my father will live longer, I don't care.

I can't even see the cursed trees on the other side. I pull upward, craning my head back to look at the endless wall that separates me from the forest. From what is to come. Each reach upward is careful, because the woods aren't the only vile thing. This wretched climb and the magic-infused vines is too.

The Shadow Wood is a fickle, dangerous place filled with blaspheming fae, brutal creatures, and trees the color of coagulated blood. If the spirits of the forest accept my offering, it will only be three miles into the White Wood instead of ten.

Then I'll be in enemy territory.

Each pull up the wall feels like it takes an hour. Time isn't something I have in abundance, so I hope the forest is kind to me tonight and my journey is short.

I'm not built for climbing, or even for adventure. I'm built for the comfort of my bed. Despite my ax, I am no soldier. Just another woman completing a task that I have no other choice but to do.

Familiar dread nests in my chest, as if I've become a home for it to grow up and grow old inside of me. I am so tired of being afraid.

Spritelight flickers in the distance. The glow gulps parts of the dark. I ease out a slow exhale, hoping it doesn't sense me. Spritelights are dead spirits, usually people who were killed violently, named after their bright, fae lookalike. There are a lot of spirits like this these days at the border between House Berrat and House Galibran. They swarm to the living like mosquitoes. The restless dead crave nothing but life.

The desperate orb shivers, as if it is both a piece of captured moonlight and moth in one. It moves closer. Closer, then it bobs just at my elbow.

"Whoever you are, go back to the afterlife," I mutter, shooing it. It continues to hang there, moving up and down. My gut twists and I look around. Gods *damn* this spirit to the fetid Otherland. I don't need it chasing after me, lighting me up like a pipe for the guards around the corner to see. I need to get over the wall, through the wood, steal what I came for, and get back.

Nisha's disapproval pecks at the back of my mind. I pretend it's not there.

I've never snuck out, but I have scaled this wall. The vines are slung across the stone to cover traps laid by our priests. My fists sweat, making it difficult to cling as I give myself another boost toward the top. During the day, this would be easy. But it also would have been impossible.

I just hope I don't grab a vine that will eat my hand.

Nisha purs, then vaporizes as she walks straight through the wall. Her thoughts press against my mind, urgent and irritated.

"Yeah, some of us aren't magical cats." I grumble.

Prickly cold plant flesh itches my skin as I hoist myself upward. Scents of green vegetation, roses, and freshly peeled oranges follow me as I move steadily toward the top. A vine hisses near me and I jerk a toe away from it.

Shit, that's a cursed bit, there.

"What's that?" A startled voice cracks out.

The call is from somewhere to my left. The spritelight follows me; this time, it tickles my hair. I freeze, flattening myself as tightly as possible into the wall. My biceps tick and strain. My lungs squeeze, but I dare not breathe too loudly. They're close. I can *smell* the tobacco on one and the sweet peach scent of another. One too-loud breath will fuck me, fuck this mission, fuck *us all*. And my father will die the slowest, most painful death, all because I couldn't control one godsdamned exhale.

My boot slips against a vine. *Shit.* A chill lips at my calf, curling downward. I grit my teeth. The cold tooths at me, trying to find a way in. The frozen temperature deepens, warming until it becomes fire. It fucking hurts. Bright heat slices into my ankle through my leather boot and I fight the urge to scream. Wetness pools in my shoe.

My foot is in a trap. One that wants to eat me. Shit, shit, shit.

"I thought I saw something."

"It's just a fucking spritelight, Ron. The dead are everywhere." Fucking Ron. *Leave.* Sweat drips at my brow. The burn of my chest intensifies. I want to yank my foot away from the thing slowly trying to gnaw my boot off.

"But—"

The nerves in my leg screech in mute agony. Fuck, fuck.

"It's a holy night. The Wolves may be monsters, but they're not heretics."

Agree to disagree.

In a way, the Wolves are the reason my foot is stuck here. And yet, fool that I am, I'm going straight into their den.

The trap plasters against my ankle. Snake-like and ridged and damp with my blood. It isn't just the pain. This wall, if left too long, will sweep me inside of it as punishment for trespassing. My heart races. I'm not a brave woman, I'm simply what I have to be. Alive. Moving forward. And I don't want my soul to be sucked into the wall to power the snares that eat people.

The guards meander away.

The vine curls up my thigh. It pauses. Pulses.... I wonder if it's listening, hearing the instructions the arcane priests coded into it. *Kill the witch*, I imagine it says.

Well, fuck that. I twist the vine around in my fist, grinding my molars together, feet still digging into the wall. My arm strains with my weight. Heat prickles my hand, dotting through my pores as my palm glows a faint pink. Bright smoke plumes from it, sparkling like cursed faerie dust.

"*Light*," I mutter. Radiance bursts from my hand in a short, hot flare. I slam it onto my thigh. The trap squeals. It squeezes me like it wants to cut off my circulation. I press down harder, willing the flame all the way through. My limbs burn, but I silence the pained sound between my teeth and transform it into a hiss. I'm not the only one in pain.

A keening, loud screech sounds at my leg as my fire singes the trap. Fuck.

It releases me, and I waste no time. I climb down the rest of the way and drop to the other side the last ten feet.

The impact vibrates up my bones, jolting my ankles and knee joints.

Dead God's teeth. I hiss through a grimace, rubbing my calves down to my toes and prepare to run to the edge of the forest instead of remaining in the open where the guards can easily see me.

The night air smells violent, as if the wind carries the promise of future battles on its tendrils.

"There's something *there!*"

I lower myself and halt, as immobile as a slab of granite. Right now I probably look like a blob of a bush. Hopefully. The cover of trees is a little ahead. I could sprint, but they would see me. Easily. The moon grins high above, lighting up everything like the Flaming Heretic from the stories. I hold myself frozen, poised on the balls of my feet, knees bent. It might not be a good idea to run, but if they see me, I'll have no choice.

"Probably a fucking faerie, Ron. It's the Shadow Wood. The Dark One's asshole. Either a faerie or a Wolf. Regardless, it's shit. Unless it attacks first, we let it go."

"Wolves. Whiny, crying bitches." The other guard laughs with bravado. Their silhouettes still line the wall above me. One leaves, footsteps clipping into the distance. The other stays. Ron, again. I'm playing a game now, waiting him out. A crack of a branch under my heel or the catch of a ray of red light could be enough to end it all.

"They know better than to try us tonight," he says to himself. *Loudly.* The words smack of lies.

Blood pounds in my ears. My leg aches where the trap bit into me. I count my heartbeats, wondering with each one if it's the last before I'm caught.

One. *Is this it?* Two. *Am I done?* Three. *Are we all done?* My thighs are just beginning to burn from holding the squat when idiot Ron finally turns on his heel and disappears.

I let out a breath, air whooshing freely from my lungs for what feels like the first time tonight. Miles stretch ahead of me, but with a little luck, magic, and a bit of blood, the world will fold itself the way I ask. I send up a prayer to Amara, to Vix, to every god and goddess of the Seven Orders and then some. *Be at my back,* I beg. I will need every scrap of goodwill the world can offer me.

I move deeper into the forest, scouting for the tree with purple buds. Everything looks different tonight, every wooden trunk could be the color of dark blood in the cavernous midnight.

Ten minutes pass before I find it. A carved bear with an X slashed through it marks the thick oak, deep grooves scarring the timber. The message is clear—don't come here, Bears. Plum-colored, unbloomed flowers curl up the side of the trunk. From there, I walk due south, ignoring the warning meant for me and anyone affiliated with House Berrat. A growing unease settles in my ribs, but I shake it off as much as I can. Nisha moves ahead, evidently confident in our direction. A series of images flash in my mind—of her, Nisha, leading me. Of her, killing a wolf-dog. Of her, lapping up milk near my bed with a flickering, pink tongue. I roll my eyes.

"Yes," I say, a laugh rolling up from my belly, "I'll follow you and then we'll be home."

[Good.] Her feline voice purrs in my head, vibrating pleasantly.

The woodland thickens, turgid coils swirl into the grooves of the bark. Though this forest sits at the edge of my House's southern edge, I don't know it like I do the Elkane Forest that rims the northern border of our territory. The Shadow Wood sets my teeth on edge. Heinous monsters live here, Cursed creatures ready to grab anyone in their path. The blasphemed fae, rejected from their courts in Otherland, a continent away, across the Sea of Mist. The cursed men of the House Galibran. The restless dead. The bastards of gods. Ancient powers best left undisturbed. Even a few of the twisted chimeras invented by the northern tyrant. Anything could be here. The old tales all whisper that the Shadow Wood holds a dark evil. And the Wolves and their violent lord want to protect it.

Something snorts.

My shoulders tense, but I move forward, hoping it's my ride into the enemy's territory. I slip past the branches, and the dappled hide of a jittery mare comes into view.

Nisha pads forward, unconcerned, and sits next to the horse. The mare is tethered to a tree, eyes white as pearls and rolling with fear. Nisha rakes her claws against the mulched forest floor, clearly mocking the creature. The mare's nostrils flare wide enough to fit three hands inside.

"Shhh," I comfort, sliding my hand along her mane. "Nisha, move away."

Nisha prances off with what I imagine is a sniff of disdain. I wait until she's out of sight before mounting the mare.

The man I paid left the creature just where we agreed. Leather creaks beneath me as I settle into the saddle. Nisha reappears in the distance, further away.

The bark of the trees remains brown as we continue. I frown, looking toward the moon. I'm not sure what the hour is, sometime well after midnight. I've a long way to go and even longer to get back. I just hope the wood is on my side tonight.

Follow the line. Straight through. The rasp of the dead stalks me, the same spritelight dipping by my shoulder. Though we've done our best to burn or bury our deceased, the occasional bone pokes out from the dark soil. Lit by the moonlight, the ivory color appears as a blushing maiden. A skull sits vigil on a passing rock, and I can only imagine that its dark sockets watch me with disapproval. Every bit of the dead is cleaned, free of flesh. I white-knuckle the reins. Fuck, fuck, fuck.

Each twitch of a leaf makes me flinch. I inhale, but it dispels not one iota of my unease. Something has been here to eat our dead. In a forest like this, it is too much to ask that it was a simple animal. Too much to ask that such a creature doesn't gain *something* from picking every ounce of meat from our fallen.

The hairs on my neck rise. I can't see Nisha, but she brushes against my mind to comfort me. Still. Despite the fact she'll run back and claw whatever evil thing might crawl out of the dirt—whether long dead or recently, whether monster or man—I can't help but choke on my own rancid terror.

With one hand I grip the reins, with the other my ax. "I will drink your blood," I mutter to imaginary foes. "I will sip it in *ecstasy*." My hand sweats. The dry crack of a dead branch splits through the air. I squeak.

A squirrel runs out, a fat nut gripped in its tiny hands.

I let out a soft laugh. My shoulders shake. And I'm *crying*. Tears slither down my cheeks and I have no idea what I'm feeling, except that I'm crazy. This is crazy. I am just—

Another snap of a twig. The little fuzzy creature moves closer. The squirrel cocks its head and...smiles? Little razor teeth glint red as it gazes at me.

Then two wings burst out of its back, as big as twin loaves of bread and just as thick. Veins pulse in grayed death. It's highly unusual that such a creature would be here, south of Ash Mountain.

The thing launches itself at me, arms outstretched, with red eyes like a vampyr. *Chimera.*

"Fucker!" I yell, brandishing my ax. My horse jerks, flattening her ears. Her hoof digs at the earth in agitation.

The wings give the chimera the lift it needs to sail into my face. The edge of my blade catches the squirrel monster, nicking its corded wing. It cries out, fumbling its nut. The snack drops to the ground. Blood leaks from the chimera-squirrel's wound and it titters, leaving a trail of red behind it. It grabs its nut and disappears into the brush.

I let out a shuddering breath. I can handle myself after all. But my nerves are destroyed. Lady Briar, scared of a squirrel. A fucked-up squirrel, but not anything I can ever tell anyone about.

You won't make it. Not without more. The thought spins and spins, unyielding.

"Don't do it," I whisper to myself. But I can't let it go.

Even though it's a bad idea to do this in the Shadow Wood, even though I shouldn't be here at all, even though I should go home and just accept the natural course of life—I don't do any of those things. Fear is nothing when love is on the line. My fingers tremble as I use the metal latch on the saddle, sawing it across my finger. I wince, but a bead of blood blooms bright like a rose. Between thumb and forefinger, I squeeze, and the drop of red falls to the floor.

I've no milk to accompany the blood. At least no offering right here. The storybooks say the fae view it as a nice gesture and are less likely to cause trouble. Sometimes, though, the only thing you have to bring to the table is your blood and your willpower.

For a moment, the forest hushes.

My shoulders squeeze, tensing against the sudden quiet. It could be anything—Nisha, the fucking squirrel. But it could also be something worse, something more predatory that has set the teeth of the wood on edge. My wooden ax handle grinds against the skin of my palm as I fist my weapon. It drinks thirstily from my finger, reddening in starved bloodlust.

Another crack. The squirrel is probably back. I ready my ax—

"Now, my lady, are you asking to be killed?" A smoky voice calls. A sound of surprise slips through my lips before I can stop it. The already skittish horse flinches underneath me and rears.

No, no, *no*—

All I see is the bright moon as the mare leans back. Stars flicker like dead spritelight.

The horse dumps me from the saddle. I fall backwards and everything slows. Skeletal tree limbs above leak maroon light between thin fingers. The smell of iron fills my nose, and I wonder where it comes from. A part of me whispers it's my power, the fae gaze that gives me the truth of it all, spiking the feeling of prophecy through me. Violence waits.

The world pulls to a pinprick and my body cracks against the ground. Sharp agony flares *everywhere.*

My chances of saving us all evaporate into nothing as the horse flees into the wood. The image of Papa's dying eyes dance in my mind. The silhouette of a tall, armed man fractures through my vision and everything stains black.

The wolves in the distance scream.

CHAPTER 3

$\mathcal{P}$ain drums its fingers at my temples. Insistent. Pattering. Annoying. *Hard.* The cloying sweetness of the Shadow Wood surrounds me, as if someone is stuffing a sticky bun of sugar and rot into my nose and holding it there. Nausea claws up my throat, and I turn over and retch.

A hand grabs at the back of my neck, gathering my hair and lifting it from my face.

My stomach squeezes out my dinner, a mixture of bile and half-digested chicken. I wipe my mouth with the back of my hand and turn around to glare at the person who held my hair.

"Barro." I squint. "Valor." It's impossible to tell them apart. At least right now.

At the second name, another figure peels itself from the darkness. The twins are both here, looming over my disgraced self like curious gilded birds. A whirl of feelings swirl inside of my stomach— anger, relief, irritation, anxiety, each battling for dominance.

As usual, anxiety comes out on top. I grit my teeth and scowl, pressing a hand against my abdomen as if I can stop the sick swell of fear there. Time is running out. Tonight is the only night this part of my plan will work—even if it's built on a bedrock of flimsy stories.

Both the twins sport ash-blonde hair, void-intense eyes, and cheeky grins. Identical white scars line their right cheeks, hooking into their mouths like fish. How they managed that, I never asked. Their walks paced the same length, so they could match each other stride for stride. Both intelligent men vacated House Ferr, pledged fealty to my father, and rose up the ranks in months rather than the years it might take others. Sharp-witted and handsome, only they themselves could tell each other apart. With one exception.

I cock my head to the side, eyes sliding over the slant of his shoulders, the curve of his brow. Something in the dip of his mouth, the way the light hit his eyes. But that isn't the way to tell them apart. "Barro," I finally say.

He smiles. "Yes, milady?" A coin slips through his mouth. Dull and worthless.

I turn to the other twin. "There you are, Barro." The other man's expression—Valor's—twists into a glare.

"How did you know?" Valor asks.

"A feeling," I reply. And magic. Where Barro spoke words of silver and copper, Valor spat out tin. Lies.

Not all the time. Sometimes not even often. But where Barro would not lie to me, Valor would do it for fun.

Barro laughs, a good-natured sound as he steps closer and slings an arm around my shoulders. "Briar, Lady Briar," he says, his voice nearly singsong. "We have come to escort you back from this ill-fated decision."

"I decline." I stretch. Pain stabs my spine. Fucking hells. "Where is the horse?" An ache pools at my back and at the base of my skull. Between the fall and the fear, I'm a mess. Doesn't matter though. I swallow and shove it all down. Sometimes, that's all there is to do.

"Gone," Barro says.

I glare at him. Obviously, the horse is *gone*. We've spent so much time together in the last year, we've gotten to know so many of each other's little quirks and unsaid things. Right now, he watches me and I know he can see the shiver that I hide between two fisted hands as I fumble to check my axes.

"Pity." A third voice says, and I flinch. The reverberation of shock flames through my body. *Not good.* This voice I know as well. Too well. I swallow, turning as the newcomer continues to speak. "Darling, why are you out so late?"

Barro's face falls, somewhere between disappointment and anger. I confess, I feel similarly, though I can't help the small amount of irritated affection that surfaces, too.

Lord Derrick Neeson looms there, feet shoulder-width apart, with one hand snagged on the sword at his hip. He raises a brow, blonde and thick, and pulls a hand through his lionesque hair.

"The Shadow Wood is no place for women."

He neglects to say that it's only fit for monsters, so perhaps some men do belong in the wood. Anger boils inside of me.

I don't have time for Derrick's petty games today. For him to try to possess me, to stake a claim on me. He's often like that, when there's an audience. I stand up, shoving the pain down and brushing off the twigs that jab into the folds of my cloak. They tumble, the way stunned birds do after they slam into glass.

"I've got somewhere to be," I say, and begin walking. Straight through as the spirits told me. I hold my breath, listening for the footsteps that inevitably follow. A hand grabs at my forearm. The flesh is cold, like a fish straight from the lake. I smack it away, but it grips tighter. Derrick. Derrick. Derrick. Always holding on when I've told him *no.*

"Do *not*," I snap. "I am the heir to House Berrat and that is a command, Lord Neeson."

His face whitens, like I've leeched it of blood with a handful of sharp words. At this moment, I regret every touch I've given this man, so much so my skin crawls to have him near me. Perhaps I'll feel differently when I get lonely, when my bed grows cold and the absence of something aches deep inside of me. But for right now, I hate him. I imagine I hate everyone.

"I'm going. Either follow or return home and leave me to my peace."

* * *

PEACE IS a gift granted only to the dead. And even then, not all spirits seem to be so lucky as to simply cease the worried flurry that marks life. The unfortunate become spritelights. The forest curls inward, and it reminds me of a cage of increasingly thick bars. Each crack of wood beneath a careless foot is the same to my ears as a spine breaking and a loud scream following the snapping bone. Too many men—by that I mean three—are here. I'm both grateful and irritated to have them.

My dark cloak snags on a sharp limb, the fabric snagging as a crooked finger might. I yank it. It cracks, jolting through the silence. My heart skitters in my chest. This is dangerous; I'm in over my head. A fresh coat of fear flecks my insides.

Derrick stalks close to me, his arm brushing mine often. A growl lives in his throat like there's a creature inside of him, ready to pull itself out of his mouth. Barro bounds two yards ahead, turning frequently—a golden dog looking back for his master's approval. His eyes find mine before he continues forward. Then there's Valor. He walks behind me and raises the hairs on my neck. I wish I could see him, if only to be assured I won't be stabbed in the back.

My scalp tingles. Why I feel that way, I can't say. But I don't like him, I don't trust him. And I admit, I never have. The man is riddled with tin, through and through.

Derrick grabs my arm, hard, stopping me. His fingers press into my bicep in a bruising grip. Nisha growls. "I'm sorry," he says. As he utters the words, a coin drops from his mouth. I usually ignore them when he speaks, like I did with the guards on the wall. I see them all the time when my Sight accidentally flicks on. But the thing falls and I can't help but watch it, notice the dull, flimsy tin.

A witch—sorceress, alchemist, an arcane heathen—isn't popular. Bad luck, they say. Unholy. Anything or anyone outside of the control of the powerful is someone to be reviled. But I can't help what I am. I'm not the Witch King, who can be who he is and rule Lumar with a steel-in-velvet fist. Somehow, *he* escapes the label of being ill luck. But then again, I am not a man. To be both woman and witch is to be burned. That, or something worse.

If anyone knew that I could see the truth and lies as coins falling from their lips, I'd either be killed or captured for someone else's use. As a lady, my freedom is sparse, but I'll take my scraps with thanks.

Still. It's hard to see those you care for lie straight to your face.

"Briar," Derrick breathes. He rubs a hand through his gilded hair. "I love you, you know that." As he says the words, a coin drops from his mouth. Silver. Truth. An important truth.

I watch the coin fall and evaporate mid-air. I can't help but wish it was tin. Or copper—the truth, but something not all that important.

"I'm not turning back, Derrick." Beneath my cloak, my fist grips my ax.

"What are you here for?" He finally asks.

A flower.

I don't say it, because it either will sound stupid or give away more about myself than I'd like. Derrick is a Bear Knight. He works for my father, but he's more than that. His flesh has slid against mine, in sweaty ecstasy. Lips have kissed mine in sweet promises. I'd seen the coins that fell from his lips turn, over time, from tin to silver. From lust to love.

His eyes bore into mine, blue like high summer skies. His gaze skims down, finding my lips. "We could go back. I can think of something to keep you occupied."

Heat slides up my cheeks.

One day, we'd probably marry. Maybe. It didn't matter to me he was a minor lord, charged—in part—with my protection. The sex was good enough, but it was the extra piece that wasn't there. A feeling I always thought I was supposed to have. Perhaps it was the faerie stories I'd read growing up. Girls with lost shoes, true kisses, and impossible tasks. As ever, they found their happiness at the end of an aisle in a white gown. Whenever I dreamed of a husband, it was never the bright, burnished gold of Derrick waiting for me at the altar.

It was darkness.

The dreams came more often now. Most nights were sleepless and agitated. I woke up, the last time with Derrick still pressed against me, dry-mouthed and with sharp visions of a wedding dancing in my skull. Jangling like silver coins.

As I paced down the aisle, blood red started to stain my white gown, and spread like a fatal wound. The bouquet I held of red roses blackened at their edges before they wilted and died.

And at the end of the aisle, a dark stranger stood, flanked by two shadows like feral dogs. I couldn't see his face; dark smoke consumed it. I didn't know his name. When he said the final words, I couldn't hear them, but I knew they marked us bound as one. The coins that fell from his mouth were shadows, too. I couldn't tell the truth from lies.

The husband of darkness reminded me of the nightly visions I'd had my entire life. A strange silhouette of a boy made of shadow with a palm spined with thorns. He disappeared long ago, lost somewhere in the space of my youth I couldn't recall. Memory is fickle like that. It protects us from ourselves, sometimes, by simply turning the nightmare of reality into a dream we can't quite remember.

I shake both the reverie and Derrick off. He lets his grip fall, frowning. There's too far to go and not a lot of time. Nisha stalks up ahead. Silent, but I feel her presence like a hot bottle pressed against a muscle ache. As I resume walking, Barro does, too. I can only assume Valor lurks as a shadow does in the understory, blending in with the poisonous plants and lying little vermin.

The trees blanch to white around us. The earth browns of the House Berrat dukedom bleach into the color of cursed bone. An imaginative scholar named this forest the White Wood. Territory here is a tricky thing. The space of Shadow Wood and the edge of the White Wood should be ours, but our enemies claim otherwise. I confess, part of me wonders why we want a piece of the Shadow Wood at all. Besides its offering of increased lumber, it's not farmable. And still, dark creatures—more twisted than the squirrel—funnel from the bizarre stretch of murky forestland that bisects Lumar, halving our kingdom. Occasionally, a creature will escape through the border at the north and slip down to this wretched forest. It only makes the feeling of being imminently eaten more oppressive.

A breath eases out of my lungs. Something about the deep wood where I can't see the evil is harder than the world of men, where malice lives in the open.

We slide through the forest; frogs croak and crickets chitter in their nighttime chorus. Loamy, earthen scents flare up underneath the pressure of my feet. Derrick walks in stewing silence next to me. His jaw is tight. A jumping vein twitches at his temple. Anger pours off of him, steaming and uncomfortable to be around. Audible huffs exhale from his petulantly turned mouth. A rejection from me, a slight, whatever—it's made him petty. Part of me wishes he would leave; the other part is grateful. I'm good with an ax, but even Nisha and I could be outmatched here, holy night or not. Man-boy or not.

A bone-like branch sweeps across my arm. I shiver. A dull ache taps behind my eyes, the headache ever present from my continued use of the Sight. Now, though, isn't a good time to loosen my hold on it. I twist a finger, yanking the arcane thread tighter to myself.

Forward, Briar. Always forward.

[Ease.] The voice comes from far away, but Nisha attempts to comfort me despite the paranoia digging into my nerves.

We are in the territory of the House of Wolves. The realm of the Duke of Death.

They say he turns to shadow and slips down the gullets of his enemy, killing them from the inside with a black magic. That his men are all cursed to become canine creatures at night and do his bidding because of his evil pact with a powerful spirit. Wandering maidens are snatched from their beds and cursed to become the Wolves' brides. That or the enemy feasts on the women's organs.

But that doesn't matter. I could be crossing the Witch King himself and it wouldn't make a difference—I'd still have to do this.

If I don't succeed here, my father will die. This is the first and last chance I have to prevent it.

Fex's flower, as some call it, blooms bright only under a blood moon. Only two nights a year can someone collect it for its magic.

Once in summer and once in winter, when lunar light bleeds as red as strawberries. A chill runs off the mountains to the northwest, cooling the air.

Tonight, the rose will ripen underneath the red moonlight. Only on the first night can it be collected for its arcane potential. Thereafter, it blooms for seven days, before rotting. Ruined.

The White Wood, they say, is the realm of Wolves and fae and ill spirits. *The wood will as the wood wills*, they say. I hope my offerings are enough. In exchange, the forest may warp its paths and halve my time to my destination, or do the opposite. I've offered milk and blood and tears for this. I am happy to give whatever I must—including splicing pieces of my mortality to ease Papa off the edge of a painful death.

A sick fear clogs my throat. *Don't be weak.* Get the rose. My grimoire, hidden away back at Gray Hall, states in tight, ancient script that the purpled petals will bloom their best tonight. Lore of long-ascended gods and goddesses clings to this revered plant. It only grows in two places—the realm of the northern tyrant, the Dark One's cursed lands, or here, in the blood-soaked backyard of our neighboring duchy.

"Briar!" Derrick's whisper snaps me back to the present. I pause mid-step.

"What?" I look up at him. The red light slides on his face, but he's not looking at me.

Not anymore.

Before I look ahead, I can't help but think of the ill luck he's bringing upon himself by letting the red light touch his skin. And then I turn.

Looming like a monster from beyond Ash Mountain is the stronghold of House Galibran. Barricading it, a twenty-foot-tall metal-spiked wall boasts statues of snarling wolves. Shock pools inside of me. We walked what felt like all night, but here, the forest didn't let me down after all.

The wood will as the wood wills.

I wish I had milk for the spirits, for the magic in the forest, but all I have right now is the red inside of me. Discreetly, under my cloak, I open the scab on my finger and press it. Three drops of blood hit the forest floor. *Thank you*, I mouth, hoping the wood understands. Playing with spirits is a dangerous game. But when the fear strangles me from the inside, I picture Papa standing behind me, showing me the balance on a blade. A slow night across from his once-healthy, ruddied face as he coached me in strategy. My finger strokes my ax. That, too, is a gift from him.

For whatever reason, Fex's flower only grows here out of all the places the forest could offer. Here, in the backyard of our enemy. Whispers of goddesses and sorceresses and curses swirl around this land, but it all comes down to one thing: the flower grows only in shadow and only blooms in blood. Of course it unfolds itself in the darkness in the territory of a terrible man and terrible people.

"This is stupid," Derrick says for the third time this night. Another silver coin falls from his lips before puffing to nothing. *Truth.* Or the truth for him. The twins say nothing, as if they're waiting. Waiting on me, waiting on the world to fall apart.

A wolf howls. This time, it's very close.

Derrick grabs my arm, then yanks. Dull pain throbs through me as he grips the budding bruises from my earlier fall from the horse. My breath settles in a fast beat, somewhere underneath my throat. Fear. Stupid fear. And rage.

"We're going back," he says. "I don't care. I'm not risking your safety."

My dagger is out and against his neck before he can yank again. A trickle of blood trails down his neck. *More for the forest.* He lets go of me, putting up his arms. A dull headache forms behind my eyes as my bicep throbs. Any thoughts I might have entertained about wanting him here—or wanting him in my bed later—incinerate to ash. "Red on a red night," he whispers, fear in his eyes. "That is ill luck, Briar."

I am ill luck, you fool.

"Tell me to go back again," I say through gritted teeth. My heart beats a wild thrum inside of me. I inhale slowly, trying to calm myself, "and I might do something we'll both regret." The dagger presses a little harder into his throat. Ill luck or not, red night or not, it doesn't matter. A chance to conquer forever only comes once. My father will not die like this, not while I live. If destiny is something that can be stolen, I will take mine in the palm of one hand while my other grips an ax. *I will not fail you, Papa.*

Derrick's face whitens, but he doesn't back down. "Briar, just tell me why, then." It's a plea, this time.

I can't. I won't. This is not a man I can tell these secrets to—even though we've warmed each other's flesh on illicit nights, even though he's asked for my hand, even though I consider him something like a friend.

The Bear Knights are not stupid. They must know their duke is ill. But if they knew he possessed Dvartha's Mark, Papa would appear more than weak. Rumors of madness and screaming deathbeds are the hallmark of the wasting disease. Black-veined agony awaited the sickness' victims, twisting their organs inside out and slowly liquifying them. But not before the months and months of hallucinations and ill temper set in. Not before those with Dvartha's Mark prayed to every god they could think of for imminent death.

If Derrick *knew*, if he *told*.... Any decision Papa were to make would be questioned. Or handed over to the Duchess. That didn't bear thinking of.

And if I tell him about Fex's flower, Derrick will know I am a witch.

And no one can know that.

"You're not a child, surely you understand how dangerous—"

"Shh." I cut him off.

[*Bad scent.*] Nisha presses a thought to my mind. The smell of men fills my awareness. The scent of fear. A shadow, a flash of metal. Nisha has seen something. *She's seen—*

"They're coming," I say. The Wolf pack is here. Barro pulls his longsword from its leather. Valor is already there, identical weapons dangling from ready fingers. Everything stills.

The quiet sends a skitter of fear down my spine. I look up once more. The wall runs high, and for a moment I imagine it reaching the moon. The edge of the statuaries limn scarlet in the violent light. My breath comes in quick gasps. Before I turn my eyes away, my gaze snags on the stone mouth of the wolf statuary. A flash of dark, red-tinted purple. I squint.

There it is.

Fex's flower.

A howl cracks through my mind. Loud. My ears tell me it's far enough away, but my heart thuds as Nisha's slides into the same urgent staccato beat.

[*BAD DOG.*]

I stagger. Derrick leaps toward me, but I jerk a hand up. He stops at my motion. His eyes shine with disbelief. He moves toward me again. A violent emotion—as if I'm filled with a dying rage—splices into me. I gesture for him to stop, but he grabs me anyways. I gasp, inhaling a long drag of air and white agony.

Nisha.

Her pain snaps into me. The strong feeling jerks me into seeing what she sees, my nerves linking with hers. Our mental bond snaps with strong tautness. The coil of thick muscled haunches, the sharpened sense of death and decay and growth and blood. Something crashes into us. Bone-jarring thud. A creature gnaws into our side, jagged jaw jamming into our hide. Our claws come out, raking the creature across the face. I blink, blink, blink. *Be Briar.* It's a hard command to follow.

The wall demarcating the border of Wolf Hall overlays with the forest, the Shadow Wood. My vision doubles. A froth of creatures teem out of the cracks. Snarling and grinding and *hating.*

Be Briar.

Wolves.

Be Briar.

A hand—Derrick's—grips me, steadying me.

Thick fear coats my tongue. Nisha's tongue. No, *mine.*

Before I have a moment to do anything—to climb, to turn, to scream—Nisha pulls away. I jerk at the sudden loss of our mind-connection. Derrick's arm wraps around me. I let him, just for a moment, be there for me. *She's okay*, I tell myself. Wounded, but running. To me. I inhale a ragged breath, blinking rapidly.

"Briar," Derrick murmurs into my hair. "Briar, come back to me." I tap the inside of my mouth with my tongue, finding it difficult to speak with the cottony feeling filling it. I twitch from him, moving back. His hand slides across my spine, reluctant to let me do what I need to, even now.

[*Hurry*], Nisha says, and the sensation of desperation fills my mind. Red pain leaks into the message. I taste blood at the back of my throat.

[*They're coming.*]

CHAPTER 4

They're coming.

The Wolves are coming.

A chorus of growls, distant gnashing. The smell of twisted creatures assaults my senses. The pounding of Nisha's feet on soft dirt, heedless of branches, her paws cracking beneath the weight of her body—it's distant, but I feel it.

[*HOME.*]

Not yet.

You go home, I tell her. *Now.* I don't know if she'll listen, but I imagine she won't.

Before Nisha can protest, before Derrick has a chance to snatch at me once again, I climb.

My fingers dig into the stone, into the vines. It's different from the one I scaled a few short hours ago. Cooler. Parts of it soften with moss, rather than warping under the soul-sucking plants blessed by the priests into viciousness. These vines are firm, but desiccated like the scraggly fingers of a dead man. A sweet floral scent hits my nose as I heave upward.

"Briar!" Derrick hisses. His hand skims across the heel of my boot, and I smash it down on his fingers. "Fuck," he grits. His eyes flash with angry longing. "Dammit, woman! What are you *doing*?"

Nisha slams an image into my mind. A teeming mass of running *things*. The pack is half men, half twisted beasts. She marks them at about half a mile away. They smell of sweat and greed and metal and monster. Fear churns in my rib cage and the sluice of beating blood in my veins picks up tempo as I climb.

Faster.

"Fold thyself for the fortune of me and mine," I whisper to the spirits, terror mangling my insides, as I seize another tough vine against the edge of stone. A bit of blood dips a dark smear onto the clump of the dead vegetation. Call it an offering to the Otherworld beyond the Sea of Mist, then. Where the dead go in death and the blessed and unblasphemed fae roam. To every spritelight, an invitation to nag me into insanity. Whatever I need to give, I will, as long as this works.

Father's face dances in my mind, gaunt and broken with wasted hope. Another image of his emaciated visage flashes before me: flesh melting until it's only bone. At once, I see my province falling to the monsters that run toward me now. The duchy losing. Then Lumar itself. The world caving in under the weight of unnatural creatures.

Nisha, somewhere far off, pounds in my direction—further away than the approaching menace. Fear and failure and everything terrible I've ever felt claw inside of me, demanding a release. The distant howls aren't enough to tell the men that have accompanied me that I know the Wolves are here. That they are coming home. That we're about to die if I don't fucking hurry.

"A noise," I call down quietly to Derrick. "Get out your weapon."

"I didn't hear—" Derrick grits from below. An ugly feeling—guilt, panic—wiggles inside of me.

"*Weapon*," I demand. We don't have time for this. Sore loser that he is, Derrick huffs back in the direction of Valor and Barro. No doubt to gripe about me. Asshole.

My arms shiver as I hoist myself up again, fingers slipping into the divot in the wall. Grit cakes my nail beds.

Nisha screams another warning through our mental bond, as I hoist myself up and meet the top of the wall. My muscles shiver, but I hold my body still before I hurl forward one last time. One last reach. I push. Muscles stretch. Pull. I hit stone. Hard rock jolts against my elbow as I scrabble at the ledge. Air hisses through my teeth against the pain. I shift to my feet, finding a shaking balance on top of yet another gods-damned wall.

It will be too soon if I never have to climb again.

I grit my teeth, quickly tucking an errant strand of silver hair into my braid, keeping the hood of my cloak upright. Beyond superstition, beyond any of this— the only young, silver haired woman alive I know of is myself, at least in this area of the world. If the Wolves thought for a moment, they'd know they had the daughter of the enemy duke—and his heir—hostage.

If they decide to take hostages at all.

I am not fool enough to be certain we will get out of here without being seen.

The pulse of Nisha's chest taps my awareness; her consciousness slides against mine as she runs. What I can only describe as cat-panic fills me. The deep desire to kill and run and win and protect expands, pushes, pulses. The connection snaps as she yanks back. I blink. My fingers slip toward the edge, and I wheel toward safety. *Hurry, Briar.* The words are an order, from me, my mind trying to get my body to move.

Wolf Hall looms on the other side of the wall. The floral smell grows pungent as I look at the manor, sprawling like a dead beast. My feet find their way forward and my breath comes in quick gasps.

Faster.

The Duke of Death is somewhere in there. I hop forward. The purple-black petals of the flower wink scarlet ahead. I pounce forward.

Harder.

[*Friend.*] Nisha screams at me from too far, too far away. The word is agony. [*Home.*]

I blink, looking at the ground. Barro and Valor are on loose alert twenty paces away. Derrick sulks near them. The Wolves aren't here, but they will be. And we're all going to die if they don't get ready.

Fuck it.

"I hear something," I say louder, to all of them this time. The word *witch* brands itself in imaginary script across my chest. Gods, I hope they don't ask questions. "Get your swords out."

Barro does, the metal of his blade singing in the dark. Valor follows suit, his own sword an echo of his brother's. Derrick grunts something that sounds like *women.*

I swallow my irritation. The Duke of Death is so close to us now. I wonder if I can end all of this. Not only the war in the north, but also the battle in our backyard.

For a moment, I wonder what it would be like to sneak in, find him in his bed and slit his throat.

His imaginary blood pours over my hands, and all of this angry violence between House Berrat and House Galibran would be over and—

A feeling steals over me—hot and dark. My gaze shifts downward. In the pitch of night, there's a pulse, like the world waits on me. I shift, swallow, and ignore the hairs rising on the nape of my neck. The rose's petals tilt toward the moon, like a pair of lips awaiting a kiss.

My fingers itch forward to snatch it. As I brush against the stem, the night-chilled stalk holds firm against my touch. I pull harder. The smell intensifies, cloying, and I taste petals. My breath grows harsh as something inside myself begs me to turn, turn, *turn*—

I do, hand still gripping the fibrous greenery, and shuffle to the balls of my feet. My breath catches.

A pair of yellow eyes blink open.

"What an interesting creature you are," purrs a voice.

I wheel back. As I do, I lose my balance, and topple off the wall.

Leaving the flower behind.

Nisha wails, from somewhere too far away to do anything. Tears slip down my cheeks as the pain in my head splits.

Fall. Falling. Air sluices around me, making my tunic, and my cloak, flutter. I'm going to hit the ground, and when I do, every bone in my body will break. All I see is my father's grayed face, creased with the grief of the final decimation of the Bears, the death of his only heir, and the cost of my own stupidity as his eyes shut for the last time. His last moments are screaming madness. All my fault.

I brace for the impact and—

Thud into flesh.

Arms tighten around me, biceps flex against my back, underneath my legs. The hood of my cloak squishes around my face, fabric flattening against my forehead and cushioning the hollows of my cheeks. A wheeze sounds above me and I look up at a man I've never seen before. We both gasp for breath and, for a moment, there's no rose scent pressing in on my nose and throat. The face of a fallen god stares down with a fissure of surprise cracking his expression. No fear slips through me, and for once, for a moment, I'm steady. I forget it all —who I am, why I'm here. For just a moment, I am lost.

But just one moment.

A swift twist and my arm lashes out. The flat slap of my palm shoves with force into his nose. He rears back with a grunt. Something scrapes the curve of my spine. I grab for the dagger in my left boot—as if I can fight my way out of whatever *this* is—but a large hand blocks me halfway to my ankle. Holds me at the wrist. My axes are pinned to my back. Hot blood trickles from the raw abrasion through my mangled tunic. The vesperi wood heats, drinking me in. Stinging pain lances the wound. The scarred man's biceps flex against me. I pull against the pressure, my arm imprisoned at my upper thigh as my fingers tangle with this strange man's.

My field of vision fills with a pair of umber eyes as he leans close. His gaze spears me like hellfire underneath a quirked brow and a shock of black hair. Beneath his left, lower lash line, a beauty mark dots his tawny skin. One irritating eyebrow, bisected by a striking scar, stays raised in mockery. Old injuries nick every bit of exposed flesh in little pink-white constellations.

"Lost, darling? Haven't you heard there are Wolves in these woods?" The scarred man flashes me a grin. Two long canine teeth flirt with the edge of his lower lip. He moves his hand from mine, the motion sending a spasm to my thighs. A howl rises up just to my right and I flinch. Shadows ripple around the clearing, and another noise screams out into the night.

I inhale, lungs filling to scream, to warn them all. "Der—"

His hand covers my mouth, muffling my warning. "Now, darling, let's not ruin the surprise."

The man's hands are hot and large, his touch scalding my skin through my trousers and my lips. I jerk against him. *Shit.* The pain from the landing in his arms still stings me, but there's something else curling in my abdomen now…something I don't care to consider.

I bite down on his palm, anger driving my teeth to clench around his flesh. Salt and iron coat my tongue. He hisses, but doesn't move it. That little beauty fleck dotting his skin twitches beneath his eye and his hand blurs. I blink, and he's shoving a white scrap of fabric into my mouth. The next second, that hand locks my wrists in the grip of his palm, while the other clasps my legs. "I was always told to have a handkerchief available for a lady," he whispers.

"Fkkyuu." *Fuck you,* I gurgle between the fibers. I struggle, but his muscles flinch around me, holding me still. The shadows slide out from the edge of the clearing, filtering in.

"Motherfucker!" One of the twins yells. Barro, I think.

The slide of metal unsheathing from leather, no doubt Derrick's sword finally freeing itself, rents the air. Laughter—some of it mangled inside of half-man, half-beast throats—caws through the deep blackness as the creatures slip from the coat of night. The Wolf soldiers of House Galibran have arrived. Nisha's snarl hisses through the air—the feeling of her claws snicking out as she barrels toward one of the beasts fills me with her feline rage.

The scarred man stares at me, as if looking away isn't an option. I want to kill him. I struggle, but he only grips me harder. His face is unreadable, besides a tiny bit of amusement pinching the corner of his mouth. No one else would hold an enemy trying to cut off their head and smile about it. The man must be a sadist.

My gaze goes to the top of the wall. The rose is there, just out of reach. I'm so gods-damned *close.*

Movement trickles around the grove, and growls rumble. Derrick and Barro stand back-to-back. Wolves—some of them fully shaped as men, the other half-beasts with furred jaws—surround my allies. Valor is nowhere to be seen. *Typical.* I shiver, a race of lightning-like fear zipping down my spine. Fuck, fuck, *fuck.*

We're going to need to fight our way out of here. But I can't leave without the rose.

Each of my boots holds a tiny knife. If I can grab one and stab this man, I can get him to drop me. Then, I can reach my ax. The image of his head rolling off my blade fills my mind's eye. Or I can cut into his neck enough to kill him. Decapitation and near-decapitation are the same thing, when it comes down to killing a man.

"Will you be good? I'd like to speak with you," the scarred man says. Carefully, he pulls the cloth from my mouth. As soon as it's out, I flex my jaw.

"It would be a pity to kill a man so handsome.," I say. "Good thing you're just an evil beast."

I snap my hand out from his grasp, slinging to my boot. His eyes widen in shock. This time, I successfully snag the metal. The leather wrapped handle is rough under my grip. I swing, arcing toward his jugular. The scarred man's fist comes up against mine, grabbing my wrist. My muscles strain and shiver, and I press down. Abs flex, and I put everything behind the movement. *Die, stupid bastard.*

He unceremoniously dumps me on the ground.

A flare of pain zips up my ankles, but I land, two feet planting onto the loamy forest floor. I fly at him, and he meets me easily, holding my wrist to stall his death. We grapple, his superior strength bearing down on me. I struggle against him, using the opportunity to drop my left hand to my secondary dagger in the other boot. My hand grasps it, and I give in.

The sudden disappearance of my struggle has him staggering forward. I shift to the side, stabbing him in the thigh.

He growls. "Vicious thing, aren't you?" Blood streams from his leg, my dagger still implanted there. That thrice-gods-damned eyebrow lifts upward again, mocking me. He winces, but he doesn't move. "Fucking grims, are you *made* of blades?"

I hiss, rolling away, not bothering to answer, not bothering to play games. I catch Derrick's gaze across the distance. Metal flashes against the light as his sword slashes the flesh of one of the Wolf monsters. Derrick's mouth twists. Then his eyes widen, and he yells something. I turn.

A furred devil streaks toward me in the dark. It lets out an inhuman scream. The scarred man watches as one of his monstrous comrades snags the edge of my cloak, pulling it.

One of the twisted ones.

I yank it away, jerking into a stumbling run. Jaws snap at me. Rancid, hot breath breathes down my neck. My eyes water. I fling myself forward, rolling and snagging a discarded knife from the dirt.

The creature knocks into me, and I tumble to the ground.

His pelvis grinds down onto mine. He traps the hand near my ax. *I'm pinned.* Fear claws an ugly talon up my belly. Saliva drips down into my face. I grab into the earth with my other hand, snatching the dirt and rocks, and toss it into the creature-man's face. Stones hit his flesh, and debris hisses in the air against his eyes.

Nisha cries out, trying to get to me. She's too far away.

He howls, grip loosening, and I jab a foot into his balls. "Fucking bitch!" The creature-man growls, voice half-tangled into something between a dog and a man. He grabs his face. Indecipherable metal coins pittle from his mouth and evaporate. I don't care about his truths right now. I snag my ax, and he runs at me. His hand reaches out. I swing and—

The blade cuts through his fingers. One. Two. Three, Four.

Four digits dot the ground, and I've never seen anything so beautiful.

"MY HAND!"

"That bitch has an ax!" Another one cries. Silver pours from his mouth, flipping like tiny flashing blades in the night. Silver truth. Important truth. His fear shows in the whites of his eyes and the bright metal pouring from his mouth. At least the last thing he says before he dies is true. I sling my ax up—

"ENOUGH!" The words pulse out, shivering the air. It's as if the forest's heartbeat shakes the ground. The scarred man steps forward, his hand grasped around the pommel of his sword. As if he was ready to use it, but refraining. For now.

"This is a holy night!" The white mark slashing his eyebrow glows; red wine light pools across the carved planes of his cheekbones. Shadows gather at his mouth and I can't look away.

I also can't move. His command freezes the air, and the very marrow of my bones chills.

The men and wolves around him halt. Some hold perfectly still, while others twitch and strain. I jerk against this ill enchantment, caught in the strange hold the man's words caused. Everything feels slower, thicker, colder. As if the darkness sludges around every joint and suggests, *Do not move, or else.* Under my Sight, a bright, dancing blue jolts around our bodies in strange spurts.

The one whose fingers I removed glares at me, face twisted into something beyond monstrous. He mouths a word. *Bitch.* Lightning-like flares sizzle at his slow-moving jaw. Blood spills off the nubs left at his hand. *I'll get you,* he whispers, though the sound doesn't reach me. I smile in response to the threat. His face darkens.

My movement is pained, slow, but all eyes are on the scarred man. He must be the captain of this unit. My pulse jitters in my neck. I swallow. His dark eyes slip from creature to human, pinning them in place, as if he is personally warning them of something. A whimper slips out from the crowd.

"Sorry, sir," says the man holding Derrick. Still, he doesn't let my companion go.

"As if we all here owe our lineage to the same gods." The man whose fingers I cut off snarls. His words slip out slowly, fangs gnashing. Blue burns all around his face as the arcane command strains against him. "Do we all need to pay edict to their ways if it is they that cursed us?"

"Shall I remove another finger?" The scarred man says. The other

Wolf only snarls in response. "That is what I thought, Bane. You'll do penance with your wounds pressed to salt blocks for your blasphemy."

A caw sounds from above us, and the Wolves jerk their heads up in synchrony, a rustle of fur and uniforms hissing in the air. A raven sits in a nearby tree, black-purple in color. Its head cocks to the side as it stares down at us. At that moment, the strange hold eases.

"The Witch King," one of the Wolves hisses.

"Lukas," the scarred man says. In an instant, another of the Wolves steps forward. I notice his eyes—the same yellow that surprised me on top of the wall—as Lukas grasps a crossbow in one hand and slips an arrow from his holster with the other.

One quick movement, and the arrow flies. All is silent, except the dull thud of the arrow striking the breast of the bird. It falls. Hits the ground.

Dead.

"If only we could do that so easily to the minion's master," the man —Lukas—says.

Whatever illicit magic that held me drains away completely under the distraction. Panic and rage dance beneath my skin.

I raise my ax. A hand catches my wrist and snaps it back, before it can arc through the air. My hood slips back, revealing my metallic-white hair.

Air hisses out between the scarred man's teeth. He lowers his mouth to my ear. "What fuckery is this?"

Fingers fist the bright loose braid and he yanks it, shoving the tangle of silver strands into the hidden folds of fabric.

"Stop," he orders quietly as I struggle against him.

He jerks the cowl of my cloak up, covering the top of my head, hiding the glimpse of my well-known hair. Confusion rattles through me before cresting into terror.

He knows.

"Remmy, Lukas, Jessa, Warren, stay. The rest of you—leave."

Deep, shaking unease fizzles through every nerve I have. *What is he going to do to me?* My breath comes in hot bursts. *And why is he sending most of his fighters away?*

There's a pause, as if some of them wait to see what to do.

"Now," he barks. He doesn't use the strange magic this time, and the response feels reluctant. Movement stirs, slow at first, but the Wolves pull back into the shadows. Those remaining Wolves move, replacing the ones holding Derrick, Barro, and Valor. One is a twisted creature, the other two fully human. Lukas casually grabs one of my axes left on the ground and holds it above Nisha's neck.

Blood smears in my mind, mixing in with my own fear. Nisha pushes, the imagined wound growing bigger as she rips out Lukas' throat.

Not yet, I say. She doesn't move, but her shoulders twitch in agitation.

Bane stares at me. Blood smears the corner of his mouth. He's less of the twisted creature now, though fur haphazardly patches his forehead. A fang glints before he leaves and the wood swallows him.

Moments pulse together. I don't know what we're waiting for. Another heartbeat. Another—

"It's *you*." The scarred man says.

Me. The daughter of the enemy. It's an accusation.

A shadow of stubble cups his lower face. Beneath that, his jaw jumps in agitation. A hard line forms above his brows. All moisture leaches from my mouth. Here he is—a leading warrior in the band of Wolves that terrorizes our border. A soldier from the province that keeps the Bears from sending more resources to the bloody front at the northern edge of Lumar. A man who cries for civil war in our kingdom. Yet, I am entranced by the curve of his lips. They're different from any other pair, soft-looking and lush. I could stare for an entire day at that mouth and not feel a moment of boredom. *Idiot*. I curse myself. Looking at him makes me so angry I want to kill him.

Fire-like rage whips up my spine, alongside another heat I don't care to investigate. Still, the feeling makes me wish I could slap my own face. Why did he send everyone away after he saw my hair? Surely he would bring me to the duke? Surely he knows. *It's you*. He knows. He *has* to. The words cycle over and over as we wait in silence.

Something isn't right here.

"So, you've come back." The words are quiet, his breath tickling the shell of my ear. I shiver and his hand digs into me.

He yanks my ax from me. I clutch at it for a moment, feeling the pull at my joints against his strength. The ax is gone in an instant. As the weapon lands several feet away, it makes a soft thud.

Fuck off, I want to say, but the words stick inside my throat.

"Nothing to say of your curse?" He hisses. He runs the pad of a finger along my cheekbone, down the thick vein of my neck. He holds it there, lightly, his other hand still gripping my wrist.

It's then that I realize that my hand is on his chest and we're both breathing like we've been running. I can't help but look at where his men have Derrick. The twins. Nisha. Derrick stares at the scarred man, hatred burning like hot coals in his eyes.

Heat rushes to my cheeks and I step away—or try to. "Beast," I spit at him.

Fear and desire crash into me as he yanks me close to him. "You call me a beast as if it's my fault?" A cruel laugh bubbles from him. "As if we did this to ourselves?"

I still don't know what he means. Surprise shoots through me. I raise my eyebrows. Odd, that there is anyone else on this side of the world that looks like me. Unless they're the Selvan enemy.

Whoever he has mistaken me for, though, is clearly not someone I want to be.

A dagger glints about five feet away in a twinkling promise. If I can fall to get it, stab him, then I can try to reach the wall again.

"I don't know what you mean," I finally say. "Release me."

When he doesn't, the rage inside my chest stokes, burning hotter.

"Why are you here, then?" he asks quietly. It reminds me of the slithering of a snake before it strikes. "Have you come to attack on a holy night? You know, they say to draw anyone's blood but your own on Amara's night is to invite Her wrath." He holds up his hand, caked in his own blood from his thigh. Proof of my own blasphemy. "But it is said She doesn't mind retribution. Much."

No, the former goddess of vengeance probably wouldn't mind a taste of blood in retaliation to violence. I lick my lips and my gaze flicks up to where I'd climbed, to where I'd nearly grabbed the flower. The chances are slim, but if anyone can do it, it's a witch with a purpose. I will succeed because I have no other option.

The grief overwhelms me so immensely that for a moment, I cannot breathe. A fool's mission this may have been, but the idea of leaving Papa to suffer without me by his side guts me. I'd prefer a slow death with a sword in my stomach. My mouth dries. I blink rapidly to look back at the wall.

The man holding me captive follows my gaze, then stares at me with unsettling concentration. He looks at my neck, staring. I wonder if he can hear my rapid pulse, if he can smell fear like animals do. If he can, he'll know I am a creature made of terror. It folds itself into my soul, settling next to the ache of loneliness that tells me I will never be good enough and that is why all the horrors slip into my life.

I'm a witch. The daughter of a hated woman. The daughter of a duke who had no business loving his wife. Everything I am is a cursed legacy. Everything I am is something that will never fit in with the rest of the world. A crazed laugh bubbles up in my throat and then breaks.

But it's not laughter at all.

A sob curdles in my chest, and I purse my lips into a tight line to keep them from trembling. Perhaps, though, I'll die here, in the hands of the enemy. I wonder what it's like to die, if I'll be able to see Papa shitting the bed, sweating with swollen black veins pumping poison into every liquifying organ, and screaming out terrible things as his mind leaves him. In a way, I wonder if it would have been better to just kill my father instead of all of this.

"Ah," the enemy says, but it sounds like a growl. He grasps the back of my neck lightly. I let him tilt my head to the side, and he runs a thick, calloused finger down the tender length. A muffled sound of protest comes from far, far away. *Derrick.* My throat ticks beneath my enemy's touch.

The scarred man finds the mark dotting my collarbone, splashing the side of my neck. From the first Duke of House Berrat to me, we've all possessed the mark—the birthmark looks like the animal we are named for: the Bear.

The scarred man's voice is low; he leans in. "No, you're not who I thought. You're someone else." A warm chuckle rattles his chest, which rests against my shoulder. I can't help but wonder at the deranged type of joy the laughter reminds me of. His breath tickles my ear, sending a quiver down my spine. "Do you remember now?"

He stares at me, waiting.

I gaze past him, to the rose. The birds sing around me, signaling the coming dawn. The scarred man looks closer, peering into my face. His hand slides in my hair the way a lover's might.

"I remember that you are my enemy," I reply. Confusion rattles through me. Who did he mistake me for? The shadows in the clearing thrum.

We don't look away from each other. His eyes are a pool of endless terrors, and some of the warmth leaks out of them. Will he kill me now?

Something shifts in his face. Silver cracks through his dark gaze, like a sudden spark of flint to start a fire. Then it's gone. The scarred man leans in, until the side of his face presses to mine and his lips tickle my ear.

"Fine, then. In the spirit of the goddess Amara and Her holy night, shall we be as She once was? We have missed the celebration." I feel his lips curve into a smile against my cheek. "I shall bargain with you as the fae, do, darling. What would you like in return for my mercy?"

"I claim the Victor's Two." I say immediately. My teeth click together. The Victor's Two meant that, in a compromise, both sides conceded, but the winner would get one additional boon.

He pauses, and the softness seems to leave him in that moment. Then he scoffs. "I think not—I have you by the throat."

"I can just as easily have you by the balls," I return.

A snort from one of the Wolves followed by a chuckle. The yellow-eyed one, Lukas, steps forward. "Aye, she probably could—"

The grip on my throat spasms for a moment and the man's eyes flare, but his gaze flicks to the speaker. Lukas immediately quiets.

"Unlikely," my captor finally says. "But...in the interest of potentially preserving *my balls*," he pauses, passing a significant look full of censure to his comrade who had previously spoken, "I promise three things. One, you may climb the wall and retrieve whatever trinket you keep looking at. Two, my mercy on the condition you draw no more blood from my fellows here. And three, a kiss."

My throat works. It's as dry as paper.

"Do we have a bargain?"

CHAPTER 5

bargain. For one, measly kiss, I'll buy the mercy of this band of Wolves for us and get the rose. For one measly kiss, I can change my life. Papa won't die. House Berrat will not fall. And if we don't fall, the northern border still has a chance of being secured. Lumar stands a chance. The province of Bear stands a chance. *Father stands a chance.* It is more than that, but the ache between my shoulders suggests I feel everything riding on this one, cursed swap of spit with the enemy.

I don't understand what he gets out of the kiss. I don't understand it at all. Kissing at any other time wouldn't matter, but this feels like a snarl of fate. Perhaps it's the witch in me, but a terrible knowing fills my chest. *Don't do it.* The words blare inside of me like the horn of the Wild Hunt in a land far, far away. I half wonder if this man is fae, or some sort of ill spirit.

My fingers spasm into a fist, and I pull back. The absence of his skin on mine cools my cheek.

"Why?" I ask.

The corner of his mouth twitches up into a smirk. A dimple appears, bold, even in the strange light. My hand itches to smack it, but I can't stop looking at his mouth.

"In part, curiosity." He pauses, an insufferable eyebrow raised. "Your choice, love."

This deal gives him nothing. He has the upper hand. He could take everything from us tonight and yet he's giving me an out. It makes no sense. If it were any other time, I'd push harder, dig deeper to understand what I'm buying into. But I need this.

To kiss someone you don't know beneath a blood moon, without the eyes of the gods to protect you, is to invite trouble. I want to shove the superstitious belief behind me, but I'm not immune to the paranoia. And he wouldn't have asked for something like this if he didn't believe in it just a little.

Or he's in lust *with you.* I lick my lips.

The only gods that watch are the ones that lie in bed with death. The spritelights around us pulse as if they hear my inner mind.

"This is a line of fate you're drawing," I say quietly to him. "Is there not something else we can bargain with?"

"Tell me, you believe in such superstitious nonsense? Kisses and princes and faerie godmothers? Good and evil?" He laughs, a bitter sound of misery. "Shall I be your villain, then, wicked witch?"

"Why do you want this?" I ask once more. The hair on my arms raises, and the gods watch on—setting down the pieces for us, asking us to play our parts for their entertainment. It is as the priests have always said, though I never thought it would happen to me. I should have known better, as the hated daughter of a duke.

It all has the feeling of a tale. A girl goes to the woods where she should not. She tries to steal something she should not. And from her, something is stolen back. This is a fickle business, full of twists and turns and ugly surprises. There are so many should-nots for women, and far too many consequences handed down from a cruel world to keep them in their towers.

The gods love their petty tricks. Still, they should not be able to watch during the blood moon. I cross an X over my throat. "I don't want to have a line of fate drawn to you, Wolf."

"If you are that superstitious, the line of fate has already been drawn, wicked witch, whether you know it or not. If you believe you can control your own destiny, though…what is the risk?"

An urgent need to run, to turn back, fills me. But I've come too far, fought too hard, and going back is the same as planning Papa's funeral. I've left the proverbial tower. But my kiss is not to be with the prince of my dreams.

I'll save myself. Save Papa. Whatever I need to do, I'll do. Nothing is off the table.

"Fine, villain." I hold out a hand. He takes it, uses it to pull me closer until his chest nearly presses against my tunic. The calluses on his hand scrape against my palm, covering my own almost completely. "You will let me get the flower. In exchange for this." I flap my hand toward his mouth, making an ugly smooching noise. His mouth drops into a small, shocked expression. "If I couldn't see that flower in front of my face, I wouldn't trust the lackey of the Duke of Death to do anything he says."

Part of me can't be sure I can trust him now. But sometimes, there's only one choice. A coiling sensation grips my forearms, as if magic courses through me. A line of fate, indeed.

I look up at him, his face a shadow haloed by the scarlet light. We're nearly the same height—where I skim just under six feet, he looks down at me from three or four inches above. The linen of his shirt scratches at my skin. My heart pounds, thrumming like a war drum in my arteries. Warmth suffuses my stomach and heats my cheeks. Derrick, Barro, and Valor struggle futilely in the Wolves' arms, held by this man's minions. Cursed strength is superior to that of mere mortals.

My chest tightens, and hot embarrassment flashes across my flesh.

[*Fight?*] Nisha presses the image of her ripping our enemies' stomachs open, red bursting everywhere and gushing between her claws.

No, I reply internally. This is nothing.

The scarred man stares back down at me. Challenging me. Something soft is in his gaze, too, like curiosity or a plea. As if he needs this. Needs the kiss. *He needs to know what my lips feel like.* The thought is fanciful, and I blink, mouth parting slightly. In a world where half the known fae were banished to live amongst the humans, where they haunt the forests and stalk unsuspecting travelers, a kiss is never just a kiss.

It is always the beginning.

Something at my chest tugs. My enemy stares down at me, no apparent impatience on his face. But no gods watch tonight to protect me from this thing. All the tales say that to brush one's lips against those of a stranger in the woods is to invite nothing but trouble. Call me trouble, then. Call me desperate. Call me half-wild.

A mixture of rage and want churns inside of me.

My enemy leans in. Mint suffuses my senses. Something warm and spicy, like clove. Lips whisper against mine. *I hate you*, I want to say. But the words stop in my throat. The press of eyes from my allies—and from the Cursed—envelope me with embarrassment, hatred, and need.

His mouth meets mine.

The scarred man's lips whisper against my skin, all soft. Nearly tender. His tongue licks the seam of my mouth. *Open.* Pooling heat slips through my core. I fight the angry urge to plunder his lips, to knock his teeth out with the clack against mine. But this is *his* bargain, not the hated daughter of a dying duke's, and I should want it to be over. To give in and give over, so I can move to the next task, the next challenge. *I should want this to be over.* And I do want this to end. Of course I want it to stop—

But part of me just wants it.

His tongue queries again, like a question, and I open for him in answer. His hand cups the base of my skull, tugs at the tendrils of hair there. The scarred man pulls the edge of my hood up, holding it so it doesn't sling back. I don't pause to wonder why, to ask anything, because that hand slips down my shoulder and my whole being tightens with confusion and desire and hate.

Anger surges in my blood. The rage is a knife aimed at him, his people, and partially at myself for wanting something I shouldn't. I want to punish him for all of it. For what the world has made me and for the deep longing and loneliness that pulse through my veins.

Though this man doesn't know who I am—*what* I am. A bargain with me is no joke. I want him to regret ever laying eyes on me, even as his fingers set my flesh aflame.

He rips apart our border, kills our soldiers. A Wolf granting mercy he may be, but I'm a witch and not merciful in the least.

He pulls away.

I sink my teeth into his lip—hard—pinning him to me. He flinches. I put all my hate into it; I want him to feel me here and think about this for days after. *Fuck you and all you stand for.* Warm iron tangles in salty sweetness with fresh mint. Blood slips down his mouth and onto mine.

The temperature plummets and he stills. Balmy summer wind cracks into a chill that harkens snow. Scents of frost and devastation fill my nostrils. I pull back just a second. The shadow across the scarred man's face never moves, but gold glows in stark streaks across his black-brown eyes. Fear slips into my body, but it's too late. A sound, half mangled between sigh and growl, rumbles from his chest. He pulls me back into him and I'm drowning.

The kiss becomes a battle of tongues and scraping flesh and deep wounds that will never heal. His hands move from the cup of my cheek, tracing every line of my body. I shudder under his touch. Fingers comb and clench my hair.

Kissing him is like kissing darkness itself.

Every brush of his lips sends a trail of shivers down my spine. Gooseflesh pimples my skin with the irate tide of desire. His mouth travels down and the trail of blood heats the thick vein at my neck. He yanks my head back and sucks. A heavy shudder shakes me from shoulder to tailbone. Then, he *bites.*

Red—having nothing to do with the blood moon—paints my vision. How *dare* he? He pulls at the skin, and I feel the curve of a smile against my collarbone. It's as if he says *mine.*

White rage bursts from me, and I pull my other dagger from my boot. My hand flies, jabbing at him, but his other hand comes up and bats it away as if it's no more than a nuisance. The blade thuds onto the soil. He holds my hand aloft, stalling my attack, but a wash of confusion ripples inside of me. His grin flashes white. He fingers the delicate skin of my wrist, caressing it as if we're lovers. Every inch of him presses against me. Pulls me closer. Back into his arms.

Want, need, *hate.* The current pulls me under, and I'm drowning in all of it.

"Bargain with me, love," he growls against my mouth. "Or have you consented to losing?" Scents of fresh mint and spicy clove spark all around me. The thrill of my fingers thread through his hair. A wanton spasm curls in my belly. My lips are on his again and our tongues dance. Nothing exists except this battle-laden kiss.

"STOP." Derrick, Valor, Barro—someone's voice comes from leagues in the distance.

His hand slides down to grip the curve at my waist, bruising. I grab him back, pressing my fingers into the bone of his hip. This kiss is a fight, and I intend to win. His other hand knots my hair. I match him, my tongue meeting his, stroke for stroke. I yank his hair like I'll pull out each dark tendril by the root.

"That's enough." The words come somewhere as far away as the Sea of Mist, beyond to Otherland, where the fae used to take children and maidens. Where the Grim Lords fly on the back of death. Mumbled, like reality calling from a dream I don't care to wake from.

My fingers snarl his hair again, pulling him close like if I fight hard enough, I can take his soul. Maybe I can. Witches can do much, and I don't know my powers by half. I gnaw into his lip again, and he gasps against my mouth. *A bad bargain, wolf boy*, I think. I want him to know it, to regret it, and to both wish he'd never asked for this kiss and wish it was endless.

It's hard to know if I want to kill him or fuck him.

"ENOUGH!" The command breaks through the lusty, bloody haze. *Derrick.*

I snap awake.

Frosty air billows around me and the scarred enemy. Snow flecks from the branches of the tree, and long icicles jab downward around us like knives. Our breathing syncs, hot exhalations swirling like cigar smoke.

The man's mouth drips with blood, and his eyes are black like a demon's. What I'd seen before, a darkness, now consumes him whole. My Sight, for a moment, flicks on. The metallic flavor of bitter truth and blood spark my taste buds. The man smiles, a twist of his lips somewhere between lust and hatred.

"You kiss like you're waging war," the scarred man whispers to me.

It's strange that I don't even know his name.

Derrick strains against the men twenty feet away. "You hurt her!" Silver coins drop from his mouth. He keeps repeating it, and the flash of light metal flips edge over edge under the gaze of the red moon, like streaks of bloodied blades. Silver, silver, sliver. Truth, truth, truth.

Lie, I think. But Derrick believes it. He can't imagine that I'd be the one to draw blood like this. The taste of iron on my tongue is the blood of my enemies, and I can only admit this to myself: I want more of it.

I want to drink straight from this Wolf's heart.

I am no innocent girl wandering through the woods. The acid taste of sincerity burns my tongue. As if our kiss was filled with nothing but the truth. The truth of what, I have no idea. My fingers touch my burning mouth. As they do, a strange shadow tucks itself against my sleeve. Dark, onyx-colored, it flutters there in a way that reminds me of cotton balls. Blobs of puffy black link together to form a bracelet. I shake it. It rattles without a sound against my skin.

"A gift," he says.

I jitter the ephemeral bangle again. It's as if someone collected marbles made of shadow and strung them together. There's something almost...cute about it. "Not one I want," I reply stiffly. It's a half lie, and I taste it the moment the words come to my lips. A spike of heat races across my skin, a small fever by a tiny degree for the lie. There's always a price to be paid. I pinch my lips together to keep from saying another one.

"Too bad," the man says. He steps away, as if to look at me fully. "A line of fate indeed."

"Are you a fae?" I ask abruptly.

"Not in the slightest."

"Then what are you?" The words hang there for several seconds. He doesn't answer. Before long, I decide it doesn't matter. Time is of the essence. "The rose," I say, my voice hoarse. I wipe the back of my hand across my mouth with a look of disgust. A smear of red stains from my knuckles to my wrist. "That was the bargain."

"And you agreed to shed no blood." He replies, a pointed look at my mouth.

"You said none of your fellows' blood." My lips throb. "You never said yours was off-limits."

A snort. The scarred man and I both look at our spectators. Various expressions of amusement, hatred, and discomfort grip their faces. The sound, if I were to guess, came from Lukas.

"Go get your prize, then."

I pause, halfway to the wall before I look back. He's still there, staring with an enigmatic expression I don't like. "Why did you want the kiss? Out of everything?"

The quiet is ceaseless, except for the cracks of shifting weight on the forest floor. The pause lengthens. I shrug. I don't care about why he wanted to kiss me as much as I care about plucking the rose before the sun rises. My chances shrink to a sliver.

"Because," he replies when I am on top looking down at the world from high above. I don't care anymore, though. I rush to the rose, gripping it hard. It struggles against me. "When I realized you were not who I first thought, I realized you were someone much more interesting."

The flower snaps beneath my hand. Thorns bite into my palm, but I don't have time to be careful with myself. A small bit of pink stains the sky when I finally tuck the fabled rose safely away. As I do, look at the bracelet made entirely of shadow once more. It slugs like lazy river water down its path. I shake it. No noise comes from it, but it hits my skin. The feeling of a cool, damp stone lips my flesh.

"What is this?" I demand of the stranger.

Another laden pause. He shrugs, a lazy twitch of mirth on the corner of his lip. *Arrogant prick.*

He jerks an arm and his comrades release Derrick, Valor, and

Barro. Nisha hisses. The Wolves discard the weapons they stole, dropping them like scraps at the tree line. The air is static, like violence might still break out. Eyes watch me, waiting for an order. At least they've decided that I'm in charge now.

I scale down the wall with less grace in favor of speed. He can't create such a scene, gift me with some dark magical jewelry, only to *leave*. "What do you mean, more interesting?" I ask instead. The scarred man, watching his people become one with the shadows, turns in their direction to follow. He moves with languid grace behind them, apparently unconcerned that my three men are spoiling to kill him.

"Don't come back without an escort unless you want to be killed," he says, ignoring my question. "If you do, you better be married to a Wolf or turned by one. Otherwise, you'll be dead." He turns, walking backward. "As for the more interesting bit, you'll probably find out later."

It's then that I realize why his mouth was unlike anything I've ever seen before. My head pounds with the strain of the Sight, but no coins —truth or lies—grace his lips.

He disappears into the darkness. The shadow on my wrist spasms.

PART II
THE BLOOD OF YOUR ENEMIES

In shadow, we find our dreams just as well as our nightmares.

-Orvellan Proverb

CHAPTER 6

BOY

he blood won't wash off. Neither will the scars. His heart is littered with wounds.

Boy realizes this in the way a bird knows when winter comes. And yet, he strangles his baser behaviors down, squishing them.

Killian, *he tries to call himself. It's hard, though. He often forgets.*

The gods love their pretty toys, and Boy is nothing if not one of their favorites. He knows this, because he understands how the magic of the world works. A mysterious, cursed son of a man who may or may not be his father. Boy has no mother. That, too, is something the divine love to play with. Killing off the parents of players in their games and watching them squirm is one of their favorite sports.

Boy learns what faerie tales are.

He learns to hate them.

Boy wakes up, always, with his sheets tangled in sweat and blood. Violent dreams ride him. New injuries pool red all over his body. Marks and ragged edges of his flesh. His aunt, Asha, learns to tend them. She's a skilled healer, but not even she has seen anything like this.

Boy knows he's different right away. Different from the other Cursed boys and girls. Whispers of why they are like this form the shape of a phantom woman—part sorceress, part goddess, all evil. Her hair spills like molten silver and burns everything it touches. Boy is still young, so sometimes he wonders if she'll appear and ask him to spin her hair into a tunic as strong as armor. Perhaps she'll demand a kiss that will bring him ill luck if he doesn't complete three fanciful tasks. He hates her.

Each night, Boy dreams of wretched things. Ghost and Erebos snarl at each other, and their fights grow more violent, leaving more wounds that never quite heal, more scars than he can count. Asha is at a loss.

Boy learns quickly that the only person that can really hurt him is himself. Except for the evil inside of him. Eventually, he realizes he is excellent at the task of self-injury. Perhaps it is the most human thing about him. His ability to wound himself better than anyone else.

Each night, he gets better at it. Each night, he bleeds a little more. The shadows in his room writhe with wretched glee. Part of him understands them. In a sense, he is them.

Boy hates sleeping, though he loves the night. Visions dance in his head, half demonic, but he learns to direct the shadows bit by bit. He learns to control that, too, along with causing himself the most pain. Boy becomes a nightmare. To everyone, but mostly to himself.

Then one day, a different dream comes.

CHAPTER 7

The flower burns against my hand through the dawn and into mid-morning. The green perfume of plants and dark soil fills my nose. I breathe in deeply. Sunlight chars its way through the glass panes in the distillery's ceiling, sparking like a cocktail of hope and devastation.

The forest let us pass through the night following our departure uneventfully. Little wounds scored our bodies, scrapes from angry thorns and petty branches, but the worst one seemed to be the injured pride of the men. My hands shake, and the angry daylight slicing into my distillery paints an ugly cast on everything. Even the little rainbows refracting off of the dainty vials and bottles on my shelves give me no pleasure as they usually would. The shadow bracelet thrums like a ring of ice along my wrist. I pull at it, trying to remove it, but my finger passes through it like it's not there at all.

My lips burn.

The image of the scarred man fills my mind—from the glint in his eyes to the sharp edge of his chin.

Vicious thing, aren't you?

You'll probably find out later.

I realized you were someone much more interesting.

"Go fuck yourself, Briar," I mutter, shaking my head. The roughness of his skin on mine haunts my mouth. What can he do, anyways? Who would believe him that Lady Briar Berrat was out where she shouldn't have been? If he knew who I was at all.

He did, part of me whispers. The look in his eyes said that he recognized me, or thought he knew something about me. A shiver skitters from the tip to the base of my spine before I shove all thoughts of my strange enemy away. Everything except the cool reminder cuffing my wrist. It's impossible to remove, because it's made of nothing but darkness. The only thing that seems to affect it at all is direct sunlight, which erases the black translucent ring ever so slightly. Concern for what it means, for why it won't leave me, jitters through me. But what can I do?

Besides, I have more important things to worry about.

I set the precious rose down at my oaken workbench, the purpled petals dark as a bruise. Small bottles, corked with dried bits of herbs and rare poisons, twinkle back at me like mischievous children. I trail a finger along an eye-level shelf, and it comes away from the surface clean. This room has no dust. No one comes here but me.

Humidity sweats in every corner of the distillery. This room juts out from the main part of Gray Hall, facing the direction of the Shadow Wood. Dapples of condensation bead and curl down the paned windows above as pinked daylight from the red season spears the glass. No sounds make their way through the thick walls, though the yammer of a chatty bird sings through from the high casement. I look up at the tickle of its feet and crows of merriment just in time to see it blob a squirt of white shit above me.

Moisture collects at my armpits and dots my forehead. A tired crust cakes my tear ducts. I haven't slept yet, and I won't until the work is done. I'm jealous of Nisha, whose sleepy thoughts occupy a small corner of my mind as she rests in my well-blanketed bed and dreams of warm meat. Worn pages of my mother's grimoire—aged over twenty years—curl underneath my fingers in a sour yellow.

Knowledge is an ocean of power. Drink up.

The words are Orvellan, written in the language of the people caught on the border war between us and the Dark One. Some of the writing is clunky underneath my gaze, difficult to wrangle with my half-fluent tongue, but I manage well enough to find the correct page with the instructions for creating the tincture in a small but neat script.

A large gap in my memory yawns like a darkened maw. I inhale raggedly. Part of me hates opening this book, even though it's one of the few things left to me from my mother. I flip the page, looking at her name written there: *Rozena*. Dead as I gasped my first breath. They'd found her in the woods, still pregnant with me, and some woman in the forest had been able to deliver me into life after my mother slipped into death. Papa spoke of it once. But once had been enough. This final act had solidified our hatred of the Wolves.

My childhood is a spotty thing, a collection of fragments. A large swath of time is lost to me, and somewhere in there is when Papa hired a tutor to teach me Orvellan, to connect me back to his beloved, dead wife.

I turn the page to another part of the book, away from my mother's name. This isn't a bestiary, but bits on the monsters of the realm decorate margins. Devoted notes detail how to kill the creatures, or if it's possible to befriend them. There's even a section on the blasphemous chimeras the Dark One creates.

Text about faerie territory—the Otherland—is short and sweet. This is likely because even Orvellan witches know little about what lies beyond the Sea Mist. The witches knew just the tales everyone seems to know, something that lives inside the blood of every person, the way we all know that there is a happily ever after waiting on the last page of a love story. It's a knowledge they kept tucked into their wicked hearts—like to never shed first blood during the Red Season, to cross an X over one's throat at the sight of ill spirits, and to never kiss a stranger in the woods unless you want to draw a fate line connecting your lives to one another.

That is a problem for Future Briar.

I sigh when I find the right portion of the grimoire. A rose with angry thorns etched in ink hatches at the margins.

This page of the book not only explains the lore behind Fex's flower and the properties of it, but it also has clear instructions on how to cast the spell in Orvellan. Doubt attempts to sink its teeth into me, but I shake the feeling off as best as I can. If this works, the spell will measure the length of my fate and snap it in two, splicing the broken piece to my father's life span to lengthen it. In the end, it doesn't stop the disease from spreading, but stalls it for much longer. What's more, it creates a channel between us—much different than my mind-connection with Nisha—and results in the shared burden of illness. One day I'll go mad, but so will Papa. And it'll be much, much later, and less painful for him in the long run. I can practically smell the stink of my own fear as I lie to myself.

But what about you? The voice in my head is the ugliest part of me. *How will you wear the visions that come with the disease? The pain? Not well, methinks.*

Paranoia scratches at my skin. It's clear that once I begin, I can't stop, or else the spell won't take. Another opportunity to grab the rose at the right time won't come for a long while—too long. Without this, Papa will be screaming in madness and pain in three months. In a year's time, he'll either be dead or wish he was. A breath hisses between my clenched teeth. Fear is nothing when the stakes are this high. The rank taste of it coats my mouth, but I'll bathe in the feeling as long as I need to in order to bend fate to my will.

The words of the incantation to start the process dance on the page. In some ways, the translation is similar to the language of many Lumari marriage rites, particularly those done by Amaran priests. I try to take confidence in that, that my barely manageable grasp on the language is enough.

Tie thine life to mine. From blood to bloom. As my heart beats, so does yours.

The words cycle in my head, over and over. My mouth moves with the unsaid words, swishing the syllables over my lips and on my tongue. A buzz hums over me, vibrating like a thousand bees barely touching me. My throat aches, but I continue to mouth the words. I can almost hear Papa's wizened voice. *Don't, poppet. Not for me.*

Too bad, Papa. I'd do anything to save him from this.

To hells with it.

"Tie thine life to mine. From blood to bloom." The words crack from my throat, splintering the air. The smell of something burning sizzles the atmosphere. A paranoid corner of my mind urges me to check the door, check it, check it, check it. Did I leave it unlocked? But I can't check. I can't.

Once I begin, I cannot stop.

"Entwined, our hearts become one. One love, one doom." Pain fissures through my hands, an old arthritic feeling snapping through them, and the ache spikes like the vestiges of a three-day fever.

No matter. It's only physical pain, and I'm used to fevers.

I split the stem in half like a wishbone, following the instructions of the text. A cool, white sap with little beads of pearlescent lavender bleeds from the break. I push the substance out into my little mixing bowl, flinching in anticipation of what comes next.

Just do it, Briar.

With my index finger, I stab my flesh into a sharp thorn.

It just pinches at first, but then the pain increases. I hold it there. Blood ekes from the whorl of my fingertip before dripping into the bowl, red dotting the mixture. The ache worsens. This, in the end, should work. I break off the torn plant fiber with the sharp edge of my fingernail, leaving the thorn embedded. It'll have to stay until Papa has done his part. The pain, though, is the test. But suffering isn't new. That's at least half of existence.

It hurts to want something so bad that I feel it in every pore. The thorn grows in the strength of its ache. My lungs catch and shiver mid-breath. What are we humans, but creatures driven by the fear that we will inevitably suffer? And who am I, but a desperate animal caught in a trap, willing to gnaw a limb off to prevent an even greater devastation?

Papa's face floods my mind. Every time I see it, I try to pull it out of my thoughts, for just a moment. I don't want to feel anything, I don't want to think about the possibility of failing in my task. A selfish streak of loneliness leadens my chest.

I pull a little bottle from the back, ignoring the jab against my thorn-ridden finger. I'm only encouraged by the hurt. It must be working. It *must*. I clench the object in my fist, but not hard enough to break it. The hand-blown glass, imported from the seaside duchy of Ferr, reveals none of the secrets inside. Nothing betrays that what I am holding would have me slaughtered in an instant, except a slight, vibrating hum of the cool material.

Tie thine life to mine.

When we are bound, I'll feel the aches of his illness. That's the price, to feel his fate.

Arcane sin whispers from the inside as my finger pries at the lid. The scent of sweet-sour foam tickles the room like bubbling water. The little distillery fills with it. I resist the urge to look behind me, to check the doors. To see if Barro, Derrik, Father, *anyone* is watching. I shove down my fear, squashing it down deep inside. My fingers hum, vibrating on the bottle. This is a different enchantment from the innate, instinctive magic I possess. I reveal things. Light. *Truth*. This spell will create a connection. In some ways, it is similar to the superstition of the kiss I shared with the strange man from the woods. Instead of a line of fate, I'm offering to split my lifeline and give some of it to Papa.

Fex's flower is all about connection, tethering one life to another. Bonding someone through life and through death. My gift, by contrast, is a paltry party trick. A flower blessed by the gods may yet be powerful enough to bend the world to my will and I can finally save him—all of us—from a terrible fate.

Magic slips from the glass, pulsing. Illegal magic, spun out of the heart of a dying fae and bought off a peddler traveling from the capital.

That is for the men, the world would say. I stare at the light, my throat hurting with more than just grief. I long to be free, to be myself. *The gods do not want your wretched womanly touch on the divine. Do you not know what happens when a witch is born? It is said three men must die.*

It's superstition, but much of what we believe is built on such whispers. We tell tales for a reason.

To engage in anything arcane, unless one is anointed by one the priests of the Seven Orders, the Witch King himself, or another powerful man—well, it's stupid. More than stupid. It means death— at least, if anyone were to know.

Death in the face of desperation, though, is nothing. And when have I ever been anything but a little girl, crawling on her hands and knees, looking for a face to look back at me with love? Despite the wealth of being a duke's daughter, I'm also the daughter of a dead wife no one wanted him to marry. It shows in the cursory nods of the Bears and their pained acknowledgements. Truly, I need my father just as he needs me. His is the one gaze I could find and see a beloved young woman reflected back in.

Blood at the whorl of my finger turns silver, and with it, a sharp flare ignites in my flesh. I flinch.

I have so few friends.

My chest tightens. It feels like whatever I'm made of twists into a spiritual agony, and I muffle a scream into my shoulder.

Gods, I hate this. I hate everything. Why does it hurt so much to stay alive?

The urgency crescendos, and I pull at everything that makes me human, that makes me *me*. It is agony to exist, to try, to be human. Sometimes, the worst part of it all is to feel this pain and know you feel it. All of it goes into the spell.

Some people are soft. Perhaps their spellwork feels like that, too. But for me, this is what the magic wants from me. I've only ever been a half-wild girl starving for love. My broken heart leaves fragments of itself everywhere I go, and my clumsy fingers ruin everything I touch with messy, desperate longing.

I choke off the loneliness with a brutal twist of the lid, freeing the bottled, forbidden ephemera inside. Tiny dots of light, somewhere between fireflies and spritelight, buzz there.

A sharp noise cuts from my throat as I slash my hand. Magic collects at my fingertips, warming and oozing down my skin like molasses into the bottle of collected light. A breath eases from my mouth.

Do this right, Briar. Do this. He needs you.

My skin tightens against the wet heat, taut and uncomfortable beneath the itch of my clothes. I select one vial of mugwort and another filled with moonwater and go back to my table. Windows twinkle as sun rays catch against them, tossing bits of color on the walls in summer merriment. The scent of the trees presses against my nose, as if I'm still in the White Wood. A trimming of brinna bark sits just left of me at my work table, and sharp smells of earthen citrus mixed with chillies spike the air.

I cradle the rose, purpled in the bright light of day, and inhale. Rustles from my skirt skim the floor, snatching an errant twig here or a petal there as I pull from my stores. Restlessness jars every move-ment I make.

Ursula, my once-nanny-turned-handmaiden, assisted me with dressing when I returned from my venture into the woods. The stinking clothes from the night prior, I shoved beneath my bed. Then I was out, blinking against daylight and sleep deprivation, flower tucked into my satchel.

Now, I'm alone, and I can't help but be gutted.

My hands pound Fex's flower to dust. Last night swirls in my head; nothing about it will leave me. The words Derrick uttered echo between my ears, an angry promise that was sure to end in a fight. *We will talk later.*

As if his masculine pride, some petty bullshit, should be anything I care about right now.

An itch grates on my back and I turn. No one stands there, no one framed in the arch of the door that I *know* I locked. A breath hisses out from between my teeth. Am I evil? Am I terrible for going against my gods, against everything I believe in, to save the one person who has loved me without fail? I scrape back a piece of sweaty hair. Are witches, like myself, as cursed as the twisted Wolves I despise?

I am my mother's child. Once a witch, always a witch. I blink back my weak tears. "Stop it," I command myself underneath my breath. I slap my hand to the edge of the table, stinging my palm.

It does nothing to stop me crying.

Grief spikes inside of me, a sword straight through my gut. Duke's daughter or not, this act of witchery will have me pinned to a stake or worse if I'm found out. But it's not the fear that hurts. My chest shakes, and I wipe a rough hand across my face, dashing away the wetness there.

Doubts don't matter. I can only move forward and, if my fear insists on coming with me, it will need to run to catch up.

I bottle up everything that makes me Briar, pulling out threads from myself and into the mixture. Intent and willpower sweat at my back. Every ache I've ever felt pools in my stomach, and my fingers shake. But I've lost people before—people I never got to know. I'm no stranger to grief, to the complicated web of hurt strung about mere mortals by a shitty fate. Though I know that sometimes, you only get one chance to make someone live.

Ironically, to do it, I have to die a little.

* * *

THE PINK LIGHT deepens into maroon. My head pounds as I trek a path back to my room, arms aching with the labor at my workbench. The tincture took all day, and the strange light during red season nearly always brings on headaches. I have to push past the wretched feeling, because I need to get this to my father. Tonight.

Alone, alone, alone.

Nisha presses a protest into my mind, but I wave it away as if it's a mosquito. Papa truly is the only person I have left now, besides Nisha. Mother has always been a dream to me—never someone to know, just someone to wish was here. My hand strays to my mourning braid. I've never not had it, have always chosen to keep this hair uncut to honor my mother. Each night I brush it out, each morning I weave the strands back together. It's often unnoticed, wound up and used to tie the rest of my hair back, but it is a way to remember a woman I never got to know.

They say she traveled from the far north, from the enemy kingdom Selva, to marry my father. Papa, who stands burly as a bear with a swarthy sun-damaged complexion and a beard black as Ash Mountain. Papa, who used to fell trees with three strokes of an ax. They say Mother glided through in elegance, by comparison, lithe as the snow cats from where she came. A woman carved of pale ice, and tall, like a fabled giant. My parents were well matched in strength of body, mind, and will.

Nisha presses her big body into me, more dog than giant cat. Her tail flicks, tickling my cheek.

"I love you too."

I go to my bed, ducking underneath the covers. The sheet hanging off the edge tickles my scalp, and I push myself amongst the dust bunnies and secrets. My fingers find a shadow, a crack in the wooden floor. Mothballs and debris fill my nose, along with the stink of sweat from last night's outfit that I abandoned here. I sneeze, and sneeze again. Nisha fills my mind with images of rats.

"If you find one, please eat it," I mutter. I find the floorboard I'm looking for, nails digging between the cracks. A hollow groan trills underneath my touch as I pry it loose.

A *clack* rents the air, and I go still. Nisha doesn't say anything, so I continue to pull the heavy board from underneath the bed. Icy marble chills my fingers as I reach into the floor. I pull the object out into the light.

The spirit board is about the size of a large melon, with light-gray marble and black veins cracking through the soft color like spiderwebs. Carved deeply into the marble are letters in a runic language from Ash Mountain. Where my mother stumbled out of the snow into my father's waiting arms.

I pull out the little piece that goes on top of the board, crafted in the same marble, though shaped like an upside-down heart. Carved on top of it is a hand—the one spirits use to pass their messages on to the living.

Apprehension coagulates in my chest. I've tried to speak to my mother many times using the spirit board. She never answers.

But sometimes something else does.

A spritelight flares near me and I flap a hand at it, as if it's a bug and not a dead soul.

"Mother, if you're there, look after me tonight. I'm...I'm not ready for Papa to join you just yet."

My breath stalls. The triangled piece doesn't move at all. The little bit of hope blooming in my chest suffocates and dies. No one is there. No one replies.

Except the bubble of spritelight. One flicks out from beneath my bed, hiding at the edge of the shadow there. It's rare to see them in the daytime, but attempting to traverse the realms between life and death —even in a mere message—usually attracts them like flies to honey.

I wait another moment. She's never responded before, but this time...this time is important.

Nothing.

I'm alone. Again.

Still.

A tear slips down my cheek. One drop. I wipe it away, hard. Crying is for fools, and I am no fool. Fex's flower in hand, I head for my father's rooms.

My mother is dead, but my father doesn't have to be.

"WHERE IS GALINDA?" I ask. An unsubtle twitch ticks at the corner of my mouth. I hide it by turning away, busying myself at the table housing the collection of strong spirits in my father's bedchamber. Darkness coats the walls, with the exception of flickering candlelight jumping on the gray stone. Tapestries hang away from the blaze; the intricately threaded battle scenes are little more than indistinct smudges in the low, burnt glow.

Amber liquid pours from the lip of the decanter, droplets sloshing against my shaking fingers in a cold spurt like the alcohol disapproves of what I'm about to do. In one sense, I am saving my father. In another, I'm damning us both.

Thou shalt not mettle with powers of the gods, fate, and fae. The unsaid words send a chill down my spine.

I don't know where they come from, but I feel each syllable on my skin like a tongue traveling up and down my body. The scarred man's face comes to mind, followed by thoughts of a fate that maybe fucked me.

That is the superstition of babes.

Nisha, back in my room, queries a question at me. *[Trouble?]*

Not yet, I reply.

[Man mate?]

NO. Go back to bed.

She settles down, going quiet. My hands shake, but I pour the whiskey anyway. My back is to Father, blocking his line of sight. The arcane tincture slips from my trembling fingers into his glass. Fat, purple-black flecks plop to the bottom before burning fire-orange. The liquid delivers a soft hiss as the substance disappears.

Papa's bed looms like the sovereign's throne in our receiving room, overwhelming and taking up most of the space. King Thaddeus' throne lives in every receiving room across Lumar. Each is identical— ornate vesperi wood carved with intricate designs. A slightly smaller set of decorated thrones is placed next to it for the leaders of each respective duchy. A constant reminder that while the duchy may have a duke and duchess, the real fealty is to our sovereign.

The bed in my father's room is thick with pillows and piled high with rich, velvet blankets. A lit sconce floats by father's bedside, a bit of arcane light gifted from the Priests of Amora. Several war texts and one popular book on courtly love rest at his bedside.

I sit, one hip on the plush fabric and a leg dangling over the edge of the bed. I hand the crystal glass to Father, willing my jittery nerves to still. The shake ticking through my hands manages to still itself, if only for a moment.

Fex's flower is a mythology tangled in terrible love and terrible power. A rose that ended wars, and also ended worlds.

Tonight, I'm poisoning myself with my father's illness.

He accepts the drink with a nod. His skin brushes mine, and it's like touching a corpse. A sharp pain cracks through my heart. His once sun-burnished skin is the color of fuzzy mold. Memories—of us riding, of him teaching me to fight with my axes, of running through the forests long before the violence that marks our borders bled into our lives—strike me like physical blows. He used to be so different. *We* used to be so different. But even before he got sick, things had already changed.

My lip trembles, and I bite it. Useless feelings for a long-dead little girl.

Father downs half of the glass with a twist of his mouth. Lines crack through his face, age and pain and illness snaking through his forehead and in the downturned edges of his mouth. Despite the summer heat, he wears a mantle of fae hide about his shoulders without a sweat. The black, furred stole hides most of it, but a sliver of a vein peeks out just below his jugular.

He waves a hand. "Oh, Galinda is with Ewan."

I frown. Perhaps I am just an ugly creature, full of petty angers and sharp edges. Ungenerous. I've been called it before. But I can't help the bloom of distrust that burgeons high in my chest at the thought of my stepmother and her son. Of Galinda's shining hair, netted with pearls, and tight smiles next to Ewan, a tall man whose pride is more swollen than his overzealous muscles. A gag grips the back of my throat at the thought of how he uses his body to lean in too close, to loom over me. Of the contents of his sick whispers.

Papa shoots me a hard look. "Don't, Briar. Not tonight."

I open my mouth and close it. There's little I can say of my step-family. They're careless. Leeches. But they don't look like the enemy, not like I do, and the Bears love them. As does my father—Galinda has made sure of that.

He sips at the drink, then a sigh eases out from between his teeth. "The Ferr don't do much for this Kingdom, but they do make a fine whiskey. At least the trade route to the sea hasn't been shit on by those rabid animals." Papa takes another pull of the drink, the liquid leaves a light trail down the column of his throat.

I fight the urge to lean forward. Instead, I touch my neck. Waiting for a sense of heat, of cold, of something, of illness to strike. I keep waiting.

A burnt umber glow with lavender edges pulses down his neck. Disappointment jams into me when I feel nothing in response. A chill? Or is it a draft? Perhaps this takes time. I grit my teeth. I may be a witch, but I am an amateur at best. I can see truth and lies, but everything else? If I didn't take to it naturally, there has never been anyone to train me because I know of no one willing to die for such crimes. Aside from that, patience has never been a gift of mine.

Papa sighs. "The king will be here tomorrow or the next day, by all reports of his retinue's progress. All of my best liquor is going to be gone." A harsh noise growls from his throat, and he drinks again. I cock my head to the side, watching him. The way he looks at me makes my stomach convulse. And I realize in that moment we both have an ulterior motive in this conversation.

There's something unsaid lying in his mouth, as if he clenches the real thing he wants to say between his molars, waiting to spit it out. This isn't my magic telling me his lies. It is simply a deep knowledge of another person, the way a thousand words live in the tilt of their head or the tap of their finger. I make a noise of affirmation, watching Papa, waiting. Silver or copper coins will ease between his mouth soon enough. Possibly even gold. I don't bother tilting the lens I see the world through, though, trusting him to tell me the truth without needing magic to verify it.

Silence stretches between us, an ugly languid thing.

"Poppet, it's time for this to end. Marry him."

He doesn't say who, but neither of us needs to name the man in question.

Derrick. Lord Neeson.

"No," I reply, taking a sip from my cup. Spicy alcohol burns down my gullet, and I can't help but wince. I touch my neck again, checking for any changes. Nothing, no sign of illness or a slower heartbeat. I clench my teeth.

His face twists in frustration. "I'm dying, poppet." His voice cracks on the last word. A gold coin flips from his lips. Pain eviscerates me, an active participant in watching someone die and being unable to do anything about it. No one knows where this wasting illness comes from, how it is transmuted. And no one knows how to cure it.

He blinks rapidly. It was hard to see a man that once stood like a redwood become bent and brittle, as if rotted from the inside. Father once walked in the training yards, besting some of our most prominent soldiers. Now, he stays here most days, the curtains drawn and the room black, with only the occasional public appearance. Galinda handles everything the duchy needs, and House Berrat has slowly become hers, from its people to its treasury.

And I have become the enemy.

"Lord Neeson called on me today."

I don't say anything. All I do is watch him intently, waiting for him to down each last dreg of the glass. His eyes shine purple. The stray light leaks out from between his lash line and the whites of his eyes, undulating like the candle next to him. Father pauses, setting the glass down.

"So?" I say.

"Poppet, you need someone to shelter you when I'm gone." He doesn't mention Galinda. Whether he loves her or not, it doesn't matter. The Bears don't care for such things in the face of what is right. Among us, the duchy comes first. Honor comes first. Love falls by the wayside if it conflicts with the interests of House Berrat.

"I have sheltered myself long enough," I snap.

His lips thin, an indecipherable look passing over his arcane-infused eyes. Guilt sours my stomach, but I don't take it back. Not even as I wait to see what will happen next. How long will this strange light passing through my father last? The trickle of fear is back and my shoulders itch, paranoia crawling throughout my nerves. If someone walks in now, the crime of witchcraft will be clear. Blasphemy against the gods will be the least of my charges. But looking at the wizened man before me, I know it doesn't matter. Nothing matters but this.

Loyalty first.

I grit my teeth. Necessity dictates my every action, but I half wonder if I am being too ungenerous to my stepmother. That, too, is part of my desperation. Galinda placates people enough on the surface, but the vague allusions to the health of my father, the empty coffers, and the scraps of rations are a slap in the face. And it doesn't end with that. It shows in her flashing jewels, her illustrious feasts for her friends. We are at *war*.

But Galinda, instead, holds court.

More than that, it's as if she's made it her sole mission to erase my mother, me, and whatever goodness lies within my relationship with my father.

It doesn't matter, though. I watch his throat, the faint glow from the remnant of the arcane whiskey alights there, like he swallowed a dying firefly. That is all about to change. All I need is a little time.

Everything depends on it.

CHAPTER 8

Frantic decorators fly through the corridors. Greenery takes on a sick cast in the pinkened light, and the smell of roasted pig, apple pie, and garlic-infused root vegetables spills throughout Gray Hall. Our sovereign's imminent arrival spikes a kind of joyous terror into the cadence of every footfall and ripens each bit of sustenance. A whiff of death sweetens life, the way one waits for fruit to age just enough to bite into it.

And here I am trying to stall time, to freeze it, to reverse it.

Father makes no appearances. Concern coils at my breastbone. The poison should be working by now—I should feel it. I check my heartbeat, pressing a firm finger to the carotid artery at my neck, wishing for a sluggish beat to thump beneath my touch. Instead, it hammers, thudding with the desperation grinding through every muscle of my body. My head pounds, an ache driven by sleep deprivation and the fear that I haven't saved my father after all. I pray it's the beginning of the magic working, that the rose mixed with the spell is finally doing its job.

The myth of the rose goes back to Amara, a divinity of love who was once vengeance. They say it was her love for Fex, her beloved, that guided her to create the flower. The purple rose was meant to cure him of a mortal wound. In the act, she bound her life to his, so she could keep him with her always. They would live together, die together, and go to the beyond together. It was this act that ultimately transformed her from an agent of vengeance hellsbent on revenge to a manifestation of love, and propelled her to divinity.

Nothing in the world is free. A bit of witchcraft like this is no different. But I should feel something. Each thud of my feet packs in the realization further, that I am healthy and hale and that the spell didn't work. I need to *make* it work. If the price hasn't made itself known, something hasn't taken.

Snatches of conversations slip around me as staff jab gold burnished leaves onto lush garlands already hanging throughout the corridors. Whispers of the king flick from mouths. Some speak in hushes of the war, but those are few. Our southern border is a turgid coil of festering violence and everyone, from the dust-powdered peddlers to the most wide-eyed children, can feel it. Some of the nobility, of course, choose to ignore it these days. Especially when this holy time offers an amount of respite and an opportunity to pretend all is well.

The Red Season is not the time for travel, but I don't hear anyone remark upon that while I pass. Not as the guards did from the night prior, but then again, they didn't know the duke's daughter was there. The king coming now…it doesn't look good for any of us.

My feet find their way toward my father's rooms once more, past the paintings of various ancestors lining the halls. Most of them remain in their original, heavy frames, but Lady Agatha must be bored. The image of my great-great-great-great-*great* aunt slips from frame to frame as she follows me down the path to the wing that houses the duke's residence. She's a tiny thing, full of angles and a back straight as a pole. A knife hangs from her ball gown, her iron-colored hair swept up into a complicated coiffure. As I round the corner, she mouths something I can't discern.

I watch her for a moment, shrugging. It's hard to know how much consciousness the portraits retain, or if it's the will of the spirit imbued into the canvases that give them their personalities. And who knows what sort of ghostly being was used to begin with. Only the priests would know, and each sect of the Seven holds their ways close to their respective orders. Perhaps, if we knew the way they did magic, we'd see they aren't that much different from witches like me. My lips form a thin line at the thought, and I think of apologizing for the blasphemy for a moment. I am most certainly not going to a good place when I die.

Lady Agatha tilts her head at me then spins, gesturing at herself as if she wants me to take her off the wall. Then she points at me. It's impossible to know if she is warning me of something or simply harassing me.

A Green Knight in full regalia—from verdant-hued cloak with gilded clasps in the shape of clawed paws to intricately braided leather vest featuring a fierce bear head—guards the looming door to the duke's suite. The knight standing there has their hood up, shadowing their face. A blade hangs from their hip in a forest-hued scabbard.

Desperation claws ugly wounds into every movement, and the tick of time wears on me. Each day could be Papa's last. I can't help but wonder if I've only made mistakes so far. My lips burn with the phantom kiss once more.

My breath stills in my lungs. I hope it's not Derrick, but even if it is, I will deal with it. There are no choices anymore. A path has formed under the chain of events sparked by last night. What could have been is dead; I can only move forward and set fire to anything in my way.

Still, part of me dreads the confrontation where he'll rebuke me, want to make love to me, and beg me to marry him so he can protect me. I don't know what I'll say to that conversation, but all I know is I am not looking forward to it. Still, I do what I must.

Loyalty first. The words beat like a second heartbeat inside of me. The hood moves, revealing the knight's stoic face underneath.

"Quinn," I say with a genuine smile twitching my lips.

"Lady Briar," she says. Age lines her face, marked by deep grooves of laughter and worry. Somewhere in the realm of mid-forties, Quinn's face is rounded and plump, despite the sharp lines of her body. She inclines her head, years of hard training evident even in the simple motion. "What brings you back so early? Were you not here last night?"

Last night. The taste of blood floods my palette. Lustful, sinful creature that I am, I can't help but feel the warmth of that man's touch all over my body. Then it's gone, and I'm here in front of Quinn. My stomach sours.

I smile, lips clamped shut. My mouth is full of lies, but not the sort that will make a witch sick. Her doe-eyed gaze stares back at me, but something sharp lingers there. For a moment, I think about slipping into the current of my power to watch her words fall from her mouth as precious coins, but I decide against it. Fatigue grinds a heavy palm against my head, thumping it incessantly. Any magic now will hurt. I need to rest..

"Can a daughter not visit her father? Duty is a pillar of our people."

"So it is."

Quinn doesn't move, and strangeness coils between us. The Bear Knights do not know of my father's condition. No one does, though whispers have begun to flutter—half-mouthed rumors spiked in fear that are quickly hushed. The only person outside of the duke's inner circle —is the blackmarket healer. A man, simply called the Hand, fetched from Veritaes at a considerable sum. But that's because the Hand is disposable, someone that can be killed if necessary. Aside from the duchess, myself, and the priest, that is all who knows of my father's condition. To everyone else, Papa studies battles, plans for the future, and tracks shipments to our border. He's not dying. At least, he's not dying to everyone else.

"Quinn, I—"

The knight's eyes alight just over my shoulder. Someone clears their throat. The high pitched noise tinnies as I turn. Bile licks the back of my throat. I already know who it is.

"Briar." Galinda says, her lemon mouth pinched. "The name has always been apt." My stepmother peers up at me, eyes flicking over my form. The way she looks at me makes me feel like an ugly, ungainly giant. "Prickly and painful."

I let a wolfish look pass over my face with a confidence I don't feel. My chest heats, twisting with anger, the emotion rearing an ugly head just by looking at her. "Duchess. How...expected of you."

Her eyes narrow as if she thought something else would pass through my lips. This repartee with her always leaves me sore in ways that were difficult to articulate. As a witch, a lie would cost me more than I had to bargain with right now. As a stepdaughter, I hate her. But as the Duchess of Bears, disrespecting her disrespects my house. Not that I am above such things, but usually it leads to other conversations that I don't have the energy for now.

Her son—my stepbrother—Ewan is no different. He has the same pinched frustration. They are bent-in people with nowhere to spend their pained jealousy for what others have. It curdles inside of them, creating spoiled rotten creatures. The price of their petty rage shows with sour lips and pinched foreheads.

Galinda and Ewan lead lives that will never find satisfaction. They toss away precious moments like pennies as they look too far ahead, never noticing their palms passing gold into gutters.

Galinda stares at me, and the air weighs heavy between us. I don't know if she realizes it, but her teeth show like a menacing animal's. Every moment with her is a bruise forming against my skin, and I wonder if she feels the same as me.

Galinda will always be my father's second wife. And she hates me, his only child, for it and for the simple fact that I am his heir. There are no children borne from her and my father, and only her first marriage to a minor lord near the northeastern border by the Wexia duchy resulted in a child. I wrinkle my nose. Ewan. A child no longer, he's just a man who acts like a boy half his age.

A piece of me feels sorry for Galinda—sorry for the expectations that rest on anyone in her position. But little sympathy leaks in otherwise, not with how she spends her spare time making me miserable.

I step forward. "Duchess," I say with a sweetness I don't mean. Like some cursed, fae-creature, witches have their ways of lying without technically telling untruths. Tone is one such tool. "I must see my father."

"He's resting." She raises a neatly plucked eyebrow. "And so should you. The king will be here soon. You look like an elderly hag."

I grit my teeth. "Duchess—"

She holds up a hand. "That's three."

Three, three. There should be no limit to my using her title, but in the way of a predator she's found my weakness and sought to punish me for it.

I know what she wants.

Both of her eyebrows angle upward. Expectantly.

"*Mother*," I bite out. The word is a blade down my throat. How I hate her. Galinda's lips twist back at me into a smile, her pearly teeth glinting. She looks like a figurine, something one might buy with a bag of gold coins and a small loan. Her brass hair shines in the candlelight. Little jewels wink like sharp, tiny fangs on her blush-colored, satin fabric. An errant hand slides down her torso, fingering one of many diamonds. The display disgusts me.

What's more, it's a lie. *Mother*. A flush of heat licks down my body. Fuck.

She takes a step forward. An elegant nail caresses my cheek and I try not to flinch.

I feel the moment Nisha wakes from her nap, down a flight of stairs and several hallways away. Violent rage from her mind echoes my own. Images of blood are more considerable from the mountain cat than from my own head. But only a little.

Peace, I tell Nisha like the hypocrite I am.

"There we go," Galinda says. "Now, the answer is no, daughter. The Duke is unavailable to visitors." She spares a significant look at Quinn, before her footsteps patter down the hall.

* * *

CAGED— that's the feeling. I lie in my bed, resting my face against the soft pillow since there's nowhere else to be. Quinn turned me away after Galinda's order. A tear slips out from the seam of my eyelid, ribboning down my cheek. Gods damned, crying little girl. I wipe it away, blotting it against my sleeve, and it disappears.

The fever takes me though it's only a small one. I wonder how something that feels so big, so huge, that the lie can only spike my body temperature up a little. I should be burning up for the way my heart hurts.

Mother, mother, mother.

The word echoes in my mind, slapping every darkened corner. Why must lies be woven into the fabric of every interaction? This is not the first time I was laid out for a lie, nor would it be the last.

When I was a little girl, I was always sickly. Children lie, after all. Poorly. Often. Even accidentally. There was no one to teach me the price for a witch's untruths. I learned the hard way, through fevers and aching bones and gut-wrenching loneliness.

I don't fool myself into believing this is the price I've paid for the spell I've done to save Papa. This doesn't feel like a splintering of my own life, but rather an extension of the same, dismal existence I've come to expect.

"Everything is going to be okay," I whisper. The words croak into the empty room, with only me and Nisha to hear them. She sleeps next to me, and at the sound of my voice, even in slumber, her big cat form snuggles closer. My fever kicks up, brightening until cold sweat licks every inch of me, and my vision sparks beneath closed lids, like flint striking a rock.

I say the words again and again, needing to hear them. *Everything is going to be okay.* Needing to tell myself that I wouldn't fail. That Papa would be fine. That I could spare him the painful death that haunts his sunken face. I speak until my throat is raw, and I have to admit, even to myself, that I am a fool. The price must be paid.

Nothing is free. Not even the little lies we tell ourselves.

CHAPTER 9

Sometime well after midnight, before dawn peeks a pinkened eyelid open, I scuffle out of bed. Flashes of nightmares spear me, a series of intrusive thoughts that only build in horror. Everything hurts, but I'm dragged out from beneath my comforter by my own stubborn willfulness and the need to change my fate right at this moment. Perhaps the shift has rotated, and Quinn is no longer there. Perhaps she forgot to pass along Galinda's nonsensical command. A foolish feeling balloons inside of me until I can't ignore it anymore. Hope is a curse that keeps people fighting long after they should have given up, but who am I to say *no* to the one thing that keeps me going?

I pull on a night robe the color of rich, evergreen trees and a pair of soft, furred slippers so my toes don't strike the cold ground. Nisha queries at me, a sleepy question tickling our mental bond.

"Hush. I'll be right back," I say. The words hurt, creaking through the air like an ill-hinged door. If I speak to anyone, they'll assume I'm sick. And I am. Sick of my own, stupid shit. Why couldn't I have just slept, rather than cradling my feelings like a broken limb and rocking myself to a fitful rest?

Floating lights line the halls, bobbing in relative stillness, casting deep shadows onto the portraits. The quarried stone wall looks like it's been dyed from the wine-colored moonlight leaking through the large, arched windows. Thick velvet curtains frame the glass panes while the view reveals the border between Gray Hall and the Wolf territory beyond.

A long tapestry stretches along a shadowed passage. For whatever reason, no bit of arcane light bobbles in cozy curiosity. It's too dark to see the images on the woven fabric, but my fingers quest over the well-known depiction of the Battle of the Death Pass, over two hundred years ago when the Witch King sealed off the territory of Selva alongside its ruler, the Dark One. It is said the two were once friends, before an unspeakable betrayal created a rift that ended the peace. The mountain pass slung between our two kingdoms has since weakened, leaving room for the war in the north. Ash Mountain has long since been carved up by the northern tyrant. This tapestry is a requirement for every House to have displayed as a reminder of our victories and why we fight.

How we once won.

I lift my fingers from it and they come away clean of dust. It was recently treated, in preparation for King Thaddeus' arrival.

The darkness consumes even the soft fall of my footsteps. Tomorrow, our sovereign will be here. The question of *why* grates inside of me, alongside a bone-tired ache brought on by the now-dulled fever.

Why would King Thaddeus come during the Red Season? Is it truly that our country is so vulnerable that only a time of peace, as mandated by the gods, can keep our king safe? A breath shakes from my throat. His appearance only complicates my goals. I need to act soon and sort this out with Papa before the eyes turn to us.

My father's rooms will still be guarded. It is such that, even though we are in our own home, we fear the arrival of the Wolves. A shiver rakes my spine. The image of a twisted, cursed body, half man, half animal floods my memory. *Bane.* The feeling of him all over me—his saliva dripping into my face, before the scarred man commanded a halt—haunts me. I skirt forward as if to leave the memory behind, the silk of my evening robe dancing over the cold stone floor.

A bobbing bit of light, a carcass of harvested spirit sealed by a

Tamoran priest into a twisted metal sconce, floats over the head of the figure next to Papa's chambers. I watch the door from around the corner. My hand curls into itself, and my nails bite my flesh. It hurts. *Good.* I'm hoping to feel so much worse soon, even as I dread it. When I inhale, it's not enough. Air fills my chest, but it's like gasping a lungful of fear mixed with self-doubt. *Stop it, Briar.* Stop. Deep unease pools in my stomach.

The fever has left me weak. I've felt it before, and not even a piece of me wonders if it's possibly the effects of the spell I performed. No, I am not so lucky in life as to be easily gifted the one thing I so desperately want. I will have to beg, fight, steal, and kill for it. I'll do what I must.

I eye the cloaked figure ahead. If it's Quinn, she won't let me pass, not with orders standing from Galinda. But if it's someone else—

The head snaps up, looking in my direction. I catch the gleam of gilded hair as the light strikes it.

"Derrick," I say quietly, peeling myself from the shadows.

He says nothing, but the hood drops back. His face is hollow, wan in a way I haven't seen. His mouth is drawn in and shadows drape in heavy crescents beneath his ice colored eyes. "Briar," his voice cracks. He moves, his arms wrapping around me. A wave of cinnamon and sweat hits my nose. He smells like a training yard filled with apple pie.

A strange mixture of comfort and displeasure swirls inside of me, but I lean into the embrace nonetheless. It's not love, but it's a cracked-porcelain of a friendship. I wonder if I can glue it back together. It may never hold water, but it is something nice to have. "I need to see him," I whisper. I don't know why I say it so softly. Maybe it's our closeness, the heat of his hands on my back.

"No," Derrick replies, words wisping my hair.

I pull away, looking up in his face. "Why?"

"Orders."

My molars crack into one another as frustration spurts into me. *Galinda. Again.* What is she so afraid of that she wants to prevent me from seeing him?

Power. It always comes down to that.

I extract myself from Derrick's arms. They tense against me, as if he won't let me go, but his hands fall away after a brief moment. The brush of light against his face reveals nothing, except a stoic, slightly pinched look of concern. He's probably wondering if I'm going to be angry with his response.

The answer is yes.

My head pounds. The light above doubles for a moment, and a wave of dizziness washes over me. The lack of rest compounds, creasing each moment into tired irritation, but I allow myself to pull at the threads of my power despite the exhaustion. The grimoire calls it opening the third eye. A small, hand-written notation in the ancient pages called it the fae gaze. Another refers to it as the Sight. Whatever it is, it allows me to watch Derrick's mouth with certainty about what is true and what is not.

"Did you ask my father for permission to marry me?"

His throat works, but I already know what he'll say before he speaks. "I know you wanted to talk further about it." Coins flip from his lips, the world going silver and copper. They fall soundlessly. I blink, trying to make the head pain and the Sight go away. Neither do.

"What I said," I bit out, "is that now is not the time."

"I just thought...the Duchess—"

"*No.*" I snap. The flow of coins ceases as I cut Derrick off. "Galinda has no place in offering my hand to anyone. We spoke of *this*, Derrick." Betrayal leaks into my voice, making it wobble in a way I hate. *Weakness, weakness.* I clench my jaw, swallowing the soft feeling. "You promised to let me think about it. To give me space."

"Briar—"

I hold up a hand.

"We're over. You need to let me through."

Emotions flash across his face, twisting too fast for me to discern all of them. But two are familiar. Devastation and resolve. "Briar, just think—"

"*You do not get to tell me what to do.*" When I push past him, he doesn't move to touch me. I shut the door in his face, catching one last glimpse of his heartbreak.

CHAPTER 10

"*F*ucking Grims!" Papa hisses. The previously dark room catches with light as the floating sconce blazes into action. When he sits up, his face twists in pain, surprise, and anger. A brass blade is in his hand, but before his eyes find mine, it clatters from his weak grip. The metal strikes the floor. I flinch. The weapon clangs, rolling, before silence metes out a strangled death to the noise.

"It's me, Papa!"

Papa's thin chest rises and falls in rapid bursts before he lets out a breath.

"Twice in one day, Poppet. To what do I owe the pleasure of your company at..." He pauses, squinting as if he can know the time simply by thinking hard enough. "...the dark part of the sun's ass cheeks?"

I bite the inside of my lip to stop the trill of laughter that bubbles through my chest. I move closer, slippers ghosting soundlessly until I am next to his bedside. "I need to know...if you feel...different." My pulse pounds as I wait for his answer. I want him to say something, anything. A small change will do. Something to let me think that this will just take its time.

Instead, new wariness dulls his watered-down gaze. "Why?" His voice rasps like dead grass.

No.

I push aside the rising tide of tears. There's been too much crying from me the last few days. Too many feelings of wretchedness.

"I tried something," I say instead. Our gazes lock and understanding passes between us. His shoulders slump, a defeated edge gripping the corner of his mouth. We don't talk about it, and truly, he doesn't know I am a witch because he *chooses* not to know.

"No you didn't," he bites back, frail torso falling back onto the goose feather pillow with a muffled thump. The fabric sighs against him, as if it is giving up. "Don't speak to me of...that."

That. The word hits me like a well-placed slap, and I blink as if he really struck me.

Gods, why am I like this? Too hard on the outside to let anyone in, too tender-hearted to not cry about a harsh word from the few I care about. But the pain sits between us, as it always does, and I swallow the hurt. He accepts every other bit of me. It's enough. It has to be. Even if the part of me he can't look at is the part of me that makes me feel closest to the woman we both lost.

It's lonely, sometimes, being yourself. But I understand why the words need to remain lost.

Tension grips my chest, tightening until it's hard to breathe. I wonder if Papa feels it, too. The same devastating curiosity about Mother that burns in my lungs every moment of every day. Did she truly cast a love spell on him, making the Duke of one of the most powerful Houses in Lumar fall in love with the strange woman that slipped from the mountain pass and into his bed? I swallow down the desire to know. To ask such a thing is to beg the past to wake its dead, and to think it at all is to disrespect the ghosts of those who have come before. To become spirits long gone ourselves.

So, we do not speak of it.

Instead, he lets me go to him, and I place the back of a hand to his forehead. The chill of icy sweat licks my knuckles. He doesn't look at me, but somewhere off to the left corner of the room with an unfocused gaze.

"There are things we must discuss, Briar."

Not poppet. *Briar.* "Okay." I croak, but I'm not fully focused on his words. Instead, I've opened my third eye, revealing the veil of magic that coats the word. My head screams a protest as I force open the Sight, but I ignore the thrumming ache of rushing blood and the burgeoning soreness that claws up my esophagus. I grit my teeth into a smile. My magic is usually easiest for seeing what is spoken, but this time I shove it into another form. Wrestling it into a shape it's not meant to be. I've done this once before, when I found out he was sick.

I can do it again.

The pain expands, ballooning in my chest as if the magic is another body forced into mine, wearing my very skin. White bursts behind my eyelids, and I gasp.

Prickling blackness coats the world.

"Poppet?" Papa says and the bed groans with a quick movement.

I hold up my hand, swaying on my feet. I inhale, a long drag of a sound. The world swims, but I hang on. My gaze snaps to the wrinkled, shadowed bed.

Papa's neck isn't the bright-orange with lavender haze left over from the residue of magic and whiskey. Instead, dull gray coats him from chin to sternum. The disease slithers in his throat, into his lungs, and congeals somewhere in his gut. There's a small spark of trailing light there, but not enough to convince me it's anything other than wishful thinking. This time, I don't cry.

The magic wasn't enough. *I* wasn't enough.

A hopeless laugh gurgles from my chest, and it feels like a sob.

Papa is speaking, but I can barely hear the words. His watery eyes don't look directly at me, but flick around the room—anywhere but my face. "...soon," he says. His voice is soft. "Perhaps we will have the year, but the winter will be hard." He lists documents, where he keeps his diary for managing our territory, and lists the lords he trusts and the ones he doesn't.

It's then that I realize I'm getting a list for when he dies. Pain, worse than any physical torture, splices through me. I am so, so tired of feeling this way. It hurts to see him like this, but the agony of watching him lay out his life like a business deal is worse. What's more, we both know it is necessary.

"Papa, no. I—"

It's at that moment, a knock cracks against the door and behind it, Derrick's haloed face appears. I open my mouth, words ready to flay him, when I notice he's not alone. Derrick's face is pale and startled, like a wild hare encountering a creature far stronger and more dangerous than he'd prepared for.

The secondary figure pushes past Derrick. A gangly youth, with skin like the pale guts of an apple. He's barely nineteen, thin-limbed and shaking. The loose fitting, verdant tunic marks him one of ours, two waved lines underscoring the emblem of the Bears to mark his position as courier.

"He's here," the man-boy says. His chest rises and falls the way a frightened rabbit's might. I rake a hand through my hair, lungs stalling mid-breath. Every bit of me—body and soul—freezes in collective terror. This isn't good. Early isn't good. *Early* makes us vulnerable. "He's here." The courier says again, unnecessarily.

For some reason, the courier stares at me. Eyes tracking over my silver hair, up my statuesque body, and on my sharp face. *You've the chin like the deadly end of a blade, Briar,* Ursula once told me. She wasn't wrong.

When our eyes meet, distrust darkens the courier's eyes. *Northerner. Selvan.* I nearly taste the words in the air. It doesn't matter if you are the daughter of the duke when your kingdom is at war and you look like the enemy. I grit my teeth. Finally, the courier breaks eye contact with me, flicking to the bed.

The young man shouldn't be in here, shouldn't see my father this way, but that is a problem for later. My hand twitches for the ax that isn't there.

The youth swallows, eyes on Papa, and his nostrils flare with a visible look of panic as he licks his lips. He's never spoken to my father, his liege the Duke of House Galibran, directly before, and the anguish of speaking to power etches itself into his eyes.

But this news? *Gods.*
Because there's only one *he* we've been expecting.
The Witch King.

CHAPTER 11

"Get out."

The courier hesitates, as does Derrick. The men share a glance with one another, a loaded look, as if they are thinking of not abiding the command.

"OUT!" I bark again. This does the job, though Derrick is sure to look at me for an extra moment, as if double checking to see if I mean him too. My glare sees him out the door. Papa huffs a weak cough, and I turn to him, shifting him so he's upright. "What do you want to do?"

"I have to receive him. Pull out the drawer there and grab the green box."

My fingers do his bidding, snapping the lid open to reveal a small sea of white powder. A pinch of it swirls and dances in the air. *Reezin.*

"Papa?" The question of why he has it sits between us, but he doesn't answer the hidden query. Instead, he takes the box from me and beckons for the little tray with a straw next to his bedside. I give it to him with shaking hands. His expert fingers form a line of the snow-colored substance, lining it up with precision. Using the straw, he inhales the drug through his left nostril until the line disappears.

"Sicilop Himself blessed this," Papa says, eyes bright. His voice takes on a booming quality. "Don't look so shocked."

Reezin is a coveted substance and highly controlled by the Seven Orders. The priests of Sicilop, the god of pain and pleasure, create it and dole it out with reluctant hands. The side-effects are uncontrollable tremors for days after use, occasional hallucinations, arcane-infused eyes, and a bitter temper. Sometimes it gifts the bearer with a small bit of magic, hence the strict control over it. It is best used for the near-dead, to give them the strength to say goodbye to their loved ones when their souls dwindle into spritelight and go beyond.

"I'd no idea my daughter was such a prude," he murmurs, wiping beneath his nose. His eyes spark, the milky white skin around them pinkening slightly. He exhales. "That is better." He tosses the covers off himself. His thin legs wobble for a moment and I lunge, but he shoots me a look that causes me to pause. Papa frowns, grinding down his teeth in audible frustration. "You'll need to come with me and…" He flinches. "I need a little help dressing. Let the lad know we will meet His Majesty in the receiving room."

* * *

BRUTAL. That's the word that follows King Thaddeus, the renowned Witch King. Little rumors about his first wife nip at him, whispers that skim his leather booted-heels. Hushed words and shushed concerns about his daughters bite the path he leaves behind. No one says anything outright, but then again, those with beloved daughters of their own do not seem to offer their hands in marriage to him.

The greedy, the reckless, and the cruel have no such concerns. Their daughters are expendable.

What does it say about me that I support such a creature? The flavor of hypocrisy is so familiar I do not even taste it anymore.

Papa leans heavily on my arm, and I do my best to make it look as if he is leading me into the room. Infrequent shakes jitter beneath his formal leathers. He looks the picture of a warrior, but beneath the drugs and the costume, he is just a sickly old man, and the father I've loved all my life.

Nisha slinks beside us. My apparent distress had her beaming straight through the walls to get to me. She only pretended to be a regular, non-magical creature when she got to my father's rooms.

Just outside the doorway of the receiving space, a scuffle inside the portrait on the right takes place. The large frame clears ten feet and is at least five feet in width. A depiction of the first Duke of the Bears proudly rears atop a white stag, a thick hide of our namesake puffing around his shoulders. Now, he calls in silent strain for the beast beneath him to heel as he pulls the reins of the pawing animal. Uninvited company crams in around him. The gilt-edged metal frame is jammed with long-dead family members in various dress styles from the last one thousand years. At least thirty of them have managed to invade the first duke's territory, and he looks on in irritation. He reaches out and slaps the back of the second duke's head, reportedly his least favorite son. Another man laughs in a muted guffaw, but it's hard to figure out if he's the fourth duke or the slapped man's brother. Lady Agatha waits three frames over and she nods to me when Papa and I pass through the doors.

On the opposite side, another painting of the same size waits. Usually, the king's portrait hovers there, watching. How they accomplished to put King Thaddeus there, animating the depiction of someone still living I've no idea. Our sovereign's image is notably absent, and yet none of my painted ancestors move into that space. Only a purple plumed raven perches, feathers flickering from deep mauve to black in a silent breeze.

Scant lines border the receiving room, four flames flicker at separate corners. A cold groan strikes the air when the doors snick shut. Ahead, darkness waits in the throne made just for the King of Lumar. Silhouettes of three ravens limn the edges of the elaborate chairs dedicated for the rulers of House Galbran. I can't help but wonder if the birds are shitting on my father's cushion.

I can just make out the puff of my own breath striking the chilled air when sparks hiss above. The chandelier cracks to life., a whirling glow that sends light shooting off into every direction. Arrows of fire strike the non-magical sconces on the stone walls, sparking to life. Bursting power rents the air, and the room burns with sudden visibility.

The Witch King leans back on the throne, an errant finger swirling over the shining wooden arm of the seat.

King Thaddeus' dangling legs splay in a lazy tangle. White skin, like sour milk, is tight across his face. Blue shadows bruise beneath his eyes. Bird-like and beady, they tighten when he marks our entrance. With bits of silver threading through his dark mane and a grim crease to his mouth, he wears his seven hundred years as if he is forty. The smile he wears looks like it will crack off his face.

Looking weak is a death sentence, and with Papa's frailty, I worry that a failed bow will end with us all dead. My fingers tighten over his arm for a second, and my exhale is low and hard as I let go. Papa gives a deep bow, folding himself nearly in half. His steadfast fist presses to his heart.

I'm in no fit state to see a king, but I ignore that, sweeping the end of my nightgown to the left as I curtsy deep, performing a similar gesture to my father as I press a curled fist to my chest.

"Your majesty," we intone. I grab my father's arm, preferring to look needy than to have him endure the embarrassment of a fall.

"Bear," King Thaddeus says. He doesn't address Papa by his title. Is it disrespectful? Affectionate? I can't help but wonder if he calls all the dukes by their heraldry's charge to keep things simpler when they inevitably die before our immortal ruler. "Should she be here?" Irritation laces the Witch King's voice.

Papa holds his gaze. "She is my heir."

The king nods, a look of displeasure clear across his face. His dislike of women is well known, ever since his wife left him. I can't help but think that, after meeting the man, I don't blame her for trying to run. Disloyalty blooms in my chest, and I try to will it away.

King Thaddeus' eyes track over my father, then briefly steal across my face. The hairs on my arms raise, and my heart skitters in my chest. *Run*, it begs. Something around the king's eyes reminds me a little of the scarred man in the forest. A hatred lives inside of him and —whatever it is—its enmity is directed at me.

Rumors whisper that the northern tyrant's–the Dark One's–spirit is evil enough to make an entire room bleed from every orifice, rumors that even shadows are fearful of him. That the air stills within a hundred miles of him, too terrified to move a single wisp of wind. Unspeakable atrocities are committed in his name every day on our border. Despite the urge to run from King Thaddeus, despite the deep unholy fear raking through every nerve, I am not fool enough to believe that only goodness can defeat evil. *Loyalty first* isn't just some pithy saying. It means more than only following an honorable leader. With these words, we might barrel straight into darkness, in pursuit of aiding a terrible man to kill a worse one.

Sometimes, honor looks ugly.

"I suppose it's just as well." King Thaddeus doesn't address me directly, but looks at my father. "I need your daughter to marry the Duke of Wolves."

Disbelief slams into me.

No, no, no.

I can't breathe.

The Duke of Wolves. *Fuck.* Whispers of another name fill my mind —the Duke of Death.

A freeze drops into my blood. Nisha hisses next to me, and the Witch King spares her an amused glance, but he doesn't look at me.

Words stick in my throat, the protest stolen from my lips. "Why?" is all I manage.

King Thaddeus turns, the focus of his attention shifting the power in the room. A frigid feeling sweats through my flesh. It's as if the sun itself turns a direct gaze on only me, leaving me chilled.

He raises his eyebrows like he's seeing me for the first time, and dread leadens my belly. *Fuck, fuck, fuck.* I don't know what is worse, that the king seeks a wife for the Bears' second-greatest enemy, or that I've been noticed.

"Don't you want to end the war...?" He trails off, snatching a look at my father.

"Lady Briar," Papa fills in.

"Hmm." King Thaddeus stares at me. "We need to quell this... dispute. And while I do not begrudge the Bears the land that is rightfully theirs—" he pauses significantly, allowing the weight of his words to settle over the room.. Papa looks wan, but not the way he did in his bed. The Reezin does its work.

Unlike Fex's flower. Another wave of raging devastation crashes into me, and I inhale a lungful of disbelief.

"I don't know, your majesty—"

"You don't know?" The words are dangerous and filled with disdain.

"I—I need time." My father finally says, and the world drops out from underneath me. Tremors wrack my fingers, and I clench them into fists until I feel either blood or sweat slick my palms. All of this, every effort, could end right here. Papa could die with a word from this immortal man. *Stop. Pushing. Him. Papa.*

It's dangerous dealing with magic, and the Witch King is no exception. The look in his eyes sends a chill through me, as if I've been shoved outside sopping wet in a blizzard.

Memory Taker, they whisper about him.

I grip the fabric at my skirt, needing something to cling to. I'm a minor witch, self-taught who can tease the truth from lies. I can bend the world, just a bit, in my favor with a little blood and a promise of repayment. I can easily see deception, a relatively minor gift. In truth, I'm little better than the Fae of old, bargaining little splinters of my life force and the world around me.

But a power like stealing memories? I have nothing like that. Who's memories has this man stolen?

Fear sizzles in me. I can't help but wonder if the Witch King will somehow look at me and suddenly know that he and I share an affinity for the uncanny. A king that sits in a gilded city while we bleed here on the border probably does not see the similarities between us. But I do.

He catches my eye and something blazes in him. Terror grabs at my throat and chokes the air there. *Hatred.* That's what the look is.

Hatred, pure and simple.

"Time isn't a luxury we have. Her, someone else, I suppose it hardly matters, but it would be fair to offer the man a decent brood-mare." He gives me a glance. "You should dye her hair. It's like you fucked one of those garish northerners. She looks disloyal."

My father's knuckles pop as he clenches them. The king decides to ignore it, because there is no way he didn't hear it.

"The rest of her..." His eyes rake down my body, and I want to cover myself. I hate it when men look at me that way, like they want me to know that they see every curve and they like it. It doesn't make me feel pretty. It feels like a violation and my shoulders itch like I'm being hunted.

"He might fuck her. We'll see. This is a peace offering, after all. And the Wolf wants...well, not forever, but I'm sure she can manage him for," he narrows his eyes, "a year and a day. It is for the wellbeing of your people, after all."

Silence grips the room, except for the caw of one of the king's ravens. It's beak snips, the noise breaking through the room. Tension grips my chest so hard it hurts as if my heart is giving out.

"It will buy us enough time to control the northern border. I'll give you until the evening after next to pretend you've thought about it and agreed to save your pride, Bear, but do not keep me waiting after that. I'll give you the opportunity to find a replacement, but it should be a woman of high standing. Anything less is an insult. You may receive me tomorrow as if this never happened."

With that, he leaves, sweeping away as if he didn't just command my life to be thrown away.

Papa clenches his jaw, then unclenches it. "That man has a passel of daughters and he has the nerve to try to make me give my heir to a monster?"

I reach out to touch him, then pull back, retreating back into myself. "Papa, I don't think we should talk about this now." Not in here. I don't know where the king's portrait is, or if one of his ravens lurks in the shadow. I don't know what other evil powers he has.

Disloyalty is something that the dead know intimately, and now is not the time to join them.

"It doesn't matter, I will find someone else," he says. A chill runs over me, goosepimpling my skin. Perhaps he will; after all, Papa is trying to secure his legacy. The Reezin still pumps through his blood, but a wanness takes root in his features once more. The next few days will be all types of hells for him, and, if this is how he will keep himself upright, Papa will continue to take the drug, regardless of the ill effects. A small kernel of hope lives in me, but flickers like a dying ember. Maybe my spell will take, though the likelihood dwindles with each moment.

But if the Witch King—the near, all-powerful ruler is willing to bargain with the Wolves to get what he wants, why would he not bargain with the Bears? The ghost of iron touches my lips as memories of my bloodied kiss slip through the sieve of memory. The Duke of Death will be much worse than a simple soldier curious about kissing a stranger on the wrong side of the wall.

I can't help but wonder if the kiss cursed me into this moment. The line of fate drawn between the enemy in the woods and myself feels like a brand all over me. Somehow, that ruined everything I tried. Certainty grinds my teeth and my eyelid ticks. I want to scream, to cry.

All the stories told me what to do, and I didn't listen. That bastard from the forest smeared a bloody hand across my destiny, marring it until there was only one choice. That's why they call it a line of fate. It slices straight through your life, making any other outcome impossible.

This path promises more violence, but I'm willing to do whatever it takes. All my options narrow to one.

I'll marry the monster.

CHAPTER 12

Scars bite into the walls of the empty room. No furniture clutters the space, aside from one abandoned chair in the corner with a frayed-green fabric. Morning light claws a ragged talon through the single window, lighting up the dim space in a half-hearted effort.

Quiet spreads itself thinly through the room, with occasional noises from the outside world as the manor bustles into motion. A soft surprise slips through me, and I can't even believe I'm feeling anything beyond the heaviness that cakes my lungs. Is this really happening to me?

The jumbled emotions in my chest swell into a complicated mess. I have another chance to save my father, but I'm likely to give up everything for it.

Marry the enemy? It's impossible, but I have to do it.

Papa's life in exchange for mine is the one thing I have that I can leverage, that I can bargain with our king for. In a way, it's not that different from what I attempted to do anyway.

Nisha slips into the back of my mind. An awareness of a dead rabbit on her claws clings to my consciousness, as if my fingers are tacky with the same blood. There's a suggestion of *don't*. Of *give up*. Of, *just stay how things are*. I shut her out.

Papa is still dying, and my plan has failed. The fucking rose, —the trip into the forest —for something that didn't even work, all a waste. Frustration stabs into me and I grab my ax, slinging it into the air through imaginary heads.

The Reezin won't do what it needs to forever. Eventually, he'll have to give in to death, and we can't have that. Some of the erratic wellness I'd seen from Papa the past year—the shiny bits of hope I clung to—now made sense. It was the drug.

I hack at the air with the swing of my practice ax. It's completely wooden but heavy enough to leave blackened bruises to anyone it hits, unchecked. Muscles along my shoulder blade extend, and I give the movement everything I have.

The Duke of Death. Marriage to our greatest enemy.

The gods are cruel.

A bark of laughter scrapes from my throat. What a fool I've been, thinking I'd be able to grind up a flower, say a spell, and make this nightmare end.

The nightmare is just beginning.

A shriek of frustration cracks from my throat, and with it, I let go of what could have been. I hack at invisible enemies, swinging my blunt wooden weapon with everything I have. Determination fills me as I decide that we'll receive the king and that I will do what I must. I stop, panting, an angry ache in my back. *Idiot.* I should have prepared my muscles better.

I use the opportunity to stretch. This is perhaps the tenth time I've been here, waiting on company, but one of countless times I have come here and been alone.

Weariness weighs on my shoulders. It's hard to be a witch. I'm slow to trust, but it is hardly a bad thing when you're someone with secrets that can get you killed.

The scratch at the door sends me whirling. White braid whips into my face, and I raise my wooden weapon, not that it will be much good. My nerves alight, as if someone will come barreling through the entrance with their blades raised.

Instead, Barro and Valor walk in, their gaits synchronized in a display of perfect twinning, then a third person—a woman with light brown skin dappled with freckles across the bridge of her nose. Her natural hair is cut short, her curls haloing her rounded face. She sniffs in disdain at Barro. "I can tell you haven't bathed recently."

"These are trying times, Daria."

"Not so trying that you should smell like an ill-mannered pig in front of Lady Briar," she says, with a significant look to me as she sketches a short bow. Barro mimics her.

Twice a week, for a few weeks now, the four of us have met. Barro suggested it, and here we are. That seems to be the way of things—he has a natural charisma to him that lends itself to getting what he wants. Why he wants me to join them, however, is beyond me.

Valor says nothing. Instead, he moves into his own stretching routine without greeting me. Daria glares at him, but his silence is not unusual.

Here, in this room, the title should fall away. For once, I agree with Valor. Who cares if you're a lady when there's a blade speeding toward your neck? My pulse throbs in my ears. Am I able to fight? Yes. Have I trained—despite the ideas that ladies should not? I have. Am I a good fighter?

That is the question with an answer yet to be determined.

"Let's begin," Barro says, vaulting toward me without warning. He whips to me, his leg slashing out. I jump over it, landing on my feet.

My practice ax arcs high, slicing toward him. He dodges easily.

"You could use more practice," Barro says. I don't need my fae gaze to know he means it.

"Well, that's what *you* are for," I return, swinging my ax.

Flashes from our fight with the enemy assail my thoughts, seeding doubt when I really don't need it. I've fought when I've had to and survived so far. Papa helped train me, but I'm no soldier. Not like Barro, Valor, and Daria who are all elite guards. The violence lurking beneath my skin hesitates, doesn't follow through the right way.

Barro continues the dance, not even bothering with a weapon. More graceful sprite than man, he slips away from my onslaught with a fluidity that shouldn't exist. He truly is near-fae with the twists of his body, enough to make me wonder if there's a long dead magic slipping through his veins. I shake my head. The fair folk are so rare, they might as well as not exist this side of the Sea of Mist. His

"You think too much." He doesn't even have the decency to be out of breath.

"And you talk too much," I huff back, with another desperate movement. The handle is heavy, and my arm is tiring.

With a quick jab, the side of his hand cracks into my wrist, sending my practice weapon skidding across the floor. Valor calls for a rest, which I am happy to comply with. We all sit, and Daria pulls out a bladder of water, offering it to me. I drink deeply, allowing the cool liquid to soothe my worried insides.

"His Majesty will be here soon," Daria sighs. "They've asked the women to...not appear." Her mouth becomes a thin line. A sour feeling guts me.

"Everyone knows Thaddeus is a misogynist." Barro shrugs. "He's just a sore loser." Valor hits him with the flat side of his blade. "OW! *What*—everyone knows he's bitter about his ex-wife."

"That's your king," Valor spits out.

Barro's eyebrows arch, mouth becoming a pert shape that makes him look surprised and a little petulant. "Briar doesn't care if we're honest. Do you, Briar?"

The words make me uneasy. Something about them is too close to the truth of who I am, what I am, but I shrug it off. "Of course not. Who would believe me, even if I were to tell of your treasonous talk?"

"Your father, of course, Lady Briar," Daria replies pertly, pushing a tendril of sweat-laden hair from her forehead. "Are we here to throw axes or just show our asses, Barro?" She looks at me, a blush reddening her cheeks. "Apologies," she says with an embarrassed cough. I incline my head, amused at her bashfulness of the swear.

Barro sticks out his tongue.

"Are you a child?" Daria asks him in disgust.

"*Yes,*" Valor replies on Barro's behalf. "Ill-mannered and ill-behaved." He pauses. "But good-looking, at least." Valor's self-satisfied smile mirror's Barro's.

Daria rolls her eyes. "Fuck you both. Ah—" She shoots me a wide-eyed glance, clearing her throat. "Sorry, m'lady."

"Please, I am no lady here." Or anywhere, really. I wave a hand, hoping she knew foul language didn't matter to me. If she could hear my string of inner monologue, she'd know I didn't give a fucking shit about the curse words. Some lady, I am.

"Anyways, why do we bow to someone like that?" Barro asks.

"That is the way it works," Valor grits out.

Barro shrugs, apparently unconvinced. Daria says nothing, seeming to give up on our purpose to actually train and goes to sit in the only chair.

I sigh. "The Dark One is worse. Sometimes, the balance of power requires a balance of evils."

Barro opens his mouth and Valor gives him a look, shutting him up. Perhaps the balance to their relationship is that Barro always says too much.

One twin lies, the other tells the truth. The one speaks often, the other only a little. Even I have to agree. Sometimes saying exactly what one thinks is a bad idea, especially in the face of something much more powerful than you. That said, the twins are strange. Barro seems to say what they both think, but Valor is the one that keeps him in check. Barro rarely says anything I disagree with, but truly, the north is a mess and King Thaddeus is the only one keeping us from being overrun by the Dark One's twisted creatures.

Are they so unlike the Wolves? A part of me whispers. I haven't seen the wraiths the Dark One creates, but I've seen the twisted hides of the cursed men near us. Rumors curl throughout Lumar that the Wolves' curse slipped like poison from the Dark One's fingers and was carried south all the way to the duchy presided by Lord Galibran. The curse dispersed like a plague, ripening and spreading. The gods must hate them to have made most of House Galibran's young people beholden to the tides of the moon and their own bad temperments.

"Let's get back to this," I say. *Before everything is different.*

* * *

A KING ARRIVING at one's home is not a small thing. The divine ruler of one's country visiting during a time of war is something else entirely. We are but children welcoming a god to our hearth with clumsy generosity and needy-approval that aches like a rotten tooth.

By midday the whispers become less discreet. A man runs into Galinda's sitting room, where I've been forced to sit with her circle of ladies and silently thread my needle with a broken smile. My stitches are neat and fine, but that's not the feedback my stepmother gives me. The man, another courier but older and more disheveled than the last, huffs with out-of-breath panic. "At—the—gates—His —Divineness."

The poor creature looks near collapse.

A joyous light enters Galinda's eyes, and it is more terrifying than her sneer. I wonder if Papa told her the king arrived last night, if this is all an act. I don't bother to pull the Sight over my eyes, her lies show in her over-wide movements and the extra gasp she sips in. Also in the extra bangles of expensive gems that drip from her wrists and twinkle at her fingers and neck.

She claps her hands once. "Let us receive His Divinity."

Then she glides from the room.

* * *

THE THRONE ROOM IS PACKED. Papa stands in stoney, unnatural stillness beside me. His eyes spark with a chaotic glaze in them that tells me the Reezin pumps through his blood with ferocity. Derrick stands next to him, shrouded in the decor of a Bear Knight. I can't help but wonder if Valor, Barro, and Daria watch from the soldiers lining the edges of the room. It's odd to be part of the center of this and to have one's friends witness it.

Friends. The word gums, unsaid, in my mouth. I don't know what to do with it, but it doesn't matter, not anymore. Today is not a day to wonder or to be soft. It's a day for tough iron and the will to survive.

I grit my teeth, wishing for the comfort of the handle of my ax. Not that this is the type of battle for weapons. Some battles call for violence in words, while others necessitate the blades of mental fortitude and to be stubborn enough to not fail.

The doors whoosh open, trumpets blare, and bright, burnished things of brass and boldness caw a song that will ring in my eardrums for days to come. Our kingdom's anthem sings into the room, each beat a joyful and stubborn thump.

The king's court slips through first. Lords and ladies that form his retinue, living mostly in Veritaes. Flashy gold spins from their hair. Little blots of arcane wonders lip at their faces, slipping around them like floating, mythic faerie circles.

The air tastes of falseness, so bloated with fake faces and put on acts that I can't help but feel all of the courtly politics scrape against my skin like a blade threatening to skin me alive. My power quests out in rogue wonder at the sudden increase in lies. My teeth grind against one another, and I force a breath out through my nose. It's a useless power, sometimes. Of course everyone here is lying a little. It's politics.

I cross my arms, holding them over my chest, and do my best to fade into the background as the festivities welcoming the king and his entourage begin. For a moment, I am no one. In a way, that's what I'd like— to become invisible to everyone else, except for a select few I let into my heart. I let down my guard for a moment, my own truth washing over me. My mouth floods with a metallic, bitter taste I've come to associate with sincerity. It's a comforting antidote to the overly sweet falsehoods.

I grit my teeth against them. I'll soak in every lie until the courtly acts wind down. Then, I'll make another bargain. Hopefully this one won't curse me to failure like the last one.

Just don't kiss a rogue in the forest, a nasty voice in my mind tells me.

I don't reply to my inner thoughts. Instead, my hand strays to the strange bracelet gripping my wrist. It bounces a little there, like a playful rabbit. Though it's just a strip of shadow, it reminds me of a cute little creature. For a moment, I think I see eyes peering back at me, but I blink and it's gone.

A line of fate. My fingers brush over my mouth.

Is it destiny? I don't know. I believe that the world will force our hand to pick between ever-slimming choices. The gods watch, to see who can play the role of their new favorite villain or a helpless maiden with limited options other than to walk the path they shape for us. The shadow at my wrist tickles, an always present reminder that I kissed a man in the woods beneath a blood moon. It is proof that I am no better than all the silly, desperate girls that have come before me, each bargaining with a fae-like creature with twisting words, and just as viciously handsome. Perhaps not all tales are cautionary, but sometimes the story is to remind us that we are not alone as we make terrible decisions—simply because we must.

I'll make a deal with an immortal king.

I wonder what I'll have to give up this time.

CHAPTER 13

*L*ady Agatha sticks out her tongue, and a bizarre gray-pink forms when she opens her mouth to blow out silent raspberries. A wagging finger marks her disapproval as she stalks me from frame to frame, following me until I near the Wescara suite.

Named for the type of bear most prominent in our province, it is the largest and most well-appointed of rooms Gray Hall has to offer. It is also reserved for one man and one man only— the king of Lumar.

I pause around the corner, inhaling to collect myself.

The king's knight waits around the corner. Everything about him appears gilded—from his bright hair, to his gold burnished skin. Even his eyes are brown-flecked with the color of the same precious metal. He smiles when he sees me, but his expression reminds me of the way a cat looks at a mouse they didn't expect to see.

"Lady Briar," he intones. He moves forward, his graceful hand flicking out to capture mine. "Sir Typhen. At your service." His words hum over my fingers, and his cold lips tickle the skin on the back of my knuckles.

"Well met," I reply, extracting my hand quickly.

Sir Typhen looks at his now-empty palm, something dark flitting across his golden-boy face. "His Divinity said that you might come by." The corner of his mouth flips up. "I'll need to search you."

"That is hardly necessary." I mean to say the words firmly, but my voice breaks halfway across the last word, snapping it like a dry stick across a knee. I don't want Typhen touching me. Don't want him anywhere near me. There's something cruel about him. It's—around his eyes and in the set of his mouth. I'm not a stranger to scorn, but this is something a little more sinister. I pull out the little knife I have strapped to my thigh, handing it over without complaint. I'm not an assassin of the king—as if a mere mortal like myself had a chance at regicide, especially when that someone was god-like in his powers and longevity anyways. What kind of weapon could kill a man that lived forever? Still, I place my little knife in Typhen's waiting hand. His fingers wrap around the hilt, holding it for a second. His head cocks to one side and he studies me.

"There, no need to go further." I let out a laugh I don't mean.

"I insist."

There's hardly anything else to do besides to submit. A chill sweeps down my spine as he steps forward. The rough skin on his palms snake down my curves, lingering too long at my hips. He gives my ass a pat. My knee jerks forward as I try to jam it up toward his balls. He blocks it with his palm, as if it's no threat. An acidic burn tickles the back of my throat as Sir Typhen's breath hisses in my face.

"Perhaps a strip search would be more...profitable." He murmurs into my ear. I shiver, disgust pimpling my skin. "Like that, hmm?"

I step away, gritting my teeth. "Sir Typhen, I am the heir to House Berrat. Disrespect to me is disrespect that will not be tolerated."

He barks a laugh. "Why, how catty you are. Apologies, then, my lady. This little game will hold for after your meeting with His Divinity."

* * *

HE OPENS the door for me, and I slip inside, then it clicks shut with the finality of a nail driving home into a coffin.

Westcara Suite oozes finery. All of the golden colors the king enjoys live here, as well as some deep reds, dark blacks, and royal blues. Everything is decorated to the Witch King's preference. Frescoed ravens fly on the ceiling, painted by Elvinescarro himself, the master painter from the Boreski Islands. Plush curtains of red velvet with gold tassels are drawn shut against the high, broad windows. An ornately carved bed—again, with the motif of ravens in flight marked into the posts—sits against the far wall. The smell of warm brie and fresh bread blankets the room, alongside a spiciness that I can't identify.

Despite the summer, a fire stokes in the furnace. Red flames lick at the fragmented wood, starving for fuel. In front of it sits a chair, turned toward the heat source. A raven roosts at the edge of it and watches me as I enter.

There's no sound but the popping of too-hot wood.

"I thought you might come." The words are soft against the harsh cracks emitting from the sputtering fire. "I'd thought you'd do it later though, little betrayer."

The nickname enrages me. "I betray no one."

"You disobey your father's—your lord's—wishes to be here. I think you know that."

An unspoken question lies at the end of his statement. I don't know whether it's the sort he already knows the answer to or not, but a pained feeling balloons in my throat.

"Tell me," he commands, standing. Silhouetted against the warm light, he's a tall statue of a man, built with muscles that are apparent even through the fine furs and elegant velvets. When he turns, looking into his face is a little like thinking one might die.

The blood drains from my cheeks and my heart stutters, tripping over itself as his gaze bores into me. It's as if he will pry everything I want to keep inside with a look like that, pull it out painfully like a warrior determined to use a spoon to kill his victim.

"M-my father is dying," I whisper, letting out the dreaded secret, the thing that could topple the stability of House Berrat and my heart.

The king laughs.

Shock races through me, and my gaze shoots up, colliding with his. His eyes are dead, despite the crinkled edges from his amusement.

The moment pulls itself out, like a slow unraveling cloth. After a minute ticks by, I wonder if he'll reply at all.

"You are all dying," he finally says.

Hot rage pools in my stomach. To an immortal man, it must seem so. "He is dying...*soon*." The last word is a whisper. I clench my fists, nails biting the flesh of my palms behind my back.

"And you would like my help? In what? Saving him?" He asks it with such careless regard that I wonder how to answer him.

Sparks of anger slip through my bloodstream, and I try to cool the feeling. One cannot simply rage in the face of power. Not me, anyways. Shaking a fist at him will only undermine everything.

"It's obvious you want something. I can feel your mortal desperation like a cloud of mosquitoes nipping my skin." He pauses. A raven flaps from the sill to his shoulder, tickling his ear. The king cocks his head. The movement reminds me of the curious and unfeeling birds that collect around him. "And what? You're willing to bargain, little girl?"

"Yes," I choke back the outrage at being called *girl*, though I sometimes think of myself as small and young when helplessness eats at my chest. But a man doesn't get to call me a girl.

Though King Thaddeus is less a man and more a god.

I snap my jaw shut. I expect to have to offer something else, something other than what he has already made clear he wants — me, marrying the enemy. But he stares at me like he's trying to see straight through me. Though I'm tired, though I'm angry, I feel like I've burned myself down to nothing—I pull on the thread that allows my Sight to come forth. A burst of nausea claws from the back of my throat, and I swallow it with nothing more than willpower and imagining the fresh smell of mint.

The king shrugs. "I'll cure him. It will cost you, though."

More than marrying a man whose people have fought ours for generations? More than exiling myself from everything I've ever known?

"Marry the Wolf. And then kill him," he says simply.

Kill the Wolf.

Laughter bubbles up inside of me, fizzing and cracking until something between a guffaw and a gasp croaks from my throat. Kill an unkillable man. *Ridiculous.*

King Thaddeus stares at me, waiting for an answer. My cheeks heat, and I open my mouth to speak, but nothing comes out this time.

"I see why you haven't yet married." He pours himself a glass of vissera. The colors of the liquid roil, shifting from red to pink to black as if it is a chimera changing shape. "You look like a barbarian and you've the manners of one."

Shame coils inside me, along with a hot and needy want to not only hide, but to earn his approval. My face reddens. I know it's a blotchy mess. I want to hate him for this, but he's my king.

The red hue of the alcohol shifts deeper. At the moment the drink becomes the shade of coagulated blood, the Witch King drinks. He takes a long pull, throat working to down the liquid. He finishes it and refills his cup, amber gaze snagging me, striking me with another bolt of burning embarrassment,. Long, pale fingers clasp another fine crystal glass, filling it and setting it in front of me. King Thaddeus stares into my eyes for a long time.

Words congeal in my throat. Under King Thaddeus' calculating look, I can't help but wonder if he's tallied every flaw into a concrete list that has proved them all correct. Beneath everything, I am coated in shame and a desperation to save my father that supersedes every other feeling. I've spent my life being made to feel like an ungainly burden to everyone who'd dared to care for me, including even Papa. Why bother, then? He loves me, that's the only answer I can give. He loves me as no one else ever has and he's the only parent I've ever known. I'll crack the world in half for him, just to have him stand next to me a little longer.

"You look like your mother. She wreaked havoc on this House."

I don't reply because I do look like her. The one picture that exists of her in Gray Hall is strangely still, as if the magic didn't quite take when the priests cast the deadened spirit into it when priming the canvas. Lady Rozena Berrat, Duchess of the Bears, was as tall as I am, but with a willowy build instead of my thicker frame. She sported the same silver-white hair, though without the midnight streak snaking through the front. The oil painting glowed as all the others did, the same ephemeral soul locked inside to animate it, but my mother's likeness never *never* twitched.

I'd spent hours staring at her face, hoping she'd mouth the words *I love you.* Or blink. What a wasted childhood.

"Thank you," I reply instead of defending a dead woman. What else to say to a king that hates your blood? My chest burns with rage. "Your Majesty, can you please say more on how to kill an evil spirit?"

The king looks, eyes narrowed, at the drink he passed to me and waits. I wrap my hands around it, then sip the pale pink liquid. A flood of strawberries hits my palette, and the world feels like a cool wind in spring.

"He is not an evil spirit. Simply a man," he growls. "Superstitious nonsense."

"They say he's had a dagger driven through his heart. That he stabbed the man who put it there with the same blade," I protest.

King Thaddeus' mouth pinches. "That, I'm afraid, is true."

That was true? I take a giant gulp of my drink. This time the red liquid filling my mouth tastes like spiced cranberries. "How?" I rasp.

"He is in possession of powers…" His lips thin as he pauses. "Well, they are not like mine. The Duke has come by his power dishonestly, no doubt. Nothing the priests would sanction."

The priests only approved of men with magic, so I doubt that they cared that the Duke of a profitable province had arcane abilities. What they would care about, of course, was that the king didn't like it.

King Thaddeus continued, again, only drinking when the liquid turned a deep midnight color. "He's a thorn in Lumar's side."

Though the king doesn't say it, it's not hard to guess that —while the Duke of Death is technically compliant with the conscription mandate, —the man's harassment of any and all provinces that border House Galibran's effects the total war effort with Selva. We waste too many resources on a puffed up wolfish-man, when we could be fighting the evil in the north.

He gestures to a little side table flanked by two chairs, and I settle to the edge of one, while he takes the other. I'm sitting across from an immortal king, about to bargain with him. It's unbelievable. It's stupid.

It's necessary.

The thrum of my blood beats a heavy rhythm in my ears, so loud I wonder if King Thaddeus can hear it. We lock gazes, and the force of his nearly knocks the breath from me. Terrible fates are dealt to mortals that dare to bargain with gods, or even with their bastard children, the fae. Let them do as they like and the harm that will befall you will be less–it is not different than dealing with the rulers of realms. No one knows precisely what the King Thaddeus is, only that he is the only kind of witch allowed to exist without penalty, with a life long like the fae and the awful powers of something divine. The shadow bracelet beneath my sleeve pulls taught, squeezing my wrist, as if it would like me to leave, to run.

Gods, I am a fool.

King Thaddeus' eyes narrow. "All these powers, tethered to creatures that do not know how to wield them."

Fear ribbons through me as the shadow bangle tightens again. The blood inside my flesh is trapped under the pressure, slowly cutting off circulation to my fingertips.

The north is home to a man who creates monsters that cannot face daylight, the chimera. Strange creatures mashed up of human flesh and animal, twisted into nothing like either. Some are lions mixed with bats, others people mixed with bears. Some are shifting wolves. Some are a bizarre concoction of squirrel and winged things, like the creature I met in the Shadow Wood.

The Dark One seeks to send them here, to Lumar. It is only the power of the Witch King and our vigilance of our military at Ash Mountain that keeps our kingdom relatively safe. Some escape, funneling down through the long stretch of forest that bisects Lumar, but those are few. The pass keeps us safe. Usually.

The Witch King's eyes glow with latent power, and he leans toward my face. Age lines his cheeks for a moment, and I blink, trying to focus on them, but they're gone like smoothed-over butter.

"Shall I save your father?" He asks.

It is a fool's question to ask if he has the power to snatch my father's life from the edge of death. I flex my purpling hand, pulling at the dark bracelet with a casual finger. "What will it cost?"

He smiles, showing sharp canines that remind me of an animal. "Clever girl. It will cost you your freedom." Copper coins drop from his mouth, plinking and piling. What he's saying is true, but to him, I'm not important enough for silver truth.

"Just that?"

He shrugs, noncommittal.

The cost may be beyond simple freedom — it could be anything from my life itself to my very soul.

I lost my mother long before memory shaped my mind. The cavern of where she should have been digs at me daily, like an empty hole in my mouth where a molar should dwell. I won't lose my father as well, much less let him suffer a death of such pain.

"I'll do it, but I need you to ease his pain now." I hold out my hand to shake his, the one not slowly being tortured by the blasted shadow thing. He looks at my outstretched offering, his eyes calculating. My mouth dries. I can't believe I offered to shake the king's hand.

Then his cold flesh meets mine, and all I can think of is the bottom rung of hell and dead flesh.

At least I don't have to kiss this one. The shadow at my wrist convulses, then releases the pressure. As if it's given up.

"A year and a day is what you have."

I purse my lips. "Not sooner?"

He releases a peel of laughter. It cracks out of his mouth, an uncomfortable sound as if he hadn't experienced joy in some time. "You already have your doubts about if you can kill him. Now you wonder if you can kill the man quickly?" He barks out another sound of amusement. "This must hold for the year, that will give me enough time to quell the monster up north. I suppose you can kill the Wolf before that time, but only try it if it is certain to work. I need the Wolves' Cursed strength." His eyes flash, and it's then that I'm certain there's something he's not saying. The mixture of tin and copper tells me he's mixed deception with what is true. "The price for failing, of course, is that your beloved father will die. So don't miss."

Don't miss. Gods, it feels like I do nothing but fail.

"I do believe you've unsnarled a knot of mine, Duchess of Wolves." This time, the coin pushes out of his lips. A warped thing, hatching like a monster. Silver, shot with something I've never seen before. Blackness swirls in the bright metal before the dark eats it mid-air. Doubt snatches my lungs and plagues my mind. What is this? A lie? A curse?

"Show me you can do what you say you can." The words curdle in my throat, but I force them out. Half-order, half-plea. I shouldn't doubt him, but this isn't something I'm willing to do on a broken chance that he can do what he claims.

The Witch King looks at me for a moment, head cocked like a curious bird. Brown eyes bloom with tendrils of shadow reaching out from his irises. They swirl, filling wall to wall with mesmerizing darkness. When he speaks, black smoke curls from his mouth with a dying hiss. "There it isss."

The smoke twists, filmy air uniting until it becomes a raven formed of shadow.

"So?" I say. It is dangerous to speak to a king this way, but I cannot afford half measures. At the same time, one doesn't say no to a king. "This doesn't prove you can save my father."

A flash and a blade is in his hand. The dagger arcs down and stabs into my forearm, straight through, pinning it to the wooden table.

Pain. Agonizing pain. The world goes white and my breath explodes out of my chest. The shadow raven flaps its wing, lathering in the pulsing power. A ghostly echo cracks from the ephemeral beak.

But everything is scarlet.

Blood. So much blood. It pools, red sluicing down my wrist.

Though the blade does not move, the sharpness radiates from my forearm.

Air hiccups in and out of my lungs. Rapid panic consumes me. Everything shakes. Twitches. Screams. Muscles. My vision. My organs. Something deeper—on a soul level, it feels like something reaches into my very essence and wants to hurt *me*. A cry burgeons from deep within me, pushing itself out from my core and rips up through my body with knife-like precision.

Make it stop. My breaths still come in a too quick beat. *Get it out.*

I can't hold it together. The pain crests and crashes.

I scream.

The Witch King presses a hand to my mouth, smothering the sound.

Throbs of nerves and nausea fill my consciousness. How do soldiers do this? How does Barro push through the pain of fighting? How does Valor? How does *anyone* endure *anything*?

In the back of my head, Nisha screams and throws herself into my mind. She takes the pain for a moment, and I breathe through my nose.

[*Kill.*] The word slips weakly against my mind.

Can't. The reply ekes through our bond like a dying breath. Cats don't understand that powerful men can't simply be put down for their cruelty. They can only get away with it.

My head snaps back, thunking against the top of the chair.

Every sense heightens. Smells of perfume and shit from chamber pots throughout this floor of the manor. Whispers fill my mind. Cold and dark things of twisted passions and dark hate. My vision sharpens. Each thread on my dress becomes distinct. A lifetime of the fiber flashes before me. It pulses with a mournful end as the cotton is plucked from the stalks. I feel its *death* as the once-plant is woven into my skirts.

A rip of pain slashes through me. Nisha can't get out of my mind. The twisting animal panic contorts my body. I scratch my fingers into the wooden arms of my chairs. Normal human nails, not claws— it should be claws.

The king cocks his head to the side. "Interesting."

I jerk back, as if to dodge a blade. Panic tightens my muscles. The urge to run grips my limbs. I need to calm down. I let out a shaking breath, trying to steady myself.

Go, Nisha. I shove her consciousness as far away from me as I can, blocking her out completely. For now. She collapses, a shuddering ball of shivering hide, her mind still questing after mine.

Instead of saying anything else, the king pulls at the edge of the shadow raven. It wiggles around his fingers, willingly—even eagerly— and he presses it to my skin like one might a cloth to staunch the flow of blood. The pour of red from my arm halts after a moment. My vision spots, but I breathe through it. Nisha purrs from her state in the ground, somewhere far away. Agony undercuts the false sense of content she's trying to project.

All I can do is look at the wet blood on the floor. Fear pulses inside of me, quick and hot.

A yank and the knife moves out of my flesh. I feel it all over again; the hot squelching pain, the burn of the raging metal. Another scream rises in my throat, and the Witch King smothers me with a fist. His hand pummels down into my mouth; his knuckles press into my tongue, pushing on my front teeth. My eyes water and there's no air. Am I to die here? The world flickers with more shadows, but these are from my vision closing in. Darkness will be a final death for me. Without a little light, I will be so afraid.

When the king removes his hand, my tongue still tastes the salt of his skin and a secondary tang of sickly blight. With pinched fingers, he plucks the shadow from my arm.

His hand is unmarred by blood— and my arm is…

Healed.

My flesh screams and burns in protest, as if the wound is still there.

"Now, the pain is just in your mind," he says.

I look up, tears washing my cheeks. The Witch King smiles at me, white pearlescent teeth gleam like bleached bone on a bed of snow. He presses a tender hand to my cheek in a caress. Soft, almost kind. It's the same hand he shoved down my gullet. The look he gives me is nearly loving, as if I'm one of his grandchildren receiving blessings at winter Holy Nights.

"Shhh," he whispers, leaning closer.

A sheen of sweat slicks my forehead. Death still washes the back of my throat at his touch.

"If you succeed, you'll win so much more than your father's life." The words tickle my cheek. "Kill the Wolf, and I may be tempted to make you mine. Possibly even queen."

CHAPTER 14

*N*o. The word screams inside of me, pounding from the underside of my flesh. My skin is too tight. The fearful tick of my heart skitters at my pulse points, beating my denial throughout my body.

No. No. *No.*

The bones of the king's first queen are buried somewhere in the Shadow Wood. I wonder if she yelled the word—*NO!*—before fleeing the king's vengeance. She was the Great Betrayer, though, I reason. The next queen will most likely follow the dead one there if she crosses this king, or god, or whatever you call a man who rules most of the known world and who has lived for centuries.

But it was betrayal, the thought flares bright in my mind. Betrayal deserves vengeance, even Amara, the goddess of love, says. Oaths connect our souls to the divine, and oathbreakers are owed the fire of fury.

I may be tempted to make you my queen.

My skin flushes in a feverish rush, and I try not to flinch under King Thaddeus' burning stare. This isn't someone who hears *no*, who understands anything except women—or anyone—bowing to his power.

"I will succeed," I croak, the words peeling out of my throat like unripened fruit spiced from its skin before its ready. It hurts.

His blue-tipped fingers trail lightly through my hair. I shiver, bile riding high in my esophagus. King Thaddeus looks to be ten years younger than my father, but he's older by centuries.

"I can assure you, my king, I am not worthy of such an honor as to be your wife. I am happy with securing the longevity of my house through my father."

His mouth thins and he looks at me, calculating something I can't define. "You are ugly," he finally says. "Regardless, if you prove yourself useful, I have no need to throw away the tools I like."

If he knew of my power—regardless of the fact that I am a witch not sanctioned by the Seven Orders—he would snap me up in a heartbeat. Either that or he'd kill me to keep his secrets. I pull at the shadow on my wrist. It lies there limply, as if it's given up on me. Despite it all, the burn of embarrassment flames my cheeks.

Ugly. I can't help but want to shrink into myself, to hide somewhere where no one will see me.

"Your husband-to-be will be arriving soon. I took the liberty of assuming the Bears would say yes. You may leave. I will decide what to do with you should you succeed in this." The king's tone is cruel, and he snaps his fingers once, all vestiges of pain ceasing, though sweat films every bit of my twitching skin. "Of course, we shall not speak of this tomorrow. Rest assured, though, you will hear from me, my little assassin."

* * *

THE DOOR CLICKS SHUT behind me.

Fucking hells. I lean against the doorframe, letting the coolness of the wood sink through my hair to my prickling scalp.

"Distressed, my lady?"

I jump, whirling. A hand grabs me and I yank it, twisting it behind the owner's back. The maneuver doesn't take, though, because at once another hand grabs me by the throat, shoving me against the wall. I thud into the stone, cracking my head. Pain lances through my skull and my eyes water.

The king's knight gazes directly into my eyes.

"My, you are a tall thing," he murmurs, his mouth close to mine. Breath skims my cheek. His eyes are the color of reddened coals cooling in a fireplace. "A bit jumpy, though."

Disgust snakes across my skin.

I swallow, blinking rapidly. He has all my weapons, and despite my practice, despite my efforts, I am a poor fighter. The only thing I have at my disposal is something that will get me killed. I open my Sight, the arcane threading against my perception of the world.

Sir Typhen smirks, holding up his hands, and backs up a step. "Woah there, my lady. No need to startle. I won't hurt you."

I can't help but watch his mouth. The faint tingle of the Sight washes over me and I shove it away. His words sweeten the air. *Lie.*

He probably would hurt me, then, if he had the opportunity, like he did at this very moment. A wave of tiredness floods me, signaling that I need to get a grip on my power. On myself. My Sight won't turn off, though, despite my efforts. It's like I'm shoving every bit of fuel into a burning fire for no reason, with not a care for winter when I'll actually need the warmth.

"It's...nerve wracking to hold an audience with the king," I finally grit out. It's not a lie, but it barely scrapes at the truth—it is overwhelming to beg a cruel man for a bone and wonder if mercy will be granted.

Sir Typhen leans back against the wall, his satisfaction at my distress is practically a rank smell. "I can help ease your distress, my lady," he says suggestively. Copper splurges from his mouth. At least he thinks he's good at it.

"I cannot help but think you are implying something untoward," I murmur in an attempt to be demure. "Surely that is inappropriate." My pulse beats in staccatoed terror. I hold out a hand. It's steady, despite my fear. "My blade, sir."

"Nothing inappropriate," he croons, ignoring my demand. Sir Typhen leans in, the tin coin pushing out behind his words like an ugly toad. "Tell me, lady, shall I come to your rooms tonight?" His hand moves, curling up to my neck. "I've always wondered what it would be like to fuck a northerner," he whispers. "You'll do."

I jerk away, knee snapping upward into his balls. This time, he's not fast enough to stop me. A howl births from his throat and a hand goes to his crotch. The other flails out, snagging along my arm and scratching a long divot. Pain splices my skin beneath his nail, and or the first time, I note the strangeness of his hands. His fingertips are a navy blue, ending in a jagged point the color of dark frozen death. Sir Typhen has a weapon built into his flesh.

Blood pumps through the wound on my arm, rising like an inevitable tide of nerve-wracking agony. There's something to his nail, something evil, and it feels like a sting of acid on my flesh.

"You'll pay for this," he hisses. Fuck the blade, I decide, then race away. Away. Far, far away. I wish I could run to a realm without kings and death and heartbreak, but I've never been so lucky.

* * *

THE BEDROOM DOOR slams behind me. The force of it reverberates against my back. I gasp for air, breathless from my dash through to the wing where my chambers resides. Nisha pounces on me and licks at the strange wound before I have a chance to halt her sandpapered tongue.. She listened, at least, when I told her to stay put. The rough pink lips at my opened skin, immediately soothing it. Even now, Sir Typhen's sharp fingers dig a phantom grip into my flesh. I'm not safe. Not even at home. Not anymore.

I frown, eyes going upward in askance at whatever gods may be watching, for one of them to please help me.

Duchess of Wolves.

If I am praying for safety, it is best to save that for when I am amongst my true enemies.

Everything is happening too fast, too quickly. I lean back into the cushions of my bed, wondering how long I'll get to sleep here after all. My days are numbered, not only in the home I grew up in, but also in the tally of my lifeline. Perhaps my time is much shorter than I'd once thought.

I cannot help but think that our sovereign—a near-deity without scruples—is afraid of the Duke of Wolves. The Duke of *Death*. Famed to have killed more with his bare hands than with his blade, he's brutally murdered and tossed our people's heads over the wall for us to see. A man who cannot die, but only metes out the end of life to others. I'll be married to the beast they say reaps death like one of the Grim Lords. And somehow I'm supposed to kill him.

My breath sticks in my chest. By agreeing to this, I won't belong to the Bears. Not that they ever wanted me. The Wolf in the wood will own me, body and soul.

Despair curdles in my belly. The only way to save Papa is with this impossible task. Kill an unkillable man. A hopeless laugh rattles from my chest. Easy, for some, maybe, but not for a mere mortal woman like me.

CHAPTER 15

$\mathcal{A}$ folded bit of paper flicks beneath my door.

Nisha hisses at the sound, body contorting in menace. She's on edge, just like I am. The morning dawned too early, and I haven't slept well in days. My skin hangs tired, loose, and dry on my face. It's my body's way of begging me to rest. But how can I rest when the stakes are so high?

My nightgown hisses against the floor as I walk to the strange delivery, each step forming increasing dread in my heart. The paper crinkles beneath my touch as I open it. I push an errant bit of tangled hair from my face.

Today they arrive. Wear this.

The door opens silently under my touch, and on the other side is a package wrapped in thin, white muslin, tied together by a gilded ribbon. A small bit of paper dangles from it. *Compliments of your king* sprawl in spiky, gleeful handwriting.

When I close the door behind me and ease the delivery open, red silk dribbles beneath my touch like the fall of water.

I ball up the edge of the dress in my fist. Fuck this. Fuck all of this.

The dark thing on my wrist wiggles. I snatch at it, trying to yank it off. My hand comes away as if it isn't there at all, and then it pulses against my flesh. A yell of frustration splinters from deep in my chest and I scream into the dress. I don't want to be dressed up like a pig and tossed to the Wolf to eat.

I hold it up in front of me. The cut of the dress is devastating.

A pit opens up in my stomach. The enemy will be here today, the same people that create this tension on our border and kill our friends and loved ones.

And soon they will walk these halls, Papa will be forced to welcome them. Not only will they be under the protection of peace the Red Season offers, but also the protection of the law of hospitality. We cannot attack unless they attack first, or we risk losing honor amongst the other Lumarian Houses.

If they find out.

Finally, I fist the entire dress as if I can strangle this blasted string of events into a shape that isn't full of despair. I toss the garment in a fit of rage, and the silk waterfalls to the floor in smooth mockery.

Kill an unkillable man. The king, on some level, doesn't believe I can do it. His eyes, his dismissive laugh told me as much, but if I don't do it, I lose. My marriage will achieve something in the way that he wants—we stall for a brief ease of tension, to turn our hearts and weapons completely toward the Dark One's tyranny. But can that possibly last? It will be a delicate balance to strike. I either need to wait until the year and a day strikes to kill this man, or I must do it with confidence earlier on. I have to kill him to save Papa, no matter what. I am not fool enough to think that our king is soft hearted. Heat licks the back of my neck. I do not know what kind of vow will be settled between my enemy husband and myself. Whatever it is, I must lie without lying, otherwise such an untruth could outright kill me.

Tonight, the monster will arrive. We will begin this cursed dance to end in death. I just don't know whether it will be mine or his.

* * *

"THEY'LL BE HERE SOON." Papa's words are a dirge that echo between my ears. The receiving room teems with sweaty bodies swathed in finery. Beneath the facade, we are not such fools that there isn't the errant creak of leather and the ting of a hidden blade. "I cannot believe we must participate in this farce."

All our bannerman—their wives, their children, esteemed soldiers—mill throughout the space. Historical figures and distant relatives pile into the portraits, the nosiest and most extroverted making their way to the enchanted frames to spy on us. Galinda caws a laugh in the corner, entertaining Lord Exterun with a flash of her smile and some inane joke. He returns the sound, bellowing it out so it rolls over both my ears and Papa's.

Papa doesn't seem to notice.

Perhaps one could call it standing, but it's an illusion. His back tucks proudly against the ivory column, double breasted green suit with ebony buttons bright against the off-white color. Leathers pad out his thin frame, offering the fantasy of bulky muscles and added protection for what is to come. His beard crops close to his face, completely gray, with hard eyes that dart over the crowd. No one approaches him. Instead, they flock to Galinda.

She's dazzling. I can't help but admit that, even as disgust rears an ugly head. Perhaps some of it is jealousy, the ease in which she moves through the rooms. Galinda was born for this. People congeal to her, as if stuck to something sweet and sticky, whereas they recoil from me. The few that have been to and come back from the northern border snap their heads in a double take when I pass. One bannerman reaches for a sword that isn't there, then goes to a hidden blade beneath his dress clothes before he blinks, catching himself. I grit out a nasty smile, too tired of this shit to be nice today. He jerks, mumbling something before backing away and stumbling into Lady Troth. She jabs and elbow into him in annoyance, and he scuttles away, clearly embarrassed for his mistake.

We are too far south for the Selvans to be here, but that never seems to matter at first glance.

Galinda greets another man, her fingers curling in a too-familiar way against the collar of the lord's jacket. Her diamond broach sucks in the light and tosses it back into the crowd, while matching earrings dangle in a gaudy jaunt.

Papa just stares at the closed doors that lead to the outside world.

The place from which the literal Wolves will loose themselves in our home. It could be a minute from now, or another hour. Violence spoils underneath the laughter twinkling beneath the pretty candlelight. Little flashes of bright blades salute their comrades, tucked into sleeves. Blood may be spilled tonight, Red Season or no. But, gods, we may curse ourselves in doing so.

"Peace will be expected, Papa." I remind him, uneasy. The way his eyes don't leave the door unsettle me. I can practically smell the bloodlust rising from him. "Honor lost is not so easily regained and we have a war to fight. We don't want to increase our tithe to Veritaes. That's what they'll be after. And Amara will be offended if we shed blood during her favorite holy time of year."

"Amara," Papa sighs, "will understand."

"She prefers love these days, they say." I slip a curled bit of silver hair behind my ear, and when I shift, a cold dagger kisses my thigh beneath my skirts. "So I am not so sure the goddess will grant her forgiveness for the blasphemy so easily."

"Then we will pay the price."

To break hospitality is to be marked with dishonor for an entire generation. Our neighboring duchies will not provide succor should we need it, which means we will nearly be exiles. King Thaddeus requires the dishonored to pay a higher price for the duchy's taxes. That said, I suppose in the end, it is only if one breaks hospitality and gets caught.

"Papa," I swallow. "I've always known that any marriage I may have might not be for love. The daughter of a duke can expect nothing more."

"That does not mean I will hand you over like a lamb for slaughter," he bites out.

"I am hardly a darling little sheep." I look over the crowd, noting a tray coming closer with bubbling spirits on it. No, best to stay sober. "I will handle it."

"I've thought about the king's offer," Papa says, ignoring me. He does not have any such compunction about the alcohol and snatches a glass from the server. He drains it in a single drag before quickly switching the empty flute for a full one. This time, he sips. "We will offer Jara."

"No, Jara is barely landed gentry. Her father pretends at lording, but he's a gambler playing at farming."

"In times of peace, all lords are farmers," Papa replies with a pert sip. He says nothing of the gambling.

"In times of peace, lords are indolent fools," I reply dryly. "And we are not in a time of peace. Lord Keswicker is none of the things he should be. His daughter is sixteen, besides." Though some marry that young, sixteen is still a child. Someone in the realm of my age— though many would call twenty-six a spinster and demand I should have already produced a passel of children—would be more appropriate. Many have claimed my Papa is far too lenient with me. A willful, Selvan-looking girl should be married and tamed by now, not wild about the castle, mixing tinctures with a large cat trailing behind her.

Father shrugs. "Then who? Lord Parelle's girl? She's about the right age, a little horsey looking, but her station makes it not an insult."

"Papa," I protest.

"No. You are not to marry the man. You are my heir." A tremor tickles his voice at that. Is he…lying to me now? The Sight I wait to use, but a coil of suspicion, of betrayal, lurks inside of me. He blinks back at me, a telltale dribble of sweat skirting from his temple to his jawline. I remember the strange taste of sweetness in his office, when my powers flailed erratically.

"Am I?" I ask, voice soft.

He doesn't reply, and my gaze snaps to Galinda. She watches, an expression molded of hate and satisfaction plain across her visage. Wretched woman. It wouldn't surprise me if she claimed to be with child right now, if Papa confided in her. I've already made my decision, though, so what does this do to it? Nothing.

"Papa. The king has said it is to be me," I insist.

"Then we will defy the king," he says.

"We cannot defy a divine ruler," I whisper. *I cannot let you die.*

He pauses. His eyes narrow. A shiver wracks his body, so violent for a moment he leans against the wall. I reach out, but he holds up a hand, stopping me. Rage whitens his already pale face. "Did you speak to the king without me?"

I halt my next words, but the pause is enough. His suspicion squeezes into disgust, mouth becoming a sneer.

"So, you undercut my will. You have no idea what you have done."

"Papa, I—"

"I think you mean *duke.*" Papa abruptly turns, his back curved like an old man's as he leaves me. I move toward him, but at that moment, the doors peek open and King Thaddeus' herald steps in. He's tall, bedecked in gold, with a gray beard braided into two separate strands. The braids are knotted off with metallic ribbon and vibrant sapphires that sparkle, reminding me of the sun glinting off a lake. I follow Papa, trailing a little behind him up the the dais. My heart thumps like a heavy gavel, each beat bringing me closer to the next event in this line of fate. The hair along my nape raises, as if a spirit trails a finger there or a god blew a chilled breath at my neck. I shiver.

Galinda shuffles in front of me as we hurry to the lifted platform, sniffing dismissively as she scooches between us. Ewan slips in just behind her. He smiles at me.

Disgusted, I circle around to Papa's other side. He won't look at me. Not even one glance.

"King Thaddeus, His Divinity, appointed by the Sacred Seven," announces the herald. He bangs his staff twice and the doors open.

* * *

Papa, Galinda, and I stand off to the side of the dais where the thrones sit, the central one reserved for the Witch King. We won't take our places in the other ornate seats until the king settles into his. Ewan, my indolent stepbrother, leans with lazy lackluster posture a few feet away. His starched collar stands stiffly, cutting angles to his jawline. A froth of frill plumes from his chest, the silken cravat overflowing below his throat. He raises an eyebrow when I catch his gaze. I want to sneer at him. I hate him watching this.

"Poppet, you don't have to do this." Papa's words come out stiffly, anger and hurt and betrayal starching them. A silver coin drops from his lips. He truly believes it.

"But I do." Pain expands in my throat like a sponge in water and I swallow it. I'll take the hurt, the rage, take everything anyone gives me, and anything the Duke of Wolves throws at me. Even if I choke on it.

I want to ask Papa when I will see him again after this—*if* I will. The words *Do you hate me?* die on my lips.

My eyes find the gaze of the Witch King as he spills into the room.

Fading pink light from the windows outside marks the room in a soft blush, except for the arcane lights that hang overhead like metal-twisted constellations. A violinist plays at the entryway, his body half-bent in obeisance as the angles of his arms strike a high tune, and then the trumpeter booms. Both of them are from the king's retinue, garbed in gold and well-practiced in the art of playing while showing their regard for our ruler.. A caw and a flap of wings strikes through the sound. Then another. Another.The king's ravens fly through the doorway behind him, soaring and diving in a raucous display.

Our divine king makes his way down the aisle cleared for him. Slippers wink as the bobbing lights strike at the gilded bits bound to the leather. A red jewel snaps at the center, grinning at me like a bloody mouth.

If I don't fail, I'll have saved my father and the marriage bond will be broken with my future-enemy husband's death. I may come back disgraced, a near-oathbreaker after committing to a man I will kill, but that is better than not coming back at all.

A quiver jerks down my arms, and I clasp my hands together to hide the tremble. "I love you, papa," I murmur, mouth going dry.

Papa says nothing. His gaze squeezes into a side eye, hurt and maybe a little hate peering out of the corner of the look. Love is the most complicated thing in the world. Someone you would fall on your sword for one moment can just as easily gut you with a cutting gaze the next.

"This is like something out of a tale," I say.

Father looks down to his scarred and calloused hands. "Tale or no, we can still turn back."

What drops from his mouth is a complicated mess of metals. Silver and tin clatter to the floor and disappear.

"Please don't do this," Papa says. "I will defy the Witch King. The Bears can handle it."

But the Bears can't. Our dead pile up by the second, and the sprite-lights at the border outnumber the stars in the sky.

I shake my head. Something in him changes, hardens, and his mouth flattens and his shoulders jerk. "If you do this, I'll never forgive you." His voice cracks, and he pushes a bit of money like a bright star out of his mouth. It's the brightest gold I've ever seen. On its descent to the ground, to some hell below and beyond, it evaporates.

I'll never forgive you.

While silver may be the truth, gold is a vow. Something that he means with every nerve in his failing body.

Pain lances my chest. I look at him, but he won't look back at me. *Better a father that hates me than a dead one.* This conversation between us is too late. My decision is already set. The betrayal will be engraved into the headstone of Papa's love for his once-adored daughter. Grief shoves itself through my core, cracking against my spine like an ax splitting wood.

He'll never forgive me, like he says, but at least he'll be alive to hate me. These days, that's all I can ask for. The lines of sickness draw across Papa's face—like a pair of creased curtains, blocking out all the light. He looks as if he's aged seventy years in the past one, as he slips a little further into the darkness of whatever comes after. A well of sadness—something beyond simple grief, because it's edged in spikes and acid—presses against my skin, filling me from the inside. Gods, it hurts so much to be human.

Galinda watches me, a smirk on her face, and Papa says nothing else. Our relationship tethers itself in a single, thin thread, ready to snap. It's been like that for a while. The ungracious part of myself hates my father a little too.

It's easy to let one's own anger rise in the face of someone else's. How *dare* he be angry with me? My hands clench. How can he doubt me? Doubt my intentions?

Galinda keeps her lips in his ear, eases doubt into his palms, which he doles back out to me with hurtful exasperation.

As the king passes us, we sink into low bows. I hold it, feeling the squeeze of my abdomen. Minutes drag and my back feels like fire. Papa holds his own—somehow—but it is likely sheer pride keeping him upright. The moment slogs, and my muscles, tired from the training earlier this morning and the day prior, tick in frustration.

The king nods to us as he passes. I unbend my body while Papa, Galinda, and Ewan do the same. Galinda's lips smirk toward me before trading a glance with her son. Most likely, she's crowing internally about getting rid of me. To the enemy no less. What use is an heir married to the enemy?

The rest of the room holds its bent pose, except for one man snaking through the crowd. The green uniformed courier reaches my father. Fear strikes his eyes when he gazes upon the king, who notices him with a sort of bored disapproval living around his mouth. He jerks a bow, his nose nearly brushing the floor, before he turns to my father. The bob he gives his lord is less deep, but still respectful.

The courier leans in, his lips at the shell of my Papa's ear, and the man whispers, "The Wolves are at our door."

Laughter and angry brutal primitive feelings surge through me. But as I clamp down on it, my chest tightens. I look at the men lining the wall. The women that also fight are gone, banished from this room, else they mill about in clothing that will hamper their movements to appease a king that has no use for anything feminine. And we have to wait. We have to pretend to be their friends. Why can't this duke just join his kingdom in this fight? We spend so much time in useless internal squabble, when we could fight the true enemy. My hand aches to hold a blade.

I bite back a howl of frustration at this frippery. The bowing and the scraping. I wish we could just kill these Wolf bastards and take them to the north to fight. Despite the holy season, the peace could crack with eggshell-like fragility beneath a misplaced boot.

The trumpet plays and the entourage steps forward through the threshold. Gasps flick through the ladies lining the aisle.

The Duke of Wolves is rumored to be a descendent of one of the Grim Lords, the heralds of death. It's an easy thing to believe by the way they say he cannot be killed. How he revels in blood.

Somehow, this tentative, temporary peace can only be guaranteed by one thing.

We will all be lucky if this wedding doesn't run red.

CHAPTER 16

*K*ing Thaddeus shifts, the plush pillow puffing an audible hiss of air as he re-settles into his seat. Fingers slide against the shining wood, once again rubbing the whorls as seems to be his habit. With the thick knuckles of a bruiser, his rings flash a smile of gilded metal. Bright jewels glint from them, some ruby, some an arcane swirl of darkness. Two ravens perch like royalty on the gold-padded mantle of the Witch King's shoulders. Shimmers of thin threads hang from the tassels adorning the metallic fabric.

Lords bend in half like felled training dummies, curled with their hands over their hearts. Ladies with delicate fingers angle their left arms out, dangling the edge of their skirts from thin fingers, with their right hands held to their bosoms in fisted delicacy. Some imperceptible movement of the king's cues the herald.

"At ease," the king's man calls. Near sighs huff through the crowd as people move upright and aching backs gain respite. The announcer clears his throat, and, despite his profession, a shiver of fear slips through his next words. "Announcing, Lord Killian Galibran, the Duke of Wolves."

The silence pools. Noises of strangled breaths punctuate the quiet. Violence claws up my throat. I've been so coiled in Papa's illness, in the king's arrival, I'm surprised by the sudden ferocity that swells in my chest.

The bodies at the border grip my mind. A hot, dry feeling aches from the tips of my toes all the way through to my nasal passage. What am I doing? *Marry* the Wolf. *Kill* the Wolf. *Kill an unkillable man.* The words jolt through me, pumping through every vein with the pound of each beat of my heart. A tingle squeezes out from my center. This is my chance to save my father, but I didn't realize that this is also my opportunity to avenge every person that has died at our enemy's hands, to bring justice for what the Duke of Death has cost this kingdom in his senseless pursuit of what does not belong to him. He doesn't own the forest like he thinks he does.

If I can do this, the winnings will be so much more than what matters most to me.

The long doors at the end of the room open with a wail, and hot air whooshes inside, rattling the clothing of those closest to the entrance.

Every sconce—both floating and not—goes out.

Darkness.

A hollow sound, the way wind blows into a cave, groans into the room. The slow-opening doors smash into the wall with a sudden burst of wind. Splintering wood cracks. Glass shatters. Screams fly through the crowd. A long winding moan hums underneath the gusting air.

This is it. My shoulders stiffen. He's there, hidden in the dark. My future husband. My enemy. My victim. Possibly, one day, my murderer.

The plunge of blackness stains the room, darker than moonless nights at the heart of the shadows. Hairs on my arms raise.

A ragged gasp of air digs through my throat, and my lungs stutter. It's too dark. I can't see. Fear punches through me, stalling my breath. Nisha leans against me, the subtle skitter of her claws on stone ekes next to me.

[Kill?]

Not yet, Nisha.

The darkness explodes. Instead of light, all the warmth chokes from the room. Frost bites the air. A single sconce by the king taps a lonely flicker. Despair slicks every figure. A shudder cracks through the room as lords and ladies bend halfway, unwillingly, but not in a bow. No, it was simply the weight of existence pressing upon their backs with an iron fist.

My knees quake, threatening to buckle, but I hold on through sheer willpower.

"What in the gods' damned hells is that?" Papa whispers in a weak tremor. He sways and I grab him while Galinda clutches his other arm. I can't see her face, but her sharp inhale cuts through the cold dark fog.

A shadow extracts itself from the darkness. Tall, far over six feet, with a swirling smoke the color of burnt plum and ribboned with deep red shadow. The room doesn't breathe. I don't breathe.

Fur curls off of the wolf, smoky with prohibited magic. Still, the display will grant no punishment. A man in power has nothing to lose, not really, because they're never punished for what they do wrong. The wolf slinks forward, the muscles in his shoulders bunching with incorporeal strength. A hiss burns through the air and the creature —disappears.

Behind the dissipating magic steps a smear of a man, the same height as the creature he follows. He's half ghost, half giant. Darkness clings to his face, obscuring his features as if he is a bride and the deep night his veil. His boots echo in the now-still room as he moves forward. Each step shakes my heart, though the thud of his shod feet sound the same as any man's. I count each footfall, knowing that this is it.

One. When he gets to the end here, we will pledge ourselves.

Two. My life will change.

Three.

I'll be a Wolf. A betrayer. And my lies to this man may kill me, if he doesn't decide to do it himself.

Four.

This is my last gamble. My eyes flick to my father, who stands in crooked pride next to me. His cheeks look like he hollows them, but it's just the wasting sickness. His eyes are pallid and glassy. I spare one last look at my king. An imperceptible nod tilts King Thaddeus' head before the sconce next to him does the impossible.

It goes out.

CHAPTER 17

"*E*nough."

The word carves into the pitch black room like a blade through flesh and bone. The gale ceases and the lights, at once, burst with flames. Terrified faces reveal themselves. Cockroaches scuttling to hide from perception, but it's too late. Lords with hanging jaws and ladies with tear-stained faces, otherwise immovable nobility to the plight of others while they are well fed by Galinda, by themselves, attempt to shove their feelings of fright back into their blackened hearts.

King Thaddeus stands. At once, a motion at the side indicates we should all bow once more. The *shh* of fabric slicks around me and I rush to fall into stance. An ache grabs my spine, but I force it away. The sweep of my hair slips over an eye, but I can still watch Duke Galibran as he moves forward until he reaches the base of the steps leading to the throne.

His face is obscured by the clinging shadow magic that coats his form, little cobwebs of darkness that flutter around him. It's nearly whimsical, if I hadn't had the experience of the utter despair that held me in a chokehold. A thread of growing fear ricochets through my entire body. *Light, please.* A damp sweat coats my skin as I stare at this monster of a man.

Rumors of bloodlust and ruthlessness follow the Duke of House Galibran like a teeming cloud of pestilence around him. He's spiked the heads of our fallen soldiers on his gates—he has even ordered them skewered onto our walls in the night. Dead faces of fathers, mothers, sisters, brothers, beloved ones forever gripped in terror by their sacrifice our cursed neighbors.

Lord Galibran is a lot of things. The cruel twist of his presence proves it. That said, I'm not fool enough to believe every bit of gossip that tickles my ears. How many people he has killed is an unknowable number, despite claims that his body count is well over forty thousand souls. Some even say that he killed Rewoan, the divinity the priests call the Dead One—the god whose death made us all mortal. It's ridiculous conjecture with a timeline that makes no sense.

Still. One thing that remains unquestioned is this: the wolf doesn't kneel.

He pauses, surveying the room, gaze alighting at various points. For a moment, I think he will not look at me, that I may have escaped him for this one moment. A soft sigh loosens from my lungs, and I shut my eyes.

Cold wraps around my neck.

I jerk my gaze up to find him staring at me. Black eyes, like a Grim, bludgeon me with terror. My heart pounds angrily, fearfully. A shadowed haze obscures the rest of his face, except for those awful, terrible, eyes. *He's letting me see this.* He wants me to see him, to see what's inside him. The cold rage. The hatred. He knows who he has come for.

He wants me to buckle.

Instead, I lift my head, letting a sneer smudge across my face. A movement next to me tells me that Papa has noticed. He shifts to the side, as if to block the impact of the evil eyes on me. Terror and rage wreck me, clogging my breathing and earning a deep sweat in my armpits.

A sense of familiarity tickles the back of my mind.

Around me, people begin to buckle to their knees. Pressure pools against every joint in my body. I fall into a curtsey, holding it there, but I keep my head up, watching my husband to-be as he looks not at me, but toward King Thaddeus.

Duke Galibran doesn't bow.

He grants the Witch King a polite nod, and the king of Lumar, of the Wolves, of Bears, of every province in our country—grits his teeth.

Nisha pushes an image of a cat playing with a mouse into my mind. *[Games.]* The word is short and grim sounding. She's far away, stalking a rat in the halls near my room. Safe and waiting until I get back. For now. Away from whatever human farce we're playing.

Yes, this is some sort of game. I'm just not sure what it is yet.

She queries at me, wanting to come, to see him, to smell this man. She can't smell him through me, the way I could if I were to share her nose. My ability to discern scents is only human, after all, in a wretched mortal body. It's nothing like a strange, magical cat's abilities.

"Forgive me if I don't kneel, Your Majesty." The Wolf's voice smacks of dishonesty while petulance and boredom drip from his words. No coin falls from his hidden lips. I grip my skirt tighter, waiting for his next sentence, waiting to see a coin drop from the cloud of shadow swirling about his head. "I fear I injured my knee and to do anything other than nod would cause undue pain." I watch his shades near his mouth and—

—Nothing.

Nothing, nothing, fucking nothing.

I fight a scream of rage. I am supposed to kill this man—and I can't even use my full ability? What kind of creature is he? Even the Witch King's—a near god— words reveal themselves to me, warped as they are. Why can I not see this blighted man's?

This is not the first time this has happened. It's the second. A chill sweeps my body as realization takes hold.

The line of fate strikes a mark down my path.

Still, denial surges in me. It was only a kiss. An ill-fated one. *It can't be him.* What are the chances that we met in the woods, that the forest pushed us together until our lips bled?

Magic always has a cost, and the cost is always suffering. Whether it is to know the burden of truth, to see someone lie to your face, or to meddle in a game of gods where a mortal should not, there is always a price to pay.

Cautionary tales coil around the wrists and ankles of little girls going to places they should not be, hamstringing us as an example for the rest. *Go back to your tower and stay there, darling. See what happens to those who do not?*

"Will you not do your bride the favor of revealing your face?" King Thaddeus asks. There's a strange quality to his voice. There's nothing to discern there with the Sight. Duke Galibran turns, our gazes locking, but the only thing visible in the teeming mess of darkness surrounding his countenance is the way that he looks at me. My stomach hollows out.

One by one, he allows the shadows to peel back. All the while, his eyes bore into me, flashing between a deep black of fear and a mellow umber like summer light dappling the bark of a tree. A high cheekbone first, sharp and angled. Jawline gripped by a dusting of stubble. The warm brown of his skin glows. The shadows dispel one by one like pieces of an old, crumbling mask.

The wisps of translucent black slide from his flesh, reminding me of the way coins disappear. Corporeal one moment, then dispersing to nothing the next without a sound.

When the last one falls away, Duke Galibran stares back at me. The denial fades to horrid recognition, leaving only an aching dread of what is to come and the phantom fingers of his touch racing across my body.

I flew too high, this time, and forgot I didn't have wings. Now all I can do is fall.

My husband-to-be's eyes flash. The shadow bracelet squeezes against my skin. My lips burn with the memory of the violent kiss I shared with a stranger in the wood, when I disobeyed gods and men.

Looking back at me is my scarred enemy from the wood.

CHAPTER 18

"My bride." The words are as smoky as his shadows. Duke Galibran holds out a hand, but no gentleman's glove adorns it. His bare skin covers my own gloved one as I accept it. A thumb rubs the back of my knuckles through the fabric. His rough calluses snag against the fine weave. Without taking his eyes from mine, he lifts my covered hand to his lips. They barely brush the soft cloth. "Well met," he says, his voice like tender gravel. I yank my hand from his grasp.

No flicker of recognition passes through his eyes. I wait for him to say something like *I know you.* I stare at him, no mark from our encounter in the woods marks his lips. My bite is gone. A fast healer then, since he walks with no sign of injury. A pity. A fresh wave of hatred spears through me. It will be a gift to kill this man.

The Witch King grins at the top of the dais. Dark velvet robes pool like shadow at his feet and a fur stole, red as the moon, hangs at his shoulders. "It's settled then. The Bear shall marry the Wolf," the king says, nearly sing-song in his cadence. Bile rises in my throat. The weight of a thousand stares presses against every curve of my body, pinioning me to a standstill.

All their hate for what has happened at our border slides against my skin. Acid burns the back of my throat all the way to my stomach.

A terrible foreboding sprawls like slow poison through my limbs. Something isn't right here. *The king knew you met him already,* the words whisper through my head, a bright bit of intuition. My gaze snaps to King Thaddeus, who isn't looking at me, but rather at the crowd gathered here. He grins. Too happy by half for such a simple thing as my marriage to the enemy.

A sprawl of lies lines this room, and I'm in the middle of it.

"We can still end this." Papa's words are so soft, there's only a handful of people that hear it. My stepmother, me, and my betrothed. Galinda opens her mouth and is cut off with a sharp wave of Papa's hand. Her jaw snaps shut, and she spears me with a look of contempt.

Duke Galibran cocks a head to the side, studying my father with reptilian indifference. "I always wondered what the man that tries to take what doesn't belong to him looks like," he laughs. Hot hatred grips my chest. Gods, I want to plunge a knife into his cold heart. "I didn't realize my enemy was so...wanting. Weak. It'll be a pleasure to take your daughter from you. An eye for an eye, then?"

Papa surges forward, a dagger from a hidden sleeve in his hand. Galinda grabs for him, her pull only slowing him a little. Duke Galibran snaps his fingers.

Shadows surge from below, darkness cast from our own bodies. But they don't go for Papa.

They go for us.

One grabs me as I shift forward. Another grips Galinda. No plan guides my movements, but it doesn't matter. The thing snags my wrist as my hand furls into a fist, joining with the ephemeral bracelet there. Freezing cold cracks into my flesh. I pull, and my muscles shiver under the strain. The other shadow wraps Galinda in a vice-like hold. It crawls up her skin, till her milk-white face reddens as the darkness chokes her. She coughs, complexion going from rosy to purple until she stops struggling. Her only choice is to watch.

Duke Galibran lets Papa go for his throat, blade slicing the air.

Frail, but likely the surge of adrenaline and drug in Papa's bloodstream gives him the strength to lunge with a grace he had a year ago.

Duke Galibran grabs the blade, hand to hand with Papa. His thick fingers wrap around the sharp edges. They look almost like lovers, close and intense in their exchange. Bright red blooms between Duke Galibran's grip as he and Papa guide the dagger into the enemy's throat. Seconds tick by, each one squelching out in slow motion.

Blood spurts from the Duke's wound, decorating the white of Papa's tunic. The stain spreads to his once snow-colored gloves until they are as red as the moon.

Duke Galibran's eyes widen, and he chokes on the blood that spews from his mouth. It sprays as air hisses from his mouth. The sound is guttural and harsh. Papa grins, a bloodthirsty look that hasn't been seen since his illness surfaced. He looks happy to incite a civil war.

The shadows ease, letting me go. Galinda lets out a rasping rattle as she hacks up nothing.

Shrieks of fear and rage erupt from the crowd of nobility.

Bannerman and their wives alternate between screaming and action. Lady Toth pulls a blade from her sleeve, and her husband does the same. Our people advance on the comparatively small crowd of Wolves. The one with yellow eyes from the woods, Lukas, smiles and doesn't even draw a blade. The woman, Jessa, in their band sighs. Her shoulders slump as if she's disappointed. Lady Toth lunges for Jessa and in a blink. Jessa unsheathes her sword from its scabbard. She holds it against Lady Toth's blade the way one lets a lazy toothpick dangle from sated lips. Horror and righteous anger dance a hot battle in my chest.

I yank my blade from its sheath at my thigh before Duke Galibran can ease out a dying breath. A bizarre feeling coils in my belly, one that feels like regret to watch the scarred man die. But this is it. Whether this is a chance or a change we'll regret, it's too late to do anything else but act.

The dying man makes a horrible, wet rattle as Papa eases the blade from Duke Galibran's neck.

The gurgling of Duke Galibran turns to a bass of deep laughter. His teeth flash, his fangs dripping with his own blood. Then it all wisps away, the red fluttering much like his dark power. His eyes crinkle with genuine mirth, and he holds up a hand decorated in little scars. His signet ring, featuring a wolf with a ruby tongue, twinkles. He pats himself down, as if he stumbled on an off day. The grin on his face is nearly boyish.

Papa's mouth drops open of its own accord. His dagger clatters to the ground.

Horror sweeps through me. The Duke of Death did not die as all the rumors warned. *What* is he?

Before I can allow a moment to doubt myself, the grip on my blade tightens. The king wants him dead, maybe this is the best chance we get, before I even have to marry the bastard. Papa has said to hell with honor and so has everyone else. I'll face the consequences later.

I take advantage of the chaos and the distraction around us. A dagger through the throat won't work on this monster, clearly, but a dagger through the heart kills even vampyrs. I arc through the air, aiming at the man's chest. Gods, he looks into my eyes and *smiles*. A joyous crinkle lines the corners as he says, "There's my wicked witch."

I don't wonder at him calling me a witch before my blade sinks into his chest. If he were to live, that would be a problem. But no matter. He was a dead man as soon as he agreed to be my husband. He just won't make it to the wedding. We fall to the floor, and I land heavily on top of him, the pressure of my body crushing the dagger all the way through his chest, finally killing the Wolf.

CHAPTER 19

I press the blade further into his breastbone. The bone cracks under my weight. He flinches with the break, jaw ticking, but his mouth smirks up like he has a secret. The crazed bastard still smiles, grinning like a madman rather than a dying one. He chuckles instead of just doing me the favor of being fucking dead. His fangs nip at his lower lip, eyes darkening as his hands clasp around my back. My grip tightens on the leather of the hilt, and I lean every last bit of my weight behind the weapon. I fight a shiver, watching the long tooth graze his mouth, dimpling the skin there. Part of me wonders what it would be like for him to press those fangs into the tender part of my neck.

Crashes of blades clang around us. I'm aware of more screaming, of people racing away. The thud of bodies hitting the ground jars me as some of the nobility stampedes toward the door. A ghastly rip severs the air near me as someone's gown shreds. Battle calls of guards bellow into the fray, shouting to protect the king, though I spare a thought to wonder if it's as difficult to kill a divine man as it is to slay this near-immortal monster. I'm also aware of the press of the hard planes of his body against the swell of my stomach, and the way his hands skirt the hills of my hips.

"My eager bride," he rasps.

"Beast," I snap, shoving against him as I get up. It's the second time since we've met I've called him that and I have a feeling it won't be the last.

"You've no idea, witch." His laugh is hollow and cracks out of his throat. He follows me to an upright position.

"Stop calling me that," I hiss. "Do you want me to be killed?"

"Not as eagerly as you would like to see me dead it seems, *witch*," he says, dusting himself off. The blood from his body disappears. I notice that the splotches of his blood blend into the red of my dress. That, it seems, doesn't evaporate. I file the information away.

"That isn't something to say lightly, Duke Galibran," I grit out.

"Apologies, then, my lady." Though I can't see anything, I wonder if I'm imagining a faint taste of a lie. It's not a bad guess. I did just try to kill him, so he's most likely not sorry. The bastard deserves death, though. His scarred eyebrow raises, reinforcing the fact that he doesn't mean what he says one bit. I don't care though, as long as he stops calling me a witch. It doesn't seem as if he knows he's right, but this man isn't something I understand at all. I eye his throat, his chest, the places those fatal wounds should be. My dagger still winks right where his heart is. Where blood should be leaking out.

I don't know how to fight him. I don't know how I'm going to kill this monster. I take a half step back, a crest of fear rising in my breast.

Duke Galibran pulls the dagger from his chest, and a liquid sound follows the movement. He winces as it leaves his body. Blood pumps from his still beating heart, gushing from the wound. It leaks in grotesque, frothy pulses. The duke holds the blade out to me, dangling it like I'm a joke. I take it. It's useless against him, but it's mine.

The flesh behind the departed blade seals itself shut, knitting together as it heals. Lord Galibran sports a collection of scars at various points on his throat, his exposed hands, his eyebrow, but the places that should have marked him from my father's and my attacks are gone. What kind of weapon could have marked this man when even the ones freshly dealt are erased into oblivion?

"No harm done," Duke Galibran calls loudly. He clears his throat, then his laughter booms, drawing attention to us. The guards Duke Galibran brought stand back to back as the violence around the room halts. People stop mid-stride, shock and disappointment and fear jolting through every face. Shame rides high in Papa's cheeks, or maybe it's rage. His caved-in cheeks mottle, a visible shake tremoring through his whole body. The enemy holds up a bland hand and turns so the crowd can see his unharmed throat. Where there should have been blood, the flesh has already closed up, as if nothing occurred. The redness dissipates from his clothes and skin. "Surely, a joke from an...old man to his future son in law. Nothing to break hospitality here, yes?"

Oh, gods.

What have I gotten myself into?

"Think of this as an early wedding gift." The words are soft. Duke Galibran looks at Papa, but his words are for me. "I won't call your father out for an oathbreaker while I am his guest. This time."

Papa's throat bobs visibly. Impotent rage whites his face. Perhaps it's the effects of the Reezin leaving his body, but worry gnaws a hole in my stomach. I move to him, but he jerks away from me. Instead, he turns to Galinda as she grasps his other arm.

"So, this is what Gray Hall looks like. How...quaint," Duke Galibran sneers. These words are loud enough for the entire room. A burst of hatred grips my chest, and my hands clench, nails biting into the soft flesh of my palm. His voice is still a little strained from the blade previously impaled through his neck. Each word rasps a little at the edges. "After the ceremony, you will be a Wolf. Remember that." It sounds like an order, and his gaze promises blood if it's not heeded.

I'll do exactly as he asks and make him regret this moment. Somehow. I've already tried to kill him, so in a way, I've shown my hand. But what else would he suspect of the Bears? We've fought for a generation, and we'll fight for a generation more. This year and a day just stalls the inevitable.

"Don't do it." Papa doesn't say the words quietly; these, too, are not for us. They carry over the crowd, grinding out from between his clenched teeth. The vein at his temple jumps, a beet red color suffuses his face. "He's a monster."

King Thaddeus watches with near-impassivity, except his white-knuckle grip on the arms of his throne. Papa will pay for his statement, of that, I have no doubt. A hopeless laugh slides up my chest. Why do I always want to laugh when I could just cry? King Thaddeus gazes at me expectantly. There's only one thing to do. I don't know how, but I'll have to figure out how to kill an immortal later.

"I will join the Wolves," I say.

There is a beat of silence, then a soft insult comes through the crowd.

"Traitor *bitch.*"

"*Whore.*"

Duke Galibran jerks a sharp look toward the onlookers. The shadows in the room throb, the lights flickering a little. A chill sinks into the humid air, and the little hairs on my arms raise. I can't see his expression, but no one says anything else. His men shift, as if they're readying for another explosive bout of violence.

My hands shake, but I pull them behind me to hide them. I won't let anyone see what the doubts do to me. It hurts, but it's not the worst thing. Not by half.

Galinda makes a display of covering her mouth and looking at me in horror. She leans into Papa, who looks at me like he doesn't know me. Should I have just laid down for this? Have done what a dying man wishes? And once more, in the face of one power and a greater one, how could I not bow to a king? Especially when he is offering the only thing I want.

The king stands. Immediately, the room jerks into a series of dips and bows. I curtsy. The plunge of the neckline of the gown shows more than I'd like to the crowd— if they're even still looking at me. The prickle at the back of my neck tells me they are. I sweep an elegant hand out, my other catching my skirt and holding it up.

"Tonight, the promise," the king intones. "Tomorrow night, the vow. Three nights of marriage at the bride's home. The final night the happy couple will be free to go to Wolf Hall."

I wait for the king to state the terms of this farce—that will prove I'm not a traitor, that I'm doing this for a *reason*. I wonder what Duke Galibran knows of the terms and why he'd agree to do this at all. Yet another bargain, a snarl, a match between two men and I don't know the rules. All the same, I'm being played. What can the Witch King offer to my betrothed to force him to marry his enemy at the behest of a king he seemingly hates?

No one says anything else. The answers to my unasked questions are out there, but there's no one I trust to voice them to. I let them curdle inside of me, part of me hoping I die a little early, before I fail hard enough to see my father shut his eyes for the last time.

CHAPTER 20

I consider trying to stab Duke Galibran again, but that seems like a fruitless effort. The Wolf lord slides toward the heavy, double doors. We skirt down the hall, which leads to the entrance of the antechamber of the pantheon's temple. This place, those of House Berrat pray to the gods of their choosing and where many oaths–particularly promises for nuptials–are conducted.. Everything feels slow, even the portraits that dog our progress pull toward our destination with the same, sludging pace. And yet the only choice I have is to move forward with my plan. Promise my hand in marriage and then later use that same hand to murder this man.

Duke Galibran's companions flock around him. It reminds me of the way birds fly. The yellow-eyed one, Lukas, tails him just a few steps behind on the left. Jessa echoes the same movement on the duke's right. Lazy, unconcerned gaits like predators that know they could kill everyone here with a swipe of one, Cursed claw if they were to shift into their canine shapes. It's a wonder that the duke didn't bring one of his ill-formed beasts here. If he thought it would win him any points, he's wrong.

He pauses, turning. I'm mid-thought on wondering if a blade through the heart doesn't work what will be my next best option when his gaze catches mine. His eyebrow cocks in mockery as he sweeps a gesture that means one thing.

Come.

A growing tide of anger seizes me. Perhaps it's petulant, but part of me bangs at the prison I've put myself in and that life has created such circumstances around me. What was I to choose except this? Should I have just let Papa die? Let us all fall at the mercy of this black tide of ill-luck? If I'm to be a sacrifice at the altar of power, let my life mean something.

A bubble of air chokes my throat, refusing to go up or down. I walk forward, ignoring the stares and the growing whispers. I know what they're thinking, what they're looking at. The child of a duchess they never wanted, practically Selvan in her appearance, and the product of a love spell gone wrong. I don't need the Sight to look at their lips. I don't want to use it at all right now. The truth as they see it will hurt too much, even if it's nothing I haven't heard before.

The duke's hand dangles expectantly. I push forward, gripping it with my own. He tucks my arm into his, as if he's a proper gentleman instead of a monster, and leans in like a lover might. "If I didn't know better, I'd think that you're displeased to see me again."

Again.

So he does recognize me. His lips twist upward. Everything about him is a waiting smirk.

I keep my face carefully blank. I haven't yet decided how to play this game, or if a pawn is supposed to have her own thoughts at all. Best to wait to seem displeased or to play an interested bride and hope he forgets that I stabbed him if that's the one I have to go with.

I can't help the grimace that crosses my mouth at the thought. I'm such a fool.

"Yes, clearly you are overjoyed." His words purr from his throat. "Trust me, we are of a mind on this. Let's just get it over with."

* * *

THE ANTECHAMBER that leads to the temple in Gray Hall glows. Warmth slides up the walls. Though there are no windows, the rooms that branch off from this space are as bright as noon in the summer.

The chamber is in the shape of a heptagon. Each wall adorning it features one of the gods from the Seven Orders, predominantly painted to the length of seven feet high by the same length in width. These images do not move, sitting as still as corpses and stare just as blankly. It would be blasphemy to bespell these holy images, as if any power--even that of the priests—could touch on the will of the gods. At least, their devotees do not reveal any moving images to the rest of us. Alongside the pictures of the divinities are smaller paintings of bowls of fruit, flowers, and even genitalia, meant to remind the viewers of their symbols. It's hard not to look towards Scillicops' portrait, which features the god himself as a giant naked man atop a horse. I'm not sure how that doesn't hurt his tender bits, but that seems to be just another impracticality skirted around by sheer divinity.

Next to him, to remind us all of his priorities, is an image of a giant penis. Not for the first time, I wonder why no vagina graces the depictions. I'm a believer, but I don't believe that the gods would discriminate as much as the priests that tell us what to think. My nose wrinkles.

More questions for all the stories one is told. Why *not* a vagina? Really. Sometimes it's the only question that demands to be asked.

Beneath each portrait sits a small altar with a bowl beside it. Each of these were recently filled, judging by the fresh ice with splinters running through the cubes. Each is a different color, to each god's preference. Vegetation sprawls in the bowls, perfuming the air and flavoring the water with the first blessing for our engagement. A hasty thing, since all of the ceremonies for our handfasting will need to be done tonight. The marriage rites tomorrow, are another matter entirely.

"You could look a little less sick," the duke murmurs out of the corner of his mouth. He readjusts my hand on his arm.

"You could be less sickening, Duke Galibran," I retort.

"Killian," he says.

"What?"

"Call me Killian. We're to be married."

"What does that have to do with anything?" I mutter under my breath. He pulls us towards Amara's portrait. Even if her portrait wasn't this looming height, the goddess obviously has a giant-like stature. She looks down her nose at us, as all the gods do, her red painted lips and copper hair brighter than the fire blazing behind her. A sword dripping with blood leans against a wall of flames in the background, a reminder of her days of vengeance and her capabilities. Fex's flower, the stupid falsehood I risked everything for, curls up her leg, staining her skin crimson where the thorns dig into her flesh. The purple bud blooms with false promises. A bitterness wets my tongue at the sight of it.

A smile, a smirk, or a promise of something one may or may not like, rests on Amara's lips. I can't say I've ever been partial to the goddess, and now I feel a type of resentment towards her for my failed mission in the woods.

"Frankly, this is going to be unpleasant for everyone involved." His voice is low. Duke Galibran's–Killian's–brow pinches in agitation. He jerks a harsh look towards the crowd that has followed behind us.

Priests from all Seven Orders gather at our backs. Galinda stands there, striking a pose like one might paint her in that moment. Ewan stands next to her, indolently eating a clump of bread.

Papa is noticeably absent.

The king isn't present, but each of the priests are from his retinue, brought especially for this occasion from Veritaes. Each wears the color of their god. Embroidery of the divinity's symbol swirls in precise stitches along the ends of their sleeves. If they were to turn, a large depiction of it would be on their backs. Some of them have elaborate tattoos carefully inked on their skin. Others possess piercings dappling their flesh in precise dots.

"Leave us," Killian orders. Unease slithers down my body. My breath hitches. Killian. Am I to call my enemy by his given name now?

The Amaran priest steps forward, the goddess' colors bright as a fresh, violent battle in the warm light. He has the eyes of a snake. "With respect, Duke, if you have chosen Amara to give the blessing, I must be here."

Killian waves an arrogant hand at the man. "This is for my future bride and I. The priest rites are tomorrow. My own devotee of the goddess will be arriving then. You will not be needed."

The priest frowns. His bald head, complete with a blooming tattoo in purple-red ink atop his scalp, shimmers with the brightness of the chamber. Without another word, he nods, backing away.

Muttering mixes with the sounds of departing feet patter out of the chamber as the appointees of the pantheon make their exit. Galinda stands there, mouth open like a fish, alongside Ewan whose expression is similar. "We are family, surely, Duke..." she says it with a twist of her mouth. I rarely agree with Galinda on anything, but her obvious displeasure for my future-husband is something that we can both concur on.

"Out," he repeats. The lights flicker. This man could rattle death itself.

She squeaks, departing quickly. Ewan follows her, stalking behind her with a look over his shoulder.

For the first time, Killian and I are alone.

CHAPTER 21

"Are we doing it, or what?" Killian asks, turning so his entire body faces me.

Are we doing *what*? *IT*?

He's tall, even taller than me, which is a feat unto itself. The hard planes of his chest are right there, his mouth just inches above mine. The taste of iron floods my palette, the memories of his hands all over me. Perhaps not the first time, but it truly hits me that I am marrying this man. A monster he may be, but he's also a knot of darkness, sex, and blood that part of me craves. The rest of me remembers that he's the enemy, that he's the source of fear and a large part of the reason the war with the Dark One hasn't been won. I want to slap myself. But still. Warmth flushes my flesh and I grit my teeth. A combination of body lust and bloodlust tightens my chest and pools in my lower stomach. Far away, Nisha's rumble of disapproval at the former desire roughens against my consciousness before I shove her completely out of my head.

The last few days have left me tired beyond reckoning, but if I'm to be alone with a monster, I need to have my wits about me. Killian is a pretty predator. The sort with a beautiful exterior to lure in his prey before he bites their neck in half.

The tired tug of magic pulls around my heart as I open myself to the Sight. The flow of truth around me pulses here, in the heart of the gods. My throat thickens as bitterness tingles at the back of it. I half-wonder if it's blasphemous to use magic in here if one is not a priest. Probably.

The scar hashing through his eyebrow pulls at Killian's brow as he scowls. He runs a hand through his thick, dark hair. Curls flip up from it, though it's tied back at some half-hearted effort to tame his waves.

"Well?"

"Do what?" I snap. That's when he smirks.

"Why, did I get a bride with a dirty mind?" His fang flashes, thes scowl disappearing completely. Killian chuckles. "We must perform the first part of the binding," he says slowly, as if I'm stupid. I glare at him. I still haven't figured out how to play this sham of a marriage, but regardless of whether I need to pretend to love him at some point, it would be suspicious to start that now. I'm free to hate him openly and I'll take pleasure in it.

"I should have realized you'd be vague and unhelpful, as well as a pig," I retort, even though he's right. He ignores this, though his mockery slips against me like a second skin. I think I'd want to kill him even if I hadn't vowed to.

Killian moves away, twisting towards the offering bowl. "Have you done this before?" he asks.

"No," I reply tersely. Have I been promised to an enemy, who is also an ass, and sworn to complete a secret mission by order of our immortal king to kill this bastard? "I haven't ever done *this*." Killian's back is to me. I look at it, losing myself for a moment in how I might get rid of him. I wonder if I can manage to poison him if that would be a good way to kill him? I've more expertise in that area than the average bride, I imagine, so perhaps that's what I can try. The best thing I can do right now is watch and wait.

Still, I swallow. The king either kills this man efficiently now so he can assume control of House Galibran and its Cursed strength or to effectively put him out of play for a year so we can win at the northern front without distractions. There's no way I'll be able to devise a way to kill him tonight, not if a knife through the throat doesn't work, nor one through the chest. I'll have to get to know him.

Know thy enemy. Well, then.

"I suppose we will learn this together," Killian murmurs. "Know thy enemy." His eyes don't meet mine. A crazed part of me worries he can read my mind.

"Why?" I rasp. I don't mean why did he send everyone away, I mean why to *everything.*

"In part, curiosity," he replies, echoing our first conversation when we kissed until we bled. "But, as ever, your choice, darling," he drawls. And from his mouth, there are only shadows that flutter from his breath. Like he took a drag of a pipe and only darkness exited his lips.

His hand swoops forward. Killian's shirtsleeves cover his arms, but the cuff lifts a little at the end, revealing a thickly veined wrist that leads me to believe his forearms must be equally decorated. He scoops the water, collecting a purple petal and the two stones from the bottle of the bowl. Amethyst and what looks to be either a ruby or a garnet. He holds it up to my mouth. "As I said, your choice."

I look into his eyes. Dark pits of mystery and despair look back at me. I search for evil, but all I find is a question. As if he doesn't know if I'll do it. Killian hides it well. Any man that slaughters people and tosses their heads over the wall for their loved ones to find is not a good man. But I am an expert on looking for the lies that people present, even if they are hidden beneath darkness. Gods, give me strength to do this.

I smile. "What are choices in times like these?" I reply honestly. He tips the water into my waiting mouth and it streams in a chilled, sweet slide down my throat. I stare into his eyes. Darkness looks back at me, swirling with little bright bits of gold. I wonder what he expects of me. A wife. An enemy. I can't help but think of our first kiss and my breath catches. A wet crawl of water slips from my messy drag of the liquid, a muted hush of the floral flavor fills my senses. This time it's not blood, at least.

The brush of the firm pad of his finger wisps at the corner of my mouth, catching an errant droplet.

"My turn," he husks.

He shifts the bowl into my hands, watching me fill it as if I am the only thing that exists in the entire world.

"Don't forget the stones," he says.

I don't reply, but fill the bowl, making sure it contains the same items. The rim of the container presses to his lips as I hold it there. He never takes his gaze from mine as he pulls the liquid into his mouth.

"Now the words."

I swallow. I avoid speaking oaths, promises, or anything like that as a matter of principle. "I wasn't told we'd have to say anything."

"This is the practice of my House," he replies. "If you prefer, you can stay silent. But this is my commitment to you. While you are mine, no harm will befall you. I swear on Amara's wrath."

Mine.

The air leaks out of the room. Out of my lungs. The word makes me feel oddly hot. It's only anger, I tell myself. And that is part of it. Definitely a small part.

"I–" I snap my jaw shut. A promise of forever, neither of us is offering. A year and a day. "I promise to give you no less than you deserve," I finally say sweetly.

His head snaps back as he lets out a hearty laugh. My chest warms at the sound.

I can't deny he's handsome, but no matter what, no matter the charm of the words while you are mine, I can't forget who he is. What he is. He can tell me everything I ever wanted to hear, but that will not change anything.

Loyalty first.

"You're violent and rude, so far, my betrothed. But at least you're honest." He walks to the corner of the room where the god Scillicops' offering waits. A bottle of sparkling wine–quallais, a bubbling alcohol that only is produced in the region of the same name, in the backyard of Ferr House—in a chilled container of ice. Two flutes of glasses designed for the liquid stand there. Killian pops the top of it, which whizzes straight into the depiction of the painted penis.

"Unfortunate," he says with a wince, eyeing the dick painting.

I can't help but snort. I slap my hand to my mouth. "We can't take that. We already picked our god to preside over the wedding."

Killian doesn't reply except to pour the drink into the flutes. A small bowl of strawberries sits by it with a little knife. He delicately slices the edge of the fruit, slipping it onto the rim before handing it to me. "None of them are watching," he finally says, "if they exist at all. They're fucking and feasting, as they have encouraged the rest of us to." He raises an eyebrow.

My blush burns to the roots of my hair. "You are disgusting."

"What?" he murmurs. "Do not tell me my wicked witch is shy."

I jerk my head up. "Not at all. Just selective in my partners." I give him a smile that is all teeth. "And sorry to disappoint you, my lord, but there is no virgin bride here."

He smiles at that. "Killian, my wicked witch. And I am only pleased to hear your thoughts are leaning in such a direction."

"They are not." I protest. Irritation and anger flares beneath my skin. My flesh feels too tight against my skeleton. The quallais sweats against my hand and I fight the urge to down the entire thing. Killian is probably right, none of the gods are watching tonight. Better, that way, as this entire engagement, marriage, and situation is a laughable sham.

"What shall we toast to, then?" His voice is all darkness and smoke, hiding whatever he is thinking.

"That a year and a day passes quickly," I say. I arch my brows, waiting. I wonder if he'll be shocked or if he knew all along.

And if he knew all along, I wonder what kind of conversation he had with King Thaddeus before his arrival.

He only nods, unsurprised at my words. "That, we can agree on."

Our glasses clink together.

The Shadow Wood is notoriously difficult to pass through, at least the section mostly inhabited by the Wolves. Chimera creatures burrow from the north into the trees, an evil from the Dark One infecting even the core of Lumar. Blood, magic, luck, and the will of the forest all must work in one's favor to pass through safely. Even the king doesn't go there, for fear of being defeated or just a claimed disinterest, I don't know. I sip my drink. The bubbles strike my palette. If Killian knew we'd marry, likely he must have known before we met given the timeline.

I want to demand all the answers, but this man is fated to die on my blade. Somehow. He has to know I hate him. I stare at him. He meets my gaze, eyes sparking with interest.

"Tell me why me," I say. Why this? Why agree to the Witch King's demands? I wait, wondering what he'll say. And what he won't. I let the quallais roll over my tongue, watching him for signs of lies. Even if the coins won't tell me, his body will. And I can still feel little changes in the air. Barely. Something is wrong with him—and my magic with him.

"Well, my witchy wife. I will level with you—we shall see if you are smart enough to grasp the situation." Anger pounds from the inside of my head and I grit my teeth. At that moment, the shadows in the room lean inwards. The one on my wrist tickles me, like a lazy finger. The cozy light dims in the chamber, but doesn't go out. "Our marriage does four simple things—one, it puts your people and mine at an impasse, allowing the king to wage his foolish war."

Foolish? What an asshole.

"Two, it prevents me from making a marital alliance with his enemies. Three, it gives him a way into my fortress. And four. It makes me look weak if my wife isn't besotted with me." So many questions gurgle inside of me. How would it allow the king into Wolf Hall? Why couldn't he go there anyways? What did the king offer the Wolf to get him to agree to this? That, I don't understand.

"Then why do it at all?" It sounds like a ludicrous bargain when he puts it that way.

"The world doesn't give us all the choices we'd like, love," Killian answers ambiguously. He leans in and those dark, aching eyes bore into me.

The gods like to play out tales. To set out pieces from stories and see what we mortals will do with them. That is what they say, anyways. What have they done, but set a villain loose on me? I wonder if that's the part Killian wants to play.

My breath sticks in my chest. The answers of why he's agreed to this farce aren't going to pass through his lips tonight. I'll have to find out for myself. In time. But maybe it doesn't matter why. Maybe nothing does, besides seeing this man on the tip of my blade. Either dead or in so many pieces he'll wish he wasn't alive to feel anything.

"I tell you this for one simple reason: do not get in my way. Or else I will make your life a living hell."

"Too late," I snap. His eyebrows jerk up and a smirk rides the corner of his lush mouth.

"This needs to look real, wife," he whispers to me.

No. I don't say it, but the word pulses beneath my skin. My pride won't let me do it. The lies soak around me, this farce, but his desperation feels true. Why does he need me to look like I don't mind his presence? *More politics.* The answer comes to me in a flash. My teeth click. I'm so tired of lies and things that don't matter. For me, it's only Papa.

Neither of us speaks. We're aligned in one thing. Neither of us really wanted this. But he's not the one betrothed to a villain. No matter what, this marriage is going to end with one of us dead. I don't ask him what social equity he'll get for having a palatable wife, or what he'll give to me for plastering on fake smiles and enamored looks. A dead man won't need that promise from me.

CHAPTER 22

$\mathcal{S}$ ilence greets us in the banquet hall. Not even the clank of a fork strikes a plate because no one is eating. Probably everyone is sickened by what has happened. Is happening. That, and no one puts down their knives in their white-knuckled grips. The oppressive tension fills the room in an angry cloud of humidity as Killian and I walk down the center aisle, passing the vertically aligned tables to the seating at the head of the room. He's tucked my hand into the crook of his arm once more. He's all grace and predatory strength. Meanwhile, I fight to not stumble after him.

Behind the table at the dais with high-backed chairs is a huge, arched window. Red light spills into the room from the moon, casting everything in a bloody glow. The wall is visible through the glass, a reminder of what this man has done to us. The rest of the light comes from the flickering sconces. Blue-black shadows pool at my husband-to-be's feet like steam skimming a hot spring. I spare a thought to wonder why he didn't use his shadows at all during our private ritual. Killian's gaze narrows at the high table, noting what I do: that there are so few people up there. Noticeably absent is Papa. Galinda, too, isn't there, though Ewan sits with a group of his goonies. A collection of half-grown men that believe in drinking more than they do anything of substance. The king hasn't appeared, but that doesn't mean he won't. It's quite possible he will arrive when everyone is comfortably seated, only to make us all stand once more. I quash the disloyal thought.

Promises take place at sunset, traditionally. Ill luck for this relationship, for all of our ceremonies to be conducted during the blood moon. The goddess Amara will not watch, despite our faked askance for her blessing of the engagement. Her eyes are turned from the mortal world during the red season, toward her lover Fex. A honeymoon, of a sort, I suppose. Her blessings will not be upon Killian and I in the way other couples benefited from. But other couples didn't need the protection of a blood moon to keep from killing one another. As Killian said, they are all doing what this time is for. Release.

Servants, decked in blue-green finery with gilded tassels, glide around the nobility assembled. Goblets of mulled wine and clear liquor press into hands. I eagerly take one, letting the harsh alcohol hit the back of my throat with thanks. I shiver. My eyes find the shape of my betrothed and hold there, wondering how many traditions we'll have to go through before we leave. Before I spend a year and a day captive. And a year and two days until this fool dies. Or until my father and I do.

Ewan stands, his posture a wavering questionable thing. He bangs his goblet against the table. Plum wine splatters across the white tablecloths. Stains spread like a wound. The room stutters to a silence. Around him, some of his friends grin. A few look vaguely uncomfortable, but in the way that they are willing to go with whatever happens.

"My sssssister." Ewan says. "My little ssssister." Bile rises in my throat. The man is a pig. And *not* my brother. "I always wondered if someone would make an honest woman of you."

He guffaws. His friends do as well. Further away, there's the titters of people that don't care for me, their unwanted heir.

Killian trades a glance with one of his men, the one called Lukas. The yellow-eyed man placed himself at one of the tables nearest to us, but not at the high table. He stands, interrupting Ewan mid-snort.

"To our peace." Lukas grinds out. "May we find that the border is less...contentious."

Silence greets his words. The other Wolves offer up their glasses to the air. A heavy pause seeps through the room and I wonder if more will raise their cups or if they will decide to raise blades instead. Finally, Ewan smirks, the affronted look wiping itself off of his face.

Killian watches Ewan, stone-faced. . The shadows at the edges of the room seem to grow thicker for a moment, but I shake off the thought. Killian catches me staring and raises an eyebrow. He pulls a silver canteen from his jacket, raises it, and tosses it back into his mouth.

It's an insult.

I frown. Ewan and the rest of the room have turned their attention away from us, or at least if anyone has noticed my husband's display, they say nothing. He takes another swig of the drink. Rage bites at me. As if the Bears would poison him right now. He continues to drink, this overtness drawing gazes and growls. The insult grows.

My hand itches toward the little dagger clasped to my arm. I'd love to stab him for this but I refrain. *Peace, Briar.* I tell myself. But there is no peace. Not really.

To be fair, Papa and I both did stab him, but that is beside the point. To not eat our food, to drink our offerings, it's a slap in the face. We couldn't get away with just a simple poisoning here. Though I do spare a thought to wonder at the man's potential concern for poison and add it to my list of ways that he might be killed.

Tonight, I get my own room to myself. Tomorrow, the wedding would take place. And the wedding night. I fight a shiver at the thought of Killian's hands on me.

Again. My lips prickle. Warmth spreads in my core.

Three nights here at Gray Hall. Three nights to kill him while I'm still here. Without having to leave at all.

Anger, frustration, agony—every negative feeling I've ever felt swirls inside of me. A petulant *why me?* whines through my body.

Nisha catches my irritation. An image of a bleeding, ambiguous-looking organ appears in my mind. A knife appears in it, then my cat friend's jaw snaps on a corner and swallows it. I snort, smiling and shake my head. So he can't be stabbed through the heart. But if the Dead One could die, a god, then whatever the so-called Duke of Death is can be slain as well.

Anything can die.

CHAPTER 23

$\mathcal{A}$ rap of knuckles on my door jolts me from my half-dozed state. At first, I wonder if it's a dream. I'd fallen asleep, nose buried in between the thin pages of the leather bound tome of illicit faerie tales after leaving the hall. This one features a gallant, dark hero and a grumpy heroine with many, mythical dragons. The urge to escape the world, to run away when the day-to-day bruises my too-soft heart, beats a frantic tattoo of insistent commands. It's more than just a want. Fulfilling the need to leave this life behind in lieu of a place where one's magic isn't punished and happily ever afters are possible is a requirement for coming back to reality and dealing with the horrors of the mundane. Thank goodness for the storytellers of the world. The well-worn paths in my mind of circling anxieties eases just a little when I am able to slip into someone else's skin on the page.

Still, tales can be dangerous. Words dictate the way we see the world and much care must be given to them. Otherwise, all the witches will remain terrible and every princess a kind virgin in a fortress, unable to touch life. Faerie tales, like the fae, are far more complicated than people would like them to be.

The fae are a lot of terrible things, creatures that are cruel and lie with the truth, but for whatever reason, we name these stories after them. Perhaps that is simply the nature of stories, to use one thing to say something else. And everyone takes away a different piece of the puzzle into their broken hearts.

Regardless, I offer a prayer to each of the Seven that I never have to meet the fae for too long.

Nisha hisses as the knock cracks again. I flinch, shaking the sleep from my tired body.

Not a dream, then.

Nisha's shoulders flex, rippling muscles stalk forward. I blearily get up, setting my book down in a slow, unhurried movement so I don't bend a page. I pull my dagger from its holster, abandoned at the side of my bed, to grip it as I stalk toward the door. It's probably Urusla, or even Derrick, but one can't be too careful when the enemy is here. It would be just delicious if I was attacked, violating hospitality, and I could kill one of them. I wince a little, the hypocrisy of my and my father's attack on Killian stinging uncomfortably. The gift he gave us, of brushing off the attack, means our honor remains intact. Confusion bubbles up inside of me with a squeeze of pressure near my ribcage. I shake it off, picturing the beheaded soldiers tossed in different directions at our border.

The door opens under my hand and the man on the other side is tall enough that I have to look up. Shadows drip across his golden brown skin, as if he's emerged from water and rivulets of darkness fall off of him. The sconces in the hallway flicker.

"Lady Briar," Killian says with a nod. Without meaning to, I take a step back. My hand spasms around the handle of my blade.

Killian moves forward a step. The rasp of his shirt rakes against the wooden door frame as he leans against it. The slant of the little light left seems to purposely find his mouth, limning it like a painter might if they were to add the finishing touches on the focal point of a portrait. He crosses his arms. The fabric of his shirt bunches obscenely at his biceps and across his forearms.

"What a big cat you have, little bear," he says, by way of greeting. His eyes flick to Nisha, but he appears unconcerned.

"The better to eat you with, Wolf."

I can't stop looking at the way his clothes gather around his muscles. A sour anger tucks itself into my stomach, alongside a heat I don't want to acknowledge.

He clears his throat. I watch his mouth again. It twists into a grimace. "A year and a day will be a long time for both of us–"

"An eternity."

"--but we will make do." Killian glares at my interruption. "Tomorrow, after the wedding, we will leave."

"No," I reply. Unease burgeons inside of me, prickling every nerve I have with tension. "We're not due to leave until three days."

"When my priest gets here and performs this blasted ritual, we'll be leaving, wicked witch," he says with finality. Arguments bloom inside of me, but I don't bother to voice them. The king will supply the priest, everyone knows that. If the priest is here to witness, it will be done the way the Witch King desires.

Killian's gaze lingers in the dark corners of my room. I wonder if his power over shadow allows him to see in the dark, if he's some sort of unnatural spirit able to take hold of nightmares. I shiver.

"Cold, darling?"

"Irritated," I retort. It's not a lie, but it's not the full truth. Confused, devastated, and exhausted could be added to my list.

A sigh heaves through his chest. His tunic rubs against the doorframe as he shifts to lean more comfortably. "This is out of order." Killian's voice simmers, low and soft. "If we'd met another way and meant this to be love—you would have gotten this long before now." Velvet words drip from his silver tongue. Brandy-warmth suffuses my stomach, pooling and soaking. Killian speaks as lovers do, with a low hum that requires you to lean in. Inviting intimacy. *Come closer,* the tone says. *I'll whisper in your ear. All day. All night.*

I refuse.

If this were love, we wouldn't be here like this. Desperation wouldn't snap at my heels, biting me in reminders of a painful loss around the corner. Promises of death wouldn't haunt me like spritelight. Hatred burns high in my chest. Rosy flames of passionate *forevers* and *I dos* instead consist of a white fire. The earth-rending desire to kill this man to save Papa. I wouldn't look at him with disgust and see all of my people he had killed.

Scorched earth is all this man deserves.

If this were love, Killian would breathe my name against my hair, let me burrow in his chest, and hold me until the world ceased its war on my soul.

This isn't love, so that's not what I get.

Metal drops into my hand, but for a moment only the whorls of Killian's fingerprints across my palm exist.

What could it have been like if he wasn't a Wolf? Then I remember his cocky smirk and the bite of his lips on me. *Nothing.* Nothing but a desperate coupling at the most. The rest of the world would still want to kill me, if they knew what I was. *Witch.*

The sound of his breathing fills my ears. Like whispers. My own exhalations pant with growing anger and my palm aches to hold my ax instead of whatever he placed there. The unfairness of this grinds against me. Why me? What had I done to offend the gods? Dead mother, dying father, nothing but a poor little witch with only her body to offer to the enemy.

When Killian steps backwards, a dainty ring glints, abandoned in my hand. The gold band is inlaid with an interlocking pattern. The center stone whirls whites, purples, blues, and reds in an endless lap of internal tide.

Moonstone.

I cock my head to the side, staring at it, letting the anger lull for a moment.

This stone, precious to the fae and to witches, is harvested only underneath the blood moon, much like Fex's flower. Moonstone possesses no magic, beyond the ability to swirl the faint mixture of colors in beautiful chaos. An arcane ghost mixing paints.

"Thank you," I say instead of voicing my thoughts. Something silly, like warmth, heats me from the inside. Beyond the nugget of anger that glows like an ever-burning coal, but I don't bother with that, instead focusing on the rage I stoke within. I was a grumpy girl that grew into an angry woman. There's no way around it, except to toss a finger at the world that batters relentlessly at my very soul, grit my teeth, and pull a weapon. For now, that is simply a smile I don't mean in the least.

My mouth stretches into a grimace.

"There's writing on the inside of the band," he says, ignoring my false expression. I twirl the ring until I see the delicate marks of the words. *Love to the grave.* Even his gifts drip in sarcasm. Love to the grave, indeed. Until we kill each other. My hand itches, wanting the feel of a blade of some sort in it.

"True love, of course," I say, looking at the ring with bitterness. Asshole. This should have been from someone who I wanted to marry, someone I actually cared for. Grims, even Derrick and his wretched jealousy is preferred to this.

"Of course," he returns. "Nothing but the best for my future wife."

The ring slips easily on my left finger. It winks there, like a cheeky child. I can't help but admire it, letting it catch the light. Small, something that wouldn't get in the way in a fight or snag on clothes. It suits me. Killian steps forward, as if he'll touch me again. We're half a foot away from one another, so close that I could just lean in and kiss him or easily slide my dagger into his jugular. Not that it would kill him anyways. The scarred eyebrow raises again, but I find myself entranced by the little beauty mark beneath that wicked gaze.

Nisha growls.

"Your cat doesn't like me," Killian observes.

"*I* don't like you," I reply.

A smirk quirks his lips. "I would say I don't like you either, but I'm not sure that's true." He leans in, his breath tickling my ear. The darkness at the edges of the room quivers and my breath catches. "I'm sure I hate you though." He says it like someone else might say *I want to fuck you.*

I shiver, jerking away. The shadows in the room lick up the corners of the wall, like an indolent tongue across a lover's flesh. I walk to the edge of my room, ignoring the itch of his gaze at my neck.

Tradition demands we exchange offerings. A token from one partner to the other in honor of the pair's engagement. I'd expected this, collecting my offering after our banquet hall disaster in the dark and before I'd dozed off reading faerie tales. The fabric slips soft against my fingers as I grab the bag at the edge of the room, left as far away from my bed as possible. I toss the velvet blue sachet to his feet. *Thud.* The cloth shimmers like a whorl of raging river water. "My engagement gift to you, my lord."

Killian picks it up, his expression curious. A hand slips along the side of the bag. I bite down a smirk. He weighs it in his palm. A crow of laughter bubbles in my chest. "Heavy," he says. "The weight of your love for me, Lady Briar?"

"No, my dear, my love's contents," I reply sweetly.

When he pulls the satchel, the string opens the mouth of the bag in a whirr. Killian stares down, his mouth opens, gaping. Shock lines the stretch of his mouth. His forearm flies up to cover his nose. The unsubtle smell of shit fills the room. "Is this—?"

I raise an eyebrow. "A fair trade, I think, for marriage to you."

"I give you a ring and you give me *bear shit?*"

I push him out the door. He doesn't resist, eyes wide with shock and outrage. "Of course not. Bear shit is too good for you. That, my lord, is dog shit."

I shut the door in his face.

CHAPTER 24

"You're too tall, dear," Ursula mumbles from a few feet away, staring at my exposed ankles. Two many bodies fumble around me—two seamstresses stretching a swath of fabric between them, Nisha, and Ursula herself. My handmaid stares, elderly face squints into a wretched look that means more than *too tall*. Today, it means *too much*.

I glare back at her, used to the half-love, half-hurt doled out from her wizened lips. Her gray hair scraggles down her forehead, parts of it making a mad escape from her coiffure. The white-ish dress the seamstresses desperately try to fit around my hips doesn't quite stretch around them and the front pulls unflatteringly at my stomach. The thing is a piecemeal mess and I imagine I look like a scarecrow. A hot race of blood burgeons at the tips of my ears. I want to rip it all off. I avoid meeting my own gaze in the floor length mirror opposite of me, looking instead toward my big cat friend licking her paw. Something between shame, self-hatred, and an unnamable feeling that shifts into a particular grief that sits heavy in my stomach.

Nisha emits a noise of disapproval in the corner of the room. Her languid form curls into a circle. Her tail flicks a violent gesture. *[Pretty,]* she insists with another swish of her tail.

One of the two seamstresses sees Nisha's movements and misses with her pin. Instead of stabbing the white fabric, the needle punctures my skin. I hiss. So does Nisha.

The seamstress drops the pin and scrambles after it. I don't try to comfort her or tell her Nisha wouldn't hurt her. I feel too sorry for myself right now to take care of anyone else's feelings.

I am nothing more than a wretched gremlin.

I pause too long, and the woman's hands shake. Guilt nudges me. "She won't hurt you now, she's just observant," I say, trying to be careful with my words. Exhaustion thickens my tongue. I can't afford another fever and I'm torn between stumbling into telling too much truth or accidentally lying. Either way won't be good for me. "Nisha's just watching me."

The woman seems to take little comfort in that, but doesn't stab me again as she fights to pin the lace at the hem of the gown to cover my ankles. We're completely ignoring that this gown just doesn't fit me, then.

Grims, this is worse than I thought it would be.

A blushing bride has never been in the cards for me. I've spent my life wanting more, never quite catching that ephemeral gift of *something* that makes a person naturally joyful. An ache lives in my chest, a soreness that never leaves. There's no word I know for the desolation of a love that never happened, but the feeling tears at my heart. A marriage for mutual devotion, for respect–all of that is gone.

When I walk down the aisle tonight, last night's dreams of darkness and blood clouding my head, I'll plan to kill my husband. The dreams I'd had for months seemed to be prophetic, then. A bitter laugh slithers up my esophagus and I fight not to let it out.

A year and a day.

You're doing this for a reason, I tell myself. And I am. Even if Papa will hate me forever.

"We could pull out your mother's…" one of the seamstresses says. The other thinks I don't see her and makes the killing gesture in a quick X at her throat. I purposely look at the decadent sleeve that doesn't clear past my forearm. My head throbs as rage inside me crescendos. Perhaps that will be one thing about this. At Wolf Hall, I'll be hated because I'm me, not because people remember my mother. I won't be the daughter of a despised woman, there. Just a woman to be despised in her own right.

"Yes, pull the late duchess' gown out," Ursula says before I can open my mouth to speak. "The late Duchess Rozena was a bit thinner than Lady Briar, but it'll have to do on such short notice."

One of the seamstresses gives a nod before scurrying off. My mother's things are on the opposite end of the manor and I wait in silence with sweat rolling down my back for some time before the woman reappears. She holds it up for us to view.

Tiny holes riddle the edges of the gown, the product of ill care and hungry moths. Hands help slip it on, firm tugs and pinches to my skin until it covers me. The odor of mildew clouds my nose, as well as the inexplicable scent of apricots. The too-tight dress is discarded and I wiggle my mother's wedding gown over my hips. Stains of age and negligence mar the ivory satin and lace.

This one, too, is still too tight, but less unflattering.

"If we drape some newer satin here and here," the seamstress who'd inadvertently stabbed me says, "we can cover up the worst of it."

"Like so," Ursula says, nodding. She pulls at another the discarded too-short and too-small gown, using it as an example as she holds it to my hip. "It'll be a long train, but why not. The veil will fit regardless."

She pauses for a moment, as if taking me in for the first time. Her gaze goes watery, before she blinks the tears away and dons on the armored attitude I'm more familiar with.

"You'll need a fishu," Ursula says instead of anything sentimental, eying my breasts that have been pushed up nearly to my eyes.

"No kidding," I mutter, my throat going sore. I don't want to feel like a slab of meat on a platter for Killian. That's what I am, though, to the world. Even if I am something different, it hurts to be seen as such. I turn to the mirror in front of me.

A wave of grief slaps me, choking off my breath. The dead-still portrait of my mother stares back at me from the looking glass. The silver-spun hair–minus the dark streak running through the front– and dress captured in the painting are the same. Even my eyes look as dead as hers do in that lifeless monstrosity. A hopeless laugh bubbles up and I let it out, ignoring the shocked looks around me. Too-much-Briar. That's me.

"We'll have to let out some of the seams here, Lady Briar, but this will work. It'll be a rush," one of the women says, her voice uncomfortable and awkward.

I finger the itchy lace at my bodice. I'd likely never wear another one like this. If I succeed, the likelihood of dying is almost certain. Tonight, after all, is the beginning of the end. I might as well dress for the occasion.

"Dye it black."

CHAPTER 25

 $\mathcal{T}$ oo many things can go wrong. I find myself winding through the castle, ignoring the looks that follow me. I should be getting ready, but I don't care to overprimp myself for Killian. I'll squirrel every blade I've got into hidden holsters, but that is the most time I want to take preparing for my marriage.

The door to the temple eases aside under my touch, opening noiselessly. Religion has never been much of a pillar of support. In the face of death and failure, though, it's nice to think there might be something powerful out there rooting for you to not die.

I settle onto the bench at the center, taking a look at all of the gods and their symbols staring back at me. I avoid gazing directly at the picture of Scilicops' giant cock.

My eyelids flutter closed. I inhale. "Amara, even Scilicops, if you're listening, please protect me."

No flash of light. No warmth. In fact, I feel colder. Why would the gods bother listening to my pleas when those I love do not?

Papa's image cracks through my mind. His look of disappointment and rage batters at me like an actual weapon. *Please understand, Papa. Anyone listening. This is what I must do.*

"Lady Briar?"

I turn, yanking a blade out of my sleeve. A priest, adorned in the color of red so deep it is almost purple, holds up his hands. Tattoos ink his bald head, intricate runes that pay homage to the god he represents. Or, in this case, goddess.

I don't recognize this Amaran priest. And just because he is a holy man, it doesn't mean he hasn't come to kill me. I don't put the dagger down.

"Yes?"

"I've simply come to meet before your wedding. Duke Galibran thought you might like to speak with me."

I scoff. "So I shall tell you my secrets and you will scurry back to him with them?"

He shuffles closer. The light pings off his head, casting parts of his sun tanned skin the color of white fire.

"May I?" he asks, gesturing to the empty place next to me on the bench.

"No," I reply. Three feet from me, he's far too close. I can't help but stare at the ink scrawled on his skull, wondering what secrets of the Amaran sect hide in plain sight. My blade holds steady between us.

"Okay." he doesn't move. "Many choose to speak to the priest representing the god before the ceremony. Couples usually do it together, but..." He waves a vague hand. This marriage is clearly different. "Killian has asked the marriage be done without blood," he says.

I pause, waiting for him to fill in with what he believes that means. I haven't been witness to many commitment ceremonies. The ones I have seen were not done under Amara's banner. If he means that no violence will occur between us, that is something I will not do. The promise itself will kill me.

"Sounds like something I'm going to say no to, holiness," I reply.

The priest snorts. "Please, call me Nord. And no, it means that all of the words of a traditional ceremony will be the same, but it will not be done with the exchange of...fluids."

I smile, showing my teeth. "If he displeases me, surely I am allowed to extract...fluid."

This time, Nord tosses his head back, belting out a loud laugh. "I shall include that in the vows then, yes?"

It's then that I put away my dagger. "Please, do, Nord." That will make my life much easier, because I never expect to be pleased by a villain.

* * *

SUNSET. The sky adorns itself with a collection of pinks, passing to deep maroon at the edges. The portraits watch me amidst the crowded frames outside of the receiving room, where the wedding waits. Truly, I look like the bride of death itself. Just my father and I wait in silence, ready for the signal that we should enter.

Black satin slicks down my hips. The gown snatches in at my waist, flaring out to enhance my robust hourglass figure. The fishu provided to me isn't worth anything. The lace triangles over my breasts, but reveals the cleavage underneath. My jaw ticks as I look down. The seamstresses—and Ursula—clearly had something in mind when they finished putting this together without me. Death by seduction, most likely.

"Kill him," Ursula had whispered to me as she helped me slip the garment on. "Kill him and come home to us."

Papa's voice interrupts my thoughts. "Poppet, you know that this isn't what I wanted." His fingers tangle in my hair, as if I'm a girl again and we're sitting at the edge of my bed. Just the two of us. A sharp pain twists in my chest. I swallow.

"I know."

I want to ask when I will see him, if he hates me. The words die on my lips. If I don't fail, I'll have saved my father and the marriage bond will be broken. The Lord of Wolves will be dead. I may come back disgraced, an oath-breaker, but that is better than not coming back at all. What's more, I'll come home to the only one I've ever felt safe with.

"I love you, papa."

"If that's the truth, then tonight you'll go to his room..and you'll kill him," he says. "Bring back his head." I look into Papa's eyes. Perhaps that is the only way to kill this creature. Remove the head. As if he's some vampyr or chimera creature straight from the realm of the Dark One.

Papa presses a blade into my hand. I grip it, twirling it in my fist. The metal is dark, darker than anything I've ever seen, as if it transmutes light into death. It reminds me of the alloyed coins slipping from the Witch King's mouth. The round bits of metal veined with an unnamed darkness.

"This—" Papa's voice wheezes and he cuts himself off, devolving into a coughing fit. I step, placing a hand across his back but he smacks it away with the flat of the blade.

Bright red wets his sleeve across the white fabric. He pulls his outer jacket further down to hide the evidence of his illness. I reach up to his face. Papa attempts to stall me, but I glare at him and he relents. The corner of his mouth smears with blood and I wipe it off. "It's gone," I whisper.

He doesn't say thank you, but he doesn't need to.

"This," he repeats, continuing as if none of it ever happened, "is grimsbane."

"What?" Grimsbane. I'd thought this was nothing but a story, meant to comfort children that even darkness incarnate could be defeated. The Grim Lords, heralds of death and destruction and kings amongst the fae, were but terrifying stories. This metal slithered through stories that promised their defeat, the one thing that might save a mortal where mere iron could not. "How did you get this?"

"It was your mother's."

The noise from the hall clatters from beyond us, but neither of us breathe after these words. My mother had too many secrets. I never got the chance to know her, but even if I had, my memories from my childhood are mostly missing, except for the smell of bright green in the cold air and warm fires. When the memories resume, I'm years older. Papa and I train with axes and weapons. Urusla grips my hair with tight fists to try to fit me into a shape I'll never be. Why is it that the edges of pain overshadow any goodness?

"She had so many secrets."

Papa's jaw clenches into a hard line. "Aye. That she did, poppet." The nickname feels like a bur, knowing that the gleam of anger in his eye is as much for me as the softness there.

"When-when he takes you back to your room, use this." The words pry from his throat. He pushes the dagger into my hands. I don't take it immediately.

"Why didn't you use this one before?" I ask.

"I did." He pauses. "It hurt him, but not the right way."

"It didn't work before, why would it work now?" Helplessness flutters throughout my limbs. I'm losing hope. Just a little. Papa's thin face looks back at me, a desperate gleam in his eye.

"You have to find his weakness. Grimsbane hurts even the fae, but it must be used correctly. Find what will hurt him most and strike it through the heart."

Doubt seizes me. He must care about something. Something has made me move forward, to go along with the Witch King's plans. I have to find it. I tangle my fingers through my hair, half upending part of my coiffure. I don't care, it's not like I'm trying to impress the stupid bastard waiting for me at the end of the aisle.

"I don't really have anywhere to put it," I gesture down to my funeral-like wedding gown. I'll take the blade. And I'll try it. Something will work. It has to.

Papa taps a fingernail smartly to my thigh. It tings with the sound of the hard edge striking metal. "I'll take this one for you for now."

A smile twists my mouth and I hike up the edge of my dress, unsheathing the weapon there and handing it to Papa with reluctant hands. He gave me that one. As much as my mother's memory means much to me, she was never the one who was there. It's always been Papa.

"I'll keep it safe until you return." His voice breaks on the last word and he slips the blade into a holster at his hip. "Unless you've come to your senses?"

"Never," I whisper with a broken tilt of my lips. He doesn't return the look. Instead, his jaw jumps and he turns away from me.

"Let's get on with this, then, Briar."

CHAPTER 26

Something isn't right.

The crowded chamber possesses an unnatural stillness. Familiar faces peer back at me. Hate, hope, confusion. My black gown is a statement that I hope my people will take into account. This is the beginning of either my funeral or Killian's. But when my gaze finds the center dais, my hand spasms against my father's arm.

"What is it?" Papa grits.

"It's a different priest."

Nord isn't there. The robes are the same, the bald head with intricately tattooed runes all speak to the Amaran priesthood. But the man there is not the one I met. Beside this stranger stands King Thaddeus and Sir Typhen. A little down the platform, but still prominently placed, are Galinda and Ewan. The holy man looking back at me raises his eyebrow. A smirk lurks at the corner of his mouth.

Papa shrugs and doesn't reply.

It takes me a moment to realize that my husband-to-be isn't there yet either.

"Where's the Wolf?" I ask.

"One can hope he's gotten lost in the Shadow Wood," Papa says. I jerk a look at him, but he doesn't return it. Have we violated hospitality again? "An honor, Divinity, to have you here."

Galinda's lips purse into her familiar lemon-like smile. Ewan's is a masculine echo of hers. "Where is the Duke?" my stepmother whispers.

No one replies.

Unease tickles the back of my mind. The king says nothing, but his face is marble smooth. A raven perches on his shoulder with preternatural stillness. The crowd lining the aisle murmurs and shifts.

A sting of rejection pierces me, along with a terror that suffocates my lungs. If the Wolf doesn't show, then my avenue for killing him narrows to nothing. If I don't try, then there's no chance Papa will survive. We're all about to die if I can't—

The doors boom open. Wood cracks against the stone walls, so hard visible splinters spike into the air from impact. Yelps litter the crowd. All that is visible in the entryway is a trio of figures.

The glow in the room dims, swallowed by dark anger.

Killian stalks forward. Each footfall produces a puff of shadow, curling in a trail of spurious smoke. The darkness doesn't dissipate, but builds. The very air in the room contracts and undulates, eating the light and oxygen left to us. Lukas and one of the other Wolves, the woman, follow the duke. Notably, their hands rest on the pommels of their swords.

Killian pauses halfway down the aisle. His eyes flash with something I don't want to place as he takes in my black gown. The fabric feels too tight against my skin all of a sudden and the room blazes. In shake out a breath, the air shudder from my lungs and hold my betrotheds' gaze as he prowls forward. The shadow along my wrist tightens, a tendril pulls itself off from the main chord to stroke my wrist. I shiver. He doesn't even touch me and I can't help but feel like his hands have scoured every inch of my body and he's slipped into my soul.

I hate it.

"So kind of you to join us," Papa grits when Killian alights the dais.

"I'd never skip my own wedding," Killian says. A layer of rage adds base to his growl. His eyes trace along my curves. The strange play of colors dance through his eyes–umber, black, silver, gold. The flesh on his cheek dribbles red blood and beneath it a fresh wound visibly closes up. He's like a supernatural abomination from the Dark One's fortress. He looks ready to eat me.

Despite my determination, my blood freezes. Tightness constricts my throat and it's difficult to breathe. All the rumors of Grims and evil spirits inside this man must be completely and utterly true. And here I am, about to pledge myself to this creature. The shadows at Killian's feet leap upwards, tendrils snaking up the shine of his boots. The wounded flesh on his face finishes knitting itself together. "Not even death itself could keep me from my bride."

His eyes don't leave Papa. Purposeful fingers grip my hand as Killian pries it out of the crook of Papa's arm. The duke doesn't look at me, but stares my father down like he's a dog fighting for dominance. The hard calluses of Killian's palm rub against the ones on mine. Someone tried to kill him. Too bad it didn't work.

"Though, death isn't something that is in the cards for me."

My husband-to-be's shoulder brushes against mine, sparking a shiver of anger and disgust through me. "Do not expect me to be your pet, my lord." The harsh words croak quietly out of my throat.

"Of course not," he replies. His voice taught with barely-contained emotion. His thick bicep spasms under my touch. "But you belong to me, now, so you will be something far, far worse."

Fear washes over me. *Mine,* he's saying. *You're mine.*

Killian's gaze shifts to the king's and his movement forces my father to step away. Papa walks with fragile pride to my stepmother, a slight stumble marks his final step. How much Reezin is in his system to make it to this farce of a wedding? Enough to nearly kill him.

All my hopes are pinned on this Grims-ridden marriage.

An arrogant smirk alights Killian's lush mouth before falling away as he looks at the new Amaran priest. I pull on the tendrils of my magic. The strain of activating the Sight grips me with a sore underlying exhaustion.

Breathe, Briar, you can do this. The words feel like lies. Little strings connecting the bits of the world to innocuous truths blink and then disappear.

"Ah, yes," the king says lazily to the unasked question. "Good thing I brought one of my own. I've no idea where your man went." King Thaddeus gestures to the new priest. Tin falls from his mouth like a cockroach scurries from the light. I bite the inside of my cheek.

Nord has to be dead.

Shock courses through me. Surely, our ruler wouldn't kill a priest? *And why not?* Part of me whispers. *This is a war and he was in the way.*

A thin sheen of sweat films against my flesh. I'm not charting my own destiny at all. I might stand the chance at saving Papa, at saving the Bears from collapsing in on ourselves, but at the end of the day I am a pawn to be played between kings.

"I'm sure you don't," Killian replies, not bothering to address King Thaddeus with proper respect. A scowl grips his entire face, dragging his scarred eyebrow downward. The coins, if any, that fall from his mouth are invisible. "Let's just do this." He moves closer to me, gripping both of my hands in his large ones.

The force of his grip on mine hurts. I squeeze, equally harsh and let my nails dig into his skin. He finally looks at me, eyebrows shooting up before his face wipes itself clean of any expression. The pressure on my joints eases.

The new Amaran priest raises his hands. "I call in the blessings," he intones. Murmurs splash through the crowd in a wave of discontent. "Amara, goddess of love who was once vengeance, we ask you to bless this union for its agreed upon year and a day. May the Seven watch and protect you both."

May they protect us all. Tin coins surge from the holy man's mouth.

The priest reaches into a gilded bowl beside him. From it he pulls out a wet, corded rope the color of sunflowers. Speckles of gray dot the fiber and something inside the cord twists like an imprisoned snake. He holds it up for the crowd below.

The priest has eyes like a predator. Endless and with a look of violence. A tight smirk flits across his mouth as he eyes Killian's scabbard situated on the duke's left hip. The holy man presses our wrists together.

"Our wishes for you are contained herein," he intones, apparent truth leaking from his lips. Aloft in the air, he now holds a wishbone wrapped in thin paper glued to the ivory bone.

Another inappropriate laugh gurgles in my chest. Yes, wishes indeed. Wishes for death and desolation in this matrimony, an early demise for my betrothed. My desires are no different than anyone else's.

The priest knots the yellow rope to our wrists, wrapping them tightly. The cord will dry, creating a painful rub against my flesh and Killian's. I wonder who came up with this ritual and if they had a bad experience with marriage.

"Do you, Lady Briar, take Duke Killian Galibran to be yours for a year and a day–to give him bread when he has none, to give him warmth when the Frost Giants breathe blue across the dying season, and to give him your body as he will give you his?"

The world pulls into a string of slow molasses.

With two words, I can save everything I've ever cared about.

"I do."

"Say the words– I take thee, husband, in this life and to the grave."

Pain convulses in my throat. I mean it all. I have to. I can't lie.

And I will certainly take my husband to the grave.

I lock eyes with Killian. Silver glints there. He looks half feral. His hands spasm against mine, as if he's waiting for me to back out.

"I take thee in this life and to the grave."

Gods, it hurts to say it. *I mean it,* I tell myself. *I mean it.* I blink, blink. I have to. *If thy word be gold, may thy tongue be silver.* The old words float up from somewhere, an old phrase that haunts the corners of my mind. Lumarian, but also Orvellan. Speak the truth, but use it to lie. The way of the witch and the fae and even the gods. Play your part, O' Pious One. It is in the scriptures of the Seven. Do as the gods will.

Killian watches me with a predatory knowing and I can't help but wonder if he means it when he calls me *witch.*

"May your bones lie beside his and your souls tangle in the wind beyond life." The priest pauses, clearing his throat. Sweat collects at his brow. His hand twitches, as if he's waiting to move it. "Do you, Duke Killian Galibran, caretaker to House of the Wolf and all its people take Lady Briar Berrat, heir to House of the Bear to be yours for a year and a day—to give her bread when she has none, to give her warmth when the Frost Giants breathe blue across the dying season, and to give her your body as she will give you yours?"

"I do," Killian growls, his eyes darkening as he gazes at me. Heat courses up my spine and flushes my cheeks. "I take thee in this life and to the grave."

"You may kiss."

Killian leans in. I don't shut my eyes. Part of me wants to pull a knife. His lips brush mine. This kiss is feather light, perfunctory. I'm left with a very different memory of our kiss in the woods. Of violence and lust. Also, somehow, I'm remembering a faint edge of a dream from long ago. But then it's gone. A shadow of a memory.

The edge of one of his canines snags at my lip. A chill races across my flesh.

But you belong to me, now, so you will be something far, far worse.

My breath catches. A supernatural glow suffuses Killian's irises. His dark gaze sparks in an alloy of precious metals. Whatever evil haunts this man lurks just beneath his skin. Whatever *thing* it is watches *me*.

A low growl peels from Killian's throat. It would sound like a pur, if I didn't catch the glint of that fang. A jolt of fear sizzles through my body and my hand instinctively goes to my hip for the knife. I could blow up the truce right here and—

But I'm not a Bear.

I'm a Wolf.

I can kill him without violating hospitality. I could kill him tonight. If I only knew how.

The grimsbane.

Could it all end tonight? No, I have to be sure. I have to know how to do it. *Could* I, though? Could I kill him tonight?

Killian blinks. His nostrils flare and his gaze snaps from me to the Witch King.

Then the Amaran priest pulls a knife from his robes. The gold hilt of the blade stings the air, a painful glint of ruby flashes as the weapon comes down.

Before I can flinch away, before Killian can extract his sword, the blade slashes across our combined forearms. Blood spurts between us. A second too late, I pull the dagger from my thigh. My betrothed—no, husband—next to me has unsheathed a weapon from his boot and he holds it now. In front of me.

I blink, blink, *blink* at the blade. Is he protecting me or about to stab me? The weapon in my hand dangles from my useless, shocked fingers.

A scream, unlike anything I've ever heard, drags the air. And something burns.

Pain lances my arm, hot like molten metal. The figure of a boiling chimera creature curls out from our blood. It looks like a curse from the Dark One himself. Black and red, it's twisted like the root of a gnarled old tree. Visible bubbles vibrate its blood-for-skin and a pinkened tongue flicks out and licks across the scrape on my arm and then Killian's.

I stab at the creature, my blade comes away clean as if the supernatural thing doesn't exist. Killian stalls my dagger. He gently grips my wrist, looking at my weapon and then at my eyes. Wordless, he pushes it away toward my hip. Killian's teeth audibly click as his jaw tenses.

Agony scrapes across the wound.

The rope grows hot and digs into my skin, blistering and branding. The creature coils around the fiber, round and round it binds us. Dripping and sputtering and sparking. It glides down my arm, looping Killian's arm to mine. I wince despite the pain, gritting my teeth against the fire lighting up my nerves. Killian's jaw ticks at the corner, but otherwise his face betrays nothing.

The thing hisses, smoke huffing out of its mouth. Sparks scatter into my skin, leaving behind little phantom scars that fade as if they'd been there a year. Killian's arm likewise litters with marks, but the marriage marks blend in with an uncountable collection of old injuries long-since sliced into his body.

I am a Wolf, a part of me whispers.

I look at Papa, hoping to find him looking back, to see the reasons I've done this to begin with. Instead, he's looking out the wide window to the sky, as if he'd like to fly out there to the heavens and leave this and me behind.

The smile I plaster to my face is unkind and as hard as armor. It doesn't matter. Loyalty, love–sometimes, those things don't have to do with the other person at all. Instead, the Duke of Death and I lock gazes, trading promises to destroy one another with a silent, loaded look.

"Until death do us part," he says, hatred riding high in his eyes. The snarl beneath his words pimples my forearms. Killian leans in, brushing a kiss across the crest of my cheekbone. "Let the games begin, wife," he whispers.

CHAPTER 27

$\mathcal{N}$o blood should have been used. King Thaddeus killed a priest to have our marriage conducted with blood. I don't know what it means, but I don't have time to ruminate on it before the crowd shuffles out with raucous murmurs for the rest of the ceremonies to take place. Feasting, dancing, then consummating.

Consummating. My naked body pressed to Killian's.

"Shall we continue this farce, *wife?*" Killian mutters under his breath. He pulls–*hard*–and my arm feels like it's going to splinter in its socket. I use my elbow to jab him in the ribs. He glares at me.

The man and the woman that had stood for him on the dais shadow us like two crows circling for carrion. I recognize them from the forest. The man with yellow eyes, Lukas, gives me a friendly nod. I don't know the woman's name, but she gives a respectful incline of her head full of frigid disapproval.

"You know the custom," the woman answers sharply.

"I know the custom, but will I *abide* it?" Killian says.

Lukas snorts. "You'd better. I've no care for dying today."

Killian frowns, but says nothing.

"Alright, my reluctant bride." He turns to me. When his gaze meets mine, it's like he's drinking me in. The cold rage cracking beneath his skin slips through his eyes, marking me with a frozen hate. I shiver. Our arms are still bound and I know he feels the twitch of my skin against his. Gods, I hate him. "Let's give the people the shit show they're expecting."

"That's the spirit," Lukas says. His grin is wide, showing his long, wolfish canines.

* * *

WE ENTER THE FEAST HALL. For most weddings, riotous talk would usually have already filtered in. Now, we were the first there aside from servants beckoning the crowd in with steaming piles of food. All is quiet right now. The shadows still at our back, I glance behind them. The rest of my House—my former House, fills in around us.

Killian and I are beckoned to the table at the top by a shaking page boy, centered there like a prize stallion and his broodmare.

No one looks me in the eye. For a moment, the impossible realization strikes me: that the tentative distrust that settled in around me since the northern border slipped into further violence was nothing. This is what it really feels like to be an outsider.

Whatever did they think? That I wanted to marry him? Would they whisper of a secret ambition?

I snort at the thought.

His hand tightens on mine and I glance down in sudden anxiety that quickly fades to annoyance.

"What is it?" I hiss between gritted teeth.

"We need to leave soon. I take it you prefer to stay?"

"Well, now that you mention it—yes," I say.

He scowls. The movement pulls the white scar slicing through his brow. I half expect him to reply, but instead he says nothing. We move to the center of the long table, toward the spots my father and I usually occupy.

Papa isn't there.

Hope slides down my throat and dies there. He didn't come.

The room fills, teeming with people to spectate the Duke of Death and his new bride. And still.

My father didn't come.

A wave of sadness flooded me. I'd never expected to be married, never really thought too much about it. I suppose if I had I would have known I'd marry advantageously for my house. But I'd been born into a time of blood and learned to wield weapons with amateurish enthusiasm, waiting for the moment I might be needed. For an opportunity to avenge what could not be avenged.

And here was my first enemy. Though his people killed my mother, the perpetrator was as faceless as the night. I have no one to blame but all of them. To blame each and every Wolf for every death, every head tossed over our walls like discarded, bad food. As if we are worth nothing to the world but to be a feast for flies.

The grimsbane blade will cut off my husband's head tonight. It's precious enough to my husband that it should do the trick.

"Potato?" Killian asks. On his fork steams the bright yellow innards of a potato. Butter glints in a hearty gob on the root vegetable.

"No." I scowl. How did he seem unconcerned right now? I'm thinking of killing him and here he is, offering me a potato.

"You were staring at me like you wanted to eat me. I thought I'd offer this potato instead," he murmurs.

A snort sounds behind us. I turn to look at the shadows that hung back, watching us. Lukas' yellow eyes twinkle in ferocious merriment.

I open my mouth to speak, but instead a tender heat fills my mouth as Killian pops the potato into it.

"Whaar—?" I say, huffing and chewing it. I force it down my throat.

Killian gives a tight smile, watching me intently before his gaze flicks around the room. He waits a moment.

"What was that?" I ask, the fatty flavor of butter coating my mouth. He hands me our joint wine goblet. I scowl, gulping down a long drag.

His head cocks to the side. Chatter is soft around us, as everyone leans in to hear our conversation. His reply is so loud and rude that the quiet is unnecessary. "I was just making sure I hadn't been poisoned." And he pops a large bit of the potato in his mouth.

* * *

THE INSIDE of my mouth aches from biting it. Killian leans next to me, stomach full of potato, summer asparagus, and a brined brisket topped with a sweetened rosemary sauce. My own belly wants to protrude with the amount I've eaten, but my gown has me cinched to within an inch of my life.

Cautious talk spins around us, but I can't bear to think of it. Looks spear me, the rub of hatred and betrayal like an abrasion on my skin. For the first time this evening, I catch the glare of withering hurt from Derrick, seated midway down one of the tables. Important enough to come, not important enough to be seen, though.

I fist the verdant-hued napkin in my lap with my free hand. I'm married now. Derrick is a prick, but guilt niggles at me like an insistent tapping finger. It's strange we never got to mark the close of what our relationship had been—whether a kiss, a handshake, or something else to mark the occasion of our sweaty nights closed.

Instead, I've a different kind of evening ahead of me.

Killian lounges indolently, as if the cord binding us doesn't bother him a bit. The flesh beneath my arm cries, hurting with the magic binding us for the evening and the drying leather sucking itself deeper into my body. His presence feels like darkness dancing in the presence of a bonfire, swirling and sweaty.

Killian's fangs flash. His teeth snap into a juicy plum. Canines pierce the fruit's meat, juice dribbles down his chin like a lazy bead of sweat. I wonder what it would be like to lick it from the cleft of his chin.

Gods, stop it, Briar. The cloth in my lap scrunches further in my grip. Heat lips at my core. Killian is *evil.*

Tension riddles every muscle in my back, winding and tight like the yellow cord on my arm. Black pinpricks dot my vision. Inky, red night pokes through our banquet hall. It's not that dark yet, but it's getting there. A smear of pink protrudes from the dark mouth of the sky, and the teasing blush-colored tongue wags at me as it retreats. As the night closes in, so does the promise of Killian's body against mine.

King Thaddeus' words whisper against my mind. *I suppose you can kill the Wolf before that time, but only try it if it is certain to work.*

Am I certain? No. But am I desperate? Absolutely. A shiver ticks through my fingers, one that won't go away. Neither will the clammy sweat at my palms. Gods, I don't want to go to Wolf Hall. I don't want to do any of this. Part of me wonders if perhaps Fex's flower did work, and this is my piece of my father's madness. A cruel laugh works its way up my throat again before I quash it. Doubtful. My mangled kiss with Killian ruined something, I'm sure of it.

It ruined your life, an ugly voice whispers in my head. That is certain.

Can I hold out in this marriage for a year and a day? Enough for the king to quell the northern front? My mouth dries. I can try. Though I have my doubts about the border with Selva. If we haven't conquered the borderlines there, completely quashed the chimeras and Selvans biting their teeth into our throats, it's doubtful a year will do it. But it's time to find out how to kill this bastard and have done with it.

A year and *a day*.

It's too long. Laughable. But the king did say that if I could kill the Wolf sooner, that I could be released from this pitiful bargain much quicker. If I can kill him tonight...my hand strays to the grimsbane dagger. I didn't have this before. It's not a chance, but it's something more than nothing.

Perhaps it's a poor decision. And who am I, but a creature made of nothing but mistakes born of desperate heartache?

My gaze lingers where my father should sit. At the empty space that serves a poignant metaphor for his feelings about my decisions. All I've ever wanted is to be loved, but it seems I'm no good at that either. If I was truly lovable, then I'd be loved. Plain and simple.

Nisha isn't beside me, but the pain from my heart wakens her from my chambers and she mewls a protest through our bond.

Silly cat.

A tap ticks at my shoulder and I turn, fisting a salad fork like it's a dagger.

Daria's brown eyes look back at me. A sad smile twists her mouth. "More wine, Lady Briar?" she asks.

"That's Duchess," Killian interjects, eyes looking into Daria's face as if he's memorizing it. "And n–"

"Yes," I interrupt, grabbing the cup with my non-bound hand and pushing it to my side. Daria leans in to fill it with the deep red wine.

"Your father sent me to wait on you," she whispers as she leans across me to pour into my shared cup with Killian. The liquid pools to the rim, full of the salty alcohol. A warm feeling suffuses my chest and I choke back a wash of tears. I stare resolutely at the now-full cup. "I'll be at your back."

Barro and Valor, most likely, were with the rest of our men. Ready and waiting to unsheathe their swords at the first sign of trouble. Because of the king's hatred of women in the field, of doing anything he considered to be unfeminine, lady soldiers—like Daria—were well placed amongst the serving staff. A small dose of relief, as if I'd taken a shot of liquor minutes ago, lightens my body.

This is the only way Papa could offer me protection. His rage as the Duke of Bears is obvious, his absence a statement to everyone that he doesn't approve. But Daria's presence means something to me, a message from a father to his daughter that he at least didn't want me to die.

"What are you plotting, witch?" Killian whispers to me as Daria moves back to line the wall. "My death?"

It won't be a surprise then. "Of course. And the downfall of your House."

"*Our* House," he corrects, wagging that blasted eyebrow at me. Gods, I want to smack him. Instead, I plaster a pained look on my face.

"When are we allowed to depart from this part of the festivities?"

"I am happy to take you to your new home at any moment, wife."

"No," I snap. "Just…don't speak to me." My voice breaks on the last word. Killian goes quiet, for once seeming to abide by what I say. The absence of my father here continues to bore a hole into my heart, despite the assurances of Daria's presence. I choose instead to look out the window as the final ray of light pink departs. The blood moon's belly bloats across the sky.

A trumpet jabs a tune across the hall. The herald at the tall, oaken doors strikes a pose. He belongs to the king, his uniform a bright gold of shimmering fabric. It's like looking directly into the sun. I blink, eyes watering a little. Rubies litter his lapel in a careless scatter. An eyepatch the same color as the gems blocks his left eye.

"Now, for the dance of Houses. Announcing His Divinity, King Thaddeus of Lumar." The herald bangs his staff–a thing of stacked ebony ravens with red eyes and burnished beaks the color of his royal uniform–three times against the floor. Any lingering chatter cracks into utter silence.

I spare a thought to note the king is obsessed with making an entrance.

The doors boom open and, this time, a cloud of ravens erupts from the doorway's dark maw. At least a thousand birds screech into the room. Screams erupt from those seated as the flock pours in. Feathers float down like dark dust. Dishes clatter onto the floor. Flutes of bubbly quallais tumble from hands and shatter onto the floor. The faces of the nobility–Lord and Lady Kesswick, their children, various bannerman and women–all stretch in horror as they duck underneath the long tables amongst the broken glass and upended platters of food.

My gaze snaps to Killian, who just looks bored. He didn't even bother to unsheathe a blade at the ruckus. Lukas and the other Wolf that have accompanied us everywhere look equally unperturbed. "What a dickweed," Lukas murmurs.

"Shut up, Lukas," the woman mutters back to him.

Daria's eyes widen and meet mine. My jaw hangs open. Lukas just called our immortal king a dickweed.

"Lukas," Killian says. That seems to be all he needs to say. His soldier's mouth snaps closed, but the man's yellow eyes stare out toward the king with hatred burning in them.

The ravens bluster up to the beams. It reminds me of nighttime, if one of the gods had replaced all the stars with the birds' red gaze. Banners depicting the Bears' sigil hang from the rafters, a lonely green color that only brings out the eerie feeling of the flock's uniform, scarlet gaze.

As the unkindness of ravens settles in above and globs of shit plop down onto the waiting food and partygoers below. A slosh of crap plunks itself down on my spoon. A nearby guard's shoulder splatters with the white excrement. I grimace.

Dinner is over.

King Thaddeus glides down the aisle. A dark furred cloak fans out behind him. The rich brocade at his chest flashes a jeweled tone of blue, trimmed with the king's favored gold.

Everyone is already on their hands and knees due to the divine sovereign's birds, so they remain there. I dip into a low curtsy. Everyone but Killian.

My hand awkwardly tugs up, connected to the arrogant bastard. I shoot him a glare, but he doesn't even bother to look at me. In fact, he jerks his arm, pulling me up sooner than is proper.

As the king slides to the chair set aside for him, settling into it as if Gray Hall is his castle in Veritaes. In a sense, it is. The collection of duchies that make up Lumar are all his subjects, people like my father are essentially just elegant servants with a lot of privileges. *A lot* of privileges. With servants of their own. And castles.

King Thaddeus gives a subtle nod and music croons a soft tune.

It's impossible to dance with anyone but Killian, but like most weddings, there's the tradition of the father walking his daughter out to the floor, her new husband bound to her, as he officially hands her over to her spouse and a fresh political alliance.

"Bear," the king's word skirts the air. A raven tips down from the rafters, diving a sharp arc toward the center table. It jerks upward, beaming itself straight at the doors.

Papa is there.

Immediately, I know this has all been too much. The wan set to his face. No amount of illicit drugs can hide his unsteady gait as he half limps toward the tall dais. I jerk, forcing Killian to walk with me and meeting Papa part way. My muscles coil and a tightness slips over my body like my skin no longer fits. I dip myself into a curtsy, one of respect and a little too much obedience. Killian tips his head to my father in acknowledgement.

I grab Papa's hand. It reminds me of the wet belly of a dead fish. A tremble runs through the delicate joints of his fingers beneath his translucent skin.

"Poppet," he whispers. It sounds broken.

"Papa, I–"

He holds up his free hand, an obvious gesture for our audience. Not for me. Not now. A titter of amusement reaches my ears. The shuffle of feet. Discomfort, perhaps, or just folks preparing for this to all go sideways very soon. Killian's presence next to me is a furnace of blazing heat and undulating shadow. The press of his arm against mine reminds me incessantly of his body, of what is to come. As if I were on the verge of forgetting.

Soon.

Our clasped grip tightens for a second as Papa squeezes my hand. His reluctance to do this–to give me to this wretched monster— pulses between us. So tangible, it feels like a boulder weighing down our combined hands. Papa blinks. The strange light in his eyes flares —the Reezin slipping through. My throat dries into a hard ache. Fear squeezes my heart. The effects of the drug are erratic, but if his eyes burn with visible magic, then the reality is that he can *do* magic. And even though he's a duke, a powerful man, the king is here to watch what may happen. He most likely won't be branded a witch, but his illicit use of the drug is a problem.

Papa lifts our hands. "I relinquish you. A year and a day." The words ring clear, though Papa blinks incessantly as he speaks. "After which time, you may come back to us and reswear your allegiance."

Goodbye.

My breath catches somewhere in my ribcage and sticks there. I can't inhale, I can't do anything, but stare at what I've just lost. But he doesn't want to look at me. Papa turns away.

Silence falls across the crowded hall. Even the crows above cease their caws. The only noise that flits through is a low groan from a wind outside.

"Whore."

The word rings clear across the room. A bright rage strikes my cheeks. The word sits there in the middle of the quiet after slitting a collective artery. Shock paralyzes the room. Then, there's the gush of bilge everyone held back.

"What of our future?" someone else cries. It grows, more and more with each yell of discontent.

"We won't have a slut for our lady!" Another yell strikes across the room, slicing my ears.

"SILENCE," my father booms. The noise settles, but a low hum of discontent tickles the underbelly of the crowd. "Lady Briar is still my daughter," Papa says. "But, for now, until her return in a year and a day— she is no longer my heir." The world could have ended, and I would not have heard a thing. Papa doesn't look at me. Silver coins drop from his lips.

A strange buzz hums in my ears. *No longer my heir, no longer my heir.* I understand the words, but they feel like *I no longer love you.*

I look to Galinda who simply smiles and puts a significant hand on her stomach.

Silver flips, end over end, through the air. The coins don't disappear right away. Metal clangs onto the floor in a sound only I can hear. My heart splinters with each snap of the coins on the ground.

This is the secret I'd tasted, the hint of it in his office. I feel it with a certainty—the same that told me the sun would rise pink tomorrow and that the dying season followed the dead season as orange leaves gave way to bleached bone. This is what Papa had wanted to tell me— and what he had neglected to say.

I am no longer his heir. It felt like being no longer his daughter.

Everything I am has never been enough. Bitterness burns in my esophagus. The candlelight flickers in too-bright mockery. My vision blurs. I refuse to call it tears, I refuse to be cowed by this, I refuse—

A hand touches my arm, tucking it into the crook of an elbow.

I look up to see Killian, jaw ticking as he clenches it. His scornful gaze takes in the room. "I suppose Bears have never been known for their loyalty," he remarks loudly. But we are known for nothing but our steadfastness.

Loyalty first.

To what, though?

My hand spasms in my now-husband's arm, but Papa's betrayal stings too much for me to defend anyone. What could I have expected, though? Of course he had to do this. Of course he did.

Killian looks directly at my father, as if waiting for him to say something. Papa says nothing.

It hurts.

I close my eyes, just for a moment.

"I think we will take our leave early to Wolf Hall," Killian says.

A pause.

"No," says the Witch King, speaking for the first time in a while. "You will not."

CHAPTER 28

"Follow me, Wolf."

The king, Sir Typhen, and two other knights pull from the room like a dirge of metallic molasses. Bowing and scraping follow the divine ruler and his men, then the flood of birds pours out from the rafters behind them. As they reach the threshold, half of them disappear in a swirl of smoke and molting feathers.

"Dickweed," Lukas says again in my ear as we depart after them. I fight not to laugh at the treasonous statement.

We're led to a small antechamber, the eight of us cramming into the space. It's ill advised to have so many people who hate each other so close together. The gods have a poor sense of humor.

King Thaddeus stands, Sir Typhen angled in front of him and the other two knights flank him like two ends of an expensive triangle. There's something about everything he does that seems planned, as if he was ready to sit for a portrait at any moment.

"I thought we could talk in private," King Thaddeus remarks unironically, as if unaware of the amount of bodies in the room.

"Quite," Killian says drily.

They stare at one another. Powerful men trading glare for glare in a silent battle of wills. Tension riddles the room, like termites hollowing out a tree. One barely-there breeze could blow this whole room apart. I don't know where to look, but the grimsbane blade feels like it's burning against my thigh.

"Sir Typhen, don't you think the bride looks distressed?"

"Quite," Sir Typhen's reply is an echo of Killian's earlier remark.

Typhen runs a blue-edged finger along the vein in my neck. It poises there, nail hovering above my ticking artery as if he has the ability to puncture it with the blunted end. A sheen of cold sweat slicks my skin. Can he open up a vein with his fingernail? Despite the risks, despite it all, I don't want to die. Not completely. Some days, only just a little.

"Wolf?" the king says. Killian doesn't take his eyes from me. "Wolf?" King Thaddeus says again. With reluctance, Killian drags his gaze from me to the king. His hand squeezes mine.

Sir Typhen runs an intrusive touch further down. Disgust twists my stomach, but it all happens so fast.

A raven flies in front of Killian's face, up to the rafters.

In that moment, a flick of paper jabs into my cleavage, past the flimsy fishu, as Sir Typhen shoves a scrap there. What is he doing? I jerk back and his hand snags against the delicate skin on my neck once more. The whole action lasts no more than a second.

The shadows in the room shiver. A roar punctures the silence. I jerk. Sir Typhen does too, his finger flinching into my collarbone. A burst of hot liquid pops from my punctured skin.

Blackness.

It's what I imagine the bottom of a lake feels like. Cold, dark. And without air.

A rush of hot air purrs against my ear. "Hush, wicked witch. You are okay."

My lungs release the air stuck mid-gasp and I shudder in another breath. *You are okay.* Such powerful words for something that is not a spell, that requires no arcane sacrifice. Four syllables that were the difference between stark terror and the ability to self-soothe. My arm attached to Killian's jerks up, roughening against stubbled flesh.

A light bursts from the ceiling. Illuminated under the glow is

Killian, knuckles white against Sir Typhen's neck. My hand cups the other side of the knight's neck, thumb hooking just under Killian's. I blink. Then I squeeze.

"Touch her again and lose your hand," Killian snarls.

We both squeeze.

What did he shove down my dress? Unease crawls all over my skin, along with the horrible ghost of Typhen's touch. I don't care, not for this moment. I remember how he accosted me outside of the king's rooms. It can't have been the first time he did that to someone. My grip tightens. The top of my thumb rubs against the bottom of Killian's. It almost feels pleasant.

Sir Typhen lets out a wheeze. It's then that I notice Killian has pinned Sir Typhen's wrist against the knight's leg. In Killian's free hand, he holds a blade. Blood dribbles down the other man's skin. I glance side-eyed at Killian, who remains focused on the bastard.

"I mean it. Today, I'll take a finger tip, I think," Killian whispers. In a quick movement, the edge of the blade comes down on Typhen's hand. The first phalange of his index finger and half of his littlest finger sever in a clean cut and a burst of red.

Blood rivers from the wounds, as well as a slice to the knight's thigh that Killian used as a cutting board. The other knights around the king jerk forward, but King Thaddeus holds up a hand to halt them and they pause, frozen. The Wolves with us just watch, as if this is a typical evening for them.

Sir Typhen screams. Killian's thumb jerks into mine as he squeezes the man's throat again. Anger and pain fracture twin lines across Sir Typhen's face. His fist whitens on his sword handle. Metal sings from the scabbard as he half-gets it out, the blade getting stuck at an awkward angle. King Thaddeus looks on, face caught between fascination and irritation. "Duke–of–Cursed–*Dogs*, do you think you can threaten a…knight of the…Witch King?" Sir Typhen rasps.

"The Witch King has decreed that I marry this woman. And I have." Killian's gaze bores into Sir Typhen, but it's like he's talking to King Thaddeus. And to me. "As my wife, I have vowed to her my sword and my life. *That means no one gets to touch her without her permission.*" A warm feeling burgeons in my chest. Then Killian leans in, boring into Sir Typhen like an ill-spirit holds sway over his body. The other man's hand jerks at an odd angle, dangling in precarious helplessness. Then Killian jerks it.

Crack.

Sir Typhen doesn't make a noise, but his face blanches.

Horror tightens my stomach. Sir Typhen's skin goes clammy under my hand. I flinch, but Killian holds us there. My hand is flat on the knight's neck, an acid feeling curling up my stomach. I can't help but flick a glance to the Witch King, who isn't looking at Sir Typhen at all. He's looking at me.

Fuck, fuck. I don't know what it means, but I feel like a thousand slugs slime a trail over every inch of exposed skin. Tension grips the space between my shoulder blades. King Thaddeus says nothing. Killian shifts his attention to me at that moment. His eyes flash with that strange otherworldly gaze before shuddering into what I can only describe as disgust.

Well, fuck you, too, husband. I hope he dies roasting on a spit for trolls. And the king's disgusting knight with him. But the bravado lasts only a moment. Killian really is a monster. I shiver.

"Release him." The command is soft. Killian's throat works, as if he's thinking about defying the king. Slowly, ever so slowly, Killian uncurls his hand. As he steps backwards, I'm forced to go with him. I delicately dodge the blood on the ground.

"My king," Killian replies carefully. "I am eager to start my life with the bride you have chosen for me." He says it as if there are not bits of finger on the ground.

The king barks a laugh. "Ah, young pup." Killian's entourage stiffens. The air crackles with withheld violence. "So eager to take to the marriage bed?"

"Of course," Killian grits.

"Then take your bride upstairs. We shall not deprive you."

"And then we may depart?"

Apparently, we are pretending the violence didn't just happen.

"Ah, tsk, tsk. It is not often the Bears and the Wolves are seen together not drawing blood. Let us celebrate this newfound peace for the allotted three nights." The words are tightly said, the king's mouth pinched into a subtle frown. It's not that I want to go to Wolf Hall, but Nord's disappearance–*death*, whispers the less cheerful part of me–is the first sign that something isn't right. Our staying longer does one thing–allows the infamously reclusive Duke of Death to remain in sight longer.

My eyes stray to Sir Typhen's flesh on the ground. He kneels, picking up the bits of his hand with angry reverence. His eyes meet mine and I know in that moment this isn't the last of this.

Killian jerks a nod of agreement

"Then you may leave after you have met your end of the agreement."

"Or if any other bargain is not met," Killian counters obscurely.

Three nights. To defy the king will be treason, open rebellion. Staying is our only option. If Killian defies the king, the king will have no choice but to call him a traitor. And what use is it to get Killian to prolong his time here? The only answer is that someone is going to try to kill my enemy husband.

I can't imagine the king has done this on my behalf. No, the killer will be someone other than me. And that means I need to do it first to get the deal I've brokered for me and my father.

King Thaddeus looks at us and smiles. "You make a handsome couple," he says before he departs.

It is, perhaps, the only blessing of approval we've received.

"Shall we go to bed, then, wife?" Killian asks, the last word dripping with acid.

"Knight," the king says. Sir Typhen stalks in pale pain after King Thaddeus. "Attend."

The room clears of the king's knights, leaving the four of us there with only one thing left to do.

"Bedtime already?" Lukas inquires. "Some of us are very eager to sleep against your door."

* * *

CANDLELIGHT WARMS THE HALL, bright and desperate. Portraits of my ancestors watch our progression to my bedroom. Stern, angry-eyed men and scornful women. Their gazes remind me of the faces in the Great Hall, the splatter of rage and disgust across the faces of people I'd known my entire life.

Lady Jesse, my great-great-great-great-great grandmother appears particularly scornful. Her nose turns up as we walk. Her portrait moves, slipping into the frame of the next—her lord husband, Erik. They whisper together before both walking into the next frame.

"Your portraits are particularly active."

I say nothing in reply. Shadows follow him, coiling at his feet. Lukas and Jessa follow behind us at a considerable distance, keeping us just in sight. Killian looks the vision of a villain—dark-eyed fire in his gaze, slick-backed hair as iridescent as raven wings, and a shadow of a beard that cups his sharp jaw. He looks straight ahead.

"At Wolf Hall, ours gossip, but it appears more tasteful than this," he says.

"Interesting, you think you understand taste," I snap.

"You do not approve of my taste? Pity, as I've married *you*."

"My lord husband, we both know neither of our tastes were consulted in this match."

He doesn't reply to that.

We get to the room. Just outside, Lady Agatha along with a whole host of other portraits overstuff the frame. Lady Agatha waggles an eyebrow at me. I ignore it.

Killian pushes the door open for me, his coat stretching and bunching against the muscles of his arms. More than a lord should have. My stomach churns. Soon, those arms are going to be around me. I shiver. In disgust, I tell myself.

I stop at the threshold, sparing a glance at his wrist level with my face. A swirl of dark ink appears at his own wrist. A finely hatched tattoo, with lines so delicate they remind me of hair. Killian's gaze catches mine. With a purposeful movement, he pulls his sleeve down, hiding whatever it is. The shift pushes us closer. We're nearly pressed against one another. So close I can see the little scars at the hollow of his throat and the rise and fall of his chest beneath his shirt.

"It's time," Killian says, voice low. "Strip."

CHAPTER 29

*S*trip.

As if he found me at some brothel. If he's not paying me, I'm not doing it. Theoretically, I can kill him without violating hospitality now that I'm no longer a Bear. My throat constricts. No matter. The king, Killian, so many others—they play an invisible game and I'm not sure of the consequences. I don't know if my next move will send me stepping into a trap or victory.

Beheading Killian still seems like the best option, but I wonder if there's been a change in what's to come. The paper shoved between my breasts burns like a hot coal. I want to snatch it out and look at it, but how can I do that with this bastard watching me? As if I'm going to let him see me naked.

It'll be a cold day in hell that I strip for this villian.

"You first," I challenge, leveling an eyebrow at him.

Killian grins, dimpling. A part of me will regret separating that cheeky indent from the rest of him, but it's a price that must be paid. "I'll show you mine if you show me yours kind of woman, are you?" A hollow feeling grips my stomach at the thought of his sparkling eyes turning dull and lifeless. Nothing like the thought of losing Papa, though. It's always sad to lose an enemy you enjoy beating. "Well, witch?"

He pulls out a dagger, abruptly slicing through our combined hands. The pressure there eases. So much for traditions. I rub the skin where the cord was, easing the ache of my flesh.

The shadows ripple around him. One rebellious tendril teases forward, lipping against my ankle, before snapping. It yanks me back and I fall backwards onto the bed. The Duke of Death leans over me and my body betrays me with a wave of heat toward my center. Fuck. I grit my teeth, glaring at him. Any trace of regret at the thought of killing him dissipates. Forever. Stupid bastard.

I pull away. Sitting upright. Primly.

"Unfortunately," he murmurs regretfully, "I'm not ready to fuck you yet. But I am ready to take your weapons. Especially since you've proven what a stabby, vengeful witch you are."

I glance at him, hiding my panic with a curl of my mouth. "You're sure you're not ready to...have some fun?"

My ring heats and I look at my finger. The golden circlet slips with a magma-like substance, glowing with brazen fire. Killian glances at my hand, then looks significantly to his own, where the wedding band matches mine with equal fervor. I swallow.

A mundane sort of marriage–the kind Killian had evidently wanted without blood–would have never had our rings react this way. The magic and the blood and the line of fate all mix into one, sloppy mess. I press a hand to his, touching the ring and feeling the throb there. Each beat times with my own heart, thumping in tandem.

And right now, my heart beats very, very fast.

"Just because—" I whisper, leaning close to him. He lets me, not moving, but watching with those endless eyes. So dark, his iris is nearly indistinguishable from the pupil, except for the bits of bright-ness, reminding me of Fex's flower itself, "—I find you fuckable, does not mean you will find yourself fucked." His chest rises and falls in rapid succession. Even the Duke of Death cannot pretend himself unmoved. My mouth lips the lobe of his ear. "At least, not fucked in that way, enemy." I pull my hand away, but the throb on my finger quickens.

With his heartbeat. His also very, very fast pulse.

In a moment, he is on top of me, flipping me so I'm laid down on the bed. The planes of his hard body mold to the soft curves of mine. My breath stalls. Killian's mouth kicks up into a smirk.

A spasm of want curls throughout my body. The enemy, I remind myself. I can't help but wonder if in the throes of passions would be the best moment, right at the point of ecstasy, I slip a blade into a keening artery and orgasm as he dies.

I smile, showing him my teeth.

"A terrifying wife," he murmurs while on top of me. The hardness of him sits at my core. Though we're both clothed, it's not hard to guess he's aroused. "Perhaps it is only what a cursed man like me deserves."

"Most likely," I retort. "Though what I've done to deserve a man shrouded in death, I have no idea."

He looks at me, an enigmatic expression on his face, before he lifts himself off of me. As he does, the dagger holstered to my thigh slides out. "Grimsbane. Clever." Disappointment and irritation slip through me and I find myself left with only a chill for comfort. "So, this is your room, wicked witch?" he asks.

"Calling someone a witch is a poor joke," I reply, heaving myself off the bed to stand. I'm not going ot ask him if he knows I'm a witch. I'm not an idiot. But I can't help but wonder. "Give me my blade back."

He shrugs, ignoring my demand. "You clearly don't like it." An evil smile curls his mouth. "I think I'll continue to call you it. Also, no. What's yours is mine. And now this is mine."

We sit in silence for a moment.

"Then give me yours."

"You really are the tit for tat sort." His eyes narrow at me. "The answer is no. If you're worried about safety, Lukas and Jessa are just outside. They'll alert us to any nocturnal...pests."

"I'm not worried someone will attack *us*," I growl at him. They'll only attack Killian. "The Bears have more honor than your folk."

"Forgive me, if I don't want to take the word of a witch who has repeatedly stabbed me."

"I only stabbed you because you deserve it." And so much more. Killian deserves to *die.* Tonight. Regret stings my throat. No matter if he's charming and handsome, that's all part of his act. Why can't I see his truths when he speaks? I snap the Sight into place, holding it there with bleary effort.

I stand up, pacing a little further away. Killian sprawls on the edge of the bed.

I recall on purpose the atrocities of him and his fellow Wolves. The heads that I'd seen tossed over the wall and into the street. Thick bloated tongues expanding out of dead mouths. Or the corpses of fallen soldiers that stoppered the streets after terrible battles. The bodies were sent back to us not just from our border with the Wolves, but the northern front– if the families of the dead were lucky to get a body of their loved one back at all. All of these deaths rested on one, selfish man's soldiers.

Why my body aches to have him touch me, I have no idea. But shame shudders through me and I jerk a step back.

"I see," Killian says instead of defending himself. Unsurprisingly, nothing falls from his mouth. I just have to learn his tics the old fashioned way. "Perhaps, you're right. I've done a lot of things that are unforgivable. Why should my wife be different from any of my other enemies?" He barks a laugh. Bitterness tinges the edges of the sound.

He's not wrong.

An evil bastard deserves nothing more, and definitely less.

Killian peers around the room. Stacks of books litter the corners. The shelf on one side of the room contains a mixture of histories, sciences, and a large dose of fiction mixed in with poetry. The books are all double stacked. With no room left for anything else, I'd had to begin making piles around my chambers.

I wait for it. The comment about why aren't these in the library. That of course is because I hate people. The library is known for its books, of course, but also the problematic side effect is that others can come in any time they like.

I cross my arms, the itch of the paper irritating my chest. I wait for the comment about how I should part with some of my precious books, but all I want to do is reach between my breasts and satisfy my uneasy curiosity.

"You need more shelves," he says instead. "Why have more not been provided?" He says it like it's a mystery. He stands, walking over to a particular stack and eyeing them.

Perhaps that is the only thing he's said that I've liked. "That is because I don't like people in my space," I say it pointedly.

He nods, ignoring my tone. "We have to move quickly soon, so you can't take these."

I snort.

"That's the most ridiculous thing I've heard. Of course I'm taking my books."

"I'm a bibliophile myself," Killian says, back turned as he peruses the spines. The paper's scrape against my skin is unbearable. I press my breasts together, using my biceps to do so. It settles the itch, at least.

"What are you doing?"

Heat jerks up my cheeks. "Uhm," I reply.

"Mm, never mind." He holds up a book. "I had no idea the Bears were so progressive." He tosses it to me. It's one of my romances, the steamy sort that would get you called an immoral slut by an idiot. *The Girl Gets the Villain.* It's a strange book, filled with bizarre contraptions I don't understand. It also had some of my favorite sex scenes. "You may take that one to Wolf Hall."

Quiet falls between us, a natural thing that becomes increasingly uncomfortable as our gazes both linger back toward one thing.

The bed.

"It is getting late." It is. And there's only one bed here.

"You can sleep there," I say, pointing toward the corner of the room where Nisha has bedded down. She uncurls herself when I speak and pads over to me.

"I think not, my bride. I'll be sleeping where you do."

CHAPTER 30

J've never wanted so desperately for there to be two beds in my room as I do now. I never thought to complain that there's only one bed in my room. Now, looking at the thing looming across half of my chamber, I know there is no way it is big enough.

Wedding night. The words spin, like an ill fated acrobat, ready to fall and shatter.

My throat ticks as I try to swallow. Something crawls in the space between Killian and I, lustful and wretched. "I did say strip, witch," he murmurs softly. Heat licks up my spine, delivering a shiver across my limbs. His voice sounds close, but he's not cheek to cheek with me. His words curl against the lobe of my ear like a kiss, whispering and wanting. The shadow bracelet he gifted me during our first kiss slithers up my arm, hooking at the shell of my ear.

"I think you need help undressing, love."

My throat works, dry like I've left my mouth open for too long. In a flash, his body is an inch from mine. His fingers snake over my flesh without invitation. But I don't tell him to stop. Not yet.

"If I kiss you, will you bite me once more?" Killian rasps. His pupils undulate, desire dragging them wide. I imagine mine must look the same. The scent of him swirls around me. My ring burns like I pulled it straight from a fire and fitted it to my flesh.

This is all a game, Briar. I remind myself. *A game you need to* win. My traitorous body is only too eager to play.

"What say you, witch?" The words peck across my neck, pimpling my skin in a trail of desire. Dark and spicy, with a sweet pinch of mint swirls around me. His scent is a drug. My mouth dries.

"*I.*" The word croaks into the stillness around us and nothing else comes out. What do I say? Something tells me that the moment I let him inside me, things will change.

A ragged breath clogs my lungs. I can't breathe.

"Regardless, I think you need to get out of the clothes, wicked girl." Deft, clever fingers undo the buttons at my back. I lick my lips. The elegant dress loosens, sagging forward and I catch it against my breasts.

Fuck, *the note.*

I blink rapidly. I forgot all about it. The hell kind of a power does this man have? That I could forget–even for a moment–what I'm here for. I can't let him see it. Whatever it is.

The calluses on his palms curve against my spine as he pulls my gown further off my body. I grip my breasts in one hand, dipping my head forward. Silver hair unfurls from the loose coiffure atop my head, blocking the edges of my vision. The paper burns in the crease of my chest.

Gods damn this.

I wasn't cut out to be an assassin, much less someone with secrets. I can't even *lie* without paying a price. I am exactly the *worst* person for this job.

Especially since my enemy smells like mint and spice and sex.

A tight feeling burrows in my ribcage. Impatience batters against me and a ravenous anxiety eats at my stomach. Curiosity bubbles in my chest in a way that feels closer to rage than anything. Every feeling I could ever have sings in my bloodstream, so much so that my vision doubles. My breath is a ragged gasp. Tensions riddles the muscles in my shoulders as Killian's hands flutter across them again.

The edge of my dress slips off my shoulder. Air lips at the naked skin there.

The shadow on my wrist stills. My wedding band feels warm.

"Thanks," I say, jerking away from him.

I glimpse the tilt of his jaw. Loose and relaxed, Killian's mouth parts in surprise. His gaze is darkness itself. Swirling with the same want that fixates itself into my core. As if nighttime peeled off its mask to reveal a naked truth that is both unpleasant and full of desire. Then the look shutters.

"Of course," he replies neutrally. As if the universe didn't just open up in his eyes and collapse.

I move to the changing screen in the corner of the room. Killian doesn't follow me, having already acquired the dagger. I don't have another weapon on me, and my plans for later are going to require that I steal it back from him. But that isn't the issue now.

The dress sags off of me. I let it drop to the floor in a heavy hiss.

"I'm not sharing the bed," I say to hide the sound of crinkling paper as I pull the note from between my cleavage. The same slimy feeling momentarily runs over my body, the memory of Sir Typhens fingers slipping between my breasts. I shiver. I carefully unfold the missive, noting the usual black color. Each movement is slow and painful to avoid excess noise.

"That is fine, you can sleep on the floor then."

"I need decent sleep to deal with you tomorrow," I call, but the words lack the snap they should have as I stare at the scrap in my hands.

Fold across these lines once across the border at solstice. The raven will take care of the rest.

The words are written in white ink, a tight neat script. Little lines dot the edges of the paper. The implications rattle through my mind. The king watched his own knight do this on his orders and watched Sir Typhen get bits of his hand chopped off. And did nothing. An uneasy feeling slicks my stomach. I fold up the dress, tucking the paper in there and take a deep breath.

My shift is nearly transparent and, despite the screen blocking

Killian's view of me, I cross my arms over my chest. Heat dances across my exposed skin. None of it matters. Not the note, not Killian's inevitable gaze on me. Tonight, I have to do it. The grimsbane can defeat a Grim Lord, so it can conquer this wretched man. All I have to do is saw through his neck tonight.

I step out behind the screen.

The room dims into darkness. I step lightly to the bed and slip beneath the cool covers.

Beside me, the mattress dips.

I slow my breath. Willing myself not to panic. My hands tighten into fists. I don't want to submit to this man, not now, no matter the treacherous desire that burns in my body. My mind says no. I say no.

"I may be a monster, but I am not that sort of monster," the words curl out of the darkness from the man next to me.

The uneasiness in my flesh sighs a relief.

Why do I trust his word here? I don't know. I don't know the answers to anything anymore.

CHAPTER 31

The image of Killian's severed head haunts me.

I can't shake it, no matter how many times I close my eyes. No matter that Nisha—eyes yellow and watching in the corner of the room—attempts to fill my brain with images of flowers and fields and forgotten things.

Sleep just isn't something in the cards for me.

Every nerve fires inside of me. Do something. Cramps coil in the sinews of my forearms. *Scream, run,* act. I don't do any of these things. Instead, I lay there with strangled breathing trying to force away the thought that I'm about to attempt to sever Killian's head from his body and it may very well be the thing that kills me. But that's not even what stills my every inch. Something about the idea of his eyes going lifeless, the quirk of his mouth stilling forever and that blasted waggling eyebrow relaxed for eternity rather than lifted in animated amusement.

Stupid girl. He's an unkillable man. You're more likely to die than he is. Despite the doubts, they feel distant. Something potent drums deep in me, a thing of brazen glory. This is how stupid people die all the time. They believe they can do an impossible thing—like jump off a cliff, certain they are about to fly.

I stare at the canopied fabric above. Filmy white cloth stretches in a gray haze. Strange that my childhood room now hosts a mess between girlhood and womanhood. The large form of my husband sleeps next to me.

My husband.

Killian fell asleep as soon as his head hit the pillow. The strange, near-tension between us slipped to nothing after we bickered about the bed. Another argument ensued that ended in my concession. For now.

That's about to end.

Soft snores shudder from his mouth. The grimsbane dagger is somewhere on his side of the bed. Candlelight wavers in the corner of the room, a small comfort that I didn't even seek out. Killian lit it just before bed, dispelling the need for me to admit a fear of the dark.

A fluttering, empty feeling fills my stomach. I need to get to the dagger. This is perhaps my one shot before I'm taken to Wolf Hall, away from all of this.

Grimsbane isn't something to be taken lightly, if the stories are true. Strong enough to kill a Grim Lord–a mythical, immortal dark creature of faerie stories. Half made of myth, soaked in godsblood. The stories say so many things about it. What the existence of the metal means is something I don't dwell on, just the little remark Killian made earlier in the night. *"Grimsbane. Clever."*

Hopefully, clever enough to save my sorry ass from an early death and my father from a painful one.

I shift silently, swinging my legs off the bed. Killian's arm lies close, as if he seeks the warmth of another body in his sleep. I move away without touching it. I keep the pressure of my arms on the bed as I shift up and off, easing the weight gradually so as not to wake him.

"Liight…" The mumbled half-word reaches my ears. I half want to know what it is, but what does it matter? He'll either be dead or as good as once I sever his head.

Tightness squeezes my throat. It's only squeamishness, I tell myself. But part of me whispers it's a good thing I am not speaking such lies out loud. Tremors jerk my hands. I clench them into fits.

My light tread makes it to the other side of the room. I'm not fool enough to think that Killian isn't sleeping with a dagger beneath his pillow. The grimsbane blade sits there, just below where his arm dangles off the side of the bed. His fingers could simply tilt down and grasp it, if he were awake enough to do so. Good thing he's not.

I let out a silent breath, steeling myself. Then I move.

My bare feet tap soundlessly against the furred rug. Easily, my hand loops around the pommel of the blade, pulling it to me. Killian heaves a loud snore. I wrinkle my nose, ignoring the growing dread blossoming in my stomach. Nisha sits in the corner, invisible, but her attention pushes against my skin like a firm hand that encourages me forward. Otherwise, she stays silent and out of the way.

The tender surrender of sleep leaves Killian's face mostly unmarred, but there's a line of care that grabs the corner of his mouth and pulls it down. Even unconscious, there's something in him that can't let go. What does an evil monster care for that disturbs even his rest?

I shake my head. Fanciful thoughts aside, I'm not here to wonder what makes this man ache. The large tendon on his neck is exposed, his head tilted ever so slightly. The grimsbane glints in the red moonlight. The ache in my throat grows, filling my neck with a phantom pain. When he bleeds, it will be the same reddish hue as the rest of the room.

I send up a prayer to the Seven—to Amara. The Wolves worship her more than any other House, but surely she should understand the necessity of this.

I move closer, leaning in. Reluctances hedges my steps. But even so, my eyes catch on the fresh mark on Killian's collarbone. My brow furrows. Strange, that it hasn't healed completely. My other hand strays to my own injury. It's a very similar wound to mine, twin to where Sir Typhen's nail sliced just below my throat.

My fingers close on the dagger.

Killian's breath stumbles and I pause. Waiting.

He shifts. I freeze. I'm so close I can see the spot where that blasted dimple forms. The sheets on the bed slither in friction against the mattress. My heart drops into my stomach.

Killian doesn't wake.

The blade captures a fragment of moonlight against its edge as I bring it up. I can't breathe. The leather scrapes against my palms. Terrible foreboding grips the back of my neck, an instinct asking me to turn behind me. I ignore it.

The hairs on my arms rise.

This is the moment. The moment that changes everything. All I have to do is stab him, immobilize him and saw through the thick sinew of his flesh. Funny enough, the memory of his slipping a potato into my mouth pops into my mind with an underlying sadness.

Something creaks.

Instead of looking toward the noise, I ignore it. Ignore every instinct that bursts into a burning sensation that screams *TURN*.

I bring the fabled blade down on my husband's neck.

[NO.] Nisha says, but it's not to me. Her panic floods me in a red wave of feline terror.

Two inches from his tender throat, Killian's eyes fly open. His gaze catches me and the dagger. His eyes focus just over my shoulder. A silver-gold flare sparks in Killian's eyes, searing me, and as a burst of bright, white pain explodes through every nerve of my body. The shadows in the room surge, rippling along the walls in a silent army. They streak toward me.

Ready to swallow me whole.

CHAPTER 32

Killian shoves me to the ground, rolling on top. The impact knocks the breath from my lungs. A gasp shudders out of me. My skull claps to the rug, cracking into the stone beneath the furred pelt. Teeth snap against each other. My elbow burns, jabbed at some point against the ground. Nisha screams out a cry.

I can't breathe.

Killian's chest presses against mine.

Air doesn't come.

Shadows gush from the walls. A deluge like a waterfall floods around us, wrapping at Killian's back. I inhale a ragged gulp. Distantly, I'm aware of the sounds of Nisha. Fighting. Someone. Or more than one someone. Blood drips from Killian's shoulder. Dripping onto my face. A droplet splatters against my cheek, rolling down the curve like a tear.

"Briar, you're bleeding," he says.

"So are you."

"No, I'm–"

A scrape like metal on metal screams in the air. The shadows pulse in a mixture of grays, royal blues, deep reddish-purples, and black.

"Fucking die!" yells a voice. A scream rents the air and Nisha's snarl cuts through overtop the strangled cry. I can't tell how many people there are, but there's got to be at least three attackers.

Iron flashes through the translucent shield of shadows as a dark figure on the other side attempts to stab through it. Another one follows. They pound against the shield. Blood continues to drip from the injury on Killian's shoulder, each splatter of red timed with the jolts of the other person against the wall he's created to protect us.

"Briar," Killian mutters. "I need you to grab the blade you dropped." He grunts as another thud slaps the shadow shield.

A firm palm comes to my shoulder and presses down hard. My vision goes spotty. Air whistles between my teeth and I look down for the first time.

Blood.

I blink, looking into Killian's eyes, confused.

"Stay with me, witch," Killian whispers. "I need you to grab it. If I move–" Another thud. He grunts. "Get it, or we both die."

We both die.

Our gazes lock. Killian seems to sense what is going through my mind and his brow darkens. "Choose, witch. Both of us or neither."

I'm not willing to die for a lot of things, but if I'm going out, it needs to mean something. Getting killed with my enemy like this isn't going to save anything. The Witch King won't save Papa if I'm not the one to murder my husband. He doesn't do favors for free or out of the goodness of his heart.

Blood pools around us and a dizziness grips my senses. Little reflections of swirling shadows dance in the low light.

Some of this blood is mine, but surely not all that?

Killian's brow smooths, seeming to read my face as if we've known each other much longer than a mere few days. He holds himself above me, allowing me to turn onto my stomach. The room folds onto itself in a dreamy, double vision. Nausea twists my stomach. I watch a steady drop of blood from the wound on my shoulder wind itself onto the floor and rivulet down my bicep. It pools at my wrist.

Killian's breath whispers in my hair. He's right behind me, crotch to ass. Another time, I'd be embarrassed, aroused, something. Right now, all I can feel is the thud as our assailants continue to try to pound through Killian's magic.

I glance behind me. Another bit of iron flashes. Is it...coming through?

"We have to hurry. Are you ready?"

I nod.

"On three, you lunge for the blade. I'll watch your back. Just one jump, wicked witch." For once, the name doesn't grate on me. Not with the stakes we're up against. I blink, wishing I could see what expression is on his face. Kindness laces his voice, something I haven't heard before. "You're okay."

It's the second time he's said that to me. Somehow, it's like he knows there's an empty ache inside of me that can only be filled with the reassurance that I would be okay. Somehow.

The grimstone blade winks, a few feet away.

"ONE–"

You.

"--TWO–"

Are.

"--THREE!"

Okay.

I lunge. Okay. I hope it's okay.

CHAPTER 33

I sail through the air. The moment slows, pulling out the seconds infinitely. Body oddly weightless. Like I'm dying. Or I've already left this plane and I'm a ghost observing the world. The pulse of Killian holding the shadow shield thrums behind me. My heart gives an extra beat. Not dead, then.

The darkness makes it difficult to see, but that blade shines like a trophy blazing for me to win. A breeze settles on my cheeks and for one moment everything is peaceful.

Then fucking hell breaks loose.

I smash into the ground. Acute nerve pain brings me back. My body yells at me. A flare of all-too-human hurt zaps through my limbs. *Not* a ghost. I'm alive. Too alive. My aching elbow cracks into the ground once more. I hiss between gritted teeth.

The ligaments in my arm groan as I sling it out. Cool metal catches against my palm and I close a fist over the blade. I snap it back.

"To me!" Killian yells.

Without another thought, I sling the blade back and then throw it forward. It slices through the air like a javelin, just to Killian's left where he holds out a hand. In a second, the shadow shield abruptly dissipates.

To nothing.

The two men on the other side fall toward us, through the shield. A tendril of darkness snakes from Killian's wrist, snagging the blade. The metal snaps against one of the men's swords. The other jabs forward, but is met with a wall of shadow.

Killian yanks the shadow appendage back, leaving the man fighting nothing. He stumbles again, falling forward. All of the sentient-seeming darkness contracts again into a pinprick. Then it bellows out, waterfalling in reverse. Killian stands in a column of shadow. His eyes glow a ravenous silver-gold. He looks inhuman.

I jerk backwards, stumbling and falling. All I can do is watch.

The invaders stumble in fear, finally seeming to realize the monster they've been up against. It's too late.

Nisha claws at the third, and a throaty gurgle grips the room.

The tunnel transforms into a swirling mass of ill-intent. The room pounds with it, as if the heartbeat of a god beats a song of vengeance that everyone can hear. Shadows surge. Higher. Taller. Faster.

The men scream in unison.

And the darkness torpedoes into their gaping mouths.

Killians' vengeance stabs into both of them. The attackers' eyes bleed darkness. Choking, gurgling comes from hthem. But it doesn't stop. Doesn't relent. Fills, fills, fills.

"Had enough?" The words don't even sound like Killian, more animal than man. Goosepimples freckle my flesh. I shiver.

One man nods helplessly. The other looks dead.

"Okay, then."

The stream of black shadows ceases, pausing like frozen liquid. The strange arcane power connects them like crystallized evil, an onyx of cracked passion and hatred. Killian smiles, one fang peeping out from his lip.

"Goodbye."

They both explode.

Flesh pelts through the air. I scream, flattening myself all the way down onto the ground. The blade drops with a clang. A roar sounds in my ears. That's all I hear. That, and the sound of dripping blood. The world tastes like iron.

All of the movement wakes the sleepy arcane light above us, which ticks on. Faint, but there, allowing me a little more light to see.

The room is covered in the stranger's flesh.

"Oh, gods," I whisper. Slowly, I get up, a little groan of pain eases out of my lips. Bits of the man are everywhere. Staining the bed. An eye, with the cord of the optic nerve still attached, dangles like a careless lady's handbag from the curtain rod above. Bits of flesh speckle throughout the room. That's when I look down and see the *thing* on my bedclothes. So much of my own blood stains through my nightgown. Formerly white, the entire thing is now soaked red from three different people. But that's not what my gaze locks onto.

A severed thumb precariously perches on the frill of fabric at my shoulder. I yelp and brush it off. Then I sway.

Nisha stands over another dead body, lapping up the blood.

Killian moves toward me, catching me at the waist before I fall. "I don't need your help."

"Aye, you do, love. We're leaving this fucking shithole. Now."

"No."

Killian doesn't respond to my refusal. Instead, he walks over to the bed and tosses the top comforter to the floor, revealing the sheet beneath. With two thick fists, he rips the fabric. The sound of tearing cloth rents the air.

Nisha tucks herself against my hip. A sandpaper tongue flicks out, dabbing at my hand.

[Okay?]

I don't respond. I don't know if I'm okay. Confusion rattles through me. How did those men get in? My *'no'* feels weak now. I bite the inside of my mouth. How can I really refuse to leave after all of this? My one chance to kill him here.

Gone.

Killian walks over to me, holding out the makeshift bandage. A thick, heavy feeling cords down my throat. I don't protest as he uses gentle fingers to pull the cloth with expert hands around me, wrapping it tightly but not too tightly. Tears well at the corners of my eyes. I blink them away before he sees. *Goodbye, Gray Hall.*

A throb ticks in my flesh, but that's not his fault. His hands are a near caress, like a lover's.

"What about you?" I ask softly. I didn't see the other man stab Killian, but the blood that stains my husband's shoulder in star-like streaks burgeons poppy-red.

"What about me?" he replies gruffly.

"You didn't make a bandage for you."

He shrugs, lips pursing as he winds the fabric against me. A knuckle brushes my collarbone, sending a small shiver down my spine. His palm flattens an awkward wrinkle in the make-shift bandage with tender firmness.

He ignores the implied question, ignores the shiver. Instead, he says, "The bleeding has stopped, it seems. But you'll be weak from the wound. You'll have to push through it."

* * *

SOMEONE—AT least two people—beat on the other side of the door. It splinters open.

Lukas and Jessa stand there, breaths coming in hard. Blood splatters their clothing. Beyond them, a pile of dead bodies litter the hallway like trash.

"The fuck," Jessa says, eyeing the room of drying blood.

"Could say the same to you," Killian replies smartly. "Where have you been?"

"Are you serious?" Lukas asks, gesturing to at least five dead soldiers behind them. A sick feeling acidifies in my stomach. Those are likely people I know. I jerk my gaze away, the confusion of the night rippling through me. Hospitality violated, a man with intent to apparently hurt me. I've never felt so alone in my life.

"We're leaving early," Killian says, ignoring Lukas. "Obviously, we've outstayed our welcome."

I open my mouth to protest, but snap it shut. There's really nothing I can say. No defense I can muster. And, despite everything, I have a job to do. Killing my husband here won't be an option.

"Get your things. You have one minute, *duchess.*" Killian emphasizes the last word. I don't know if he's making a claim on me or reminding me of the fact that I no longer belong to the Bears. Either way, I don't like it.

I choke off a protest. I have to go with him. I can't stab him here, with others to protect him. What's more, I've seen his shadow magic at full force. An ache grips my throat. He could just burrow darkness into me and explode me from the inside.

Kill an unkillable man. What a shit bargain I've made.

I can't dwell on that right now. I try to think of Papa, but all I can see is the hatred sparking high in his eyes. There's no safety anywhere for me, no anything at all. Heartbreak fractures through my chest and I want to cry and scream. But now isn't the time for any of that.

Killian, Lukas, and Jessa speak in low tones in the corner of the room. I use that as an opportunity to pack the belongings that my mother once owned into a satchel–the grimoire, the spirit board, a pack of fortune telling cards, and a few other items that I needed. My axes land in the pile. A dagger. Two books. As I shift through a few clothing items, a crinkle of paper hooks my attention.

The paper from the king.

Something that, when I'm at Wolf Hall, I can use to call for reinforcements.

I stuff it into the growing pile of things, the nasty feeling of slime slicking my skin as I do so. Every time I touch the paper I think of Sir Typhen's hands on me. I shake the feeling off. The grimstone blade chills my palm when I grip it. The weapon slips easily into a sheath I latch to my thigh. I pull my nightgown over the weapon. As I reach down to slip on my boots, my head swims. Dizziness pulls at my consciousness.

No. I can't afford to pass out. I let out a shuddering breath and finish pulling on my boots.

A patter of footsteps thuds to the doorway. The trio's heads jolt up toward the noise. Every one of them shifts their weapon. Jessa jolts forward first, a grimace across her face. Lukas next, a wild look like joy stretches his mouth. Killian follows last, pulling shadows around him like a cloak trailing after a king.

A silhouette fills the doorway. And another. And another.

Jessa lunges first.

It's then that I recognize them. Daria, Barro, and Valor.

"NO!" I yell, throwing myself forward. The dagger is out before I can think. Daria holds her sword across her body, wide eyes taking me in as Jessa's sword sails toward her chest.

A shadow snaps into the darkness. It splits itself midair, the turgid coil snagging my ankle and yanking me back before diving beneath my falling body to stall my fall to the floor. The second tendril snaps against Jessa's blade. Holds it there.

Everyone freezes.

"Stop–" I begin, but the shadows dissolve. I fall the rest of the way to the floor. Jessa's sword doesn't fall like I do. Instead, it is gently returned to Jessa's waiting hand. Killian's eyes take on that silver look, before shifting to blackness.

"No," Killian says. "Begin."

CHAPTER 34

*D*aria surges forward. Blood covers her forearms. Who's blood, when most of the Wolves inside are in this room? I have no idea. No scabbard dangles by her hip and she still wears a servant's clothes, rather than the green fatigues of a soldier's. Her sword meets Lukas' with a shattering clang. The metal screeches. Lukas bores down on her, all the strength of the Cursed coursing through his rippling muscles. The hair across his forearms visibly darkens, becoming coarser in seconds. A long tooth lengthens from his ever-smirking mouth. His strength is superior, all animal, and Daria shudders under it.

Jessa and Barro meet, weapon to weapon, with a similar sharp sound echoing the air.

"Why, grandma, what big teeth you have," Barro grunts.

"The better to rip your balls off with, *Bear*," Jessa snarls.

"Ew," Barro replies, swirling. He's the sort that likes to taunt in a fight. Annoying his opponent to death with little wounds that make them bleed out. Too bad he's fighting something much worse than a human. Jessa's figure distorts a little around the shoulders, muscles veining with supernatural strength.

Gods, these Wolves are different from the others we'd seen in the Shadow Wood. They can control their power in increments.

Fuck.

Valor and Killian stand back. Eying one another. The shadows in the room boil on the walls, whipping in a frenzied lather of darkness. Curls of the deep colors fleck onto the floor. They don't dissipate, but build into agitated puddles of Killian's rage.

Jessa rips forward, one hand elongating into that of a clawed animal, the other hoisting her sword ready to dive into Barro's gut. My head pounds and a scream crawls up my throat. Daria pulls forward, spinning and lashing into Lukas. He parries, a bored expression leaks across his face.

It's then I realize we can't win. I don't even know who *we* are. My reluctant alliance with Killian and his soldiers? I need to go with them in order to save my father. My *friends*—the word leaves a thickness on my tongue–ready to lay down their lives for me? I can't sacrifice them to the literal Wolves.

[*Stay back*], Nisha tells me. She slinks into the corner, thrashing her tail. [*They don't need you now.*]

Blood throbbing at my shoulder with pain, I jam forward. A cotton flavor coats my mouth. I lurch into a fighting stance, the metal singing from my sheathe. Grimsbane flicks a dark reflection onto the wall. The shadows on the wall shirk from the strange dance of deep light. A fanciful thought. I shake it off. Little dots form in my vision like a mass of flies clothing dead meat. My breath rattles out of my chest like a dying woman's might.

"Stop," Killian says. His eyes track me.

"They belong with me," I rasp at him.

The very room seems to hold its breath. The darkness coiling along the walls instantly stills, waiting on Killian's word. I wonder if they're sentient, or more like an element like water he can control. Do the shadows revel in death? Or do they just administer it?

"You'll come without a fight then?" His voice is soft, as if he's whispered it into the cuff of my ear as we lay in bed. A shiver pebbles my skin as his words skim over me. No matter that he is over ten feet away from me, it feels like he's breathing on the nape of my neck. My body betrays me in a gush of want. He feels as familiar as a gulp of air, as if I've been holding my breath all this time and now I'm finally allowed to breathe. The thought is ridiculous, but I can't help but feel that part of what I've been missing all this time is the long shadow of his presence.

My teeth click together. "Yes," I grit.

"Fine. If they behave, they can come. Just to the wood. They may not stay at Wolf Hall. Then, it will just be *us*."

The way he says *'us'* causes my heart to stutter.

The words shift the room's attention to Daria, Valor, and Barro. The three exchange glances, then turn to me. Waiting on my word. It occurs to me in that moment, that they have given me their allegiance, not my father. A wash of tears weakens my gaze and I blink them away.

"Agreed," I say, the word breaking in half like a thick bone finally giving way. "They'll behave."

WE SLIP THROUGH THE HALL. I step over dead bodies of people I knew, shoving down the rage and sadness. A growing puddle of hatred leaks in my stomach. My shoulders pinch together and I put my head down. Nisha slips away to follow from afar. She poofs through a wall, disappearing.

The portraits are mostly empty, the figures of my ancestors hiding somewhere where the fighting isn't. I'm not sure if a torn canvas is something that can finally kill off the strange magic embedded into the paintings, but I don't blame them for not risking it. I pass a smaller, rounded portrait comparable to the size of a shield, if it were made for an eight year old. A grayed head peeks in. Lady Agatha.

When she notices me, her eyebrows hook upwards in twin arches. She gestures at herself, then at me.

"Take you with me?" I ask, stopping.

Killian's head snaps to look behind him. Silver-gold eyes glint in the coiling darkness. He seems to know exactly where I am at all times. Discomfort and confusion burn in my belly.

Lady Agatha nods.

"Hurry, witch," Killian says, stepping back toward me.

I quickly yank the portrait off the wall, tucking it beneath an armpit. The movement causes a jolt of pain and dizziness. No time for such things though. I blink, breathing through it. My other hand holds a bag full of my things.

"Foolish woman," Killian mutters, grabbing the bag from me and tossing it over his shoulder. His wounded one. His face doesn't change at all as it hits the injury. Perhaps it's already healed. Wooziness settles into my steps, but there's no choice but to move forward. Killian's declaration that I'd lost too much blood is probably true, but at this point, staying will only risk losing more. It's either stumble forward or fall down, dead.

We wind through the oddly vacant halls. A few portraits see us and scatter at our movement.

"Where is everyone?" I whisper.

"No witnesses," Killian replies grimly.

I see. The bloodshed is just beginning.

* * *

UNEASINESS SUFFOCATES ME. It feels like a ragged, dirty cloth is stuffed down my throat. I gag on the non-existent thing, bending over and dry heaving. Acute nerve-pain pulses at the wound on my shoulder. A weave of dizziness swirls my consciousness. My stomach convulsions.

The streets are empty.

Summer air with a taste of fall breeze rattles through the alley. Deep shadows grow longer around us in the red light. A strange comfort softens my anxiety. Darkness brings its own gifts. I lean my head into the cool stone as I'm struck with another wave of pain and nausea.

"Weakness." The word tumbles out from ahead. It rolls around in the silence, louder for all of the quiet around us. "Disgusting." It's a woman's voice, and I know Daria wouldn't have said that. I grimace, mouth opening again as I throw up nothing. Weakness isn't something I want to claim, but it's hard to get the words out between gags. "Also, going to get us killed, Duke."

"We don't have time for this." Killian grabs my arm attached to my uninjured shoulder, pulling me forward. Valor jerks forward, jolting in front of Killian. "And we don't have time for this, either." Killian hisses. The shadows around us snap, a long tendril grabs Valor, coils around the man's arm and yanks him out of our path as Killian drags me forward. "Do I need to carry you?"

I inhale a ragged breath. Valor jerks his arm away from the shadow. "Valor, stop," I say. We have to keep going. "No," I reply to Killian. "I can make it."

"Then stop trying to throw up our wedding dinner," he replies with a grim smirk.

After a few minutes, my nausea abates. Valor and Barro fan out behind me. Daria takes to my side, ready to either defend or catch me.

We reach the wall, only encountering one civilian from the city, who skitters away. This isn't right. A cloud of premonition hovers over every movement, choking each footfall with dread. I can't imagine the rest of my company doesn't feel it too. Something is *wrong*.

"Motherfucker," Daria says, immediately covering her lips and looking at me. She truly has a soldier's mouth. "Sorry, lady." I'm about to tell her that I'm not a lady and I've heard and said every terrible word out there, but another voice cuts in.

"Duchess," Killian corrects her absently, tilting his head up to look at the looming wall in front of us. The celestial light catches the planes of his face, casting each cheekbone in stark relief. He reminds me of a depiction of a god, all unattainable beauty and deadly grace.

The hairs along my nape pull upright. It's amazing—outrageous, even—Killian brought just two people with him. The fact that we haven't encountered anyone after the altercation in my chambers doesn't bode well.

I look at the wall again, the foreboding increasing in every inch of me. The vines will be what does us in. I breathe in another rush of air. And this time, I can't use my magic to free myself from a trap unless I'm willing to admit to everyone here that I'm a witch.

Why would my father, the Witch King, anyone—just let us get all the way to the wall? Possibly because of the vines and their powers meant to stop intruders or criminals, but even that isn't a guarantee.

"Hospitality," Killian replies. It's then that I realize I must have spoken out loud. "When we get to the other side, we'll be attacked. Brace up."

CHAPTER 35

"Papa wouldn't do that."

The denial comes easily, but the sweet, metallic taste of tin floods my mouth. Another wave of wretchedness shivers through my body. The Sight slips over my vision and I attempt to wrestle it to the shape of my will.

My power flicks on and off in erratic spasms. I don't need to know if *I'm* lying. In fact, it doesn't really matter if anyone is lying right now. All that matters is getting over the wall and eventually killing this man. Out of habit, my eyes flick to the mouths of those around me, watching for truth and lies in a situation that is only life and death. I don't need it right now. All that matters is getting over the wall and to the safety of Wolf Hall.

Gods, who have I become to think that Wolf Hall is where safety will be? My stomach convulses again and I wish I had something cool to lean against. Clamminess beads against my skin in a tight, wet frigid chill. I don't know what is the truth, but my body is caught in a wicked tangle of confusion and power.

"Of course he would," Killian says absently. Nothing except a puff of shadow slips from his mouth. I hollow my cheeks in frustration, watching his lips as if I can force a coin through them. I want to know *something* about this man. Darkness pools around him, liquid black and it swirls like a glass of wine. The shadows solidify. Glass-like, the darkness hardens into an onyx staircase that leads up to the parapet.

Barro and Valor both make an X at their throats at the sight of it.

"Are you a witch?" The words pull from my mouth unwillingly and I want to snatch them back.

Killian looks at me, cocking his head to the side. "Not quite," he replies. "Looking for something to relate over, wicked creature?" The last words sound less like a pet name and more like a curse.

My jaw aches from clenching it. I don't reply.

We sweep up the created staircase. I half expect each footfall to send me tumbling to the ground. Below, the shadow steps are all filmy translucence. The vines on the wall writhe at our movement, but are unable to touch us. Killian is one step behind me. A hand grips my arm.

The moon above us yawns red.

"I can do it on my own," I snap under my breath, pulling away from Killian's grasp.

"Really?" The hand doesn't move. Killian's eyes scan ahead of us. Jessa and Barro lead, with Daria just a few steps behind. Lukas and Valor walk nearly step for step behind. Watching our backs and each other.

"Now."

"Unlikely. You'll barf up nothing and split your head open below. Then no one wins."

"And what is it you want to win again?" I grit, wanting the answer. I still don't know why he agreed. Not really. Yes, the politics, but how could the Witch King have coerced this man half made of shadow into the light of day and forced him to do his bidding? That doesn't make any sense at all. "Well?"

He stares at me for a moment, as if he might answer, if only I said the right thing. But I don't have answers, I never have. The shadow at my wrist itches. Killian is the one to break our gaze.

"Your heart, clearly," he replies sarcastically. "Now, shut up, witch."

I open my mouth to argue, to say something else, but we crest to the top of the wall. The shadow steps become hard stone and a sigh of relief blooms in my chest.

"What now, Kill?" Lukas asks. The wind feeds the silence. A sweaty loop of hair blows in front of my face and I push it back. Kill. What a great nickname for this murderer.

"The others are on the other side," he says after a moment. "We don't have a choice. We go down and we see what happens."

"So the usual plan, then," Jessa says, sarcasm dripping from her words. "Lovely."

This time, when Killian's eyes flash with the use of his power; a growl groans from his throat. His neck burns silver at the center. "He's done," Lukas says to Jessa. She nods.

"Done?" I ask.

"Spent," Lukas replies.

Killian shoots him a dirty look. "I'm fine."

Instead of a set of stairs, a steep slide appears. At the top of the wall, the world looks dark and pitiless. The forest, full of chimeras, vampyrs, and evil, opens up below like the endless maw of a monster. A shiver of fear wracks my spine. Do all of the evil players from the gods' stories live there? They say every wretched witch, dark fae, and malevolent spirit from the faerie tales calls the Shadow Wood home. I'm going with the man that is the worst of them all. Murderer. Enemy. Villain. My husband.

Killian's hand on my arm softens for just a moment, but then grips me with a firmer touch. I wonder if I imagined the change.

A howl cuts through the night.

Jessa cocks her head. "Remmy, I think." Her brow furrows. "We need to go."

Killian and his soldiers exchange a loaded look. Without a sound, Jessa sits down on the shadow slide and slips off into the infinite blackness below.

"Surely we're not going to slide down?" I whisper.

"Don't worry, wicked one, you're not going down alone."

Barro scowls at Killian before following Jessa, no doubt deciding that it would be a good idea to have someone on our side out of the mixed group waiting below. Daria follows. Lukas and Valor stand behind, waiting.

I look up at Killian. He watches me, an enigmatic expression masking his face. There's no argument to make. There's nothing else to do except what I'd sought out. I've no choice but to go to Wolf Hall and learn my husband's weaknesses so I can kill him to save Papa.

Loyalty first.

I sit down, scooting forward. Killian *envelopes* me. I inhale a sharp breath. His legs fold around mine, his inner thighs flattening against the outside of my legs. A hand wraps around my waist, his mint scented breath tickles my hair.

His crotch presses forward onto my ass. My throat feels tight, like I'm getting a cold. Everything about us is different. He's all hard angles and I'm a creature of soft curves.

My cheeks heat. His one hand goes to my hip and the other drifts down. He pulls me into him, jerking me back. I press my knees together, the sensation of him behind me is all I can think of, all I can feel. Except for the twist curling low in my belly.

"Have something to say, wicked witch?" The words rumble low, buzzing over my pimpling flesh.

"No," I choke out. I start scooting forward and his body follows mine.

We tip over the edge.

Wind rips over my face, fluttering my nightgown. My hair scraggles in my face. We're all speed. Killian's hands grip me. I'm tall, but he's taller. He tucks the top of my head under his chin. I'm completely enveloped by him, burrowed in the protection of his body and shadows.

"When we get to the end, don't leave my side," Killian says into my hair. I nod, unable to speak.

No words pass between us again until we get to the bottom.

A dozen shadows step out from the wood.

CHAPTER 36

The darkness peels off of the figures, revealing a crowd of Wolves. Some are half-human, snarling things. Others wear the form of normal people, but the hairs along my neck rise. They could transform into their canine forms at any moment.

Daria stands, posture ready to fight. "Peace," I say to her. For now.

I scooch forward. Daria moves to me, grabbing me by the hand to help me up. I'm acutely aware of my backside in Killian's face. For the thousandth time since I met him, heat flushes through my body. Killian seems unaffected, quickly standing and brushing himself off, ready to deliver orders. A young man approaches us. Heavy hair adorns his face, more than a normal beard would. He smiles at me. Instead of appearing friendly, it looks like a snarl, but his eyes are kind. I swallow, fisting my hands together to hide how they shake.

"Errol, head off to the western border. Spread the word amongst the Pherrans that the Berrats have violated hospitality. Hit the network, they'll do the rest for the other regions of Lumar."

"No–" I begin.

"Yes," Killian hisses back at me. With each breath the words grow louder. "*I* know that we were attacked. *You* know that we were attacked. They *don't even like you*. The way those *fucking* assholes carried on. *Why do you insist on defending them?!*"

They don't even like you. The words skewer me in a way no blade ever could. It doesn't matter that I can't see the truth falling from Killian's lips, it's clear he believes his words. What's more, he's right. But that doesn't mean it doesn't hurt.

"Uh, Duke Galibran?" one of his men asks. Killian doesn't seem to hear the man.

"Duke?!"

"*What*, Remmy?"

Snap.

Killian's gaze slices to the trees when a branch cracks in the distance. My heart thrums in my throat.

"Shift now. If you can't shift, you'll be carried." When Killian says this, his eyes crash into mine. I open my mouth, but he makes a sharp motion. "For tonight, you ride me, *wife*."

My jaw drops open. I snap it shut quickly, but not quickly enough.

Lukas snorts. "Nice."

"Shut it," Killian snarls. "We need to hurry."

Barro steps forward, his voice deep and steady. "We're coming with her."

Killian's eyes flash, that strange sort of look that reminds me of something feral. "No."

I lay a hand on his arm. "Just until…we're further in? We might be attacked."

Killian's arm twitches against my touch. Silence spreads between us, the only sounds are the groans of men and women becoming animals. Finally, he gives a short nod. "You will not enter my home. Coming with us–being seen with us–may make you traitors to your kind. I hope you know that. We only let in fellow shifters or our wives. Unless it's truly a special event." His eyes glow that strange silver-gold color, brightening until they remind me of coins the color of truth. His body ripples. Snapping noises crack from his joints. No noise of pain grinds from his mouth, but it sounds like every bone in him breaks. I half reach out, then snap my hand back.

The hair on his arms darkens. The clothes on his body absorb into his skin, disappearing through the thinning flesh. There's nothing desirable underneath, his body half-crouched like a mewling baby, half standing like a soldier. His jaw lengthens. The strange swirling ink I'd glimpsed at his wrist reveals itself at his ribcage.

Nisha slips out from the darkness, watching Killian intently. She doesn't say anything, but I can practically feel the fur along her body raise as if it's my own.

The tattooed image of a wolf whirls against his skin. It moves, in a way reminding me of the enchanted portraits in our halls. The creature cocks a head at me, black lines rippling. Silver eyes slit themselves. Then explode across his body.

Killian's head snaps back. A spasm ripples the skin at Killian's throat, like something tries to claw its way out. His jaw jumps as he clenches it in silence. The men and women around us let out the painful howls. But Killian swallows the sound whole.

His body hunches again and elongates and grows. Fur rapidly grows over his skin, black and dark. Killian's Wolf form lays on the ground, panting in rapid bursts. When he shakes himself and stands, he's the height at the dip of my hip. He leans against my waist for a moment, nudging his head at my side.

Nisha hisses. Killian growls back at her.

We go, watch though. I tell her. She doesn't reply, but an angry cat feeling slices into me. Later, she'll make me regret this.

I climb up on Killian, fisting clumps of fur. The warmth of the animal body underneath me ripples, each sinew of muscle stretching with an unimaginable strength. An ache that has nothing to do with my injury coils inside of me, spasming around my heart. The enormity of the task in front of me looms. I want to lay down and surrender to my hopelessness and let the Seven take me to the afterlife.

A spritelight flicks in front of my face, zooming into the direction of the forest.

Without a word, all the Wolves paw at the ground. One bark comes from the front. For a moment, I imagine it's Lukas. It might very well be. I blink, noting the figure on top. Daria. She looks back at me, a frightened expression plastered across her face.

Barro and Valor both sit atop large Wolves. Identical looks of fake boredom mask their faces, but I watch them both shift and touch their weapons frequently. A rumble vibrates in my thighs, drawing my attention back to Killian beneath me. A golden eye with a silver iris eyes me. I must be imagining his displeasure at catching me watching the twins.

At that moment, the pack moves in unison into the forest. The Shadow Wood swallows us whole.

* * *

"WE HAVE TO STOP THE NIGHT." The woods should be for us, but I wonder if it's *me* it's against. Over a day has passed and the forest shows no sign of conceding extra ground to us. Not like when I trespassed into Wolf territory and the forest floor accommodated each step like an eager and welcoming friend. Now, the Shadow Wood has a growl that reverberates in every corner, rattling the stray stones nearby and deep roots of the dark licorice hued trees. Each footfall of the pack produces more displeasure. Whispers of movement tickle my ears. Each time I turn to see if anyone is behind us… nothing.

There's no one there.

That doesn't mean no one follows. Killian's earlier proclamation that we would be attacked never came true, but I can't help but think we're being tracked.

Hesitation limns my bones. Fog curls up from the ground. A howl rises up in the distance. The Wolves appear unconcerned, even though it's clearly not from anyone in our group. We'd traveled for several hours. Only small chimera creatures—rats and squirrels—had been sighted, but they chose not to fight an entire pack of Wolves. So few of the chimera make it down to this region of the world, most of them are barricaded in Selva by their maker north of Ash Mountain. The Dark One. I shiver.

Our entourage shifted back–for the most part–to human form and now we settle in a small clearing in the Shadow Wood.

I must do this, I have chosen to do this. Killian's eyes–flickering in their myriad of colors—stare at me through my mind's eye before finally going dark, as if he's died. A chill slips down my back and my teeth chatter.

Soldiers work to set up camp. Smells of wet dog and sweat clog the air, but no fire sparks the night. Lukas gives me a tentative smile. "Your lodging, duchess, courtesy of the Wolves," Lukas says with an elaborate bow. Next to him is the man Killian referred to as Remmy. He gives me a puppy-like smile, his bright blue eyes crinkling with genuine warmth. I can't help but give a small smile back.

Killian looks at Remmy and Lukas, blank-faced. His throat works in silence, making me think he's fighting another one of his growls.

Beast.

The heraldry of the tent flaps on the side, cross swords with a wolf howling in victory.

"Where's my tent?" I ask.

Killian looks at me, a long dark stare raking up and down my body. It feels like he's trailing his fingers on my bare skin.

"Our tent is there."

"No." I shake my head. I'm so tired. I want to be alone. And what's more, I don't want to be near Killian. Anger seizes me from the inside. I didn't want any of this. Not really. Nothing was fair. My father becoming so ill. Watching him waste away in front of me, the flesh shrinking day by day from his body. The wan color of his face and the light dimming each day except when he snorted Reezin. Then my stupid bargain with a man more powerful than a god. I want to rage, to rip up the tent in front of me. What's more, I want to rip apart the man standing in my way who represents it all.

"I can assure you, I'm not letting you out of my sight."

A growl rises from my throat and I toss myself at him. A flaccid weakness deadens my limbs, but the rage is stronger than the blood loss. I don't stop to wonder why I can still move, despite the injuries. Anger bursts through me, enough that my lurch forward is forceful enough to thud against my enemy. Killian catches me easily, but my fist connects with his cheekbone. He twists my arm behind my back. My shoulder screams and my eyes widen. Killian's face twitches, flinching as if he feels my pain. He releases me, shoving me from him.

"Either you're in the tent willingly or tied up unwillingly. I'll let you choose. Tonight, I'm not playing games."

* * *

THE TENT IS COZY. It's not elaborate, not by any means, but it's more than a standard soldier's bunk. A cot stretches out on the ground. Big for one person, slightly on the small side for two. An arcane light bobs in the middle of the tent, high up enough to light the entire interior, reminding me of an intimate fireside chat. A light sheet adorns the sleeping spot, since it's not cold and no furs are needed for the night.

"Get some sleep," Killian says from the entrance of the tent. He holds the end of one flap with a fist, eyes dark and enigmatic.

"Why is it taking this long?" I ask as he turns to leave.

He pauses half-way out, shoulders twitching. He comes back into the tent, the canvas slapping down and hiding us from the sounds of camp. Killian doesn't answer immediately, but pulls himself close to me. Gentle hands pull at the cloth that binds my wound.

As the fabric falls away, I gasp.

Half-healed. It's impossible.

Killian's face remains passive as he wraps the wound once more with a clean bandage. My heart heaves an extra beat. His lips are carved in a perfect bow. I can't stop looking at that little mark beneath his eye. For such a hardened man, such a thing looks soft on his face. My hand moves before I have conscious control over it, touching the freckle there. He flinches when I make contact, but doesn't move away.

Shock spikes through my body, zapping every nerve. I let out a slow exhale, pretending to wipe something from his upper cheekbone. The pad of my thumb slips across the beauty mark and an unwanted tenderness softens something in me. I hate it.

I taste the lie on my tongue even before I say the words, but my pride won't let me do anything else. "Blood," I whisper. "Blood was on your face."

A breath shudders out from his clenched jaw. He jerks away, leaving my hands touching nothing at all.

"The woods knows they're coming," Killian says, finally replying to my earlier question. The moment between us goes unacknowledged. Heat blooms all over my face. Fever, I tell myself. "It's helping us lose them, but it adds to our time." He tucks the end of the bandage in, firmly positioning it. "Your wound is healing nicely, though. It should be just a scar in a day or so. Not sure if it'll stay." He shrugs.

I stare at the white cloth at my shoulder, unable to look away from it. Witchery, of course, but how? I don't have that kind of power. Just a paltry trick of seeing what people don't want me to.

"How?" I rasp.

But when I look up, he's gone.

CHAPTER 37

I wake to the smell of burning flesh.

The acrid smell of death hits my nostrils and I choke on it. Darkness coats the room like the film that sits atop a pond. I sit straight up, hand going to my nose and mouth to block the smell. Yellow eyes flash at the mouth of the tent. Lukas.

I flick on the Sight out of habit. "What is it?" I whisper.

"Your people are attacking us." Metal flashes. I blink. Tin somersaults onto the ground before disappearing. Lie.

At that moment, Daria and Valor push into the tent. "Lady, we need to move." Valor orders, lips silver. Daria holds her sword stiff in front of her body, immediately walking toward me.

"Duchess," she corrects.

A scream rips through the air.

"MOVE," Lukas says. His body shudders. Muscles twitch and elongate in front of me. A terrible gnashing sound groans from his mouth and he hunches. A muffled scream cracks from his mouth. White, long teeth slice against the low light. His clothes disappear into his skin, revealing his naked body which rapidly is covered by fur.

I quickly pull on my boots, a thick leather hide, and strap on my weapons. My ax stays in one hand and the grimsbane blade goes to the holster at my thigh.

The tent flap opens and I step through. Screams and battle cries fill the forest.

"Where's Barro?" I ask Valor.

"He's coming," Valor replies, but even if the twisted metal hadn't spurted from his mouth, his tone was unsure.

"Go find him," I order. Lukas stalks in front of us, making a snapping sound. His head jerks. Towards the forest. Nisha appears, her cat shape coming together like smoke solidifying. She presses herself to me, hissing at Lukas.

"Lady–"

"Now," I order Valor. "Find him." Valor gives a rough nod. His sword raises, iron refracting against the dregs of the blood moon.

Daria nudges my ax. "Get ready," she says. "I've got your back, duchess."

"Likewise." I hoist the weapon up. As best as I can, anyways. I shove the doubt down. I'm no soldier, like Daria, but I'll do what I need to to protect my friends and myself.

We push through the crowd. I don't recognize anyone–but I don't know anything anymore. Uncertainty leadens my muscles with hesitation. Dangerous.

A blade lashes toward me. Nisha and Daria jump toward my attacker as I dodge, stumbling. Daria's sword meets the end of the other slashing metal, blocking a fatal wound. My ax swings out catching the man in the side. He goes down. As he rolls, Nisha pounces on him and rips his throat out.

In the distance, a figure surrounded by shadow pulls the darkness toward him.

Killian's sword slices through the air. The weapon comes down on his opponent's neck. Wet slush squirts into the air—blood. Killian has already moved onto the next when the enemy's head hits the ground. Another falls in its wake. Shadows around him spear the people through the stomach, like a pronged blade to the gut, leaving them bleeding out in a painful death.

A Grim Lord made flesh. Each movement slices the air without hesitation, without fear that their swords will catch him. Killian moves as if death means nothing to him.

My ax is in my hand, thudding into flesh. I don't recognize anything—none of the corpses left behind belong to the Bears. At least, no familiar faces stare back at me in forever stillness. It's the only thing that comforts me.

Three converge on us. They wear all black, no House colors to identify them. They spring toward me, but Daria is there again, as is Nisha. "GO!" Yells Daria. Guilt and shame swirl inside me. I can fight, but I am no fighter. "RUN, DUCHESS!"

She says as two bear down on her. Nisha swipes at the third, grabbing with her sharp teeth at the man's wrist and biting down. He screams. I imagine she bit off the appendage.

I rush to Daria, but she shoves me away. A hard look enters her eyes. "Go, now." She grunts as a blade swings down. I attempt to forestall it, slashing out my ax toward the attacker. He easily dodges it. "You're in the way, Briar! GO!"

She blocks a swing with her blade, growling as she shoves it back with her own weapon.

Briar. She called me Briar.

The same ugly, oily feeling pools in my stomach, like clumping shame and dread. I stumble backwards.

Gods, I truly am useless.

I run.

I near the edge of the clearing into a thick copse of trees, fighting my way out of the cloud of battle.

A Wolf, half twisted between animal and man, limps toward me at the edge. Nisha barrels into the attacker on the left, slashing at him and ignoring the approaching Wolf.

"Duchess?" The word groans from his vocal chords.

"Yes, we're going to–"

His sword flashes out at my side. One second. That's all it takes.

CHAPTER 38

I hiss as the metal rakes my flesh and I swing my weapon. But it's too late. Always too late. And too useless. My opponent lunges forward, face dragged into a snarl. Smells of battle pinch the air with brittle death. "Why?" I croak at the Wolf. But he doesn't reply to my question and it's an easy guess. Because I should never have been married to this man's lord.

Once again, I'm a woman to be hated.

A shadow streaks out of the forest, solidifying into a javelin-like weapon. But it's not needed. I sling my ax in an arc, catching the man in the leg. He screams.

I did it.

I got in a hit.

He jerks away and pulls himself into the forest when Nisha appears. Blood gums the fur at her mouth. I gesture for Nisha to wait. Weakness titters through my limbs. The edges of my vision grow fuzzy. Everything feels heavy.

I watch him leave, waiting until my gaze blurs completely and I sway.

"Duchess?" Daria inquires. I blink. Not Briar this time. I wish it was Briar. I'd like to just be Briar to her.

"Let him go. We don't have time for him." Still, it takes me a moment to pull my eyes from the place in the forest the man disappeared to. A distant throb hums at my side. "Have you seen Barro and Valor?"

A painful thump beats in my throat. Are they dead? They'd be here. This section of the forest titters with unease, but at least there are creatures here to be uneasy. Daria shakes her head in response to my question.

This is all my fault. I've pulled them into this mess. I should have made them go. Not that they would have, but maybe. Just maybe.

Shame grips my stomach like illness. Why am I not a better fighter? Daria fights like she was born to it. She's smaller than me, but she's all grace and fighting glory.

"Thank you," I whisper to her. For being with me. I don't say it, the words clog somewhere between my heart and the back of my tongue. Nisha scratches the ground next to me. *You too,* I tell her.

[They are okay.] She assures me. It feels false.

Can you smell them? I push a picture of the twins together into her mind.

[Too much blood everywhere. Will look.] She disappears, puffing into smoke.

The screams die down in the distance. "The fight is winding down." Daria's face reminds me of a ghost. I stare into the knot of violence, a gross unease wrestling its way through my body as I look for any sign of the twins.

We wait there until the crack of a branch breaks the silence. Daria stands, sword fisted and ready to defend. Two Wolves I recognize pull out from the branches. Their faces are set to enigmatic expressions. One seizes my arm, the other seizes Daria's. They pull us back toward camp.

I jerk from my captor. The last Wolf I saw tried to kill me.

He slaps the ax out of my hand. I immediately grab for the dagger on my thigh, but he grips my other hand easily and pushes me forward. I hear Daria's struggles behind us.

When we break back into the clearing where we set up camp,

there's blood and bodies everywhere. At the center of it all, stands Killian. He looks at me, hatred pooling in his eyes as if I'd planned this.

Honestly, I would have if I'd had the resources and time. But I would have made sure all my friends got out alive. Tonight, I can't say that they are.

I pull out of the grasp of the Wolf. He lets me, that's the only reason I'm able to free myself. I rub my wrist, looking at my husband. He gives the man who held me a dirty look, but doesn't chastise him. "You can run anywhere in the world, *wife*, but I will always find you."

So. He thought I was trying to get away. I don't correct his assumption, for whatever good it would do. I'm not going to run off until I kill him.

"Now we know your people have no honor," Killian spits at me. "And I know what to expect of my wife now."

"That was not my people." *Papa would never do that to me.* Confusion rattles my nerves, but I convince myself I'm not lying. Still, it's probably better not to speak. Nisha queries a concern at me. I feel her pounding closer to me.

Barro and Valor?

[No.]

"You violate hospitality. I knew the Bears would pull some shit like this." He pushes a hand through his dark hair. "That or *the bastard*." The way he says the last word, I can't help but think he means the king.

What's more, I couldn't tell my new husband that honor is something I believed to be an hour long-since-passed. Not now, not after new blood waters the border between our homes. Our wedding had sapped away whatever dregs of goodwill that existed between our Houses, like the abandoned leavings from a burnt pan of a misbegotten meal.

Whatever the Witch King's plan was here, it was going horribly left. At least from what I could see.

"You will never truly be a Wolf," Killian says, as if it's an insult. A hard laugh rises in my throat. *Of course* I won't. He thinks that I've already decided that his people are mine. As if I'd give up who I am so easily to the enemy. Stupid asshole man.

"Of course not," I say, my vehemence is equal to his. *Honor.* That is what we discussed here. And vengeance. "But I'm telling you, the men that attacked us were not from House Bear."

"Then who?"

"Can you think of any enemies you have?" I counter his question with one of my own.

"I'm far too charming to have many." He smirks. Gods. Hatred blazes through my skin. A hot, tight feeling condenses over my collar bones and my bicep jumps like it's about to move. I fight the urge to slap the expression off of his face. My hand itches horribly.

"And yet, we had to have a wedding underneath the blood moon."

"Just because I hate some of my neighbors doesn't mean I hate *all* of them."

"And just because *you* don't hate them doesn't mean they don't hate you," I reply. And truly, I do think all of his neighbors hate him. Handsome or not, clever or not, the man is a prick.

Bad blood has boiled between our people. Wolves have chipped away more than just pieces of the forest, taking it over as their own. Stealing land, stealing women.

It began years ago, before I was born, and half the forest was set afire. The aftermath only poisoned tensions more. Women had gone missing occasionally since then, but it was nothing like what happened before. And it was hard to get enough people to care in a world that didn't value women enough to find them, much less fight for their safety.

This order from the King—one of our women to marry a Wolf—is more salt in the wound.

What's more, lumber for the war effort is taken by *them.* The bastards snarl and kill for every tree, but don't give a shit about actual people. Familiar rage rises, rippling through every sinew and joint.

The Witch King plays a game with the Duke of Wolves. If I'm to survive—if I'm to kill him—I'll need to figure out what it is. Killian is a man with secrets. The scars across his flesh, when he can seemingly heal without a mark. The reasons he decided to marry me in the first place—all questions that sit uncomfortably in my belly. The answer to how he must be killed is partly the grimsbane blade, but it has to be done the right way. I have to find something he cares about—more than his precious head, more than even the safety of his men. The viscous interlude in my bedchamber was, in some ways, a blessing. It was stupid—*desperate*—of me. I needed to plan better.

Next time needed to be the last time.

Now that I was away from Gray Hall, I would need to wait a year and a day unless a too-good opportunity presented itself as a gift straight into my lap.

My breath comes hot and angry. A sheen of sweat dapples my forehead, alighting along my arms, and tucking into the folds of my skin.

White pinpricks dot my vision. That's when I realize it's not just rage. It's more than just the rapidly-healing-wound at my shoulder. More than that. Much more.

My hand goes to my side. It comes away sopping wet.

I hold it up, marveling at the pool slipping down my fingers. I peer at my side. "It's like a lake," I say finally.

"What is it?" Killian asks. I blink at him, holding up a red hand. Killian curses. "Let's get to our tent."

Our tent. I swallow whatever rises up in me. White scalds my vision. "Thought there were two," I mumble, pointing toward the shivering tent. It's doubled. And shivery. The world is pulling slowly away from me.

"Obviously, there is only one tent, Briar."

Killian's voice sounds far away.

"Grab the healer, wherever he is, get him here *now*."

"But he's—"

"No. We can't have her dead already, the truce will not last and neither will we."

He turns to me, eyes blazing. Everything feels hazy, distant, and not quite real. I think I see pixies, but that seems impossible. Pixies haven't been seen since the time before the Mist Wall went up around the Gilded Sea and someone renamed it. The Sea of Mist. Regardless, most of the fae are just tales for children. And the ones that are not are so rare they might as well be.

Occasionally, one might see a troll beneath a bridge, but that was a fae creature easy enough to spot and often kill. The pixies buzz around Killian's ears, whispering things that sound like threats and prophecies of my death.

His head snaps over and he yells something. The words gurgle as if we're underwater.

"You're beautiful, you know," I tell him. He looks at me, eyes intense. The pixies pause, then resume chattering and swirling. Killian waves an arm, dissipating them. "Perhaps my favorite enemy yet." I whisper.

"Don't you dare die on me, Briar. I'm the only one allowed to kill you." Killian barks, slapping the side of my face. The sting of it burns my cheek. "Wake up! Don't sleep!"

I fall into complete darkness. My eyes close.

The flat of his hand hits me again. Shock jolts my body. I'm awake. For just a second. "SOMEONE GRAB A LIGHT!"

Yes, that sounds good. I am afraid of the dark, after all. A light would be nice.

Another face is shoved into mine, my eyes flutter. Killian is so close to me. He turns his head.

"Where's the healer!" Killian yells over his shoulder.

"He's—"

"Lukas, get—him—the—fuck—over—here!" Killian grits then turns his attention to me. "Somebody dies tonight, aye, wicked witch?"

"Who will die, besides me?" I whisper. Papa. Definitely Papa. I grimace.

"Bring me–" Killian cuts himself off, bringing his nose close to my wound and he inhales. Killian's pupils dilate. His irises flash between black, silver, and his natural golden brown. "Lukas, here." Lukas comes to my side, breathing in. He gives a gruff nod before bounding into the forest.

Killian's hands press into my side, stoppering the blood.

The lake. It's on his side too. Killian drips gore. His face pales.

"Are you dying, too, enemy?" I croak.

Killian's brow pinches before thundering into a glower. "I'm unkillable, haven't you heard? And while you're mine, so are you."

"Am I yours, though?" My voice trails off.

"Yes," he gruffs. His eyes change again, this time looking just like the first time I met him. Golden with a hint of silver. The color of truth. His eyes shift back to that warm brown. "Mine, until I say otherwise."

At that moment, Lukas pulls a man from the forest. The one who made the sopping wound at my side. Jessa follows, more gently cradling the Wolf called Remmy in her arms. Remmy shakes like a dead leaf ready to release from a branch. So does the other Wolf in Lukas' custody.

Both men might die, but for different reasons.

Killian growls, a low sound in his throat. If his human form had hackles, they would certainly be raised. My enemy husband stands, stalking toward the man Lukas holds and grips him, one-handed, by the throat.

"That was the man, wasn't it? The one who hurt you?" Killian gestures toward my side and back to the man, but everything blurs. It feels like iron weighs on my eyelids, pulling them down. Rippling red pain passes over me. My side burns. And I can't feel my feet. Why can't I feel my feet?

"*Who did this to you, Briar?*" Killian's words are angry. Hopeless sounding. I must be dying.

Why does he even care?

"Because you're my wife!" he says. "You are the worst wife in the world, but it is my job to protect you as long as our vow holds."

I sigh. Men are stupid. Why can't more of them be fictional? None of this would be happening, otherwise. Books are so much better than real life.

He gives me another look. I can't stop looking at his lips. Why don't coins fall from his mouth?

"She's not making sense anymore!"

"Kill– there's blood on your–" Killian cuts Lukas off with a sharp look. His figure swims, doubles, triples. Lukas' lips purse into a grim line.

A figure pushes forward from the small crowd. He wears white, like a healer, though his robes are slashed crimson from the dead and dying.

Killian turns his head back to the man he's captured and inhales near the man's throat. "You smell like cowardice. And like her blood."

The man snarls. Lukas snaps forward, grabbing him and holding his arms behind his back.

Killian looms like a shadow stretched by the setting sun. He releases his hold on the man's throat, but tucks a finger beneath the betrayer's chin. He pushes it up and their eyes meet. The darkness around us shivers, rattling the air and shifting the night in a mirage of rage.

"No one hurts my wife, understand?" Killian whispers, a growl reverberating the bass in his words. The Shadow Wood shakes around us, as if it belongs to my husband and expresses his ferocious anger.

The other man nods, a quick desperate gesture.

"Good."

The world jitters on and off, like a flickering light. Killian lurches forward. Blood flies mid-air as Killian slices the man's throat.

And then my husband collapses, too.

CHAPTER 39

"KILLIAN!" Lukas yells, rushing to him. The world swims but I roll, trying to get up. Confusion ripples through me. Concern for my husband. Why do I feel that? I shouldn't feel that at all. He needs to die. But I need to be the one to do it. My vision blurs.

I grit my teeth.

"No, duchess." The healer is suddenly at my side and I inhale a ragged breath. He pulls back the fabric of my gown that Killian had kept a hold on. The wound gushes, but less so than before. "You're–"

Nisha jolts forward from the darkness, knocking into the healer and hissing at him. Her tail lashes.

"Nisha, let him."

The man wraps a tight bandage around my side, mumbling while he does so. Another wave of disorientation washes through me and the back of my throat tastes like snot and death.

Lukas hovers over Killian, hulking over him with visibly growing shoulders. His body twists and a groan peels from his throat. "We need Asha," he says. "Gods, I've never seen him like this." His last words contort into a half-swallowed growl as he shifts.

"I'm here, Lukas, not dead," Killian says, obscured by Lukas' rapidly twisting Wolf form. "If you're bringing me, bring *her*."

Her.

Me.

* * *

KILLIAN and I are shuffled onto Lukas. His coarse fur sits beneath me, not quite like a porcupine, but certainly unpleasant. I try to itch my gown down, but the movement sends another spasm of dizziness through me.

Killian's eyes are closed, his skin blanched from sudden blood loss. Will he die? The little scars on his face, the white nicks on his knuckles and exposed skin, stand out. How can a man that cannot be hurt have so many old wounds? Killian was stabbed—I stabbed him— and nothing.

He healed so quickly.

And now I hold a hand to his side, stalling a bleeding wound even though I'm woozy with my own. Somehow, I'm the strong one right now.

It takes me too long to remember that I want him dead. His head leans against me, his breath so familiar it's like we've done this a thousand times. My throat hurts watching him.

Nisha follows us, rushing in near tandem. When she comes across an obstacle, she disperses her body into a peel of smoke and mist, only to come together again as she bounds forward. The world slides sideways. I think I feel myself healing, but it's strange because I'm the one sitting behind Killian, holding him up.

Why am I holding him up? I hate him. Hate all he is. And his people—his *father*—they're responsible for the death of my mother. What am I even doing here?

Papa, I remind myself. Remember Papa.

[Stay awake.] Nisha orders. But I've lost more blood than I should have. Killian groans in front of me and I clutch him tighter to my chest. Lukas' wolf form bounds over a fallen branch, jolting us on

him, and I clutch my husband closer. We've left enough blood behind between the two of us for the wood to use. Now we see if it's accepted. Another burst of wooziness clutches at my consciousness.

The wood will as the wood wills.

We'll see if our offering means we approach Wolf Hall soon. Where I'll be trapped until Killian releases me. Or until the marriage dissolves on its own. Until I kill him.

The grimsbane blade is cold against my thigh. Could I just...take it out? I never did get to try cutting off his head. Weakness cuts an undercurrent to my thoughts, but I slide a hand to my leg.

My ring tingles on my finger and the shadow bracelet tightens.

No.

Wait.

The word comes from deep within me. A voice of intuition. I have no wish to die. Or I at least want a chance to live. Even if I might be willing to give it all up for my father, the slim shard of a future dangling ahead of me is enough to stall my hand. I need a moment to escape after I kill this man. And there's a strangeness to his wound—a man that supposedly cannot be killed is leaking blood in my lap. If it comes to it, I'll kill him when he's on his deathbed, even though it seems unlikely such a creature could die this way. I'll take the credit and run.

But until it comes to that, I'll stall my hand. For now. At least until I understand this strange connection and what it means for me. A pulse patters at my side, where the wound is. Was. It hurts less, but my gown is still wet.

Killian's hair tickles my arm. He looks nearly peaceful, if not for the pinch of care between his brows. I run a finger over the scar there and he sighs. The line nearly disappears, and he mumbles something under his breath. "Light." His mouth moves, but the rest of the words are lost, half swallowed by his dreams.

I let out a breath and clutch my husband closer.

* * *

LUSH BRANCHES of burgeoning silver and gilded leaves slip away until we enter a clearing. Wolf Hall hulks there, like the worst sort of man spreading his legs and leaving no room for anyone else to exist. The ramparts with the statue wolf heads grinning in predatory stillness stand tall. The view of a parapet walk between a corner tower and the large portion of the keep is visible and looks different now in the daylight.

It's hard to believe that only a few nights ago, I'd wandered all this way here to grab Fex's Flower. Or whatever it was. Fucking false flower.

The steady rock of Lukas' movements makes me want to sleep. But I keep my arm clutched around Killian, holding him around his middle. Somehow avoiding the mutually painful wound at his side. I peer around him and my husband's face shifts to look at me. He gives me a baleful glare, as if I've inconvenienced him.

"Fuck you," I whisper just for the hell of it as I meet his gaze.

"Likewise," he replies as Lukas' wolf form stalls.

Flaccid weakness jiggles my limbs and people appear like phantoms. I wish Nisha and Daria were here. Anxiety jerks my stomach.

[Coming. Following you.] Nisha says from somewhere far away.

I wonder why the wood isn't as fast for them. Perhaps it's the amount of blood we gave to the carnivorous forest. I wonder how long I'll get to see Daria before she's turned away. I recall that moment–what feels like an age ago–right after I shared that first, fateful kiss with Killian. The Wolves only let in other shifters or their partners. I shiver.

We're greeted at the front by a host of servants, bedecked in purple, red, silver, and gold. More hands appear, lifting me off of the wolf and onto my feet. Someone assists Killian down. I find myself steady, if a little woozy. I look once more at Killian. I should be wooing him and convincing him I bear him no ill will, but I'm finding it difficult since I'd rather slam the blade of my ax into his thick skull.

"What happened?" I mumble. "Why...?" I gesture to our wounds. They're the exact same. Killian shrugs, not answering. "Did...where are Valor and Barro? Were they found?"

Killian shakes his head, unconcerned. "They're most likely lost in the woods. Or…Well. We'll know at some point."

"How can you be so callous?" I demand. I step forward. A wave of dizziness slips through me, but I square my shoulders and put my stance wide.

"They mean nothing to me," Killian says. The people around us–a handful of folks, but none that I've ever seen before–pause. He turns unsteadily, as if that's the end of it. A man that looks like a butler from the cut of his coat and proud shoulders steps forward, as if to grab him. Killian shoots him a dark look. The edge of his fang flashes in the pink light. The butler takes a step back. "They will either die in the forest or be returned to you. It makes no difference to me. They were only with us by chance."

The image of heads being slung over the wall back at Gray Hall pierces my mind. Killian has killed a lot of people. And he didn't care if they trespassed into his woods, their heads were forfeit.

"If they come back…are they safe?"

Killian shrugs and says nothing else. Desperation fills me. I am in over my head.

"My things?" I should have kept that paper on me. My fingers itch, as if now is the time to send the missive. It's not. Not until the equinox like King Thaddeus said. All my bravado about not wanting to be a girl stuck in a tower becomes ash on my tongue. Now, I'd like for nothing more to be saved. Valor and Barro are most likely dead. Dead. Dead, dead, dead.

Grief hooks its teeth into my gut and bites down.

"Whatever trash you brought is with your…lady's maid," Killian says. Lady's maid?

Daria.

I close my eyes. At least she's safe, as is Nisha. "She's following. As quickly as she is able, I imagine." His mouth twists. I worry my lip, a deep unease clouding everything. I take a step forward and falter. Killian moves to me, hands slipping at my back and on my uninjured side, as if to forestall me from collapsing. I grit my teeth.

"The Duchess is injured,"Killian states to the butler. "Get Asha."

The man scurries off. "Your lady's maid may come this far, but I will send her back to her fate after this."

My stomach drops. What will become of Daria when she goes back?

I shake my head. A sharp pain greets the movement and I hiss between gritted teeth, swaying. Killian's hands spasm around me, but he immediately lets me go after I shove him away.

Mere minutes after the man leaves, he's back, a petite woman in tow. She has a spine that looks like it's made of straight iron, the way she carries herself. She flicks a grayed-blond braid over her shoulder. A slight glow suffuses her fingertips.

"Asha, my aunt." Killian gestures toward the woman. She's perhaps in her forties, maybe early fifties. Blonde hair shot with gray sleeks back into a neat bun. The slate dress she wears is modest, but well-made. A white apron with an embroidered corner at the bottom left hugs her waist. "She's our resident healer, you'll go with her then return to me."

You'll return to me.

My stomach drops as I watch his back and he stalks away. Rage sparks off of him, palpable as if it's a coat he wears.

"I'm fine." The dizziness is there, but it's bizarre. It's like my body can't decide if I've been injured or not.

Asha sighs. "Pay him no mind, dear. He's such a homebody that it's hard for him to leave the estate."

The statement is laughable to me. The brooding, evil-eyed Duke of Death described as a *homebody?*

Lukas bounds up to us. "Mama, you are as gorgeous as ever." He slaps a generous kiss on her cheek. My eyebrows shoot into my hairline. The Wolves are free with their affection here.

"And Lukas, you are just as mischievous as the day you were born." She sighs, consenting to his kiss on the other cheek. She shifts her glance to me. "He took a day and a half to come into this world. I should have known then he'd be giving me trouble for the rest of his life."

Lukas only grins.

"Where's your shadow?" Asha asks. "I don't see Remmy."

My stomach twists. Remmy. Lukas' joy dims instantly, a serious look taking over his face. "Remmy is with the other healers now. He's —he's in a bad way."

The woman's face blanches, bleached like bone. She starts forward in the direction that Lukas had come from. Her son holds out a hand, stopping her. "No, Mama. He'll be okay...it'll just take time."

"That bloody king," Asha hisses. "And all his demon servants." Her look cuts to me and she silences herself. For some reason, shame leaks into my gut. As if I'm responsible for this. Perhaps it is good this way, though. I'll kill their lord and they'll hate me regardless. Why not be grouped in with the Witch King? She gives me a sharp look, something between rage and disgust ripples across her face. "I'll tend to this one, then, and then I'll see if I can lend my skills to Remmy."

Asha and I walk to the infirmary in silence.

CHAPTER 40

$\mathcal{I}$ purse my mouth, trying not to look like a traveler in a strange land. Asha ghosts a little ahead of me, footsteps no heavier than a falling leaf. Little lights–like spritelights, but not–blink in the dust bunnies corners of rooms we pass. I reach out for Nisha. The tug of her magic jerks at me as she runs straight through the forest, puffing through trees like they're made of wind.

[Coming.] Her voice provides a lull to my fast beating heart.

Be careful.

[I'll kill them if they try to stop me.] She replies, which sounds exactly the opposite of careful.

My pulse kicks up, but I bite the inside of my cheek. Will she be able to get past the Wolf sentries like this? Injured and while they are on high alert? An ache of worry knots in my stomach.

[The female is behind me. Smells like meat.] Nisha delivers an image of Jessa, snacking on a drumstick with one hand and half a loaf of bread in the other. The background of the memory is familiar, from Gray Hall where Nisha must have glimpsed Jessa putting away an obscene amount of food. I let out an uneasy laugh. My stomach growls.

"What is it?" Asha asks, whipping around. Her blonde-gray hair is pulled back so ruthlessly I can't imagine she doesn't have a headache. I look for Lukas in her face, trying to see where the family resemblance is. Their color is similar, but the mischievous waggle in his eyebrows evidently didn't come from his mother.

"Just…" I pause, choosing my words carefully. "Just thinking about food."

"Soon enough. We can have a tray sent up to you and the Duke."

We enter the room. A breath eases from my lungs. An array for books stretches from floor to ceiling, sorted in the color of the rainbow. At the very bottom, all of the tomes that are black and dark brown sit, while at the top there are two rows of white spines of varying widths. The ceiling is high, with little floating air plants, bobbing much like the way dust would in the wind.

I open my mouth and close it. Open it again. It's hard to know what to say.

"Before you ask, I had the books re-covered, so the order not only makes sense to my mind, but it is done because it pleases me." She grabs a bag as she speaks. Asha directs me to the table at the center of the room and gestures for me to sit. I do so and her hands tugs at the bandage around me. It pulls, sticking to my skin in stiff peaks before giving way from my flesh. Asha's mouth turns down. Then her index finger glows.

Glows.

It looks like truth in color, but with a hot center, as if a light burns from inside the tip. She eases the edge to the blood-ruined makeshift bandage and it falls away from my side like her finger is the sharp end of a blade.

I jerk.

"Ooh, careful dear," she says and her skin dims to a dull glow like a dying ember. "I should have warned you, I suppose."

"Are you a witch?" I whisper. Asha's eyes jerk to mine. Narrow.

"I'm something less restrictive." The bandage clings like a snaggle tooth to my skin before releasing me. I look down. "I'm what they call a fractured spirit."

"What does that mean?"

"Hmm." She doesn't answer me. Instead, we both stare at the wound. Or what should be the wound.

A pucker of a scar is there. That's it.

I bite in a sharp breath, my gaze jerking to Asha. Her face blanches, a tick jitters just under her eye.

"My gift doesn't come from the blood of gods or fae. Not anymore," she answers obscurely. She stares like her eyes are glued to my used-to-exist wound. "It seems there is a different sort of problem with your wedding than we thought to expect. Let's go see your lord husband now. He's waiting for you."

* * *

KILLIAN IS SETTLED on the other side of the desk. Claw marks of various sizes shred the corners, but other than that the redwood shines with fresh polish. Wolf heads are carved into the legs, sleek bodies rippling in mid flight. Two are visible from where I sit. One wolf flies forward with death in his snout, the other flies forward like a dog excited to see his master. A root from the wood slips down into the floor, as if the desk is merely an oddly shaped tree.

I feel oddly naked without Asha here.

Or maybe it's just that I feel naked when I'm alone with Killian.

He shifts in his seat, not looking at me. The feeling of unseen eyes slicks down my neck, raising the small hairs there. Breathlessly, I turn. Nothing.

"A drink?" Killian asks, getting up. His chair shrieks against the wood floor. The decanter gleams behind him. Honey-colored liquid sloshes into a crystal cup.

"Ye—" I cut myself off, then shake my head. I don't know the perimeters of this game yet. What I wouldn't give to see the coins fall from his mouth. The ability has saved my life–at least, politically speaking–many times over. Why it fails me with this man—that is beyond me.

He snorts, pulling out another glass anyways and filling it two fingers up. "We both need it and we both know we can't kill each other."

Yet.

The unspoken word drops between us.

The strangeness of this connection–of what it means–grips me with uneasy paranoia. I don't want to die. Not really. Not yet. And right now, I'm not sure what our mutual wounds mean.

A candle burns in the corner, squashed down into a near-nub of wax. The wick weakly sputters. "You need a new candle." I state. He pushes the glass to me, the alcohol lipping towards the edge of it with the force of his push.

His eyes narrow, pinching to near slits as if he's looking deep into my soul rather than just my face. "Perhaps you owe me one or two, then."

"I don't owe you anything," I snip, confusion rubbing my brow into creases. "Just stop burning candles when it's light out." It's strange to think he would need them at all.

Killian's jaw ticks and whatever softness might have been in his gaze is hidden under a dark, hooded look. "They're not for me."

A pained feeling blooms in my chest, half warmth, half chill as a flood of goosebumps drag themselves down my arms. "Sure, why would the Duke of Death, master of shadows and immortality, be afraid of the dark?"

"There's as much to be afraid of in the dark as there is in the light," he says with an obscure wave of his free hand. He takes a swig of his drink. A silence, not uneasy, settles between us. It's worthless to wonder at Killian's secrets. I just need to survive long enough to do what I came here for. Now that I've arrived, I must wait. Piddling away energy on this man's mysteries are a waste of time if they don't pertain to how to murder him.

"You killed the man that gave me this." I say, breaking the silence. My hand brushes up against my side. *I saw it.* I don't say the words. The blurred memory of blood whipping through the air, the swift choke of death. Killian collapsing. My stomach somersaults. The image sits uneasily in my mind's eye.

The flesh at my side stretches as I shift in my seat. The pain is still there, but dull.

He shrugs. "As far as I'm concerned, I'm the only one who's allowed to kill you. A threat to you is a threat to me. For now." I put the edge of the glass to my lips and sip. It burns all the way down my throat. "At this moment, it looks like if you die, so will I."

CHAPTER 41

The ghost of the injury on my ribs pulses. "What?"

Killian's brow crashes down. "Your injury, it's the same as this, is it not?" He lifts up his shirt. For a moment, the room tilts and the walls lean in. I blink through the haze of Killian's lean stomach that takes all my attention and the striking V forms an arrow like a sign that says *go this way*. A thin trail of hair flecks the flat of his abs. My mouth is dry like I haven't had water in months.

A whirl of ink peeks from around his side. It moves. I can't tell what it is, but I glimpse the edge of a dark image of a creature before the tattoo pulls itself back to hide at Killian's spine. I've never seen anything like it. But I've never seen anything like Killian, either.

I shake my head, focusing on where his finger points at his side. An identical scar to mine.

"We're bound. That's the risk of mixing blood, magic, and marriage. I'm not sure if my injuries affect you the way yours do me, but I suppose we'll find out." Killian grimaces. "Thaddeus planned this."

"Planned it?"

Killian's eyes narrow. "He wants me dead. I'm a threat to him in more ways than he'd like to admit." In what ways? I don't for a second think that Killian will tell me if I ask, so I keep the question on my tongue and let him continue to speak. "So he's willing to kill priests now to get a little closer to my demise."

A little ache blooms in my heart. Nord. He was kind to me, at least. He didn't deserve to die.

"Do you really think he killed Nord?"

"And why not? He needed our marriage rite to be conducted a certain way. We just have to wait it out a year and a day. But first, we have some things we need to discuss. Rules." He lets the edge of his shirt fall down, covering his body once more.

"Rules?" I laugh. "Sure. Tell me, enemy, about what I may do while I am your captive."

"I think you mean *wife*," he corrects, irritation lining his face.

I don't reply. I said what I meant.

"But in name only," he continues. His throat works. "This is not a love match—we both know that—and we will live together until the end. Then, we will part ways. Our marriage will dissolve on its own and we will pretend this farce never occurred."

The marriage bond would dissolve on its own. Without the right ritual, a year and a day dispersed into nothing. I eye the ring on my finger. That, too, would dissolve. It was not often that the Old Rites were performed anymore, because few knew them. Because few had the means—or the inclination—for such magic. After a year and a day passed, the promise would have been fulfilled and the bond broken. The itching irritation at my finger—likely from Killian's own unsettled feelings—would be gone forever.

Good.

The strange shadow on my wrist squeezes. He put it there, back in the forest. I add it to my list of questions to ask him—when will he rid me of this?—but I have other thoughts pressing on me first.

"Tell me, then, O' husband of mine, what a mere woman like myself is allowed to do?"

"My darling wife, I thought you'd never ask." He pauses, taking a sip of the honeyed liquid. His lips shine with an extra droplet and I watch as his tongue swipes it away. "First, this side of the house, let us consider it mine for the hellish months ahead. You can have the other half of the house."

So, it's like that. "Shall we draw a line, so we may clearly delineate our territories?" I ask with a pert raise of my eyebrow. He ignores me. As he opens his mouth to speak, a knock raps at the door.

"I'm busy," he growls.

A voice muffles through the wood. "There's been an issue at the border. Bears one side, chimera funneling down the middle. You're needed, Duke."

"It never ends." Killian rattles out a frustrated sigh. "I'll be there in a moment." His gaze zeroes in on me, continuing as if he hadn't been interrupted. "Yes, we will have our territories, with a few exceptions. You'll meet with either myself or one of my lutinents—like Lukas—to train. You're a liability to me. Your mastery over swordcraft is...well, there's much to be desired."

I open my mouth, but he blazes on.

"Second, do what you please, fuck who you please, but do it quietly. I will not be embarrassed." This, he says with a blank face, as if he's watching for my reaction. "If you want to fuck *me*, you only need to ask nicely, darling." At that last one, he grins. Mid-sip, I choke on the burn of alcohol. He throws his head back and laughs. I glare at him. "Things always sound better in threes, don't they? I have a feeling that I'll need more than three rules with you. An entire book, likely."

"No one ever mentioned the Duke of Dogs is enamored with his own jokes."

"Then you have not heard the truth of me." He leans forward intently. "And it wasn't a joke, *Duchess* of Dogs. I'm your husband, I'm happy to fuck my wife whenever she pleases. I'll just have you searched for knives first."

Blood runs hot on my cheeks at the thought of being searched before going to bed with my own husband. It's the indignity of it, I tell myself, but I can't help but imagine Killian stripping me bare and my ears grow hot.

"What I wouldn't give to see what's inside that head of yours, wicked witch," he whispers. "Feel free to send a message if you need an escort to my chambers." He leans back, shirt stretching against his chest.

"Don't call me that," I snap.

He carries on, ignoring me as if I didn't speak. "Next rule, don't leave the grounds unescorted. You're a liability to me. The woods, its creatures—as well as the people here—are dangerous to you. With that in mind, when you've recovered, we'll begin the training. The Equinox is approaching, and we Wolves typically celebrate it. You will attend at that time and we'll try to look our part as a married couple. For now, though, we'll do our best to avoid being seen out so we don't give it away that we hate one another." That eyebrow of his arches up as he says this. "Now, I'm afraid I have business to attend to. That dirty mind of yours will have to wait."

CHAPTER 42

*R*age fills me, as if I've been doused in it. I open my mouth, but Killian is already buckling on his sword. The room surges with shadow, but it seems as if the darkness is careful with the candle flickering in the corner of study.

Fire hazard. Truly. I let it burn, hoping the flame will snatch at something it shouldn't and burn this whole Grims-ridden place down.

An issue at the border. Likely, it's more of the same—a frustrating territorial dispute. There can't be the number of chimera the man claimed.

No one seems to care about the Red Season, or the dwindling end of our holy week. A sour feeling, with the weight of a slimy brick, settles in my stomach. The attack on the way here–that wasn't nothing. But I also know it wasn't Papa.

He wouldn't do that.

Not to me.

And chimera? There are so few of them this side of Ash Mountain, it seems unlikely there would be more than a handful of any significant size to fight. That wretched squirrel pops into my mind and I scowl.

Nisha, sensing my rage and confusion, presses a picture of the moon into my mind in an attempt to calm me. I breathe out, pivot, and walk out of the study. I'm halfway down the hallway–the echo of Killian's door slamming behind me ringing in my ears–when I hear a "wait!"

I whip around, my hand still itching. That man makes me want to kill something, so when I see Lukas, who seems to be not just his cousin, but perhaps Killian's closest confidante, I think about killing him too. Lukas approaches, eyes widening at my expression.

"Woah, woah!" He jogs to me, but there's a cautious set to his face and he holds up two hands. "Lady Briar, if you want to hurt someone, definitely choose my cousin. He's a good leader, but he's definitely in my burn book after what he did when we were six." He looks at me seriously. "He ripped Felicia, my teddy bear. And don't even get me going about what he did when we were two—" He leans in conspiratorially, "He stole my slice of cake for my birthday. Can you believe that?" Little copper coins fall out of his mouth as he speaks. Inconsequential truths.

I watch him. I like him.

And I don't trust him.

I remember the little bit of tin splurging from his mouth earlier, but that doesn't stop the small smile twitching at the corner of my mouth. Everybody lies. I just don't know why he lies to *me*.

Lukas waggles an eyebrow. I snort, the killing edge dying down in me. "Yes, I'm sure you haven't forgiven him. You're biding your time before you kill him, yes?"

"Just like you, right?" he says it lightly. No coins fall from his mouth. It's neither truth nor lie, but I can feel the importance of his words and his quest for my answer as if a thousand silvers spewed from his lips.

"I'm thinking about it," I say truthfully. I can't afford a fever right now. Especially not after my recent injuries, despite how quickly they're healing. A little lie would make me unwell, but to lie about murdering my husband—I'd either be bedridden or it would kill me.

We stare at one another, as if we're opponents sizing each other up before a fight.

"I can't tell if you're lying or not," Lukas says. His blonde eyebrows shoot upwards. He looks nothing like Killian. "It's scary." He falls into step beside me. "So where are we going?"

"I am going to figure out what is in this gods-forsaken place. I also need to find my room and where someone put all my things."

"Would you like a tour?"

"Actually, yes."

We walk through the halls. Though technically it's still summer season, with the Red Season ending in just a few weeks and the world will resume its normal coloring wherever the natural light touches. Everything smells like cinnamon and pumpkins. Little lights flutter up and down the hallway, casting a warm autumnal glow along the passages. It makes my arms ache for a blanket to wrap myself in and a book I can fall into and forget about all my problems. A shiver tip-toes down my spine. When the Red Season is over, any of the ill-enforced peace will immediately end and violence will delineate our territories again. It occurs to me that now there really should not be a problem from the Bears at the border. So who is doing this?

Because it's not us.

I have too many questions and it's not like an instruction manual on mariticide was delivered to me when I exchanged vows with my husband. It would have had to be a lot more complicated than the standard husband-killing directions. The inclusion on how to politically maneuver around a kingdom essentially fighting two wars—while hiding one's ability as a witch without accidentally killing oneself by lying about something too important—would have been a critical addition. Also, how to end the life of a man who cannot die in a timely manner so your morally ambiguous divine king doesn't get bored and let your father pass into madness and a painful death. Yes, it would have been nice to have a little more of a walk through on this.

Lukas points out various rooms as we walk and, stupidly, I only half pay attention.

Wolf Hall is oddly…normal. Cozy, even. Unlike Killian's claim, the portraits scurry from frame to frame, jumping and leering at me to get a glimpse of the new duchess of Wolf Hall. I grimace. We pass another portrait and Lukas stops, eyes flicking up and a strange expression passes over his face. His lips whiten as he creases them into a firm, thin line before the expression wipes clean from his mouth. All that is left behind from the brief, solemn look is an expression akin to a happy golden dog, if the creature possessed sad eyes. The shadow on my wrist lips against my skin.

A picture of a man sits in the frame. He lifts a brow when he sees Lukas, and wags his finger. Lukas swallows, giving him a smile. The man follows us down a few frames at a stately pace, looking stern.

Lukas blows him a kiss, which devolves back into that tight, sad smile as we continue on.

We walk away.

"Who was that?" I ask.

"Ah— my father." He runs a hand through his hair. "You know the soldiers at the northern front…We used to get letters."

That's all he says.

My heart drops like quarry stone.

"I'm sorry," I say. That's all there is to it.

The northern border was a mess. The king conscripted people from the different Houses, whittling down men to bleed and die at the Selvan front. It was strange Lukas' father had been chosen rather than Lukas himself.

"That's what everyone wonders,." hHe says, voice bitter. I didn't say it, but it must have shown in my face. The usual jovial tone is gone. "The Witch King, though, picked *him*. You'd think you'd have wanted someone with the Wolf Curse. But—" he cuts himself off. Silver falls from his mouth. His jaw jumps as he grinds his teeth. "It's not important."

But that's not true, because a mass of tin coins fall in a sound of rushing rain and tinkling bells.

I can't help but think of my mother and her absence in my life.

Lukas just lied to me. Again. First, at Gray Hall. Second, just before battle. The third time now. It's not as if I trusted him, but it set my teeth on edge nonetheless. I let the lie pass.

I don't mention my mother, don't mention I'm a witch. Of course it's important. Sometimes, we tell the world the biggest aches in our hearts don't matter. We have to, so we can continue to live. Who am I to dig into his pain about his father who is probably dead by now? I understand what it's like to lose.

* * *

"So, what do you know of Wolf Hall?" Lukas asks, after most of the tour. The autumnal scents fill my head like a heavy drug. Concern for Daria, Valor, Barro, and Nisha convulses through my body. What's happened to them? My throat pulses a dry ache. I pinch my lips together.

Lukas still needs to show me my room. An overwhelming feeling of despair, exhaustion, and hunger surges through me. Gods, this is a mess.

My stomach gurgles. I clutch at it.

"Mine too," Lukas says. "Let me show you where the kitchens are. It's the most important place in the castle anyways."

We wind through the halls. I mark the passages with my eyes, noting jade vases and thickly curved columns depicting rarely seen fae. A face whirls in an etched, dark wood panel before quickly disappearing. I blink, sure I imagined it. Finally, we find our way to the kitchens. The main marker of this is the hot smell of fresh bread. A woman stands there, bright, plum colored kerchief tied to her head like a flag waving before battle. She rattles a wooden spoon on the edge of a counter.

"Quickly! Melt that cheese! And where are my hot peppers?" Her voice sounds like the crackle of a fire and woodsmoke.

"Tessa?" Lukas intones, voice tentative.

The woman snaps her gaze to him. Her clever eyes alight on me, bore *through* me, before moving back to Lukas. "Aye, the troublemakers are back then." To the single staff member in the kitchen she'd yelled at to melt cheese, she gestures her spoon. "Send a platter up to His Grace," Tessa orders. "He'll be plotting this time of day."

"Plotting?" I ask, speaking to her for the first time.

"Aye, all week it's been getting worse." She waves a hand. "The border, as you know—" She cuts herself off, a sharp look entering her eye. "Well. You do know."

This time, we are not talking about Lumar. We are talking about Bears and Wolves, games of honor, games of Houses. Throats slit and hearts lost.

"Yes," I say, the same edged look on my face. "I do."

"He already left to deal with something relating to that." I say, a quiet unease tensing my shoulders.

Tessa lets out a frustrated snort. She shoves a plate at me, filled with triangle shaped handheld pastries. A jumble of berries sits on the side. "Well forget it, he won't be in his rooms anyways. Take this with you then on your way. Hope you like pie."

CHAPTER 43

Only fools don't like pie. Lukas takes most of the plate in his hands, scarfing down his own personal pastry. I'm holding the warm, handheld crust of another and huffing air around the hot innards to try not to burn every bit of skin in my mouth. A nearby portrait eyes me with a stuffy look, her hawkish nose and eyebrows are raised disdainfully. If I could hear her, I'm sure there would be an audible sniff. I swallow the pie in just a few bites, scalding heat be damned.

Jessa possesses a similar steeliness to her spine that Daria does, though Daria has a kind consideration for others, whereas Jessa doesn't seem to give a shit. "I brought you your...lady's maid." Jessa says the words like she ate something bitter.

Unease fists itself into me, bullying its way into each pore and burrowing through all my nerves. It's amazing they let Daria in this far, amazing that she hasn't been killed for trespassing into our enemies' precious Wolf Hall. I slow my breathing. *Stop panicking, Briar,* I scold myself. Words of forced calm don't mean much, though, when your mind swirls with every disastrous outcome. Our party is quiet after Lukas finally hurries off with excuses to meet with Killian. Probably because our walk feels more like a dirge.

"Thank you, I don't know what I'd do without her," I reply sincerely.

"I guess you'll need to learn quickly. I'll show you to your room."

* * *

As promised, the manor is large enough that Killian and I won't need to encounter each other much except for his mandatory…training. Whatever that means. A clammy wetness collects along my armpits and forehead. Paranoia grips my neck, like an ill-spirit claws at the nape and squeezes and squeezes *and squeezes*. My throat ticks a dry convulsion as I try to gulp down the fear. I don't remember the last time I drank water.

Sickness washes through my belly. Valor and Barro, where were they? What happened?

The woods aren't something for even the bravest of soldiers to venture into. Still, we were with reluctant allies—something the Shadow Wood might have valued. A common goal between people that hate each other? That's something the gods would love. The opportunities for tension and betrayal, it would make a valuable show for them. And all of the tale set in the Shadow Wood—a pit of despair and evil wasteland. It was the perfect set piece for the divine to watch yet another mortal story play out. For them to put down more pieces and hope we'd pick up their favorites, and fulfill the fate the gods give to us.

It makes me wonder if I were to bleed out in its center, if the forest would give me back my friends. But it's a fruitless hope, an empty gesture, because I can't do it. Not with so much more than their lives on the line. Shame guts me, souring my insides.

I don't want to believe that the Shadow Wood swallowed my friends whole, but I can't help but close my eyes for a moment and inhale a ragged breath that fills my lungs with grief.

I can't help but think they're dead.

Fuck the gods. And fuck this place.

Daria walks to my left, Jessa ahead of us. I can feel the scowl Jessa has on her face, even from behind her. I wonder if Daria does too, because her hand often drifts to a weapon that isn't at her hip. It was probably confiscated by the party we arrived with. No one took mine. The rushed entry and urgency robbed the Wolves of a chance to make sure I didn't have anything to gut them. Either that or they don't really view me as a threat.

Which is also likely.

I frown. It's hard to feel like others see you as soft when you're the sort that envisions killing people that wrong you and those you care for. I'm not as poor with a blade as Killian made me out to be, but I'm hardly the soldier Daria or any of my other friends are.

Were.

Fuck.

I bite back the tears that clog my throat, shoving them deep down. It's too dangerous to cry.

My boot catches on the lip of something and I stumble. I catch my balance. Daria jerks toward me, as if to catch me, but then she falters too. Her shoulder jams into me, into the tender place the wound used to be. I hiss in pain.

"Ah, what–?"

Jessa tosses a look over her shoulder. "The house doesn't seem to like you. Careful. None of us take too kindly to outsiders. Here's your room. I'll leave you here to say goodbye, then your friend must leave the grounds."

* * *

It's magnificent.

The click of the door snicks closed behind us. Daria and I stand there in silence, taking in the high vaulted ceiling. The walls are light blue and above, a gilded ceiling casts everything with a subtle, yellowed hue. The floors sport a plush carpet, thick and light gray. The sort of thing that makes aching feet give a sigh of relief after a long day. A tall bookcase stretches from base to ceiling. It has only one book on it. *The Girl Gets the Villain*. The tome from back in my room at Gray Hall. Killian must have brought it and had it delivered here. For a moment, I can't help but think back to us, bantering back and forth in my room back home.

When my life was normal. When I understood what would happen next. A sharp splinter of alloyed anger and anguish pierces me from every direction. I run a hand through my hair. If it weren't already white, I'd say the stress of the last few days would have made it so. Daria shoots me a questioning look, but I ignore it, looking around the room.

A still life of a carrying candle, with a base of old brass, flickers with low light in a thick, brassy frame. The base where the light pink candlestick drips its warm wax is intricately designed. A scene of a fox and a moon and a field of flowers is shallowly painted. The oil paint brims with life, as if it's a real flame that won't ever go out. I swallow the swell of relief that thickens my throat. I hate the dark. I wonder if the little movements from the candle's light will stay when the date sputters into night.

"What am I going to do?" The words come out of my mouth by accident.

Daria sighs and moves over to the bed. She pats the space next to her.

"We need to find out where Valor and Barro are," she finally says. "And we have to kill the duke. So that's what we'll do." I jerk my head, looking at her. She lets out a low laugh. "Don't look so surprised. We can't go home until we kill him. We'd never never be forgiven for giving up on an opportunity like this."

I open my mouth, close it, open. "I have to do it," I finally croak.

Daria's eyebrows shoot up to her hairline. "Really?" she asks. Daria says nothing else, most likely because she's trying to be tactful. If any of us were to be the one selected to kill the duke, it would make more sense for it to be a soldier.

"Yes, it has to be me." But there's no rule that someone can't help me. Like a friend. "I need to deal the final blow. And..." I swallow. The rules here are clear. "You won't be able to stay much longer."

Daria's eyes narrow. "Alright, Duchess."

I grimace. "Yuck. Briar, please. We're far past titles."

She shrugs, a sly smile on her face. "Alright, then...Briar. Are you going to seduce him, then? That won't be so bad. I saw how big that wolf boy was." The look shifts to an outright grin. How she goes from surprise to easy belief is beyond me, but it warms something in my chest.

"Daria!" I lightly punch her shoulder, feigning outrage. We dissolve into a fit of giggles. "Yeah, he did get kind of large. As a wolf."

We snicker for another moment and we both lay backwards onto the bed. The swirl of gold above reminds me a little of the king's colors, which is odd. But even dukes can like gold, even if that's one of the favorite colors of his mortal enemy.

"Get to know the staff here. There doesn't seem to be that many." Daria's brow pinches. "I'll look through the wood for them."

Them. Valor and Barro.

"Are you sure? The wood...it's not safe."

She shakes her head. "I'll be clever about it. You've been injured. Rest for today. Even if..." She swallows, her eyes going shimmery. Daria blinks, shaking her head as if discarding the emotion. "Even if we can't do anything for Valor and Barro...you have to do what you came here for. "

"Why did you come all this way just to have to turn back, Daria?" I ask. A sick feeling of guilt and grief grips me. "You didn't need to come."

"Of course I did...Briar." Her lip tips at one edge, a lopsided smile as brief as the tears she hid. "We've been friends. Even if we didn't quite realize it until now and...what's more, the Wolves have cost me more than–" She cuts herself off, jaw ticking. "I'm happy to help you end them, is all I mean. I have to go now, but I'll find you when your marriage is ending. I'll be there for you. And I'm happy to kill whoever you need me to. What else are friends for?"

CHAPTER 44

*C*leverness begins with magic. A tenacious, smart girl can make a lot of things happen, if she reads the right tales and takes the correct path. And sometimes that road she must tread is the one that everyone tells her not to go down. I bite the inside of my lip, giving it a viscous suck with my face skewed in hard thought. It's difficult to think like a god and what kind of path I can mold to my will using their tools. For a time, I stare at the ceiling wishing my life would fall into place around me. I wonder what stories Daria uses to guide her. Aside from curse words, a sword, and a bloodthirsty smile.

The bed is soft beneath my back. I can't help but wonder if there will be a moment when I get to lay down my worries. That time never comes. Every fear I've ever had grows inside me like a rising tide and all I can do is choke back the tears of frustration, devastation, and burning need to kill something.

Daria left hours ago. Off to...not give up. She's strong and talented, with a streak of intelligence leagues wide. *What else are friends for?* I bite back a laugh. Of course Daria would say that a good friend will be there to kill whoever crosses me. An edge of grief splices through me. I'm alone and she's...gone. She's gone.

Hopefully the woods won't eat her whole.

But we all have our part to play. I roll over, curling my hand into a fist and settling it against my stomach. As if that will stop the ache there. I think back to all the tales I've read when, inevitably, the band of heroes splits off. Each with their own task. But it's not like we are fighting the Dark One here. This is what the gods will. We each must grow or die by the edge of a blade and our own wits.

Gods, who am I? A terrible woman who lets her friends go off to die? Who doesn't go to look for them? I bite the inside of my lip hard until it bleeds. The tang of iron coats my tongue. Papa is the only one that matters, though, at the end of this. More than just my love of him, but the fate of the Bears lives in his veins. I am not going to be a good enough substitute for them. Not now, not yet.

Probably not ever.

I sit up. The ache at my side is still there, but the injury is a pinkening scar that looks lighter by the moment. My healing is a physical manifestation of my connection to a monster. One with an unsettling gaze that seems to know me more than should even be possible.

A sick feeling claws up my esophagus.

I need to do *something*.

I swing my feet out of bed and go to the pile of my things in the corner. I can't help but wonder if anyone went through my bag or if Daria is the sole person who had them in her possession.

What if *Daria* went through them?

Dread unfurls low in my belly. What would she think if she found out I'm a witch? I want to hope that she'd accept me, no matter what, but the ugly voice in the back of my head tells me that's just wishful thinking.

I can't help but remember how my father acted—knowing he knew, but also his denial of the fact. His willful ignorance to admit what I am and how much that hurt.

I put the feeling away into the dark place that I keep all my hurts and pull out the spirit board. I ignore the other items that traveled with us through the woods. The fortune cards in the velvet bag, the portrait of Agatha that sits in leather wrapping, even the bit of paper tucked into all my things that I'll need to send off closer to the Equinox. Cool marble slips against my skin like ice as I clutch the board. I shiver, the press of the dead weighing on me. This manor might very well be haunted.

No, I can't think of that. Goosepimples spread, skimming my exposed forearms.

But I need to know if Valor and Barro are dead. Maybe then if they are…I could find Daria before she gets too far in. Send her back all the way home. But to what? To be judged as a betrayer? Would our people say she had consorted with the Wolves, that she had done the wrong thing in aiding me? Gods, I am not thinking clearly. Not at all. My hands shake.

I slow my breathing, trepidation tickling the little hairs along my entire body. The memory of tripping, of feeling like some*thing* had tripped me, when Jessa led me here shoves itself into my mind. I put the planchette onto the board.

The spirit board shifts, a small eek of grind marble on marble as if a heavy hand presses the planchette, shoulders over fist. But spirits don't have shoulders. Or fists. They shouldn't. Still, calling in the dead for help is rarely something recommended, but here I am again reaching into the afterlife for answers. Begging for a mother that never answers, always getting static unless another ghost hears. An ache of a motherless daughter slinging out her fear into the world, howling for someone to finally comfort her.

The hairs along the nape of my neck rise.

It's not my mother. Her silence is a fact.

Who? I spell out.

No spirit is compelled to tell the truth. And I wouldn't know if they were lying to begin with. What kind of power can work on the dead, to compel them to never lie?

The planchette doesn't move. Then it streaks across the board so rapidly I can barely catch the letters beneath it.

F-R-I-E-N-D.

A friend? Of mine? I suck the inside of my cheek. Valor or Barro?

N-O. The planchette continues to shift. Letter to letter, spelling out in quick succession. *A-L-I-V-E.*

For now.

Papa?

It spells out the same word once more, but says nothing else. I stop, hand hovering halfway over the board. I move to ask another question, but the planchette begins again. It scuffs in rapid movement.

D-U-K-E. The marble piece pauses. Then it bursts into another string of movements. *S-T-U-D-Y.*

Killian's office. *What is in there?* I use the marble piece to ask.

Y-O-U-R. P-A-S-T.

Nisha hisses. My teeth chatter as the room fills with the feeling of frost forming. A burgeoning horror–like something is watching me presses everywhere on my flesh. I jerk to look behind me.

Nothing.

But the building ice doesn't stop.

The crevices of every corner of the chamber cracks with ice. Something yanks my hair. "OW!" My hand goes up, toward the roots. My eyes water. I turn, head snapping back. The pulling doesn't relent and I grunt, grabbing the hair near my head to halt the jerking sensation of something trying to yank the strands out.

A low hiss, like water tossed onto a fire, builds in my ears.

"FUCK!" I yell, as another ruthless pull threatens to tear my hair from my scalp.

Nisha pounces, swiping at nothing. A low thud drums through the room, as if she's hit something. A squeal peels through the chamber.

The chill breaks in half, splintering and singing in pain. I grind my teeth. Nisha howls and a rake of red appears at her shoulder. I pound forward, knocking into whatever is there.

Then the cold disappears.

I watch the curl of my breath fade, breathing hard. Nisha's tail shifts in agitation. She doesn't say anything, except to move into a ball and lick at her shoulder.

I'm not afraid of spirits. Some don't want to refer to anything magical that isn't something that the priests of the Seven deem holy.

I'm a witch, so that doesn't bother me. I pull my hand up to my hair, wincing a little. Still, it doesn't mean I always like magic. Or whatever that was.

The frost. The cold. Wolf Hall is fucking haunted.

* * *

RED DAYLIGHT PEELS AWAY, leaving dim light and nothing but the strange portrait in my room featuring a low-burning candle. Relief swamps me. It would have been humiliating to admit my fear of the dark to Killian, to anyone here. Why I am so afraid, I could never parse out. My memories don't tell me shit, most of the time. Nothing terrible had truly happened to me, not as far as I know, but it didn't stop a strange taste of blood at the back of my throat, as if my body holds the answer to a question I'd long asked. And whatever that answer is, it isn't something I would like.

Part of me is afraid that whatever attacked me will come back. I rub my head again. But it's been hours and nothing has come back. Yet.

My throat stings. Dryness, like sandpaper, coarsely grinds against each breath. I sit up in bed. The pillows around me feel like a tender hug. I yawn. Nisha grumbles in the back of my mind, reminding me to be quiet and that the ghosts will die on her watch.

I snort.

[Not a joke.] She says, our connection feeling sleepy. I quirk a smile in the dark, but a tug of fear loops around my lungs. Soon, I'll need to figure out my angle on this. Seduction seems like an...option. A bizarre sensation floods my lower belly, a combination of terror, desire, and hope. But the need for water grips me harder than any confusion I need to parse out. Something to deal with tomorrow.

I slip out of bed. As I do, my eyes alight on the pile of things I came with. Not much. I'll need more things for day to day wear, but the wife of a duke will easily be able to get such items. I lean down, brushing a hand over the leather wrapped portrait and undo the bindings that hold Agatha. She blinks open her eyes sleepily. I watch them focus on me, her face slipping from joy to a scowl and back to something in between. She mouths something I don't understand. I shrug at her. "Sorry," I mumble. "I forgot. You can go look around now, though, if you'd like."

She scowls again, turning away from me. I'm not sure if she's going back to sleep or simply pissed. Probably both. I don't blame her. I didn't mean to forget she was there. And she'd spent all that time, wrapped in the dark. I push a hand through my hair, wincing a little as it hits a sensitive spot on my scalp from my altercation with the ghost. Or whatever that was.

Water, though. My throat is unbearable.

I strap on the grimsbane blade to my thigh, just in case. My feet pad over the floors as I make it to the door. Daria, gone. Barro and Valor, gone. Just Nisha and me. And at the end of it all, I'm the one that needs to kill my husband for any of this to have been worth it at all.

I shuffle out the door, thoughts submerged in turmoil and a heady feeling like shame and thick self-loathing coating my insides. The kitchens would have water. I make my way down the hallway, dim light from passing windows guiding my way. I clutch my arms around myself.

Down a flight of stairs. Round a bend.

That's when I see him.

Killian stands there. Back from the border. Nothing but his trousers, which sling low across his hips. That strange cast to his eyes glints in the shard of moonlight that splinters through the wide rose window. Shadows pull in turgid coils along the walls, whipping and snapping the way a storm intent on capsizing a ship would. A finger of darkness trails across my collarbone. I freeze. My breath stalls in my chest. The little shadow bracelet hasn't left me since our first meeting. Now, it tenses against my skin.

My flesh pimples as a fresh chill ices through the air. The cusp of summer dies in this room, leaving only autumn's rattling breath. Fear snakes through my body, winding and trickling into every flinch and involuntary movement.

His eyes.

I need a light, beyond the tiny fragment twinkling through the high up window. Darkness is the unknown. Darkness is agony. Whatever memories my mind doesn't want me to remember lay there and I can't force myself through the pain of shuffling through the past. Not yet. Not now. And never without a glow to guide my way.

My hand itches. My power is limited, untrained. Perhaps if I'd had a coven the way my mother's grimoire mentioned to guide me through my powers, I'd have come into my own. But all I do is shed a bit of light on the darkness, whether it's to discern the truth in a vat of lies or to create a burst of luminescence to show what the shadows hide.

A strange crackle patters through the room—like someone stomping through a field of dead leaves. The smells of the dying season tickle the air. A curl of cinnamon and smoke and heat wafts under my nose. I watch Killian, unblinking.

He stares back at me. Caught between something—as if he can't figure out if he wants to kill me tonight. My hand drifts to my thigh, where the grimsbane blade beats like a second heart. My father's voice rings in my mind.

Killian steps toward me. He's close. So, so close that when he licks his lower lip, I can practically taste the sweetness from his breath on my own tongue.

He watches me, head cocked to the side. The posture reminds me of a dog—a wolf—that watches something that might leap on its prey and rip it apart. A slow smile spreads across his mouth. A fang flashes. The scent of dead wet leaves on a deep night curls beneath the smells of a dark fall.

"The gods are kind," he growls. "Amara does favor the Wolves."

"Why? Because her lover is your ancestor?" My voice rasps.

"Yes. And we keep our promises, wife."

His fang slips against my throat. Pinches. Warm blood slicks from the wound. I squeeze my eyes shut, my hand slips up to the side of his neck. A reciprocal wound on his skin leaks against my palm. My ring heats.

I hold my breath.

"You didn't bring a light," he whispers. "The one I keep is back in my room."

My throat works. His room. I imagine a large bed, silken sheets spilling like a shining liquid off the sides and mussed from...something. Warmth heats my cheeks. "I forget to bring a light often,." I say, wondering if he knows more about me than he should.

The lie about the light pinches me from the inside and a small fever fires in my blood. I don't forget to bring it at all. Usually, there's a candle, lantern, an arcane orb, or something in the halls. That, or I expect to be able to make my own light myself if I need it. My palm itches, as if it wants to cast a spell now.

"Of course you forgot." His voice is bitter, even hateful.

Something strokes my hair. Tangling tendrils and teasing each strand like a lover might. Killian, one of his shadows, perhaps a ghost? It's hard to say.

Darkness swirls deep in his gaze. Silver. Then the black deep again. The normal color of his irises is gone for a long moment and what looks back with his eyes isn't him. I can't see the soul that is Killian in there at all.

"Go," he rasps. His eyes flick silver. "Go before I kill you."

"You won't kill me," I challenge him, stepping closer. The message from the mysterious spirit dips into my mind. Ripples through me like a rock disturbing a once-smooth pool and changing everything it touches. My past is in his study. An answer. I need his trust.

That's not what you're here for, an inner voice says. Which is true. More than his trust, I need his life. I may not be as adept with a blade, but there are some other tools I can use. If I want to.

You want to, something sly inside my mind says.

"Won't I?" His head dips. The heat of his breath hums in my ear. Tightness convulses in my throat. If it was dry before, now it's more like land that hasn't seen rainfall in three generations."I'm a killer. A monster, wicked witch. Don't you know not to walk around in the dark alone? *Something terrible could get you.*" The words hiss against the cuff of my ear. They fold into me, slipping against some primal fear. And some deep-seated hot feeling I don't want to look at.

I forget how to speak.

His tongue flicks against the blood at my neck. A wave of desire unfurls inside of me.

"Are you a vampyr, then?" I choke out.

"No, darling wife, you married a Wolf, but you bound yourself to something so much worse."

Dread leaks through me, slipping down my ribcage into my core. I'm going to die. There's nothing else to it. How did I ever think this was wise? I should have left when he told me to.

Shut up, you're not a helpless girl. I tell myself. *You're a woman. Stab him. Then* run. *Or do something else about it.*

The voice is wise, but there's so many questions I do have answers to. When I'm hurt, so apparently is he, but is the reverse true? That I haven't yet seen evidence of. Still, perhaps I could stab him and drag myself to my room. The perks of being connected to a monster is the rapid ability to heal from impossible injuries. The thought of fleeing from him, though…part of me wonders if he truly is like a dog, that running will only make him chase me. And worse, he'll enjoy it. And this darkness inside of me wonders if being pushed to the edge is something I want—that even more awful than him enjoying hunting his prey, if I'll enjoy getting caught by him.

Perhaps.

I turn my head toward him and he pulls back. His eyes don't look like how I've come to know them, but I shove the unease down. I curl a hand up to the side of his head. If I'm to kill him, I need to get close. And perhaps, what I should do, is let myself transform from a reluctant wife into someone eager for his bed.

Something other than fear wiggles into my stomach.

Not all of it would be a lie.

Killian stills as I move my lips against the thin scruff of his beard. The stubble bites at the tender skin on my mouth and I trail my tongue down his neck, up to his earlobe. He lets out a groan.

A hand comes up to the side of my breast, caressing me.

"Gods, I've waited to touch you," his voice smokes into the dark. "All I've done is taste your blood. But I want to taste so much more than that."

Desire claws through me. The apex of my thighs grows wet. Killian shoves me against the wall. As my spine hits it, a portrait clatters down. The people portrayed in it—a man and woman decked out in fine jewels and illustrious lace—lurch in silence at being jostled from their perch. They watch us and I can't help the moan that growls up from my chest.

Gods.

"You like that, then, wicked witch?" Killian gasps into my ear. His hand moves down, cupping my sensitive nub beneath my nightgown. "And no underwear, either?" He leans in. "You really are a wicked girl."

He eases the shoulder of my gown down, exposing my breast. The light is dim, but alights on the curve of it. His mouth is on me in an instant, tongue lipping at my nipple. A burst of white sparks the edges of my vision and my head snaps back. A laugh rumbles up from his chest.

"You like that then?"

I gasp, nodding.

"Then what do you say?"

"More," I rasp. The world is nothing but the two of us. I don't remember needing water, when my thirst is slaked like this. I don't remember needing to kill him, not when his hands make me feel so *alive.*

He blows on the spot he just licked, cooling my flesh. My nipple puckers, taught and high. My center squeezes.

"MORE," I order. My hand goes down, attempting to touch my clit. His hand grabs mine, squeezing. Forcing me to look him in the eye. I don't know who—or what—is looking back at me in this moment. I have a sense that Killian is there, but so is something else. Something dark. And something that wants me to submit, but also something that wants me dead.

"More, what, wicked witch?" This time, his voice is dangerous.

"Please," I finally say.

Killian growls this time, in satisfaction.

His fingers swirl at my clit again, another slides into me. And another. He pumps his hand, knuckle deep as he pays homage to the bundle of nerves. The pair in the portrait watch us—watch me—unable to look away. The man in the portrait has the woman's gown down, just like mine is, and he swirls her nipple as he watches me. Her mouth gapes open and her head leans against his shoulder. I make eye contact with the man there, just for a moment, and he smiles.

A feeling builds inside of me, rippling up from deep within.

Killian abruptly halts, fingers slipping out of me. I gasp. Anger ripples through me.

"Don't stop," I say. It's supposed to be a command, but it sounds more like begging. Frustration rattles my teeth until I clench them.

I watch him slowly, without breaking eye contact, dip his finger still slick with me into his mouth.

"How does such a bad girl like you taste so sweet?" he husks.

"It's a lie I don't get in trouble for," I reply truthfully. I pull at him. "Please," I say again for the second time this night. I hate myself a little for it. *But this will help you kill him later*, I tell myself. Be seduced and seduce in return.

I'm not sure these are words I'd speak out loud for fear of what might happen. How much truth lives between us, two people that should have never met that have been forced into a strange bargain? I bleed, he bleeds. I wonder if the same is true of the reverse. How closely connected are we? Does he feel everything I do? My ring is hot against my finger, burning with our shared desire.

Killian's hand leaves a hot wake of sensation as the pads of his fingers rake down my thighs. He shoves my nightgown up. The wall on my back is cool, which is welcome. Heat flares through me. A growl of frustration rips from his throat as my nightgown alights on his head. He pulls back.

"I want to see you come on my tongue."

All I can do is nod.

The shadows around us surge. A tendril rips from the wall, slicing toward us. I flinch. It scrapes up the front of my dress, cutting through the front as if it's a blade. The fabric parts behind it, exposing my thighs, my stomach, and my breasts to Killian.

He stares at me for a moment. "It makes me wonder what a monster like me has done to deserve such a gift."

And then his mouth is on me. I thread my fingers through his hair. My gaze alights to the portrait with the pair watching us. The man there is doing exactly what Killian is. The woman's dress lays wide open, exposing her breasts. A thick hand of his massages the nipple. Her unfocused gaze meets mine and she smiles. She blows me a kiss.

"Look at me, wife, not them. I get to be the one that you watch when you come this time."

I meet his gaze. Killian's tongue flicks out. My clit puckers beneath his attention. He strokes me, swirling its tongue and he sucks. My head snaps back, cracking into the wall. I don't even feel it. His hand clenches against my hip. Another wave rolls through me. Each breath will be my last, glorious one. He moans against me. My vision goes dark at the edges and part of me wonders if this is part of his shadow magic. To make the world go dark for me and for me to not be afraid of it.

I crest another wave of desire, each stroke of his tongue bringing me higher and higher. I grab his hand, settling it against my breast and I ride the final wave. "Killian," I choke out.

I look down. At that moment, the gaze I meet isn't what I expect. His eyes flicker out of the warm brown, replacing it with the black-eyed and molten metal gaze looking out from where my husband's soul should be. One for each eye.

I shiver, a shudder running through me. My breath still comes hard and fast. I pull at the edges of my ruined nightgown, sliding a little away. Killian's departing warmth leaves me cold.

"Who are you?" I ask.

A pause.

"That was delicious to watch." Another voice says with Killian's mouth. "We all enjoyed it."

Desire quickly drains away, leaving nothing but fear.

"*What* are you?"

"Something dangerous. And something that hates you. But you taste delicious. Your cunt and your blood." The eyes that look back at me are dark and pitiless, and nothing like Killian, even though whatever *this* is wears his face.

I think the eyes looking back at me are from a creature that really will hurt me. Bedamned of the consequences.

My body chokes into a shuddering stillness, convulsing only in the little shakes of fear. And maybe, just maybe, a little of the leftover desire as I open my eyes and watch Killian's eyes bloom black as he licks the bead of blood off his bottom lip. His eyes shift again, and this time I know it is my husband speaking. "I will close my eyes, but you need to run. If I watch you flee from me..." His face shudders. His eyes squeeze shut, hiding the darkness in them. *"GO."*

He shoves me away. I stumble backwards. Towards the room filled with the phantoms of my past and ghosts that hate me. It's either ill spirits or demons tonight. And I have to pick.

I run.

I run, run.

My breath comes in short, desperate bursts. I stumble. Nisha is sleeping, but my fear wakes her and her cry rattle through my mind.

Things pull at me, trying to take me down to the ground. The shadows along the wall slices out like a rolling fog over water. A dull roar groans from behind me and there's a crack of shifting bone.

A howl cries down the hallway.

Killian is becoming his Wolf self.

My breath comes fast now and I sprint down the hall. Up the set of stairs. The door to my room sits up ahead. My nightgown twists against my legs. I stumble, falling.

My knees come down hard on the ground. Bone cracks into stone with brutal force. I hiss, coming down hard onto the flats of my palms. The sting of impact zaps up through my wrists to my elbows. A scrape burns overtop a blistering bruise. I try to get up but my knee twists.

"Fuck!"

Fear. Rage. Confusion. The feelings ripple down my center,

tearing into my ribs and eating at my stomach. Who is this man to think he can touch me, to seduce me, then to push me away? Husband, enemy, villain? Darkness itself? I curl my hands into fists. Asshole. Definitely.

The pound of feet follows me. I ignore the pain.

Tossing myself forward, I open the door and slam it shut behind me. A few words follow me, leaking in through the little gap between the wooden frame and the floor.

"Next time, bring a light. It's the only way to fight the dark."

I sit with my back against the door, breathing hard. The ache of thirst intensifies, but there's no way I can leave. Not tonight. Not with my...husband out there.

There are so many questions. What spirit deigned to speak with me? What is in the study that the ghost wants me to find? Is this manor haunted by crowds of deceased? Do the evil dead slip into Killian's veins, is that the stranger I see looking back at me when his eyes shift? My heart races and my breath rips through my lungs in quick bursts. If the *thing* is some ill spirit, how am I to survive this? How do I seduce him, be vulnerable with him, when any moment my exposed throat could be slit? The only comfort is that if he slits my throat, he slits his own.

But those questions all feed into one other query, the thing that spills into my heart and fills it with iron resolve. *How do I kill my husband?*

I have to find out what he cares for, as my father said. That's what will ultimately end his life, with the help of a blade formed of myths made of death and godblood. And, Grims, isn't that always so? There's always more than one way to stab someone through the heart.

In less than a year and a day, I'll be able to kill my husband without it hurting me. For now, it's hard to guess what a wound to him will do to my body. It's a risk I can't take, not with so much at stake. Papa, House Berrat, even Lumar itself tethers itself to the noose that is this marriage.

CHAPTER 45

The next day dawns, and it's like nothing happened. The next time I see Killian, it's nearly a week later and he looks at me like he didn't make me come apart on his mouth and then try to kill me afterwards.

More clothes appear, including a brand new nightgown, in my room without a word, though. A silent acknowledgement of what happened that makes my cheeks redden.

I spend the days stalking the hallways and the immediate grounds, waiting for a ghost to attempt to attack me. Nisha rarely leaves my side. Something seems to bother her, by the near-constant gnashing of her nail and raised hairs between her shoulders, but she refuses to address it.

The immediate area around Wolf Hall begins to fade into fall. Green leaves redden with the growing chill. Whenever I approach the gates—even to see where Killian and I first encountered one another—a guard sends me back. The message is clear.

I'm here until our marriage is over.

I find the infirmary, where Asha putters around the workroom. There's one cot in the corner of the room that houses Remmy. He gives me a weak smile.

"Are you...okay?" I ask stupidly.

He shrugs. "Yeah, hardly a great impression I've made on my new duchess, though." Remmy quirks a pained smile. "I swear, I'm stronger than I look."

If he's a Wolf, of that I have no doubt.

"The Curse generally keeps us healthy and hale," he says with a twist of his mouth. "But iron infused with a bit of the divine...that will do it. Takes a bit to recover afterwards."

"Grimsbane?" I ask.

He shakes his head. "No, grimsbane is...well, no one knows exactly what that that is. A mixture of reality and un-reality. Of tales and today. There's godsblood involved, still, but also fragments of desires and fiction and every feeling. It's hard to describe and everyone has a different story about it." The blade feels hot on my thigh as Remmy continues to speak. "Doesn't matter. It can kill anything, if you stab the right thing through the heart."

"What do you mean?" I ask, half knowing what Remmy is going to say next.

"Ah, you know, find what someone cares most for–" He stops, eyes narrowing. "Well, so the stories say. Duchess." He pauses, changing the subject. "The Cursed are hard to kill, though, so let's hope that whatever stabbed me doesn't have the final say."

"How did the Wolves become...this?" I ask. I want to cover my mouth the moment the words leave my lips. They sound rude. A prickling feeling pinkens my cheeks.

"Don't worry," Remmy says, sweetness eeking through a sad smile. "We were born this way. A witch or sorceress cursed this House. Every one in three children is born this way for the first thirteen years since the Duke was born." Remmy swallows. "He blames himself, of course, but he didn't cause this. No one...no one knows why she did it. But it happened so long ago, and the duchess died the day the curse fell over the House. She was gone after that, just gone. People thought–" He cuts himself off. "It isn't my place to say. Asha was there, of course, but she doesn't speak of it. No one really does. But we haven't had a new Cursed in so long. Most of us are pretty grown.

Lots of us conscripted for the Selvan front. The king," Remmy practically spits the word, "loves to bring us there. And take our loved ones and the forest from us for the war effort."

Asha steps back into the room, a thunderous look across her brow. "That's enough, Remmy."

Confusion twists inside me. I've spent my life hating those that owe their fealty to House Galibran and those that govern in. And yet, they live their lives with their own desires and destinies to fight for. I choke down the protest that I want to spit out, because it's hard to argue with the fact that everyone has someone they love that they will do everything to protect. Even if it means doing terrible things to those that get in their way.

* * *

KILLIAN TAKES ME TO A SMALL, private courtyard that leads out from his room the next day. "We'll meet here every day. If I'm not here, Lukas or Jessa will be. Maybe Remmy, if he recovers." There's an aching pause between the end of this sentence and the next. "You have to improve. If anyone is somehow able to make it beyond the trees, or you're taken, you're a risk," he says, a tight swallow undulating his throat. We don't speak of the incident in the hallway. Not how he felt on me, not what happened after. My body remembers, though, by the tightness in my core when I look at him.

"Improve?" I raise an eyebrow, ignoring the flush on my flesh. "I think you're the one with some personal renovations to attend to, Killian."

"My dearest, wicked witch." His lips smirk at my scowl. He knows I don't like it. Part of me wishes I'd never said anything to him at all. Killian is a predator, sniffing out weakness and biting a vulnerable spot. "I had no idea you were watching me so closely."

"Of course," I snap. "Who doesn't watch a monster stalking toward them?"

He closes the distance between us in a few quick strides. "Some," he whispers, "don't watch. They run." His breath stirs the hair by my ear. "How interesting you choose to stay."

"I know my duty," I reply stiffly. My skin feels hot, too tight. The sweetness of his breath, mint and sugar and spice, skirts the edge of my ear. I shiver.

"Then in the interest of performing your duties," he pauses. "I need you."

I need you.

He moves and I'm greeted only by empty air and the stumbling feeling of free-falling now that the thing that keeps me solid has left. What a silly, fanciful thought. My stomach twists as I right myself and find my footing. *I need you.* The words echo in my ears. I'm so distracted by my own thoughts that I flinch at the clang of metal at my feet.

A dagger.

Another clang. A sword.

Killian is at the edge of the wall, tossing very sharp objects at my feet.

"What are you doing?"

"You're my greatest weakness," he says it carelessly over his shoulder. "You bleed, I bleed." His voice now twists to a sneer. "This means you need to learn to defend yourself."

"I know how."

"Not well enough. Your duties are now to rise with the Wolves, train with us, and then we'll see if you can become not an opening by my ribs. Come here tomorrow."

"What is it to a man that cannot be killed?"

He gives a brutal laugh. "Oh, wicked witch, anything can be killed."

* * *

EACH DAY RATTLES by with the force of a Frost Giant trying to shake the stars from the sky. I grit my teeth. The Red Season ends, as it always must, and blood flows freely at the border now. Whispers of the contentious line between Houses Berrat and Galibran creak through to my ears, even though no one speaks to me.

Killian is secretive. So is everyone else. I check the cards, the spirit board. Whispers tickle my exposed neck. The hairs rise, as if something is behind me. A curl of warning explodes from Nisha's throat and I turn, whipping out the blade holstered at my thigh.

Nothing.

A titter sounds somewhere in the room.

But nothing happens. Nothing at all. Unease fills my belly. There's no safety for me here. I don't feel like I've ever really been safe at all.

*　*　*

WOLF HALL truly does feel like Killian and I stalk through our separate halves until we met to train. My body aches, the semi-frequent practice with Daria, Valor, and Barro are nothing compared to this. Every morning, I wake before dawn. Every morning, I'm guided by a shadowed *thing* to Killian's rooms. Usually he isn't there.

Today, though, he is. And he works me hard. He knocks me to the ground.

Once.

Twice.

Thrice.

My arms burn with effort. Swords, ax, every kind of weapon has clattered out of my hand.

My back aches with the hardness of stone on one side of me and the feeling of my husband against my breasts.

Killian's body presses against mine. "You let your guard down," he whispers, breath skirting the shell of my ear. The hot planes of his chest friction against my tunic and my nipples tighten beneath my undergarments. Heat slicks my core. Every nerve points to the grind of my hips against his.

His eyes darken. That otherworldly look lurks at the corners of his gaze and a smile lifts the corner of my mouth.

My dagger points into his stomach. "Hardly," I reply just as quiet, letting the tip of the blade press into his body.

He laughs. The vibrations roll up his body, shivering into mine and he lifts himself off of me. "If that were a real fight, you'd be dead."

"So would you."

"Doubt it, witch. Shall we try to kill each other then?" His eyes flicker in that moment, as if the ill creature inside of him wakes up.

Abruptly, he turns, a blade slices the air as it leaves his palm, straight at my face. I duck, swirling to the side. As I do, he lunges. Catching me and knocking me into the wall. My spine thuds against it and with the force, pain and lust rake their claws down my body.

"Enemies can still have...benefits," he husks at me. His knee nudges between my legs and I part them. The press of his thigh stokes a fire against my core. One of his hands grasp my two smaller ones, pinning me at the wrists.

A shadow from beneath us wisps out, like smoke. It curls against the side of my cheek, hooking the corner of my mouth. Tender and cool, it moves around my mouth, as if it's a finger exploring. I let it, shivering.

Killian dips his head down, inches from my lips. I hook a leg around him, pressing myself to the hardness beneath his trousers.

"What kind of benefits do you mean?" I ask innocently and smile.

His eyes watch my lips, tongue licking his own mouth.

"Uh...Duke?" calls a voice. Killian curses. He jerks, levering himself off of me. The other man holds up his hands, as if to defend himself. "Baron Verrikov is waiting to discuss tithes."

There's always an appointment, always a situation at the border. Frustration curdles in my core, rattling through the muscles in my forearms as I clench my fists.

I'm not sure I want my husband to go.

When Killian departs, leaving me alone in the courtyard, dying orange leaves fall around me. It's then that I realize I'm cold.

I need to learn his weaknesses. That's all.

"Fuck!" I curse, slinging an arm over my forehead. How am I supposed to learn anything about him when there's so little time I spend with him? How do I get close enough to his heart to stab it?

CHAPTER 46

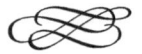

The days slip by like molasses, pooling in slow speed toward an inevitable end. Nisha stalks the castle with me as my own personal shadow. That, at least, hasn't changed. I learn the grounds. The people. But there seems to be few to speak with. A cook. A maid. A butler. One of everything. But just one.

Not nearly enough personnel to run a place of this size.

Everything about the Wolves is a knot of mystery.

The Equinox is coming. Then it will be time to call in the king. I bite the inside of my mouth. There is still so much to understand and not enough allies to tell me what is happening. Or what *has* happened.

Is my father okay? A bargain like this, King Thaddeus has to be upholding his oath? I can't help but think of the line of fate that has tethered me to this path. There have to be consequences for promises broken. I shiver. Though in words, I have not betrayed my marriage oaths yet, the spirit of the agreement is broken. There will be events yet to deal with for me. Papa's face dances before my mind. The new lines, the hollow cheeks, the frail way he moves—all of it in such a short timespan since the disease manifested.

I can't think of it. I can't think about Papa too much, or the fragility of my heart will undo me. Even with the gaps in my memories, all of the good one's I have are with him. Or Nisha. He's the only one who ever spared affection for me, aside from the little moments from Ursula. My mother was well despised and I inherited every vile look and barbed compliment that would have been given to her if the Wolves had not found her in the woods and murdered her.

I shut my eyes.

There is so much retribution to deliver to them. Even if I understand them a little more now, they are owed nothing but vengeance. "Amara will understand," I murmur to myself. Love sits so close to hate. Any warmth I have towards these people will need to be put aside when the time comes to slaughter their Duke—and anyone who gets in my way.

I can't help, though, but wonder at what arcane workings the Witch King has managed to work on Papa, if my father has given up the Reezin in favor of a healing hanging on the edge of my blade, or what is happening back at Gray Hall in my absence. *Don't think about it*, I tell myself.

The slap of my feet echo through hallways, pattering against the stone floor like lonely rain. Despite the lack of staff, no dust crowds picture frames at the manor and elaborate spreads featuring various foods—from roasted duck to jelly cakes—arrive on time and are cooked to perfection.

Most of my days, I spend in my room, alone, except for the company of Nisha. Unless I'm training with Killian, Lukas, or Jessa, I'm in my chambers or furtively scoping the place. The memory of Killian's body against mine, him conquering me as my sword clatters to the ground, shoots a flush of scalding rage through my body. I shiver. The hot reminder of his mouth on my clit clings to my dreams. Every night I wake with the very shadows on the walls quivering and my wedding band hot like I'd left it in the sunlight for hours.

Killian and I don't speak of it, though, and my aim at seduction seems far off for the amount of time we spend together. When I try to find him, he isn't anywhere. And I can't bring myself to dare into the dark once more. Not yet.

Papa's face haunts me. His too-bright eyes dance in my mind, high with Reezin. *Stop,* I command myself. The intrusive vision of him slices into my mind day after day. It doesn't matter the ugliness he dealt me before I left. I love him, broken heart and all.

The summer has whittled away, moments twirling away from me like wood against a sharp knife. Days still flash hot, but by evening a brisk chill leaks through the wind. A false fall. A fool's time.

My chest feels cracked inside, a deep grief burgeoning there as if someone has already died. It promises to be a cold, hard winter. My bones whisper it to me. And still, I've no idea what I'm to do.

What am I even doing here?

An ache of loneliness unfurls like a poisonous bud inside my heart. I've hardly been here for any time at all. I should be gaining Killian's trust, but instead, all I've done is foster a mutual resentment. And lust. He *wants* me to try to kill him. I see it in his eyes when we train. There's a mockery there that makes me grind my teeth, and a desire that makes my legs clench together.

All letters I've written to Papa return unopened. Not because he hates me—though that may still be true—but because the Wolves do.

Scrawlings I address to anyone—father, to Ursula, to Derrick, they wind up crumpled up at my door. I address some to Daria, but those I have little hope of being delivered to begin with. Perhaps the letters will be seen as proof she did not betray the Bears, that she didn't come with me. The spirit board tells me little, except an oft meandering planchette spouting vague warnings of the carnivorous forest.

Then one day, I find it.

A crumpled up letter in my chamberpot. Amidst the piss there, lies a letter addressed to my father, begging him to love me. Telling him I'm alright. And never delivered.

Rage courses through me. The utter *disrespect.*

So much has been taken from me by the Wolves.

Then, to find words I poured out from my heart onto the page not only open and read, but tossed in a chamberpot, as if my feelings are nothing but shit. I know exactly who to blame.

"How *dare* he."

The killing edge rises up inside of me. Hot rivulets of rage ripple throughout my body. My forearms shiver, my fists clench. Fucking Killian. In my mind's eye, my hands encircle his stupid neck and squeeze, squeeze. I don't see why I can't try. It's not even like that's trying to kill him, really, since I know it won't work. If I'm fucking trapped and miserable, Grims, I'll make sure he is too.

I wipe a rough tear leaking out of my eye and grab the chamberpot with both hands.

The door slams behind me, a clap of thunder breaking a clear day. Startled servants—the few I see—jump away from me as I storm to the side of the castle I'm not allowed in. A nosy woman painted blue hops from portrait to portrait to follow me. Whispers follow me that become louder as I approach my destination.

"Does she—"

"—chamber pot?"

"Shit!"

"Lady—" Someone calls, but I ignore them. I hoist the chamberpot —a blue and white porcelain—on my hip. My hand grasps the doorknob to my husband's study and the door flies open with my rage.

Killian looks up casually, as if he isn't surprised at all. Rage brightens across my cheeks. My teeth clench painfully, snapping against each other.

"Killian, see here—"

"My lady," he says, cutting me off. "This is Lord Wesley and Lord Tyron." His eyes take in the chamber pot in my hand and an audacious smile crosses his mouth. His eyebrows quirk up to his hairline. "I believe that I forgot we were going to...look at the chamber pot design throughout the castle. She has an interest in things like that, you know," he stage-whispers conspiratorially. A flush heats my cheeks and I just know my ears have turned into the color of beets.

The two men stare at me, their faces blank with shock.

"Now, my lady, I can't very well tell these men that chamber pots are more important to me than the tax issue or the land dispute..." He looks at the men, one of them laughs. "But, I do believe, that as a newlywed, pleasing my wife ranks quite high in my priorities."

There's a slight pause as the men decide to handle this.

"Happy life, happy wife," one says before congenially getting up. My hand aches for a weapon. *Happy wife, give her a knife,* I think.

"We will continue this conversation, my lord? I understand newly-weds need…time together." He laughs and the other man joins in. I flick on the Sight. Tin coins rattle out of the man's mouth. The other has little coppers clink to the floor and vanish.

"Of course, Lord Wesley," Killian says.

They leave quickly.

Killian and I stare at each other over the chamberpot. My piss sits in it, alongside my letter.

"I'm afraid to ask—have I graduated from a bag of shit to a bowl of shit?" He looks significantly at the chamberpot.

Suddenly, I realize I've stormed through the castle holding a chamber pot and busted into Killian's office like a mad woman.

"Oh gods,." I say.

"You can sit," he invites, gesturing to the now vacated chairs. I plop down in one, a hand going to my face. I've made a fool of myself.

"Jokes aside," he says. He comes around, close enough to touch me. He leans against the edge of the desk, arms crossed over his muscled chest. His boot taps into my slipper. "What has happened?"

I wonder why he's not berating me first, for coming to his side of the castle.

That's when the door behind him opens. Killian turns, eyes narrowed. "Close the door," he says to nothing. The door snaps shut. But not before I catch a glimpse of what's behind it.

Two women peer from above an empty fireplace. One is tall and lean, and looks just like Killian in her elegance. Golden brown skin with deep eyes that look like they're made of whatever the universe is born from. Even from here, her mouth has the same smirk as Killian's, as if it might parse out a secret if you ask nicely enough.

The other woman—

Silver haired, rounded face and lush lips. Killian's mother only comes to her shoulder. The silver-haired woman's eyes seem to stare straight through the portrait, as if she can see through the paint, through the fog that settles around the Sea of Mist, straight to Otherland itself.

A ragged claw mark streaks down her face. The tear looks like rage.

My breath shudders to a stop. This can't be. Why would she be here?

Why, out of everywhere in the world, would the Wolves have a portrait of a woman they killed?

My mother.

CHAPTER 47

"What is it?" Killian looks at me with fire-bright eyes.

"Hmm?" I ask noncommittally, avoiding a direct lie. A nervous ache swells in my chest. There's an intentness to his gaze, one that reminds me of direct sunlight on metal. My ring feels the same beneath his eyes. All the rage, the bluster that I came in with drains away with the realization that not only was my mother killed by the Wolves long ago—somewhere in the lineage of this stupid territorial dispute–but that she *knew* them. And they knew her. Enough that there's a portrait of her ripped with rage hanging in one of the most important rooms in Wolf Hall.

The cascade of information hollows out my stomach.

I know nothing. I've never known anything. And every time I turn around, there is another secret to find and another monster waiting beneath my bed.

"What is wrong?" Killian asks. This time, he leans forward. A thumb presses to the corner of his mouth. I can't help but stare at that finger, cradled against his full bottom lip.

"Ah, nothing."

FUCK.

Two words. They slice down my throat like a blade.

I swallow the urge to scream. Lie, lie, lie, lie. And, what's worse, an important one.

My mother. Perhaps the most important mystery that's ever wormed its way into my life. A sense of unwellness curdles low in my stomach.

Witches, like the fae, cannot lie. Or—perhaps, unlike the fae—we can, but not without consequence. Fever. Illness. A low grade temperature and a subtle unwellness served as consequence for some untruths. A large lie—that could kill a witch.

I swallow.

Killian isn't stupid, as much as I'd love to think my husband is. His gaze sharpens on me and a tiny chill ticks up my flesh. The weight of his attention feels like he's holding me down, choking me with it. I shiver, clenching my teeth against their urge to clatter.

He'll figure out that I lied. He'll connect the dots and figure out I'm a witch. The fever that is going to overtake me soon is going to out me as what I am and, what's worse, there's a defaced picture of my mother hanging in his secret study. He can't kill me yet, but I am entirely at this man's mercy.

Questions will go to staff—what was her day like? And the truth is, I didn't speak to anyone until I spoke to the Duke. He'll think back to this moment, when it all started. He'll comb over every word. And he'll know that my nothing isn't nothing.

The only thing I can think of to cover up my lie is to lie more.

"I've been thinking, my lord husband," I move around the desk. Sickness curdles inside of me but I push it away. "We should get to know each other better."

"Oh, really?" he asks, his eyebrows shooting up to his hairline.

I move a little closer, the cold seeps into my bones.

"Yes, I think I'd like to take you up on that offer," I say. A curdle of fear slips in my stomach. I'm about to say it.

"What is that?" he asks, a low growl. His pupils dilate and the darkness swirls in his eyes. I slip a hand over his shoulder, letting it rest on his chest. Let it skirt up the edge of his waistcoat, teasing the collar. Then I scoot into his lap, wiggling a little there. His hand goes to my waist and spasms there. An echo of our bodies pressed together in the hallway, all the little moments training together, press between us.

"I think you should fuck me," I whisper in his ear. My stomach squeezes uncomfortably when I realize that is not a complete lie. Despite the strange feeling of the lie-fever beginning to boil in my veins, another warmth rides low inside of me.

"Really?" he asks. And that finger, the one that had thumbed his lower lip transfers to mine. He presses it against the bottom of my mouth, staring into my eyes as if he looked to a magic mirror revealing the secrets of my soul. "Are you sure you're ready for that?" he husks. "Do you remember yet?"

"Yes," I say. And finally, a complete lie. I shiver. I'm not ready and I don't know what he means. Remember what? I remember nothing. Its the one thing that scalds me. The darkness. And I have married the night.

Fever or not, goose pimples make their way up my arms. Why do I feel this way for my enemy? "Sometimes, I wonder if our marriage wasn't the best possible thing for me," I say. Ah, there it is. The feeling of wooziness lips at me. The one lie was already too great, two too much. But I wonder, still, if I should lie about one more thing. Just one, just to be sure. *"I would never hurt you."*

Freezing. Chills.

He sweeps his mouth in for a kiss.

But even then, the word falls away into nothing.

CHAPTER 48

When I wake up, there's a weight next to me. At first I think it's Nisha, so I cuddle to the warmth, expecting to thread her fur through my fingers. Instead, my hands slip across a man's naked chest.

I jerk up, looking down, my hair spilling around my shoulders and onto my shift.

Killian looks back at me with his fire-bright eyes and a smirk adorning his mouth. Dick.

I scramble upwards, to get out of the bed and away. "No," he commands, grabbing my arm in almost-gentle firmness. I scowl. "You've been sick," he says. And he doesn't mention that I'm a witch.

I pause. Waiting for it to come.

It doesn't.

"Until we know what happened to you, you need to be careful."

I know what happened to me. It's only a matter of time before Killian does. How will he react when he knows I'm a witch? Does he know now, and he's only pretending not to? The scorch of shame fires down my spine and leaks into every organ. I want to cry. Because all I can do is see my father's face.

He knew what I was this entire time. It's only more proof that I'll never be loved for who I really am. And Killian, though love has never been on the table, will find a woman with this much power either reprehensible or too dangerous. Such is always the way.

A thickly callused hand curls against the side of my face. I turn toward it, looking deep into Killian's eyes.

"Do you think if I stabbed you now, that it would kill me too?" I whisper.

He smiles, but it's more teeth than mirth. "You could certainly try." He pauses. "But wouldn't that ruin everything you've worked for, wife? A doting husband, hmm?"

He leans down and a fang rakes its way down my neck, careful to not break the skin. I shudder.

"All my nightmares have led to this," I retort. And truthfully, I can think of standing at the altar of my dreams, a man shrouded in shadow beckoning me into what I fear. The dark.

I don't know if it'll kill me to stab him. But I wonder about trying.

Slowly, ever so slowly, I take the blade that is still strapped to my thigh. Killian never moved it. "Why?" I rasp.

"I thought you'd need something to fight your demons with," he replies, eyes never leaving mine, despite the dagger waved in his face.

I inch the blade down, waiting for him to react. To tell me to stop.

He doesn't.

The edge of the grimsbane blade settles against his skin. I watch Killian's flesh dip as I apply pressure, right next to where a little scar rests. Still, I wonder with someone who heals so quickly how he could have such an impressive collection.

Blood peeks out of the wound.

I look to my arm. We both do.

Nothing. No wound. Killian's hand moves to the unmarred area, caressing my skin with his thumb.

My chest hollows out, like a wide cavern that groans in grief and utter emptiness.

The blood from the injury soaks back into his skin, which closes up without a mark. "If you're to kill me, you'll have to find something I care about, witch. Stab it and make sure it dies for good."

A monster like him, doesn't he care for himself? The words feel false in my mind, especially with the soft touch causing a ripple of tenderness through me. I need to wake up.

This information is what I needed. And yet, I wish I didn't have it. I can hurt Killian without causing harm to myself. At this moment, everything is all timing. He's teaching me how to kill him, one training day at a time. Every time he defeats me, presses his body against mine, I learn a little more. One day, it will be his undoing.

"Do not leave your room today, wicked witch," Killian says, moving away from me. "The forest is uneasy."

"Don't call me that," I rasp back. Nisha purrs in the corner, useless, seeming not to even mind Killian anymore. "Why is the forest uneasy?"

"The fair folk know there are unwelcome guests," he murmurs.

"The fair folk...as in *fae*?"

"Aye."

I think of the rumors of a green troll that once was said to have inhabited the space underneath a bridge on the way to Veritaes. The creature quickly had been killed—supposedly—after asking unwelcome riddles or requiring coin for travelers to cross. Few fae found themselves on this side of the Sea of Mist. Only those banished from Otherland. That said, the ones here were discarded from their fellows, after all, and assumed to be creatures of ill intent to have earned such a penance.

"But...there's hardly any left. How could there be so many as to make the forest uneasy?"

Killian throws back his head to laugh. "Witch, who do you think the blood is for? The trees aren't the only ones who are thirsty. Who do you think makes this castle what it is? That does the linens and cooks half of the food? Wolf Hall would need quite a few more hands to make it run if not for the goblins, elves, pixies, and such. Who do you think put that letter in your chamber pot?"

Fae are *here*? I think back to my hair being yanked and the invisible things I'd tripped over. That had tripped me. That were sabotaging my efforts to communicate with home.

"I thought it was haunted," I whisper. I'm not sure that this is any better, truthfully.

Killian doesn't laugh like I half-expect him to. "That is up for debate." He pulls the thick quilt over me. The fabric slips against my skin, like a heavy coat of tender flesh. A guilty feeling lances through me, from stomach to heart.

If this place is haunted, it's by my husband.

"If you're better later, I'd like to visit your bed." The word *bed* lands between us as if he's just thrown a stone in the middle of a pond. All I can do is watch the ripple his words cause. "Think about it. Now, do as you're told, witch, and stay in for the day. You'll need rest for what I have planned."

I open my mouth to snap something else at him, to ask another question, but he's already gone.

In his place, there's only a wisp of shadow, coiling behind him. That, and the growing anger of being told what to do.

CHAPTER 49

Fuck Killian.

The wind cracks overhead like a whip. Slicing clouds in half—a broken egg with gray yolk sliding out of porcelain pieces. The gale howls.

I hate this place. I hate it all. The fae, the people. I hate my husband. I hate his tenderness and I hate the lust that he makes me feel.

Now, do as you're told, witch.

The words snap in my mind. I imagine smashing them like gnats as I stalk away from Wolf Hall. My body shivers like the nerves only know how to twitch. Whether it is exhaustion or cold, I hardly know. I don't care, either. All I want to do is defy something—to be in control. To grasp something for myself.

Fool that I am, I walk toward the uneasy wood.

My ax sits in my hand, itching like it wants to be used. I don't go into the woods without a weapon, but I suppose that I'm stupid enough to wish to do violence with it. To find something to kill.

I always knew I'd get married, be bartered away like a fat hog. But all I ever wanted was to seize my own destiny. The words inscribed on my mother's grimoire float up in my mind's eye. *Live like destiny is a decision.* As if the gods weren't dangling little toys on strings for us to fight against.

But if the divine have no control then I'd make this fate for myself. For the chance that my father may yet live. I'd risk it all, racing to the end of each day for those I love. I will not be a pawn in this game my husband plays with the king.

I'm tired of being a pawn between men. Today, I need to clear my head.

Killian's bloody arm fills my mind's eye. That, and his rapidly healing skin. I wonder at the mythical blade, how it sat in Gray Hall all this time and Papa finally found it. Is it just another set piece from the gods? Is it something else?

I need to stab something Killian cares about. If it doesn't work on himself, it has to be someone else. I think of Asha, Remmy, Lukas.

Gods, perhaps I am the monster instead of the Wolves.

Confusion rattles through me. Just one foot in front of the other, Briar. *You have time.*

But I don't have time. I don't know what is happening with Papa. I don't know anything anymore and no letters have been sent. Killian didn't offer to assist. Now that I know there are fae, I can only assume some have taken a dislike to me and the letters that have gone astray have been mislaid by none other than the fair folk. What kind has been invisibly in my rooms, I can't say. I wish I had the type of Sight that allowed me to see them. Or if I did, I wish I knew how to use it.

Nisha stalks next to me. Images appear, rapid-fire, in my mind's eye of a chandelier falling on Killian's head, Killian collapsed with lips blue-white and a berry cobbler clutched in a hand, Killian at the bottom of a staircase with Nisha slinking away after tripping him.

A smile twists my mouth. Perhaps.

Nisha slips an image of tripping Killian down the stairs in my mind and I smile. I couldn't help but praise Nisha for her thought process, though. "You are so violent and lovely, my sweet." I stop and plop a clumsy kiss to her forehead. Her fur tickles my lips.

"I could say the same about you," a voice says.

I whip around.

A man I never expected to see again.

"Barro," I whisper. The ax in my hand falls to the ground.

Golden-bronzed hair and sun-pinkened skin, nothing marred his flesh that I can see. I run to him, joy overtaking the rage I felt earlier when Killian ordered me to stay in my prison.

I slam into him. The hard plane of his chest crashed into mine. Thick arms enveloped me. Warm, solid. Alive, alive, alive.

"Barro, what happened?" I cry. Fat tears stream down my cheeks. A horrible feeling—like a storm flying into everything you once held dear and smashing it to unrecognizable pieces—explodes in my chest. "Where's Valor? Daria?"

"Sorry to disappoint you, Briar," he says, tilting my chin up. The words sounded stilted, awkward. As if he hasn't spoken in some time. "Why are you crying? Do you wish I was dead, lady?"

Lady. Duchess. Why can't I just be Briar—or someone more than that? I want people to see me for someone capable—someone fierce and sharp.

I jerk away from him. "Don't be stupid, of course I don't wish you dead. But I thought...." That Valor and Barro had disappeared. That they were lost, taken, killed. So many possibilities.

He shrugs, as if it truly is of little consequence. "I didn't die, though."

He looks like Barro, sounds like Barro, *feels* like Barro, but something isn't right. I flick on the Sight, waiting for the telltale sign of truth and lies.

I tilt my head and look at him, eyes narrow. "Where did we first meet?" A chill slips into the space between us. He cocks his head in the way he always has, but something in his eyes is dead. "Barro?"

The smile starts small, and for a moment it looks just like his normal smile. But then it grows and grows, stretching into a grotesque mask that takes up his entire face, pulling past his eyes— even his ears—into a slick, blackened maw. A veined creature the color of infected greenery peeks out. The flesh that was Barro pulls back like the skin of a fruit, bloody and raw. Not Barro. Not even Valor. Something else.

"Well, sorry to disappoint, Briar."

Barro's flesh lands around like someone dumped a bucket of liquid onto the ground in a single slop of gore. Boiled bones crumble around me and blood slaps into me.

There's screaming.

Loud shrieking. It hurts, everything does. The noise, my eyes— they burn. And my throat. Gods, my throat. It feels like a hot poker shoved itself down through my gullet and into my heart.

I scramble back, realizing the screaming is me.

Nisha pounces forward, clawing at the thing that was Barro. "NO!" I cry. She swipes at it. The creature knocks her aside and she lands with a thud. A green-black sludge marks where the mouth-like thing touched her.

She screeches and steam rises from her.

Ax, ax, ax. I dropped it when I saw him. Where?

The creature stalks toward me, leisurely. It reminds me of the way a cat might play with its food. I catch a glimpse over my shoulder. Even the walk is still Barro's. That steady saunter. Barro is probably still dead, has always been dead. And whatever this evil sort of monster is—it probably was the thing that killed him. My mind goes blank.

I need to get to Nisha. I need to get my ax.

My foot catches on something, and I stumble falling face-first into the ground. The wind knocks out of me and I crawl, catching sight of my ax. My bloody, bloodthirsty ax. The wood hasn't eaten in weeks and will want blood. Almost as much as I do.

I see it. Shining, bloodthirsty, and somehow half-hidden by a holly plant. I lunge for it, my palm landing on the handle. Somehow, there's blood on my hand. A minor scrape, but I feel the vibration of the wood against my skin, hungry for more blood.

Something slithers against my ankle.

The word turns upside down. I manage to hang onto the ax as the creature that-was-Barro dangles me from an impossible grip. The thing's face twists into an upside down smile.

"I've been looking for the perfect way into the Wolf's den," it says with my friend's voice. A finger slips down my chin, a claw more than anything. For a moment, it brushes at the necklace Killian gifted me. Toying with it. "And I think I've found her."

The creature tucks a nail at the cleft of my jaw, tickling there and then presses until a sharp pain explodes and my vision goes white.

I'm going to be eaten.

I'm going to be eaten and there's nothing I can do about it.

The creature leans in, kisses me softly on the mouth. Its wretched tongue slithers down my throat, lapping at the blood from the wound.

Helplessness consumes me and all I feel is self doubt. I've never been able to do anything in my life. I've always been waiting. Waiting for someone to save me. Every brave thought I've ever had is beyond recollection, somewhere far away and false. I've only ever been a girl, waiting on a prince, waiting on a mother who died too long ago, waiting on someone to choose me, to love me. None of that will happen now.

My death will come, and I'll still be waiting.

I am going to die here, eaten by the same thing that killed my friend.

Eaten—

The blood dribbling down my body hits my ax.

The wood burns my hand. *Burns* it. It's hungry, hungry, and it demands more. I sling the blade up with the last of my strength. A wet smack of flesh reverberates as it hits the creature in the back.

The thing gives a cry, a sound like a rasping, reverberating crow.

I drop to the ground with a thud, narrowly avoiding falling on the sharp edge.

I roll, dropping away, but something about my neck can't move anymore. I flick a look to Nisha, who contorts in silent agony. She groans, muscles sleek and shivering.

The creature stares down at me and a slip of drool drips onto my face. Slips down. In its wake, my cheek grows numb. Paralyzed.

This is how I'm going to die.

"The master gives his apologies, by the way," the creature says, in

Barro's voice. "But even witches need to die to save the dark fate of Hisself."

The cavern of its mouth grows wider, wider, pulling until most of my vision is filled with the dark maw of its throat as it drags itself downward toward my face. Rank breath slips against me, watering my eyes with the foul, acid stench.

"Goodbye," it hisses.

Saliva drips onto me and the teeth scrape at the tender flesh of my face and—

"DON'T HURT HER!"

A voice I never thought I'd hear—at least not for another year.

Derrick.

He charges the thing, sword drawn and shining like an elongated tooth. He stabs at the creature, but the thing catches it with the edge of a forearm, a spined glossy blue like a navy night. A sound, metal on metal, cracks through the air and the creature shoves the sword away, knocking into Derrick. He falls to the ground.

I scream. Something snaps closeby and a growl grinds through the air.

Wolf.

Giant, with fur like coarse midnight and gleaming teeth of sharp stars.

Something about the saunter, the way he moves. I can't say what it is, but I know it's Killian. I get to my feet, hesitating as I shuffle closer to Derrick. He groans, a dribble of blood snaking down his temple.

My ring grows hot in my hand, steadily warming until my finger scalds with the intensity. Rage. It can only be rage. I lock gazes with Killian's wolf-shape. Then the creature screeches with Barro's mouth, barreling into the wolf. There's a yelp and I freeze, indecision paralyzing me.

This is perhaps one of the only ways I can think of to greatly weaken my husband before a year and a day is up. I need to do what I'm here for.

I grab Derrick and move away, limping as fast as I can away from where Killian's wolf form fights the creature. As soon as we push through the first ring of trees Nisha evaporates, like smoke. I look over my shoulder, catching the wolf's eye once more.

If wolves could hate, all of that feeling would be leveled in that stare. And maybe they can. People certainly do.

For a moment, I'm torn. I could turn to help my husband. For the tender moments we shared. But I don't. Though I need to destroy something he cares for, it won't hurt to try to destroy this man a little before I find that soft spot. I'm glad the paralytic from the creature numbs my face, because otherwise I'm not sure if I'd smile or cry. Derrick leans against me, nearly completely limp.

Killian is still my enemy. And Derrick, asshole that he is, is not.

I leave Killian to die.

CHAPTER 50

I pull Derrick forward by his shoulder. The strange blood from the creature slips across my chest, my fingers. Ax now attached to my hip, I jump at every errant sound. The forest seems more dangerous now. Each crack of a branch is another of those strange, flesh-wearing creatures, reading to find me. To eat my flesh.

Barro. A tear leaks down my cheek as I trudge resolutely forward. To have him given back, for just a moment, then taken back. He is well and truly dead. That means Valor is and likely Daria, too. Maybe. Gods.

Everything around me dies.

Derrick groans and I struggle forward, thigh muscles shaking. He's heavy, like a chunk of iron. Burly muscles. Lots of hair. I bite the inside of my cheek as my thighs burn. I find myself questioning my choices.

Eventually, we reach the castle and the sun has dipped to the underworld, but then. Darkness presses chilled breaths across the autumn night and I swallow, looking around. Where is everyone?

The halls of this haunted, cursed place are entirely empty.

I wonder if the Wolves are all out in the forest, slipping in amongst the trees to find the Duke of Death and bring him to this blasted burial ground they call home.

I'm able to get Derrick to my room, the portraits follow us. Agatha pops in from a reddened frame, hopping into a black one and down the hallway after us. She doesn't try to say anything, but follows either out of concern or entertainment.

I wonder if all the dead Wolves' ancestors would yell, like angry fishwives, because their expressions of haughty disapproval follow me like the stink of a skunk.

My muscles burn by the time I lay Derrick on my bed, heedless of the sheets and their state. Killian has enough money to buy a god, I think, judging by the elaborate decor in Wolf Hall. I look at Derrick and he shivers like he has a fever, a green pall to his skin.

"Fuck," I mutter. I don't know what to do. I could get Asha, but then she'll tell Killian. Doubtless Killian will be excited to find my former lover in my bed, injured or not, but I'm not sure what else to do. Nisha appears, like a cloud of smoke.

"Where have you been?"

She gives something the equivalent to a cat-shrug and presses a thought into my mind. Flashes of the book and the spirit board flip through my brain. *Ask your mother*, she means.

I dive underneath my bed and grab the items Nisha suggests. The marble cools my skin as I place the planchette on the board.

The planchette moves rapidly, my intentions and questions splurge through my shivering fingers.

P-A-G-E. 2-7-3. The instructions are spelled out across the marble in quick, hummingbird-like movements.

Page 273. I flip through the grimoire at my side, the old paper a thick parchment that reminds me of callused skin. The closest thing I have to a coven, the words and magic from witches past is stitched into the leather of the binding.

The page is blank. Then, ever so slowly, words begin to form.

The Dark One, of Erebos. He, who was once Death now Dead.

I read on.

Erebos will split Himself thrice. Once at Death, twice at Life.

Prince, King, and Dead God. Lover, killer, and to eat.
The Witch King is only one such foe
Ready to end and to try to defeat
The dead shall die, only to rise. By summer sun, take their eyes.

I pause over the words. Most of them don't make sense to me, but what I do recognize is clear. The spirit board is telling me perhaps one of the things I don't want to hear.

The Witch King tried to kill me.

My gut churns. An image of my father, the Bears, everything I cared for flashed through my mind in quick succession. Why were the terms set to a year and a day if he'd wanted me to kill him sooner?

Why had he tried to kill *me?*

Because he wants Killian dead now? Or something else? I haven't used the paper he gave me. Not yet.

I press my palms into my eyes, blotting out every word. Everything has gone wrong. I have no earthly way of divining how my father is doing, which is the entire *point*—

I pause.

I've used my marble spirit board already today. It doesn't like to be overused—the answers grow foggier and murkier and the spirits' interactions ever-snarkier. Whoever is on the other side. I've tried before, to no avail. The marble hadn't answered.

I pull out the other way of connecting I have—my cards.

The fortune cards are thick. painted paper passed down from my mother. Perhaps her mother gave them to her. I like to think that there's a legacy of witches I come from, each passing supernatural memorabilia down the matrilineal line, similar to the grimoire.

I pull out the cards, meditating over them. A single question, in the form of my father's face, looms in my mind.

I run my fingers over the cards until one grows hot in my hand. I pluck it.

A Nightmare Fae.

Another .

The Grim.

And the last one is—

Death.

Too many mysteries swirl here. I can't help but wonder if everything is connected.

The Witch King. My marriage. My mother. The sliver of her face I'd seen in Killian's room—before my lie ravaged me with fever. I lay back onto my bed. Derrick groans next to me.

The cards are about my husband, my marriage, and the state of where I am right now, but I have no earthly idea what it means.

The door crashes open, wood slamming against the wall.

The cards that are on the bed fly up in the air as I jerk upright.

Killian.

Blood smears the side of his face and rage contorts the rest as he looks from me to Derrick on my bed. Rippling abs flex as he stalks in the room, shirtless, except for the white bandage wrapping his torso. Red stains it, trickling down his side. He's breathless, as if he ran to my room as soon as he was patched up. I can't help but feel the flash of concern that ripples through me at the wound, but that soon evaporates when I see the hate smeared across his face.

"Get the fuck up," he growls. I do. "Not, you. YOU!" He yells at the sleeping form of Derrick. He stalks over, shoving the other man. "What are you doing in my wife's bed?"

"Killian, stop!!"

He doesn't seem to hear me. In fact, when I catch a glimpse of his eyes, they're not human at all. Dark and that flashing quicksilver and yellow-gold, like a rabid wolf.

He shoves Derrick, still injured, off of the bed. Derrick lands with a thump, jolting awake. He groans.

A clatter is at the door and I move in front of Killian, blocking him in case he throws himself at Derrick. He crashes into me and I see the glimpse of a small crowd at the door. A flush heats my cheeks at being the subject of a scene like this.

"You're mine," Killian hisses in my ear. He clutches me, fingers almost claw-like and I see that the enemy I had married is barely there. Something else is inside of him.

Duke of Death, they call him for a reason. And he wants to possess me. Or whatever *this* is wants to possess me. A shiver rakes down my spine and I clutch him back, pulling him away from Derrick.

"Say it," his hand goes to my throat, squeezing lightly but the threat is there. I lick my lips, a heat of an entirely different sort skimming down my flesh.

"I'm yours, Killian." And somehow, no chill shivers through my body. "For now," I say, to make sure I don't fall into illness. And that is the truth. I will play this game until one of us is dead.

His mouth twists, but he doesn't push me further. *Wicked witch.* I can almost see the words playing across his face. His eyes shift back to what I've come to think of as him, but they remain mixed with the tortured color of *other*. He leans down, his breath brushing against my lips.

He takes my mouth against his.

Killian fists my hair, the roots pull and he forces my head back. I open my mouth for him. Hot desperation grips me, reminding me of our first kiss out in the woods. Gods, I want him. The need grabs me from the inside. Killian hoists me upwards into his arms. His hands cup around my ass and I can't help but roll my hips.

His hardness heats against my core. Wetness pools there as my desire crescendos.

He twitches, and abruptly jerks back.

He pushes away from me in disgust. Pure shadow looks back at me. That, and a hatred that lives in the narrowing of his eyes and the curl of his mouth. Killian turns to the crowd behind him. "If you're here to spy, you can at least be useful." His voice feels nasty, as if he wants to hurt anyone who's witnessed this. Killian has never claimed to be a hero, so perhaps he does. The desire inside of me curdles into shame and rage. "Grab this fucking Bear and toss him to the wood."

"NO!" I yell, throwing myself in front of Derrick.

The people around us stop, except two of the guards that push through. They wear deep purple uniforms, each adorned with a silver-carved wolf snarling as a badge of honor at their left shoulders. They pause, waiting for Killian.

"Dungeon," Killian says instead. The stoic guards exchange a glance with one another—one that not only I see, but Killian does as well. He turns his gaze to me, all heat and rage. I've made him look weak. And that is not something that will be easily forgiven. "You," he says, "can go too."

"NO!" I yell. Nisha springs upwards, pouncing in front of me. "We won't go."

The guards drag me away. Nisha swipes at one. The other brandishes his sword. "Out!" he says to everyone.

"Nisha!"

Everyone backs out of the room. Nisha rears, and the door slams shut. Her body pounds into it. I don't say anything, that Nisha can re-materialize at will.

She presses a thought into my mind. Her, killing all of them. I have never been really good at exchanging thoughts the way she is, but I try to press the rage down for a moment, despite my shaking hands, and project *later*. Images of made-up dungeons scrawl through my mind. When the pounding stops, I only hope that she's gotten my message.

This man, I hate him. Killian looks at me, eyes hooded and emotionless behind the shadows thrown up on his face in the hall.

Every fiber in my soul heaves with barely-contained loathing.

I can't wait to kill him, flesh and spirit, and burn his body and toss his remains to the Sea of Mist. His squelching flesh feels hot in my hands, as if it's a near-memory, and it's the only thing that lets me control my breathing and walk with my head held high. Promises, my lord husband.

As I'm pulled past him, I spit in his face.

Saliva slips down his cheek and he wipes it off with a careless hand.

"My wife has clearly been possessed by an ill spirit on her way out in the woods," he announces loudly. "Keep her for three days in the bowels of the house and summon the Satyr."

Lukas looks up, jerking his head and his face paling. "Kill—"

Killian gives his cousin a dark look. "I think you mean Your Grace," he hisses. "Do it, or go pick out your own cell, Lukas."

PART III
TWISTED HEARTS

The world spins and spins again
Yarn for yarn and lie for lie
If you have a bird in hand, let it fly
To the moon and back
And beyond the grave
Little girls die that misbehave
Boys will be boys who become
men who will be men
The world spins and spins again

–Old Lumarian Nursery Rhyme

CHAPTER 51

BOY

*S*he appears in his dreams.

With hair like spun moonlight and a streak of darkness fracturing down the thick tendrils, a Girl waves at him. Girl circles his mind, her presence wrapping around him like an embrace. She comes every night. Each dream she visits, she gives a shy waggle of her fingers. Girl is tall, but not as tall as he is. She smells like rosewater and thyme and sunshine. She doesn't talk much. But Boy is okay with that.

He looks forward to sleeping, because Girl is there. She brings a peace he's never felt. It's worth the anger of Erebos, for just a little bit of ease.

But Girl is so scared of the shadows. He thinks she must also be scared of him. Boy is darkness, after all.

"I can't," she whispers at night, shaking. "I can't see."

"I'll leave the light on," he tells her in one dream. He likes the shadows, they make him strong. The light fractures his powers. But for Girl, he would do anything. "I'll always leave this burning," he promises, candle in hand.

He learns that a light in his room where his body rests will help him have a lit flame when he dreams.

The candle in his room burns low, often only a nub by sunrise.

Boy finds that when he wakes, sometimes he has more scars than before Girl arrived, but his sleep feels tender. When she finally asks him his name, he remembers. Finally.

"Killian."

When he asks for hers, her mouth moves and bubbles erupt from her pink petal lips. Iridescent orbs float up and pop above, scattering rainbows all around them. Little bits of darkness puncture the dream.

Killian wakes to a pain in his hand and a strange purple flower he knows he's not supposed to touch. Father has told him so. Many, many times. He wonders why, and his only solution is to blame the gods.

Killian unfurls his fist. His palm is riddled with thorns and the flower disappears, but the feeling of the spiked stem never quite leaves. Erebos and Ghost snarl inside of him and he learns to keep this part of himself tucked away.

Sometimes, when he feels the pain, Killian thinks he hears the gods laughing.

When he dreams next, she isn't there, but he thinks he smells the scent of cold snow off the mountains.

The girl made of thorns is gone for years. For years, the girl made of thorns doesn't come.

Killian grows up. Sometimes he forgets his name, but then a phantom pain stabs his palm and he remembers it: Killian. Whenever the name comes, it's always because the girl made of thorns reminds him. Even though she is long gone.

When the word escapes him, though, he no longer calls himself Boy. He's Man now.

Erebos and Ghost fight, the way they always have. Killian learns that the other Cursed do not have a Ghost or an Erebos inside of them. They're called by the moon and their own souls. They don't have to share a body with self-hatred and evil. Killian learns to fold the pain inside himself and pretend he is the same as they are, when all he can see is how he is different.

The blood on the sheets is proof.

Still, the wounds grow a little less each day. Erebos is less vicious at night, though he works to kill Ghost and probably Killian. When he's quiet, it's only because he's thinking.

Killian still wears out the candles every night. Sometimes, he catches the smell of the far flung mountains and Girl's scent of rosewater, thyme, and sunshine in tight whiffs. He wakes up with skin the color of poppies, leaking from a thousand tiny wounds.

Then, one day, Girl comes back.

She's tall and rounded by womanhood and hardened by years, but it's still her. He catches the ice in her eyes and his heart heaves an extra beat. Not Girl anymore. Just like he is no longer Boy.

"You're back." Killian's voice is deeper now, but he hopes she remembers the cadence and the promises shared in their youth.

When she turns, his stomach drops. She reminds him of the witch—the sorceress, the trickster goddess, the fickle fae, whoever she was—that cursed his House. He's seen her portrait and learned to hate her.

Killian blinks and he sees the dark streak in her hair and convinces himself he's seeing things. The mark on her neck is still there, shaped like a rabid bear. Girl turned Woman is still made of thorns. But she smells of mystery, misery, and mountains now.

"Do you remember now?"

She says nothing.

"Where did you go?"

And she looks through him. She doesn't see him at all.

No one sees a man clothed in shadows. Not even himself.

Killian tries to show her the light, the candles he's burned for years and years waiting for her to come back. Thousands have melted into nothing. Killian would buy every wick in the world to keep the light on for her. And still, she won't even meet his gaze. Killian's stomach twists in panic. He reaches for her, but it's all a dream. Nothing is real. And still, she gazes straight through him.

I'll never know peace again, *Killian thinks.*

She arrives in his dreams infrequently, and he watches her grow up in tandem with him. Ghost and Erebos are restless and get worse each passing day. Something is coming. A reckoning. He can feel it. His palm hurts with invisible thorns.

Killian learns to control his shadows. He becomes a weapon. There's no other choice. The Witch King tries to kill his people and Killian every day–he hates Killian's House and Killian doesn't understand why. Others do, but they purse secrets between their lips.

When Killian becomes an orphan, he knows that the gods are watching and smiling. He inherits a burden he never asked for–to care for creatures that hate him, for fae creatures he hates, and to hide the hatred he has for himself. He's a Duke now. He must be invincible. Killian becomes an unkillable villain, more myth than man.

He makes himself into vengeance, like Amara did before she fell in love. Sometimes, he dreams of the girl made of thorns as his bride. Sometimes he thinks she sees him, but his throat is a cobweb of shadow when he tries to speak.

Then the Witch King comes. He's a wretched man–a killer and a threat to agreements Killian has already made and promises he's inherited. So Killian makes the man a bargain, as one might expect of a villain playing the hero. He agrees to marry a woman he's never met in exchange for a truce for a year and a day.

It will give him time. And he sorely needs it. Still, if he had a heart, it would break as he gives up the dream of his girl of thorns.

The king tells him that the woman Killian has agreed to marry will be in the forest soon. How he knows such things, Killian doesn't ask.

When Killian's future bride appears, his palm aches as he sees Girl turned Woman. Still made of of a brittle, beautiful sharpness, she demands something he can't give. So he kisses her with false promises and feels his chest ache with the little betrayal.

But just the same, for the first time in ages, Killian is happy. He knows it won't last, but a year of false joy is more than he's ever had. It is more than enough for a cursed man.

When he kisses her, the metallic taste of bitter blood coats his tongue.

CHAPTER 52

Frigid stone leeches all heat from my body. My feet are still bare.

"Fuck this." I whisper, rubbing my palms against my arms. The dry rub of skin on skin is all that sounds through the dungeon, joined only by the steady drip of water elsewhere and the skitter of rats.

If I hadn't planned to murder Killian before this, he would certainly be on my list to kill now. What a fickle bastard. And all because I made him look bad? I swallow a pebble of regret. I didn't do it intentionally, but for the Dukes of the various Houses, appearances matter.

Also, I left him in the woods to fight an evil beast.

But I don't. Not when I'm down here without a scrap of warmth to heat up my blue toes.

A groan echoes in the cell next to mine. "Briar?"

"Derrick!" I say.

"Briar, I-I've come to save you," he mumbles. I roll my eyes. What an idiot. Sweet, but stupid.

The man likely has a head injury on top of everything else. In the dim light, I can make out a fresh bandage that I am nearly certain I did not apply. So there's been some amount of wound tending, even if a blanket hadn't managed to materialize on a list of priorities.

The only thing I was provided with was a window that provides a single sliver of moonlight. It slices into the cell, keeping a little darkness at bay, but not my fear.

* * *

CLICK.

Click.

Click.

I swallow a dry, festering feeling inside of me. It feels like I've lied a thousand times and all that is left of me is a ravaged sack of flesh. Why hasn't Nisha come?

The clicking continues. Comes closer.

Then I hear voices.

"It's good you put her in here," the voice says. It's not one I've heard before. "If she's a witch, as you say, you could have been in serious danger, Duke. Which means *we* are in danger."

Killian appears, and the shadows pool around him in loving caress. I haven't seen his shadows in some time, but here they are now. A shield. Against me.

The other figure is as tall as Killian's shoulder. No supernatural darkness spools around him, so I can see him clearly. His skin is white, like a fish belly, with auburn hair streaking around his bare chest and clumping at his nipples.

My eyes travel the rest of the way down, stopping at what appears to be hooves. .

They call him Satyr because he's just that. A fae. A legend that hasn't been seen on this continent since…well, ever. I've never heard reports of his kind in Lumar, not like the occasional troll, hobgoblin, or dryad. He belongs to the Otherland, which means if he's here, he's wronged a lot of the fae folk.

"You've honored our agreement, it seems. Lord Protector suits you nicely," Satyr says. "Our long-awaited hero, finally fulfilling the bargain your House struck. Though it took you long enough."

"I can assure you, Satyr, I did not know."

Satyr makes a tutting sound, and his hooves click closer to me. "You might have sought to give the witch a blanket before tossing her in here."

Killian growls, stalking toward me. The shadows still linger across him. Not for the first time, do I wish that I could see coins slipping from his mouth to know what he truly meant.

His eyes turn yellow as he watches me. Pulsing black irises fight against the jaundiced color, thrumming back and forth as if a battle wages inside his head. "Guard," he growls. "Get a blanket. A hot bottle. Soup. Tea. *A light.* Whatever else. And call the fools that threw her in here without those things to my study. I will deal with them later."

The retreating feet of the guard slips away and Killian enters my cell. He piles me on top of him. He's a furnace compared to the cold stone.

"That—Duke—is not what I was expecting here," Satyr titters.

Killian shrugs. "I may hate her, but it is hardly right that she freezes to death." I shiver against him and his arms spasm around me as if in reply. The warmth of his chest eases the ice in my spine.

I hate you too, I think, but part of me hesitates to say it.

Satyr clicks closer, still on the other side of the bars. "Well, witch, what do you have to say about the Puca?"

"What?" I rasp.

First a satyr now a...puca?

At my hoarse voice, Killian growls. "When did you last get water?" he asks.

"I-I'm not sure." His only reply is another growl and to pull me closer.

"Relax, Duke," Satyr says.

"It's not me," Killian replies cryptically.

"Ah." Satyr pauses. "In that case, I think I must ask you to leave."

"No."

"Yes. This pertains to our agreement, in which you have vowed to uphold. I think it is best you leave. Unless you want the terms to be worse at renegotiation?" Saytr inquires. It sounds like a threat.

The hairs along my arms rise as Killian tenses, a rising violence inside of him that slips between us as if we share a skin. I put a hand to his chest. I don't know what to think or what to believe. The same man who tossed me inside a dungeon and ordered me soup as soon as he saw what had been done to me. Right after I'd left him to die to save another man.

At that moment, a clatter rattles the air and Lukas appears, bearing the requested items with Asha in tow to help.

"Thank god this madness has ceased," Lukas says.

"She's a witch," Saytr says.

Asha and Lukas both still.

"Ah," Lukas says finally.

"And apparently there is a Puca about," says Killian, his chest reverberating against me.

"Well fuck me, that explains the nightmares," Lukas says.

"Language!" Asha admonishes.

"Sorry, mama," he says with a shake that reminds me of a dog. "Turn it down, Killian. Your alpha dickheadedness is messing with *my* wolf."

"I've asked him to leave," the Satyr says.

"And I have refused."

"Look, there's soup here, she can warm up while they talk. I hear that you've sent Gaspar and Julian to your study. I think I should accompany you so they don't get beheaded."

"They deserve it."

"Surely we can just cut out their tongues," Lukas jokes, but Killian tilts his head as if he's considering it.

I move away from Killian. His hands tighten around me briefly before letting me go. "I'll take the blanket. Is there anything for Derrick?"

Killian growls again. As if he's about to shed his human form any moment to become a full wolf.

"Let me take care of Derrick," Asha says. "Now is not the time to...

test the master, dear." I accept the soup from Lukas and for once don't push.

"I'll stay here until the Puca appears."

"What's a Puca?" I ask finally.

Killian looks at me, eyes calculating. We stare at one another long enough that I feel a prickling at my cheeks as I blush and a heat gathering lower. His nostrils flare, as if he knows. "A fae of ill luck."

"And we're waiting for it? Then will I be released?"

Killian says nothing, and for a moment I think I won't get an answer.

It's Satyr that speaks. "I've been told that you have a large cat from north of Ash Mountain."

"Yes."

"With fur like the burnt refuse the mountains are named for, with eyes like shifting gems, and teeth like ivory swords."

I shrug. It sounds silly, but Nisha is a beautiful creature and people like to spin yarns about anything they are unfamiliar with.

"So we will wait for Nisha, as you call her. The ill-luck creature in question."

Nisha. They think Nisha is a faerie.

CHAPTER 53

"*N*o," I say.

Denial floods me. She isn't...this can't be real.

I had no real interactions with the fae, apart from the hauntings that Killian told me were supposedly them. But to say that Nisha is one—that she'd been lying to me my entire life—

The Nightmare Fae card from my deck.

The floor feels unsteady beneath me as I shift. Killian tucks himself around me. His arms are strangely comforting.

Nisha? I query.

For a moment, I'm not sure she's heard me. As if she's too far away... But then our bond reverberates, as if she replies, but I don't hear anything. I only feel something.

Shame.

When Nisha appears, she's all milky skin and long, sinewy limbs. Something about her still looks the same, minus the fur. With bright lips and feline eyes, she blinks at me the same way she always has. Even her gait still has the same smooth, cat-like grace.

The room watches her as if she might attack.

Betrayal burns high in my blood. I look at Nisha in her woman-like form. Nisha of the fair folk.

"You knew," I whisper. "You knew my pain, you knew what it would have meant too speak with me like this," my voice rasps in raw rage. I touch my neck, as if to communicate what it would have been like for her to have been human and spoken to me directly. A fae of ill luck, they said. Ill luck indeed. "Why? Just tell me why you lied."

"You know the fae can't lie," Nisha says. Her voice half growls. A strange lilting alights the words, like she's still a large cat that has only just now learned to speak. She clears her throat. "I never meant to hurt you."

"Then tell me why you did."

"I–can't. Not yet," she amends. She flicks a tongue out, licking the back of her hand and tilts her head to look at me. Her eyes, still cat-like, stare in unblinking contemplation. "We've more curses to break, little one. Some answers are for another day."

More curses to break? I let out a hollow laugh. As if she was cursed instead of just willfully playing pretend. A fae trick, nothing more. "There are too many curses in the gods forsaken life. I can barely manage the curse of living, much less the failures of those who have come before me." I eye her and for once, she seems to be cowed.

"If you are fae, then you are old enough to remember my mother. Tell me of her," I order. I shift forward. The room watches us with bated breath, but they all fall away as my gaze focuses only on Nisha. I don't feel Killian behind me, not Derrick moaning in pain in the next cell over. I don't hear the shuffling awkwardness of the remaining guards.

It's just us.

Nisha shakes her head. "It's more complicated than that." Her voice is dry as bleached bone.

"Which means–"

"All witches come from fae, who come from gods. We are all the children of living deities, if we have a bit of magic at our command." At her words, she snaps her fingers. A strawberry with an inner blue blight perches between her thumb and index finger. When she bites into it, it turns into a tightly rolled scroll. Red juice dribbles down her mouth. She pulls the now-stained paper from between her lips. Another snap and it disappears.

I pull on the Sight, shoving the veil of magic over my eyes.

"Don't waste your magic, sweet one," she says. "I only speak truth." Gold coins pour from her lips. Bright and blinding, I blink several times. A hot wash of betrayal burns like bile at the back of my throat. "It's the only way you have magic, if you are a descendent of a living god. Most mortals are descended from The Dead One, so they live short, magic-less lifespans. Witches are simply descendants of at least two gods. Most of you still die as humans do, but with a little more… sparkle." She smiles at this, a brief twist before her face goes blank. "I–" she cuts herself off, scowling in a frustrated manner at the ceiling. "There are so many snarls to speak around," she finally mutters.

I don't care that she is bound by curses, that she cannot speak of all of the things that I wish to hear. It is the betrayal, the years–the life-time of it–that soaks my heart. No apology will ever be enough to make up for the sheer weight of loneliness. "Don't bother then. I want to be alone."

"Briar–"

I hold up a hand. "If I want to speak with you, I'll call for you." She begins to nod, but my mouth opens. I want to hurt her. "Watch me, watch for my truth."

Nisha's eyes track mine, cat-like pupils widening as I lean in. Cold seeps into my bones and the scraps of warmth I've collected for myself fall away in the face of my freezing rage.

"I'll only want to speak with you when I'm dead."

No fever spikes my blood, no shiver against my skin marking me a liar.

"Well, then." There's nothing left to say, so Nisha walks through the wall, leaving me. I don't bother to acknowledge anyone else when they eventually depart. I'm alone. Lonely.

Lonely, lonely Briar.

Eventually, guards shuffle me out of my cell. Nighttime grips the halls with vice-like strength. Little spritelights flit across the windows like moths, but other than that, no glow spares my eyes from the vast, utter darkness. "I can't see where we're going."

A panic settles in my chest as the last spritelight fades away.

"You're going back to your room, Duchess," one of them says, a fist cupped around my arm. I snort at the title.

"I still can't see."

"No one can," the other replies. I want to toss my head back and laugh, but the darkness keeps me quiet.

Of course.

Killian doesn't want the world to know he locked me up.

CHAPTER 54

I'm scarcely in my room before I leave it.

Agatha leads me down the hallway, hopping from frame to frame. Her weapon swings at a jaunty angle from its scabbard and a strand of her hair unfurls itself from her updo. She's perhaps my only ally in this bedamned, grimsridden hellscape. I half wonder if she will betray me, too. We wind through the hallways, crossing the invisible line that for the past several weeks had delineated my side of the house from Killian's.

Fear rattles through me, mixing with betrayal and rage. There's no one here for me. No one is on my side except for myself. That's the way it's been my entire life and the way it will always be. Nisha's—I jerk inwardly against her name, as if she's trying to get in my head—explanation of my mother grips me hard. My mother. There's an answer in this house about a mystery that's plagued me since the Wolves killed her, and I'm going to find it.

The dark decorates Killian's study, broken only by a small boost of sallow light from the moon peeping through the wide window. Moonlight casts a jaundiced eye over the room, alighting only on the shining bits of gold and silver. Flowers sprout from a vase with gilded edges and the portrait that sits across from the desk is none other than Killian's father, the prior lord of Wolf Hall. Duke Reginald Galibran.

Hot hatred burns through me at the sight of him. He's the one responsible for my mother's death. For all my pain. If I'd had her, someone would have been there to understand who I truly am. And help me become who I was meant to be. As it is, I'll never know that woman with the life I wish I had lived. She's as dead as my mother.

I can't help but notice Duke Reginald Galibran doesn't look like Killian at all. Agatha stands next to him, poking at the side of his cheek. He ignores her, but as he moves, the edge of his formal coat shoves her halfway out of the gilt frame.

The portrait of the Duke stares at me, his emotions behind a mask. His head cocks to one side in silence. I wonder how much the portraits can think, if they understand things like secrecy and thievery. The portraits spy, but what do they do besides gossip amongst their own?

The former Duke of Wolves is not the painting I'm interested in. The door behind Killian's desk looks like a black cave, the wood so dark it's as if it was built from a burned tree. I swallow, pressing a hand to it. The moonlight glints against the gilded door handle. I push it down. The door—

—is locked.

Nothing I didn't expect.

I don't use my witchery often, but if ever there was a time this is it.

Killian's father puts a finger up and presses it to his lips. *Shhh.*

A flutter of panic grips my stomach. What game is this portrait playing?

The low mumble of voices slips through the crack in the door. I glance at the portrait again. He nods his head to the large desk. I don't trust it—I don't trust him. Why would Killian's father—portrait or not —help me?

The room isn't built for hide and seek. Everything is wide open, as if to prevent something like this from happening. Everywhere, I can be seen—everywhere except one place. I dive underneath Killian's desk.

Footsteps patter into the room. Two sets. One a hard tread, the other like light rainfall. A swish of fabric slips to my ears. Those who entered are silent for a moment, then the door shuts. Gods, do I hate this. Once again, it seems I've well and truly fucked myself.

"You look weak," Asha says. Her voice is harder than I've heard it. There's a rustle as she moves, a thump as she settles into the chair in the corner. "You're thirty, thinking you're twenty, but acting like you're ten. Such is the way of stupid, ridiculous men."

"Don't spare my feelings, Asha," Killian says sarcastically.

"I never spare the feelings of fools," she responds crisply.

The thudding tread reverberates the floor as he moves. *Don't, don't.* He walks around the desk. The dark black of his trousers is all I see. For a moment, I hear the clink of glass. More drinking, my lord husband? But all I feel is relief. He's just getting them drinks—

The chair scrapes. Fuck.

"Ouch," Killian says. As he sits down, his long legs jab forward. His knee nearly brushes against my nose and I rear my head back, squishing myself as small as I can. The flutter of panic rises inside of me like a building scream. What in *the hells* have I gotten myself into?

"You are feeling sorry for yourself and it shows. It's a poor look that generates no respect. That girl will have someone in her bed in a second and—lord or no—do not think that Wolves will not challenge your position. A Wolf whose wife looks elsewhere doesn't take care of his family, and therefore cannot take care of his people. Weakness, as I said."

"You're not even a Wolf."

There's the swift sound of Asha rising, her skirts brush the floor and feet thud to bring her closer. I hear her rapid breaths as she leans over the desk. A slap reverberates in the room.

Asha just smacked Killian. My mouth falls open a little, but then I shut it. *Good for you, Asha.*

"Don't you dare," she hisses. "I gave up my life to come here, to be with your uncle. I raised you. You do not speak to me with such disrespect."

"I'm sorry, Asha." He takes an audible breath. "What do you think I should do?"

"Just like in the wild, an alpha does not let another fuck his mate." Her voice is scornful. "What were you thinking?"

I fight a protest. I didn't do anything with *anyone*, like I said, but looks matter in the world of courts, kings, and lords. And Wolves, apparently.

She continues, even as Killian opens his mouth for a rebuttal. "The Equinox ball is a good opportunity. The house will look gorgeous. You must show her off. Show that you want her. And, more importantly, that she wants you."

"What makes you think I want her?" he asks.

"I've seen your type," she answers, just as a blush settles across my cheeks. *Type.* As if finding someone attractive makes a difference when you want to kill them. "That woman is a series of hills and valleys, just as you like it. Plus, everyone saw you nearly shift for the second time in a day when you thought she might be fucking another man. Not only that, someone saw her running naked down the hall a few weeks ago. Now go woo your wife, Wolf."

We're enemies—*fated* enemies. Even if we weren't born to the Houses we were, it's so much deeper than that.

I wonder about letting him woo me. The memory of his mouth on me settles against my skin, igniting it.

"Fine," he says. "I'll make sure she knows she belongs to House Wolf now." My stomach squeezes.

The door shuts as Asha leaves, but Killian doesn't move. Not yet. The scrape of a quill scratches in my ears as he writes. He lets out a frustrated growl, crinkles the paper, and tosses it to the floor.

It drops, rolling a little.

A little too close to me.

I swallow.

I hold still, wondering if he'll pick it up, but he doesn't. He doesn't move for a long time.

"Well, wife? Do you know who you belong to?"

"No one. And certainly not a monster." I crawl out from beneath the desk. Killian says nothing, but the eyes of a demon follow me.

CHAPTER 55

The missive slips under my door, the *shhh* of paper reminds me of a skulking rat. I stalk to it, grabbing the folded parchment between two angry fingers, and open the note.

Dinner. At 9th bell. The words are spiky, aggressive on the paper. No please is written there.

No please? For me, that means no thank you.

I tear the paper up, taking satisfaction in imagining it's Killian's head I'm ripping from his stupid neck, and drop it back outside my door. My stomach gurgles, but I ignore it and toss myself onto my bed.

As if that man gets to throw me in a dungeon and expect that I'll dine with him the next day. I snort. My belly protests again and I press my hands against it, glancing up to where Nisha should be. She'd be somewhere in the corner, having fetched something, no doubt. At least she'd have tried to bring something to my door.

I bury my face in my pillow, letting the tears fall. A faint query quests to my mind and I slam my mental walls shut. Nisha. The betrayal and agony from all these years explodes inside of me as I sob harder.

I should have answers. From Nisha, from Killian, from my fucking dead *mother*. Years ago. The oppressive loneliness that has haunted me my entire life turns to kindle for my rage. How dare they? Everyone that has ever been in my life. That left me to the cruel fingers of my stepmother, the wandering hands of my stepbrother, and even the well-intentioned neglect from my father. I viciously wipe the tears from my cheeks. The anger builds until I can't stand it anymore, and I stalk to the door, ripping it open and—

On the other side, Asha waits, hand raised as if to knock. My chest rises and falls in rapid succession. Fists curl at my sides and I blink back the tears that cloud my eyes. Instead, I let the rage curl over my mouth.

Asha's eyebrows raise as she takes in the scowl on my face.

"Feeling better?" she asks.

"No," I reply with gritted teeth. "What is it?" I swallow. Asha didn't do anything to me, yet I don't apologize for my rudeness.

"I've come to help you dress for dinner. It's in an hour."

"I'm not going."

Asha's eyebrows disappear into her hairline.

I don't want to be rude to her, but this isn't the time to exchange pleasantries. "I-I'm ready to see Satyr." I venture. Rage still curdles inside of me, and a deep hatred has slipped inside my heart. For everything. For everyone. But that creature down there will have answers. I sorely need to clear up a few questions.

Asha eyes me with calculating gray eyes. She looks so like Lukas, except for the height and the absence of thick, veiny muscles. "He's currently drinking all of our spirits in the cellar, so it will be a good time."

* * *

WINE BOTTLES GLARE, holstered to the floor-to-ceiling racks. Splinters of low light strike the cloudy glass. Satyr sits on the floor, hairy legs splayed out like a rag doll as he leans against the wall. He hasn't bothered with anything but the bottle, though stemware perches untouched on a small, elegant table.

"Gettout." He belches and wipes the back of a hand against his mouth. Driblets of red slick down an ashy blonde beard. A pink tongue flicks out to grab the errant drops. It reminds me of a worm.

"No thank you," I say.

He looks up at the sound of my voice, and a bushy eyebrow raises. Then he throws his head back and laughs. "So the witch comes to speak to Satyr." He snorts, tosses another glug of alcohol into his throat. "Nothing good can come of that."

"A good way to start," I say, frowning, "with an agreement to speak plainly."

He shrugs, waving a careless hand next to him as he gestures for me to sit. I walk to him, stepping over the abandoned bottles and plop next to him. My skirts spread out. He hands me his bottle andI sip it. "You are not committed," he says, pressing the lip of the wine bottle to my mouth. Liquid splashes. It's old, not decanted, and I get a mouthful of sediment. I start to choke a little, but can't pull away as he grips the back of my head and keeps my mouth pressed to the bottle. Acid and deep earthen flavors coat my tongue. I chug it, letting it go in and in until I haven't breathed for a minute. My eyes water. He finally releases me. Rage flares, hot and hard in me. So much anger grinds up from my bones, wanting to pulverize everything in my path.

I choke on the win and on my rage. Some of the wine dribbles down my chin. Before I can catch it, it drips to my dress, staining the light green fabric. Satyr shrugs. "So, I'll only speak with you if you continue to drink. I don't care to talk to sober people at the moment."

I grimace, bringing the bottle back to my lips. If I can get past this initial barrier to a pleasant sense of tipsy, I'll be able to drink without thinking. I open my mouth to speak, to yell, to something, but something tells me that screaming at this creature won't be in my favor.

"So, which curse have you come to inquire about, then?"

My face swelters. "Well, any that affect me."

"I've only enough alcohol to talk about one, witch, so what will you pick?"

How many curses snarl around me?

"I want to talk about Nisha."

"The Puca?" He raises a brow. "Wrong choice, but as you wish." He leans back. Leg bumps into a bottle, which sails across the floor in a cantankerous rattle. I take another swig from my bottle. "Although, it may surprise you to know that I believe in fate, so your arrival has brought together the knot of all these curses. The living gods and such are obviously bored."

"How many are there?" I ask.

"How many what?"

"Curses."

"Well, if you want to boil it down, it's just one. *Being alive.*" He tosses another swig back into his mouth. It glugs audibly. I count under my breath. I get up to fifteen before he ceases drinking and his unfocused glare finds my face. "But, technically, I can count five." He holds up seven fingers.

Truly, how much I'm going to get out of this conversation is going to depend on how fast I can get him to talk before the rest of the alcohol catches up to the both of us. "Tell me about all of them. Tell me about my mother."

"First." He holds up a finger. "Life. It'za bitch. And I hate it."

I take another drink, wincing.

"I miss my home country," he sighs. His breath hits the top of the empty bottle. It whistles. Something strange shifts the air. A change. A magic. It's Satyr, his sigh swirling the bottle and whistling a mournful tune. Illusions of dancing petals fritz through the air and I smell them. Soft and floral. And then they and the feelings they evoke vanish, leaving a sour smoke. Saytr takes another drink, frowning at the now empty bottle. He blows again and another sound, like a woman singing, slips from the neck of the glass. The room shimmers as if rain fell on a day of full sunlight.

I finish the bottle in front of me, letting the last of the liquid lick the back of my throat. I hand it to him. He lifts a corner of his mouth, blowing once more. Another sound, higher than the last–this one like a young boy, but just as sad–hums in the air. As he speaks, I can smell something.

It's not a scent that is as simple as cherry blossoms or the land after it rains in a deep forest, it's more. It reminds me of all of those things, but also of a memory as my heart aches for a place I've never known. It's the sound of a dream that you've always had, but one that is fated to die inside you and curdle your heart until the world becomes a bitter peel of once-sweet fruit flesh. "The cursed fae. The banished fae. That is the first ill I will speak of. It also relates to your mother."

The whistling continues. He pops another cork, hands the bottle to me, and pops two more. As he drinks, he speaks. "First thing is that living forever is a curse. I clock that one under just living in general, but having to endure with no respite, that is cruel. And the fae are cruel. I am cruel." He slices a sharp look to me. He waits until I put the drink to my mouth and chug it. I'm not sure I'll ever want to drink wine again. The world feels strange and pulsing, but if I want answers from someone, this is my chance.

"Why is living forever such a bad thing?"

He ignores me. "Across the sea, beyond the Mist Wall, Otherland waits for us. I can hear her when I wake up. The only way to silence her is to drink. There, most of the fae live. Some humans, but that is another story for another girl." I frown at him. "I suppose, it relates to you in a way. Your mother must have been fae enough to live there, but human enough to make a mistake to get banished. And fucked up enough to damn us all. If she's dead, I'm glad of it. But I've never been lucky." He snorts.

Of course she's dead. Anger drips through my veins at the slight against my mother, but I quell it with a twist of my lips.

Something shifts in Satyr.

A cruel streak, a flash in his eye. "Drink, little mortal witch, if you want more answers."

I frown.

"If you can drink enough where you don't feel the pain, I will tell you a secret."

With that promise, I down a bottle. And then another.

"You'll—" I begin, but my mouth is dry and cottony. The world is spinning. Above us, I see a swirling world and people shimmer there, singing a sad song for a homeland they'll never have again. "You'll need to tell me more than that," I mumble.

"How about this, witch. You've had a bottle and part of another. Drink as many as you'd like. For each one, I shall tell you of a curse."

I drink. I keep drinking.

"Your dear puca will tell you only so much, but like all the cursed, she has her own agenda. She'll not tell you another secret for another year."

Another bottle.

"Your husband has been cursed and he holds an agreement with the banished fae. One that if he breaks, will kill everyone here. *Hold the wood*, tis' his only task. And yes, he's the bastard you think he is."

As I drink the next bottle, acid clings to the back of my throat. I eye the remaining bottles, deciding in the smear of consciousness to ask, "What makes you think my mother got banished from Otherland?"

"She's the reason we all did. A long, long time ago." He leans closer and my eyes flutter closed, the haze of alchol-fueled stupor riding my body. "So best be careful, little witch. Human and fae alike want you dead." He delivers a soft kiss to my cheek. "I do, too. Just not yet."

I close my eyes.

I wake up in darkness, the cellar dim and empty. The collection of bottles sit around me, as if I'd decided to drink it all alone. Sickness washes through me as I stumble upstairs. The world wiggles like streaks of water on a dirty, hazy window. I stumble through the hall, looking for my room.

Killian finds me. I look at him. He raises an eyebrow. "Asha did say you'd gone to see Satyr."

Every wrong in the world boils beneath my skin and the world spins in a coil of my rage. "Fuckger wolvesanfae," I gurgle at him. Then, I toss up everything in my stomach on his pristine boots.

* * *

When I wake up, I'm not in my room.

"Mine was closer," a voice says from a chair.

I'm in Killian's bedroom. I groan, head pounding. The mirror on the ceiling shows me how awful I look. Around me is a cascade of red silken sheets.

"Leave me alone," I groan. The cool fabric calms my skin. But not the nausea.

"Less than a year, witch."

I grit my teeth. "Do not call me that."

"I thought witches didn't like lies. Why would I not call you what you are?" I can practically hear his eyebrow raise in mockery.

"Then what shall I call you? Bloody bastard," I grumble. Something flashes in his eyes and he's abruptly in my face.

"Never call me that," he hisses.

I struck a nerve, then.

"What do you want?" I ask. He doesn't want to be called a bastard. It makes me think of the portrait on the wall, the little resemblance between him and his father. The former Duke of Wolves. I wonder then if he truly is a bastard.

Too many secrets. Too many curses.

"I had thought to check on you and make sure you were alright. But I forgot what a sour woman you are."

"Your taste is noted," I reply.

"You've no idea about my taste," he growls.

"Speaking of taste, where is Lord Neeson?" I smile at him.

"You don't get to fuck your lover in my house," he snaps.

I snort. "You gave me permission."

He says nothing else except to lean toward me. The shadows in his eyes grow. "Embarrass me again, and I'll kill you. Truce or no truce. Vow or no vow."

"What hurts me, hurts you," I remind him. I give him a tight smile, though a shiver of fear rakes bloody claws down my back. "And likewise, husband."

"And when have I embarrassed you?" he asks.

I hoist myself out of the bed. The world still spins, alcohol still racing through my blood. I can make it, I decide. I can get back. And away from this blasted man. I need to sharpen my axes for the moment I get to bury one in the back of his skull. That, or stab him through the eye with the grimsbane blade.

I cock my head to the side. It occurs to me that I can hurt him without killing him directly. I wonder how far I can push the vow.

"Wife? Tell me when I've embarrassed you like you've shamed me," he growls.

I toss my hair behind me as I open the door. "You embarrassed me the moment you became my husband."

CHAPTER 56

I stay in my room the entire day. Nisha paces, scratching at the floor. I glare at her every time I hear a noise in her direction.

I don't forgive her. Not one bit.

She hasn't chosen to retake her human-ish form since we last spoke. She hasn't tried to speak with me either—neither with lips nor the presence of her mind. Why she's still here is beyond me.

I leave my mental walls up, letting them crest high enough that even I wonder what I'm feeling.

"GO!" I finally yell. She watches me for a long moment after that.

She tries to push something against my mental walls, but I block her so completely that all I feel is a distant whimper of pain and all I hear in my mind is a faint whisper of Nisha's cry.

"LEAVE. And don't come back!"

The last glimpse I have of her is her tail wisping through the wall as she disappears.

Derrick's placement elsewhere is a mystery. Asha claims Killian removed him from the cells underground, but for all I know Derrick's corpse could be lying there, a frozen husk right where I left him. I shiver. There's no love lost between us, but I can't help but feel loyalty to him. The age-old whisper of the Bears burns a brand through my core: loyalty first, loyalty first.

The world becomes so much more complicated when one must figure out how to be loyal. Or to whom.

And yet, Derrick is someone I grew up with. The chokehold of who I am—*was*—grips my throat in tight-fisted urgency. For the simple fact that he is of the Bears and so am I.

Was. I am a Wolf now. Perhaps.

It's hard enough to know what House I even belong with, much less *who*.

The ring grips my finger in another hot pulse. Killian's anger—frustration, insecurity, whichever—pulses through the metal like a molten breath.

A flutter of paper sounds underneath the door. Another missive comes and goes, the same arrogant request written on it.

I've never seduced a man, but I'm not sure I have it in me to do it. To pretend I don't want to kill him. I wonder if I can keep my temper long enough to pretend to like him. I wonder if I can just stab him. Does it count if I don't kill him right away?

Witches don't—can't—lie, after all. Not without consequences. Perhaps it's the distant fae blood, where with more power comes more traps. A way to level the playing field. I can lie with my body, but as soon as he expects a direct answer to a question, I'll be leveled out on the floor. Again.

A knock sounds on the door.

"Just leave it and I will get it later."

"No." The voice is dark. I swallow, knowing exactly who it is.

"Since you don't have food, I'd prefer you leave," I call.

"I do have food," he says. "And I would like to eat it with you." My stomach growls.

The lock on the door clicks open and Killian pushes through, picnic basket in hand and a baby blue fuzzy blanket in the other.

When he opens the basket, pixies—the periwinkle and navy blue varieties—fly out. Small hats, made of acorns, adorn their heads. I can't help but stare, marveling at the light dripping from their pores.

The stems atop their acorn hats glow with a candle-like flicker. Inside the basket, another bit of fabric obscures what is inside, except the flipped-up corner revealing a bright, waxy green apple.

"I thought we could get to know one another."

"The different sides of the castle works for me."

"I'm afraid that doesn't work for me any longer."

"And why not?" I know why not, but I wonder what he will say to me.

He waves a hand. "It doesn't work for my image," he says succinctly. "I can't be known as the lord whose wife is repulsed by him and fucks other men."

"I didn't—"

"It doesn't matter if you did or didn't. All that matters is appearances. And what it appears to me is that I am humiliated. You've broken our deal," he says accusingly. He doesn't say anything about my foray into his office. Or about our ugly conversation earlier.

Honestly. As if I ran from that vile creature and immediately had sex with Derrick in my bed.

"You threw me in a dungeon," I reply, finally plucking the beguiling apple from the basket. I run it along my sleeve.

"I got you out."

I snort. "Why, thank you, my prince, for saving me from the villain." A wet crack rends the air as I bite into the fruit. My tastebuds alight with the sour-sweetness. "Oh wait," I say, mouth still full. "I guess that's you."

Killian sighs, leaning backwards. "I think—" He swallows, as if this is difficult for him. "I apologize."

"You think you apologize?"

"Yes," he replies, threading a hand through his dark hair. The shadows slide around the floor, ticking as if they're irritated. "Though, you did leave me to die."

"How was I supposed to know that was you?" I counter with a question. Not a lie. A sleight of hand.

He levels a look at me to let me know he knows better.

I shrug. "Fine, tell me about the snacks you've brought me, then."

He opens his mouth as if he'll say something else, closes it, then opens it again. "Nothing more to say about your marriage to a villain?"

"Anything to say about your marriage to a wicked witch?" I reply.

"Fair enough," he says. "So here are the snacks I have brought you." He pulls back the blanket. As if he's been waiting for this moment, his eyes are on me like a weight of stones pressing against my skin. I can feel it, but I'm not looking at him directly when he peels the fabric back and another host of bright pixies burst from the basket. It looks like all the magic I felt when I was a girl.

I swallow, a sudden rush of tears in my eyes. A few pixies float nearby the array of hard cheeses, handheld pies, fresh fruit, and wrapped bread. I place a hand to the loaf; warmth rises up to meet my fingers.

"The kitchen just pulled that out of the oven," Killian says, peering in. I hope the bread didn't melt any of the cheese. There's a gouda and cacio e pepe, as well as a spreadable goat cheese. There should be jams somewhere in here…" He digs through the basket. He pulls out a little bowl filled with dried mango and a tin with a smear of brown on the side. I pop it open, noting two chocolate cupcakes. Killian continues to dig through the never-ending feast, looking for something it seems may not be in there. His finger knocks into a pixie, who turns an angry pink and gives him the middle finger. "Apologies, madam."

Looking at him here with all of the food he's brought me, it's almost enough for me to invite him into my bed to fuck me.

"Ah," he says, pulling out a jar. It's red, like blood, with tiny seeds visible through the translucent glass. The lid comes off with a sharp snap and he slips a finger inside. A wet sound fills the space between us and he doesn't look away from me. His eyes take on that fire-bright quality and my ring burns hot on my hand. Desire rises inside of me and I know his wedding band on his finger must be burning with the same hot temptation. How easily between us it can become lust.

He pulls his index and middle finger out of the jar and the jam slips down his fingers in a slow promenade. He licks the edge of his finger, tongue lashing out and catching the dribble that threatens to slip between the crevices at his knuckles.

"Delicious." His voice is more wolf than man. "Care for a bite?"

I nudge closer to him, breath stilled somewhere between my heart and throat. Heat flares in every region I can think of, as if I've just told the largest lie of my life.

He slips both fingers back into the jam, the contents of the jar lapping against the digits like frantic tongues. Killian slides them back out, never looking away from me as he lifts his hand to my face. The pads of his fingers tease my lips as he presses them to my mouth. I open for him and suck the strawberry flavor. Bright, tartness pops on my taste buds and I flutter my eyes closed. My lips suction his fingers. He stares at me as if I'm a siren who's transfixed a ship of his men at sea.

"Perhaps this is the first thing we can agree on," I reply, licking them once over before leaning back against my elbows in a careless gesture I don't feel. My body shakes with want, but I shove it down. "Now, dear husband, have you come to seduce me or was there something else you had in mind?"

His eyes hood themselves as he stares at me. His gaze lingers on every curve of my body and I know he's imagining the same wicked things I'm feeling. My wedding band burns like a brand. "I had come to propose a truce, but seduction works just as well." His voice sounds like silk sheets and moans at midnight.

"Tell me about this truce," I counter.

With a pinky, he swirls the jam, letting the bits of strawberry collect along the digit before popping the finger between his waiting lips. "I'd rather talk about the seduction."

I snort, but don't reply.

He sighs, as if giving in, but I'm not fooled. My wedding band slips not one degree cooler. As I look at him, not for the first time, I wish I could see the coins slipping from those seductive lips.

"I need you," he says. The bedroom voice slips away and I look at him directly. This is the Duke speaking. "My bannermen, the lords… they will be coming at Equinox and if my wife finds me distasteful, I will appear weak. I need you to appear...to like me." He grits out the last part.

How it must gall him to ask this. The Duke of Death needs me. The man I need to kill, the man I've been wondering how to seduce, he's thrown himself right into a hole I didn't know was there. I toss back my head and laugh, a full hearty cackle. The band on my hand cools abruptly, plummeting in temperature along with Killian's apparent desire.

"Witch," he mutters.

"Are you asking for a faux courtship, Your Grace?" I tease. It's like something out of a novel.

"Of a sort," he grimaces, scooping up another dollop of jam on his finger and plopping it in his mouth. I watch his lips. It's hard to know if he realizes how erotic his mouth is. How is it possible for lips to look so delicious? And his eyelashes—

I jerk my gaze away. Instead, I tear off a hunk of bread and shove it in my face.

"I would like you to be seen accompanying me about Wolf Hall and to be seen on my arm for the Equinox Ball we will host. To introduce you to the Wolves as my duchess. And appear to...enjoy it." He says these last words with a tight smile.

"That will cost you extra," I say around a mouthful of bread.

"Yes, to cost." Killian tangles a hand through his dark hair and leans back on his elbows. I can't help but look at the sweep of chest hair that peeks out, the stretch of the fabric on his pecs. As my gaze goes back to his face, his eyebrow raises. "I'm happy to service you with my body, of course."

My cheeks burn. "Despicable," I reply. I'm not sure if I mean it in a way I don't like.

"Delicious," he counters. He sighs, but then scoots closer until he's right next to me. "That is part of it, though," he continues, voice dropping an octave. "I'll need you to appear to find me attractive." He pauses, as if he's chewing on something. "Well, at least show your cards a little, darling witch." He holds up his hand with the wedding band on it.

I swallow, my cheeks slipping to scarlet heat.

"I want my freedom," I rasp. A truth worth a thousand silvers.

"I thought you might ask for something like that." He pulls out a key, the sort that time grinds its molars against. A bit of rust flakes from it. Looped through a chain, it swings like a pendulum. Killian holds it out, waiting for me to put my head through. I do. As he lowers it, his knuckles graze against my collarbone. "This will take you anywhere—except my study. "

The one place I want to go. The one place he knows I want to go.

"That, as ever, is private." He pauses, eye burning. "The Wolves are free with their affection," he continues, and as he says this, a light hand trails down my arm. "While you are mine at the Equinox Ball, a part of the agreement is that you allow me to hold your hand." He traces a finger on the center of my palm, slipping it back up to my wrist and rubbing it. Images rush into my mind of him, pinning me against a wall, a bed—*anywhere*—and those hands everywhere. "Or hold whatever you ask me to," he rasps.

"We'll see. As for Derrick..." I trail off, watching the annoyance ripple across his face. "You can't keep him in the dungeon."

"He will stay there until he deserves to be released."

I open my mouth and shut it. Derrick hardly deserves to be held against his will for a long time.

"I can give him to the woods."

That, too, seems a poor choice.

"When I go home to visit..." Killian growls when I say these words. "...allow him to go with me."

"If I ever let you go, perhaps. Until then, I'll have him set up comfortably enough." Killian's eyes burn darkly into mine. "I'll see you tomorrow at our usual time then."

And after, I'll find out what my mother's image is doing here in this den of blighted wolves. I smile at him, but it's more feral than a dainty lifting of lips. Killian doesn't know it, but he's already lost whatever game we're playing. And so have I.

"Wait. The portrait..." I almost swallow the question. But maybe he'll answer it. "The portrait of the woman with white hair…tell me about her."

He laughs, a bitter sound. "Of course, there's a connection to her. After all this time."

"What do you know of her?"

"She's the reason I am the way I am."

"Cursed?"

"Yes," he rasps. "She did this to us all. And you must belong to her, for you torture me more than she ever has."

Something tender breaks through a soft, malleable bit of me. I lean in and brush a light kiss to his mouth. "Tell me more."

"That's enough," he says, voice breaking. "I've told you more than I wanted to."

I press another kiss to his lips, but he doesn't move away.

His lips slip sweetly against mine. Killian feels like he's everywhere, but worst of all, he feels close to my heart.

The time to seduce him ticks by, to get close enough to learn what he cares for enough to finally slaughter him. My breath quickens. I will have to do it. But the confusion between what I know of my mother and what he's saying is far too much for me to bear. I don't think he'll be honest with me. The one person I need the Sight for, it doesn't work. And I don't know why.

I slip from his side and Killian doesn't protest. The door shuts gently behind me as I leave my room, the feeling of his warm lips on mine haunting more than any ghost ever could. The time to seduce him ticks by, to get close enough to learn what he cares for enough to finally slaughter him. My heart gives an extra beat at the thought. I will have to do it. But the confusion between what I know of my mother and what he's saying is far too much for me to bear.

CHAPTER 57

*K*illian and I lay down in the courtyard that has begun to feel like a sanctuary. The weeks that passed never ended without him seeing me at least once a day. Fall cracked summer in half, leaving trails of dead leaves on the wind and a dead chill that promises winter is around the corner. After the equinox, our marriage will run full-tilt towards the halfway point.

I find myself trying to shut off the piece of me that demands blood and demands answers whenever I look into Killian's eyes. Something strange has broken between us. Maybe it's the changing of seasons, but part of me slips into a tender and willful ignorance as I try to force the future away. Each day brings a little more of a transformation between us. It doesn't seem real that the blood moon was months ago.

I lean into Killian, fall air crisp against my nostrils as I breathe deep. He slings his arm around me, face slipping into my hair as he inhales.

"Did you just…smell me?"

"Yes."

He says nothing else.

I lean into his armpit and give him a whiff. "Yuck," I say. His tunic holds the scent of sweaty musk and something spicy. I kind of like it, but I wrinkle my nose anyways. A faint pain, like the beginnings of a cold, squeezes my throat with the tiny, white lie. The ring on my finger flares as warmth suffuses the metal. It brightens the way a hot coal does just after a fire goes out. When I look up, Killian is staring at me.

"Yuck?" he questions, eyebrow raised. "Lies aren't good for you, wicked witch."

I don't reply.

"You know this can't last." His breath skirts my face. Butterflies flip in my stomach.

"What do you mean?" I ask. Deep inside, I know, though.

"I know you care for me. I can feel it." He rubs the ring at his finger. A spike of fear flares inside of me. He can feel what, exactly?

"I care to kill you," I say. The little band at my finger itches.

He sighs. "Briar, can we just pretend for one moment that we're not enemies?"

Witches can't lie. Not with our tongues, anyways. Not without consequences. He knows that. He's *seen* that. But still. I can't help but yearn for what he's asking. A break from this endless war.

"You are..." I pause. He leans in, eyes bright with interest. I can't help but stare at his lips. Want stirs in me. We may have been placed at the opposite ends of the chess board, but that doesn't stop me from desiring his mouth on me. On all of me. "...you...are my favorite enemy." I finally say with an impish grin. It's the truth. No fever boils in my veins at the words.

He quirks a half-smile, but something shadows in his eyes. "Of course, I am. Of all the villains, I must be the most devastatingly handsome."

"Are you looking for an award?"

"That depends on the prize." He pauses. "*Is* there a prize, witch?" His fingers find my arm, swirling at the sensitive skin on the inside of my elbow. I fight a shudder. Letting my body ache with want is allowing him to win this little game.

"For an enemy?" I scoff. Willingly giving him anything would be an affront to everything I believe in. A loss. I am playing the long game here. "Never."

He frowns, turning away. "What villain plays a game where there is nothing to win?"

"What villain expects to win when he can just take what he wants?" I counter. The words drop from my mouth before I have a chance to think of what I've said.

A dare.

A wolfish grin alights his mouth, his eyes nearly burn with a white fire. The strange otherness flickers before he shudders.

"I've no use for cheap trinkets." He presses a quick kiss to my cheek. "The most valuable things in my life have been years in the making."

Killian suddenly shifts away from me.

"I need you to meet some important people tonight. There will be a small dinner. Some entertainment. I expect you to be there."

He leaves before I can say anything else.

CHAPTER 58

$\mathcal{I}$ walk into the dinner hall. My dress swishes around my ankles, liquid silk, and all heads turn toward me. Dark sapphire fabric slips against my skin, with a few dots of crystals beaming at the hem as if the seamstress pulled the bluest section of the night sky and decided to give it to me. The cut curves in a graceful loop at my collarbones. A black ribbon ties around my neck and a cameo of a pixie made of white ivory beams against an onyx background. A thin, simple bangle adorns the same wrist the shadow bracelet rests on. When the bangle shifts, it moves right through the shadow.

My neck prickles with the feeling of being watched. I feel naked and I fight the urge to cross my arms, as if I can cover myself or become invisible. I walk down the aisle toward the center dais where there is my chair and an empty one beside it. The feeling of eyes on me intensifies, and I turn.

There he is.

Killian peeks out from the velvet black shadows. His hooded eyes watch me, lazily lapping up the length of my body as if we are the only two people here.

The people around the room lean in. Wolves, bedecked in casual garb, grab drumsticks and cobs of corn. The sound of clinking glasses abruptly ceases as attention narrows to the space between my husband and me.

Gods, this is torture.

Blood rushes to my cheeks and I grind down on my teeth. Titters follow him as Killian stalks over to me. He takes my hand, placing it on his arm as he moves me toward where he was sitting. I move around the table and sit at my seat, and he slips next to me, unconcerned.

Lukas sits at a nearby table. He raises a glass in salute and turns back to his companion, an attractive blonde woman. Remmy, looking much better than his time in the infirmary, sits next to Lukas with a spoon dangling from his mouth.

"So, my wicked witch." Killian looks ahead as if he's not speaking to me. His goblet hovers in front of his lips. "What game shall we play this evening?"

"I have no idea what you mean," I reply, likewise lifting my goblet. The gilded surface slides across my lips and I take the opportunity to let the mulled wine lap at my mouth. The taste of clove and cinnamon wet my tongue, and warmth spreads through my chest. I want to get drunk. The inclination is unwise.

"You know, Briar, I am not opposed to bedroom games. However, I do not share well." This he says with gritted teeth.

I smile, openly turning to him. "Then I suppose we should not play such games."

His face darkens, brow crashing to just above his eyes with barely a centimeter of space. Our earlier ease is gone, replaced with the feeling that Killian is almost here, but not quite. Or if his soul is truly looking out of his eyes, he has company. A sick feeling passes over me as I look at him, noting the darkness looking out. With that, I decide I don't mind trying to hurt him. Killian's jaw ticks in frustration. Good.

"Where is Derek staying? North side of Wolf Hall?" I ask, daring to play the game he warned against. "Or still in the dungeon?"

Killian turns to me. His mouth stretches into a false smile. The gleam in his eyes makes him look more wolf than man. "You know, *wife.*" He says this last word with special emphasis. "I do think that we should play that special sort of game. In fact, I think a new living situation is in order."

The volume in the large, echoing room quiets as if everyone inside has pressed their ears to the wall to hear what we are saying.

"I think," Killian says, "from now on my wife should share my chambers."

I down the rest of my drink in one large gulp.

He pulls me close, as if we're truly lovers, as if he spends his free moments thinking of sweet nothings to tickle my ear. His breath rasps against my skin, hot and dry. "I will not be made a fool of. You don't know what game you are playing, my darling witch, but this is too important for me to let you fuck this up." His teeth skate down my neck. Eyes watch us, and the press of what feels like a thousand gazes envelopes my skin in a tight, hot bubble. I shut my eyes and try to shut it out, except my body betrays me and I shiver. "That's a good girl," he whispers. "Finally, a good witch in my grasp."

I inhale. I could fight him on this, but I don't. This doesn't affect me at all.

Thank the gods witches don't burn for lying in their own heads, a nasty voice whispers in my mind. I want to stab her.

"Come with me to the hall. I need to speak with you," Killian growls.

He pulls me away. His palms scrape against my arm, trailing down to lightly clasp my wrist. A tremor tickles down my spine. He stares straight ahead, like something races on our heels. As we pass, the people in the hall crane their necks to watch us as Killian leads me out. There's barely the scrape of a fork on a dish and the entire hall runs silent.

Killian lets go of my wrist to press the doors shut behind us. Through the wood, there's finally a burst of noise—sudden chatter and music. I turn away, walking a few paces forward. Tension settles between my shoulders, stiffening them. A mixture of anger and want cracks through my heart.

A thick hush settles like a layer of snow between us.

CHAPTER 59

The hallway is empty. Then Killian's lips are on my neck. Despite the anger, or perhaps because of it, lust rakes an insistent hand down my body.

Something intoxicating slips through my veins, like *var*, the drug that made people believe they'd been granted their deepest desires. That, combined with an aphrodisiac.

Killian presses behind me. The hard planes of his front are tight against the soft curves of my back. A hand grips my ass.

"Gods, do I love this," he whispers, squeezing me.. His other hand comes up to cup my other cheek with a dull smack.

"Someone may see," I hiss, shivering. The anger I'd felt earlier doesn't matter right now. Not when he's touching me like this. We're barreling toward a miserable end, why not enjoy the ride?

His hand trails leisurely along my body, as if he's the king and he can do what he pleases. A finger finds my neck, slipping down to thumb my nipple through the thin fabric of my gown. I swallow hard as my breathing quickens.

"And would that be so bad, wicked witch?" he murmurs in my ear. "What if I want them to know you're mine?"

Possession.

I shiver with pleasure. I shouldn't like it, shouldn't want to be his—anyone's—but I can't help the thrill that the words *you're mine* send through me, even as I reject them. I shouldn't want to be anyone's but my own.

Why not both? a devilish voice asks.

Because, I argue with myself. *We're not here for that.* I'll kill him soon enough.

"I think you'd like it," Killian says, dropping the bedroom voice. He means it seriously. He spins me around so he can look me in the eye. "Briar, you know if you want to try anything we can talk about it."

What is this? Part of his plan to seduce me? Confusion wars inside of me with anger and want. Am I being used? A pawn? And yet, this man is nothing but a pawn to me. Why shouldn't I use him back? Still, the level of seriousness in his voice swirls my doubts inside of me. Why should he even care about what I like?

My breath hitches. Sex wasn't something I ever talked about with anyone. I had it, sure, but we didn't *talk* about what we liked. Or what I liked. Even with Derrick.

"I think you like the thrill of getting caught." Killian's bedroom voice is back. It's as if he can't help himself. Killian is always trying to seduce me. "Of being seen."

I shake my head.

"Really?" Killian purrs.

Someone could come out at any moment. The opera singer in the dinner hall belts out another note in a language I can't understand. Killian moves, pulling me with him. No one, not even a spritelight, haunts the hall. Killian pulls me to a window seat and nestles us behind a curtain. Shadows buoy out from the thick velvet, cocooning us. He pulls at the top of my dress, quickly undoing loops to reveal my breasts. His tongue finds my clavicle.

Anyone could walk in. Through the curtains, around the corner. They'd see a wall of shadow, they'd *know*. Heat threads through my veins.

"I think," he whispers, pulling me back further into the little alcove. "I'm right."

"Of course you're not right," I rasp. "I don't want to be caught."

"Not yet," he says, "you merely want to be almost-caught."

And I can't help but see us, clothes half undone, in a passionate twist and ecstasy, when the applause crescendos.

"Shall we test that theory?" Killian asks. A silky smile stretches his lips. His dark eyes light up like fires in the distance, warning the enemy is coming. "Or are you afraid I'm right?"

I push my hand down the front of his trousers, feeling the hard, silken length of him.

"I want to be inside you," he whispers.

"And I want to speak a thousand lies and eat more cake than my stomach has room for." I murmur back into his ear. "Shall we compromise tonight? I want you to show me your throat, Duke."

He leans his neck back as I stroke his cock. I spit on my hand, wetting it. He groans in my ear as I work up and down his shaft.

"Touch me."

The shadows surge through the alcove, as if I'm the one that has control over them. One feels warm and wet as it tangles beneath my skirts, sliding up my leg. I shiver as it touches my sensitive place.

"Are you sure you don't want me inside of you?" he asks, voice shaking. "Because I'm about to come."

I'm not ready for the level of intimacy required for us to join like that—not yet. Later, perhaps.

But I *am* ready for him to come.

"Come for me, master of shadows," I whisper. I shiver as the shadow continues to stroke me, but he loses control and the portraits around us slam to the floor. Nearby, a large vase shatters, and shards of porcelain torpedo toward us. Killian shifts at the last minute as he comes, taking the pieces in the back. His hands move under my dress, as if nothing hurts, and he uses his thumb this time on my clit, quickly moving me to ecstasy.

I come apart in his hands.

For a moment, everything is quiet except the distant sounds in the other room and our heavy breathing. The smell of sweat and sex swirls around us.

The door to the hall opens. Noise filters in and we freeze. Clothes undone, *I'm* undone.

"Who's there?"

The curtain pulls away from us. Killian's shadows block me, but the lord's eyes already widen with the brief glimpse of my naked breasts.

The lord lets out a low whistle. "Looks like you aren't being cuckolded after all, Your Grace."

Shame poisons my gut. A game. It was all a game. To what end, I don't know. Perhaps to prove himself after all. To everyone that he was wanted.

"The Duchess does have nice tits, though," the man says.

The shadows swirl around us, still blocking the man's view. Killian pulls away from me. Again, the sensation of whenever he leaves my arms only gifts me with a frigid chill.

I wonder if he'll lean in, smirk with the man.

Instead, he punches the lord in the face.

CHAPTER 60

Killian brings me to his room—now *our* room. Silence stretches between us.

"You think I planned this?"

"I know you did!" I yell. "I heard you and Asha! You have to seduce me so your people don't think you're weak."

Killian is silent for a moment. "It's not like that," he finally says. "It's more than just people thinking I'm weak…" The edge of his inhale is a jagged jerk. His hand slips through his hair, brow furrowing, as if he's not sure if he should say what he's thinking.

I don't reply. Waiting. Hurt brims at the corners of my eyes, blurring everything.

"You *make* me weak, Briar." He cups my face.

"Then kneel," I say, wanting to torture him.

At first, I think he won't do it. Killian's eyes darken and a growl crawls up his throat. He shoves me backwards, my spine thudding onto the bed. A reverent expression passes over his face as he hikes my skirts up past my hips. Satin pools across my stomach and a chill strikes my now-bare skin. Killian leans in, teeth scraping at my flesh, followed by clever hands. Hot fingers leave streaks of fire down my legs before hooking at the corners of my knee.

Then he yanks.

Positioned right between my legs, we're a mesh of tender valleys and firm lines. The soft curve of my inner thigh heats against the hard, outer muscle of his.

"You want me to kneel, Duchess of Wolves?"

Yes. Desperate fire claws at me. I want *him*—want him to kneel, I want him inside of me.

I can only nod at his words. *Kneel.* And gods, do I want him to kneel. Heat slicks me. His finger whorls at the soft back of my leg. Circling. Thinking.

Slowly, ever so slowly, he sinks to the ground.

Finally, after all this time, the Wolf kneels.

"Just because you make me weak, just because I want to worship you, it doesn't mean you've won." Killian's words have the force of a sword's swing, intent on drawing blood.

Yes it does, I want to say, but I don't want him to stop.

I will win, in the end. I have to. I've never had a choice. What he thinks I'm going to win, I have no idea, though. I only know that I must claim victory only granted by his death.

Kill the Wolf.

He presses his mouth to my center, teasing me over my underwear . Lightning jolts my core and a warm pool of want slides its fingers inside of me. The world—everything that brought me here to this moment—snaps away from me with a zap of need.

"Do I make you weak, too, Briar?"

"Never," I breathe. The lie burns through me.

His hands grab my underwear and pulls. Something catches, rips. "Fuck," he curses, mouth pressed to me, finding my clit. His tongue slips in circles, around and around. I grip the sheets, white knuckling them as another wave of want rides inside of me.

Killian, Killian, *Killian.*

"Not weak at all?" he asks. His finger thumbs my entrance. I shudder.

"Don't stop," I order. My knees press into his head, as if to bring him closer. He pulls away.

The hard planes of his face shadow. The light flickers in the corner. The brassy carrying candle's base shines. It's the same object depicted in the painting in my chambers.

I can't see Killian's expression, but the way he pulls back— I know. Whatever lives inside of him, whatever hateful thing, it's back.

And it wants me to lose.

"*Submit to me.*" A voice like curling smoke and midnight devils. A firm hand grabs my hip, hard, the other cups my other hip gently, circling the knob of bone there.

"I don't submit to demons," I say. Fear and want war inside of me. It's still Killian. But the demons that pull at him from the inside are there, too. Whatever evil resides inside my husband slips out in both dark and silver-gold fragments. The bits of the man I've come to know are so little right now. Killian is at the mercy of his personal demons.

A ripple shudders his face, his eyes draining of the deep shadows that haunt him. "I kneel only for you. Tell me you submit. Tell me you're mine." Killian's gaze takes on that umber look that's truly *him*. His teases my clit with his tongue and I swear I may come right then. "Tell me."

"*No*," I finally say, a shiver riding my body.

He freezes. I grab at his hair but he pulls away again.

"Then I will no longer kneel to you," he says with a vicious look in his eye.

These games we play. Sex deals and marriage politics. Demons and kings and wolves and witches. I lean back in frustrated silence. Something inside of me protests. *Just lie*, a voice whispers. *Tell him you'll love him forever*. I wonder what such an utterance would cost. Would I find that the price I paid in shivering fevers is less than I think?

Would it even be a lie at all?

I don't speak it. Not for fear that I'd contract a fever, but for the stark terror that I won't.

"Wait," I whisper. "Killian."

He stills, staring at me..

The room tilts as desperation chokes me. I can barely breathe past the feeling, as if all I am is a frayed braid of desire and ugly fear that he won't want what I can offer. "I'm yours. For the night."

The air settles across the space between us in a thick coat of silence.

At first I think he'll leave, but then he turns. A shadow uncoils itself from the thick canopy that drapes along the back side of the bed. Soft and cool, it trails a translucent finger down my cheek. My nipples tighten.

"Then that will be enough."

CHAPTER 61

*T*onight won't be enough.

"Lift your hips, wicked witch," Killian rasps in my hair. I do. His hands snake over my curves. I'm pulled closer as the shadows do the work for him of slipping a pillow beneath my ass, angling my body upwards. The silk chills my skin, but my husband's hands leave trails of heat as he idly strokes my body.

Killian poises above me, completely naked. The low light limns his muscles, alighting on the planes of his chest and the roll of his biceps as he hovers above me. The muscles bunch at his chest, with a thin layer of dark hair. Want burns inside of me in a way I've never felt before. I brush a hand across his face. His eyes track my face. Taking me in. The light in the corner flickers, as if the candle is fighting to not go out.

"Don't let it go out," I say. It's more than just being afraid of darkness. Perhaps I'm not so afraid of what the shadows hold, not with Killian here. No, I just don't want to miss the look in his eyes when he comes. I shiver again, my flesh pimpling. "I need to see you."

"Darling, I'll always leave a light on for you. I wish–" He cuts himself off. His jaw ticks. "Tonight," he says. "Give me everything. At least once."

"Okay," I whisper.

"And don't forget." His hand pushes the hair out of my face.

I don't respond. I don't know how I could ever forget this man.

He leans down, lips trailing from my collar bone back up to my lips. His lips are soft, at first, reminding me of the tender petals. The breath he exhales is nearly a sigh, full of lost things and dead futures and brittle joys that cracked long ago.

Then he smiles into the kiss.

Just for tonight. Let us just have one moment where nothing else matters.

I smile back at him, letting myself shed all the worries and the doubts about tomorrow. And somehow, it works. A small laugh bursts from my lips, and his chest rumbles with amusement as our teeth click together.

Here we are. Grinning like fools.

He strokes the birthmark on my neck then he leans down. Fangs flash. The edge of a tooth snags a thin line of desire down my neck, not puncturing the skin. Killian's hand reaches between us, finding my clit. The smile fades from his mouth as he cups me, swirling the sensitive nub at my center. My breath hitches. More.

Wet heat slides through me. He presses a finger inward. "So wet for me. Will you be a good witch for me now and come on my cock?"

"Yes," I gasp.

"Mmm," he murmurs in my ear, leaning down. The sound of his pants shifting down rasps between us. His cock comes free, thickly laying against my thigh. "I think you might not be good at all." Killian's tongue licks at my throat. He shifts, positioning himself at my entrance. Then he pushes forward.

"Fuck," he groans.

His cock slides in further, filling me. My hand travels up to find his head. I grab at his hair as I arch. A wisp of shadow snakes out of the darkness between us. The cool touch feels hot against my clit as it swirls, swirls, swirls–

"Oh, gods," I say. Killian pumps harder into me. The bed groans under the force of his thrusts. "You feel better than I imagined."

The orgasm grows inside of me, imploding like a star. White coats my vision as I come.

Killian growls as I convulse around him. His eyes stay that same brown, but little fresh scratches–none of my doing–redden against my fingers. Fresh marks from whatever haunts him. "Briar," he moans into my ear as he pulls out, spilling across the sheets.

We lay like that, in tangled sweat, for a long time.

* * *

THE EQUINOX IS SOON. Just a few days away. If I'm going to do this, it's time.

I recall so long ago, that struggle with Sir Typhen. I must never forget that I'm here to kill my husband. Excuses bubble up through me, desperately wanting a way out, but there's no escape to be found. After our fervid coupling, betrayal haunts me. I need to do it now. Before I can't.

Either Killian dies or my father dies.

And the only reason for Papa to die at this point is if I'm no longer amongst the living. I'll be an ill spirit haunting this earth before I give this up. My breath stills in my chest, heavy like a gravestone as I creep back to my room.

I pull out the items brought with me from Gray Hall. The cards, the spirit board, bits and mementos from what feels like a lifetime ago. The bit of paper crinkles between my fingers as I pull it out.

Now that the time is here, though, the time to use this paper to send a message to the king–resistance stalls my fingers. I close my eyes, breathing out. I have to do this. I must.

He tried to kill you. I shake my head, a painful throb settling itself around my temples.

Confusion rattles my lungs as I heave in a ragged inhale. I don't know. It doesn't matter, though. A bargain is a bargain and I have made my own fate. Or the gods have. Whichever, the path has settled itself into one, tight line forward.

I grab the paper, writing as instructed. *King Thaddeus, you are invited to the Equinox Ball.* I scribble. My handwriting is barely legible, my fingers shake so badly. But I have to do this now.

A hollow feeling splits through my stomach. Disgust slicks through me.

The memory of Sir Typhen's fingers against my chest, his nail slipping against my skin, Killian's heated declaration–*touch her again and lose your hand*–lives inside my body. Little images ingrained into my very flesh, alongside everything I'd shared with Killian. He's been inside of me, but it's more than just an exchange of pleasure. Killian has reached through me, past my heart, and into the essence that makes me *me*. He's seen it, the ugly parts, the darkness. A man half made of shadows, he isn't the type to see darkness and fear it. He'll let it be night until I am ready to see what the shadows hide.

I'll leave the light on for you. The words still cling to me.

You love him. A voice whispers.

I don't.

You will.

I look up, staring at the departing enchanted paper flying out the window.

Perhaps I could love him a little. But it's not enough.

CHAPTER 62

*E*quinox. Another celestial event, this one marking the halfway point to the celestial year. My lungs expand like they don't fit in my body. The flitting bit of paper tickles the edge of my memory as it escapes the window. What will happen after that—who the king will send in his stead—I don't know.

Fae lights twinkle at the vaulted ceilings in the hallway leading to the ballroom, bobbing up and down like little leaves in a near-still body of water. White, gold, blue, silver.

There's a translucent pixie waiting just to the left of my door. Her organs are visible beneath her see-through skin. When she smiles, the muscle tissue in her face stretches, revealing pointy little teeth. A high squeal sounds in my ear. Pixies are strange creatures—at once human enough to make you think that they can understand you, and on another level, they're carnivorous tiny bitches who would be more than happy to eat your finger.

She gestures for me to follow her, but not before she grabs her tits, honks them, and then titters a laugh. I snort. Pixies.

Everything smells like pumpkin and cinnamon for the Equinox Ball. Even though the tables where the food will be served are in another area entirely, scents of roast meat and pie tangles my senses.

My stomach gurgles.

I follow her toward the landing, where the herald waits. He's a stoic sort, with a mustache that pulls his whole face into an expression of disapproval, regardless of the circumstance.

Below, bits of greenery bedeck the room. Potted trees with snarled roots float, suspended by magic above the corners of the room. A few simply sit in pots on the floor, not infused by any magic, though their containers are painted with the same wondrous enchantments that allow the portraits to move. Along the bases, active scenes of wild hunts and romantic kisses play out on the fired clay. Bright orange ribbons, suited to the turning season, hang from the ceilings. Carved pumpkins lit from within dot at intervals below the tall windows, grinning crazed and wild smiles. Strong smells of cinnamon and bread and warmed chocolate reach my nose.

Despite the fact that I am meeting the bannermen of the House Wolf as their lady, despite needing to kill their lord, despite the rough kisses Killian and I mistakenly exchanged—I'm excited. Bird-like flutters fill my stomach and sweat collects at my armpits. There's a lovely shawl around my shoulders that I'm grateful for. It hides the pit stains on the green silk dress I wear.

"Duchess Briar of the Wolf," the herald calls.

The delighted chatter of the crowd downstairs fizzles out.

Fuck.

I plaster on a fake smile, letting my lips stretch in a pleasant affectation as if I'm happy to be seen. I wish I could be invisible. The people of the Wolf eye me with unpleasant suspicion. But it's different from the type of distrust I've grown up with. I don't blame them. I'm the enemy, even if I've married their lord.

Then an arm slings around me.

I jump, hand spasming as if I'm going to grip a dagger that isn't there or an ax that is several flights of stairs up. A familiar grin stretches below shining, mischievous eyes. Lukas.

"If it isn't the Duchess of Wolves," he proclaims loudly. "May I be the first to offer you my fealty?"

I laugh, though the sound is stilted. "Of course, but I think that's what the ceremony is for," I reply.

"Of course. Already my liege lady, putting me in my place." He places a hand over his heart. "If only I had gotten to you first, Duchess Briar, I would have married you in an instant. I need someone to keep me in line."

"And we shall find you one," growls a voice next to me. I freeze as a hand takes my arm, callused palm placing it atop the well-muscled forearm of the speaker. "But you may not have mine. I do not share."

I shiver as my gaze flicks to Killian. My stomach tightens.

He looks at me, taking in the green silk against the orange of the autumnal decorations around us. Little fae lights high above twinkle like little stars against a dark night. "You forget, wicked witch, that the Wolves wear purple and red."

"I wore that when we met," I retort, thinking of the spill of wine-colored silk the king had given me.

"As I recall, you were doused in the blood moon's light, so that is true," he whispers in my ear. A shiver runs up my spine and his hand curves down the slope of my waist. "Next time, wear our colors, love."

Next time.

There wouldn't be a next time.

I plaster a smile on my face. And perhaps I should have worn the red, though it would have felt like a lie. And though I can't lie with my tongue, I've lied every day that I've been here as I've sought ways to undermine the enemy. The reddish purple would have been a simple concession, a show that would have allowed me to wiggle further into his heart. And yet, I hadn't been able to bring myself to do it.

The lights above us surge. The opposite of when Killian came to Gray Hall. A yelp sounds. A pink candle explodes, the warm wax slinging out into the crowd. Dozens more that limn the room meet the same fate, as hot wax pops everywhere. There's a shriek from a nearby lady as the wax splatters her. The twinkling fae lights wink out, as if fear causes them to vacate. Only the arcane infused lamps blaze brighter. Silence leaks through the room, except for the hissing breaths of fear.

Except the steady knock of something heavy against the door from outside.

CHAPTER 63

As the doors fly open, the lights flare bright–so bright it's like looking directly into the sun. A flock of birds sweeps in, diving into the crowd. Raven after raven caws, streaking through the room and roosting themselves in the rafters. Screams and growls shiver through the room as lords and ladies get ready to hide or fight. Musk and cinnamon scents fog the space as Wolves transform into their animal states near the potted trees and some beneath the floating ones.

The Witch King stalks forward.

Whispers flick up through the crowd, a gust of wind exploding leaves into chaos. The Witch King, the Witch King, the Witch King. I swallow a poisonous feeling deep in my gut. I'm the one that invited him, but I can't help the shock that numbs my extremities at the sight of his face.

I thought he'd just send someone, truly. Rather than come here now.

Whatever game is being played is going to play itself out tonight.

"Peace," Killian orders.

A curling coil of leaves follows King Thaddeus, tilting toward the man—if one can call someone who is practically a god *a man.* Bits of autumnal decoration turn to him as if he is the sun itself. And, like the sun, the bits begin to burn when he gets too close.

Smoke wafts into the ballroom, clogging it. My eyes water, and I cough. I don't remember him doing this at Papa's, which only leaves me with the conclusion that King Thaddeus is doing it on purpose.

"Your father sends his regards," the Witch King says, looking directly at me. He smiles.

Warning me.

Papa will die if you don't do what you've committed to.

Kill the Wolf.

CHAPTER 64

I stand there, stockstill. Until a hand pulls me towards its owner. Terror slithers down my throat. One more night, perhaps. One more night. I look at the person the hand belongs to.

Killian.

"What are you doing here, King Thaddeus?" Killian's greeting isn't warm.

"Your bride invited me."

Killian doesn't betray a flicker of surprise. "I thought she might. I'm glad she did. You can enjoy our happiness," he says instead. "The festivities are for everyone who comes in peace. Anyone who doesn't...well, there are a lot of hungry creatures here that are happy to feast on an interloper's misery."

"Killian, I–"

"Don't," he murmurs. He stares at the king, who doesn't look away. They hold gazes for a long time, until the Witch King shifts his attention to me with an enigmatic look.

"I suppose I shall await your ceremonies then, Wolf. I cannot wait to see your...traditions." King Thaddeus tilts his head. I notice a little dot below his eye, similar to the one Killian has. They're of a similar height and they stare each other down with the same mix of confusion and hatred. I flick on the Sight, wondering what he will reveal. "I have come to witness." Copper.

"And my father?" I ask. A scrap of anything.

"He was...waiting for news, I think." The king watches me, eyes dark. Dark the way Killian's become.

I see.

"You will be welcome as long as you keep the peace, King. I must speak to my bride privately. Enjoy, our traditions take all night."

* * *

WE SLIP AWAY FROM EVERYONE. Away from the world. Just one more night. Just another moment. Leaving the Witch King and what his presence means behind.

"Killian," I say as the ballroom door shuts. "I'm sorry, I–"

I was just doing what I must.

"Briar," he says. The sound of my name on his lips gives me pause. Not wicked witch, Briar. "I understand. We have all done what we must here. I only hope that...forgiveness always lives between us. For whatever we must do in the face of impossible tasks. I've kept my secrets, too."

I can only gape at him before nodding.

"We'll have to come back in a little," he says, voice rough. "But I can't see you like this and not do something about it."

"See me like what?" I ask, half dreading the answer.

"Beautiful. Delicious. And...devastated." With the last word, his gaze bores into me, as if he knows everything I've hidden. As if he knows I'm here to kill him. And he must know. He must. And yet he does nothing. Of course, to an unkillable man, I'm nothing more than a gnat. The light tenderness from him in the face of it, though, is nearly more than I can bear.

Try me, it's like he's saying. *And see what I will do.*

But the blade Papa gave me–the one handed down from my mother–it means something. It's a tool, a key. And I think I have finally found the lock.

I look into my husband's eyes once more. The fringe of his eyelashes lower as he leans down, brushing a kiss to the crest of my cheekbone. I will simply wait just a little longer to open the door. And maybe, just maybe, I can force my way into a happy ending. If I can't, I'll simply be another girl starring in yet another cautionary tale. *Don't fall in love with villains,* old women will tell their granddaughters. Fathers will whisper to the young ones they keep, *don't go to the forest. The adventure is not worth the fallout.*

And what's worse, young women will tell themselves this: *never, ever think you can defeat a king.*

And the gods will smile, having gotten their entertainment regardless of what happens at the end of this story.

"I hate you," I breathe. My heart drums a forceful beat forward. My blood ticks up and a shiver ravages my body. I swallow, letting the illness take hold. A small thing. Such a little lie. A small part of me whispers, *this is the end.*

"I hate you, too." Killian says, the words trailing at my throat before he sinks his teeth there. I feel his smile on my skin. My ring burns hot. Passion, passion like hate. Or love. Something shifts between us. Our so many *almosts* and *not-quites* converge into a *yes.* His hands grab me, as if I'm a scrap of air he needs to breathe. My hands are in his hair, tendrils tangled between my fingers as they raking across each strand and dig into his scalp. "You have undone me. You betray me, and I still can't stop–" he cuts himself off with a shudder. So he does know. But he also doesn't think I can do what I have sought to do. His fingers grip me, torn between passion and possession, love and hate.

My favorite enemy. Something like that.

"I know you like it in the near-open, wicked witch, but I want you in my bed again. " He guides me out of the alcove, large hand pressed to the small of my back. As he whispers in my ear, I catch that ever-present scent of mint. "Don't worry, though, there's still opportunities later to be watched." A shiver passes down my spine.

The Witch King is down there, somewhere. Yet Killian doesn't seem to care. As if honor is something that can keep us both safe. That hospitality will hold when it didn't before. Honor like one promises to have and to hold, to protect, to entwine one soul with another. Honor is nothing.

He pulls me down the hallway. The noise from downstairs is distant. Servants brought in just for this occasion, both human and fae, dodge out of the way. The portraits Killian once claimed to be less nosey than the ones at Bear Hall pile into one another's frames as we pass.

He puts his rough, callused hand on the back of my neck, enveloping it as we walked forward. His thumb caresses one artery while his middle finger strokes the other. I shiver. If we weren't bound such as we are, all it would take is for him to squeeze and keep squeezing until I was dead. Still, all I want is for him to take his hand and slither it to every part of my body. I am a traitor to all I have loved.

To my husband most of all. Later, later. The Wolf will die, just as King Thaddeus decreed.

Lukas rounds the corner. "Killian, we're out of those tasty little biscuits downstairs, do you—"

Killian's eyes pin him with a glare, glowing like arcane obsidian fire. "*Don't,*" he says.

Lukas holds up his hands and backs away, taking in my half undone dress, and backs around the corner from where he came. I let out a small laugh, genuine mirth slipping through the haze of dread. For the next space of time, I'll shove all of it away. I can have one more taste of something beautiful. Killian eyes me with the same death wish stare. Something in his gaze belongs to something else, though I don't understand it.

"Killian, I—"

"Shh," he says. We round the hallway. He releases me and leans against the door. He rakes a hand through his dark air. It flops in front of his face. The words he says next grind as gravel does under a wheel. When he looks up, his eyes glint an otherworldly gold. As if an animal lives inside of him. "Briar—don't walk through the door if you don't want to be fucked."

Sometimes all I want is to be held, to be cherished. To be given kisses that grant wishes from far off fae. Dreaming up visions of pretty white dresses and true loves and prince charmings. Happily ever after, some kisses can promise. Each lick a slick sliver of silver slipping together something shivering and wanting and full of need. Part of me wants those forevers.

The other part of me is okay with being fucked.

"It doesn't have to be anything but you and me in there. No feuds, no wars, no Witch Kings. I want all of you."

We are always doing this. Pretending that tomorrow won't come. That this isn't going to end with one of us dead. Tonight is probably the worst night to give in to this.

My body falls into his.

"Killian," I breathe. I grab him and my lips press to his.

He pushes against me one more time, his lips whispering against mine. "I mean it, Briar. My wolf wants you. You go in there, and you belong to me."

The door flies open and slams with a finality of a jail cell locking into place. I'm not sure who does it—him or me. It doesn't matter anymore because there doesn't seem to be a difference where he ends and I begin.

There's not enough of him to cover every inch of me and every place his hands vacate leave me breathlessly cold. More, more, more. There's not enough. Not enough of anything in the world to fill the aching hole inside of me. But damn, will I try.

Hold me, I think. *Love me*, a small part of me begs. I squash her. There's no room for love between Killian and I, but surely there's room for whatever this is. There's room for right now. Our present runs out, passing through my fingers like sand. Autumn leaves a dying world in its wake. Frost kills everything good and leaves slip into a death as they crunch beneath feet. Winter will be here soon and the seasons will pass. Then summer. Killian's teeth trail down my neck.

Summer.

When all our promises are fulfilled. It will be when the oath 'til death do us part cleaves us in half and I'll always wonder. Time will empty itself of what could have been soon enough. I'll not wait for this moment to pass. No one in my life has offered me forever, this isn't any different. He grinds into my core and it's all too much. Too much. I need his clothes off, I need him naked and mine. The yellow-eyed stare is back in his gaze and I know his wolf is riding high, wanting to claim me. I lick at the big vein in his neck and Killian growls.

My fingers fumble at his vest, brass buttons coming undone in a flurry. Now, now, now. A plea sings inside of me. As if coming together will make me feel whole.

And maybe for a moment it will.

And with that, I force myself to let go of all the other things, to be in this moment, with this man. Villain or no, husband or no—witch and wolf.

I groan, rocking into Killian. The hardness of his cock presses into me through the layers of my gown. Too many clothes. Too much between us. I grab his trousers, tugging them down. Our fingers fumble against each other. His grip is bruising, possessive. The look in his eyes flashes like a wolf, something dark and needing flicks through him.

He moves to rip my gown.

"If you rip my dress, I'll stab you through the heart, binding vow or no," I say, smacking his grabbing hand.

He lets out a growl of frustration, working at the little buttons on the back of my dress with impatient fingers. As he does, he nips at my body through the fabric. Desire ripples my flesh in his wake. My legs shake. I reach around, threading my fingers through his hair and pulling. "Hurry," I say.

His eyes track the holster that holds the grimsbane blade on my thigh. His lip tips up into a smirk. "Still made of blades, I see."

"The better to stab you with if you don't *hurry up.*"

I pull at the buckle, dropping the dagger to the ground carelessly. Killian frees the last button and the dress slides off. I kick it away, completely naked. He stops and stares at me for a moment. A blush rises up and I force myself not to cover myself, as if I've never had a self conscious thought in my life. As if no stretch marks redden my hips or my stomach has no curve to it. His hands reverently slip down my body, as if he's seeing me for the first time. "It is a sin," he whispers.

"What is?" I whisper, half afraid of what I'll hear.

"Such beauty should only belong to the stars themselves." And the way he says it—it's as if he means every word. I fight a sudden rush of tears, swallowing them down for later, for the doubts of another woman. Tonight, I want to be what he sees.

He guides me to the bed, and for all our fervor, we move slowly now. The pads of his fingers whisper at my skin, flitting from the crook of my arm to the curve of my hip. As if he can't stop touching me.

But then he stops.

He looks at me once more, as if he can't believe his eyes, and then he shoves me back onto the bed. He lets out a growl of frustration, kicking off his own pants. I shove the rest of the fabric off of his hips. Undergarments, shirt. The tattoo I'd seen before, the one of the shifting wolf glints against his skin. It watches me, slipping its head askew as if it's curious. I run a finger over it. A growl pries out of Killian's throat as I do.

Killian's cock comes free, hard and between us. It sits on my stomach. Killian's mouth lavishes my neck, down to my breast. Each kiss leaves a shiver in its wake, as if the touch of his mouth is something that expunges every sin and leaves me baptized in Killian's need. "More," I rasp. More of everything. More of him, to drive out everything that has ever hurt me.

"Look up, wicked witch," he whispers.

I do. And I see us. Above, playing out in sweet ecstasy is a mirror.

"I plan to do this a few times tonight. So I'll be generous. I'll let you watch yourself come on my cock first."

The mirror above shows his back and my mouth widening as he slips inside of me. "Oh gods," I murmur, unable to look away.

"It's Killian, witch," a laugh rumbles his chest. "Call my name instead. Now be a good little witch and take what I give you." A shiver slides down my spine. Heat pools in my stomach.

This time, when he slides into me, every tender moment is there, but also he drives forward like he's trying to exorcize the demons inside of him. Above us, the vaulted ceiling shows his rippling back and muscles, the wolf on his skin contorting in time with his pleasure. A cascade of feeling flares through my body and I clench my knees against his side, shoving my hips up and rocking in time with him.

The look in his eyes swirls between him and whatever haunts him. Silver, black, gold, brown. Every color I've seen inside of them swirls, as if every good and ill thing inside him watches me come on his cock.

He slides into me again, again, *again*—the shadow swirls at my center, bringing me over the edge at the same moment as he cries out. Around us, shadows grow like a burgeoning storm. They flare out, snapping into the dark. Something falls with a crack, but that moment we both gasp again, riding the wave that wracks both of our bodies.

We lay there, breathing hard. And I can't help but think this is all about to come crashing down.

CHAPTER 65

Killian's hands write letters across my skin in a language I can't understand but can only feel. Killian trails soft kisses down my collarbone to the hollow below my throat. He stays there a moment, lapping at the divot there and blows a sweet chill across my flesh. I shiver. We need to get back. I can't believe the Witch King is down there and we took this time to fuck. To make love. Whatever it is.

But I know that it's just me, prolonging this moment until the end. An idea takes root in me. *Kill the Wolf.* I know what to do, I don't know if it'll work. My husband cares for me, but is it enough to do what I need to do?

"What are you thinking, witch?"

I don't answer for a moment, letting the grains of thoughts and feelings swirl like sediment in the bowl of my mind. What am I thinking? What am I doing?

"Too many things," I finally reply.

"I hope at least some of those things have to do with what I can do for you." His hand grips my hip possessively.

"Some of them," I reply tartly.

"We'll need to go back soon."

"Just one more moment. Tell me what haunts you," I finally say, my fingers touching the tattoo of the wolf. Killian shivers as I make contact.

"I was born wrong."

The words feel stilted, as if they'd lived inside of him his entire life, but had never been allowed to breathe fresh air.

"The darkness of an evil creature lives in my soul. From...from my father." He pauses here, but doesn't elaborate. "A witch, a sorceress, whatever she calls herself–owed my mother a favor. Whether a debt or friendship, but when she attempted to make me whole, she cursed this entire house. Now, my fate is tied to two unkillable things. A wolf spirit—Ghost—as well as an evil worse than him are inside me— Erebos—are tethered to my soul. And all they want to do is to kill each other." He snorts. His hand gestures to his side. "Ghost lives both in and on my very skin. This is where he feels most alive."

I press my hand to his ribs. The wolf depicted there ripples the flesh as he turns towards me, head cocked. It doesn't seem possible, but it feels as if he tries to press himself closer to me.

"Erebos and Ghost," Killian says carefully, "are both my greatest curse and my greatest gift."

"What do you mean?"

The space between us grows fraught and he pulls away for a second. It takes me a moment to release him, my reluctance to be apart from him, for even a moment, drags my fingers against his skin in a needy gesture I don't like.

What I'm going to do is either going to save him or betray him. I don't have to make that decision until we're in front of the Witch King again. I am hoping that I am a clever girl instead of simply a stupid one.

"Had I not been a man riddled with darkness, I never would have found you. You don't remember, you never have, but I've known you longer than that moment in the forest. I've dreamed of you my entire life. Then you stopped seeing me. You simply were...gone."

Gone.

"The line of fate," I whisper. The blank spot in my memories... Confusion furrows my brow. "You think that I came to you in your dreams? That we were fated for this?"

Killian barks a laugh. "Perhaps. Fate, gods, or strange luck, it's hard to say, but you've been mine all along, even if you never remembered it."

I want to, though. I want to remember so desperately. And when I do, I want to never forget again.

Killian holds me to him, the warmth of his chest presses against mine.

He pulls away slightly, looking down at me.

"Are you plotting?" he asks.

"Always," I sigh into him.

"I told you many of my secrets, and yet now you're hiding something from me," his voice rumbles.

"Always," I say again. I swallow. What have I done? This strange affection between us. Killing him—it has grown from something I craved with unquenchable thirst to a near-impossibility. But killing him can save us both. Or just him and Papa.

An impossible task. Just like this marriage has been.

I'm falling in love with you. The words burn in my throat like bile, like impossibility. Like a near death as a life flames out at the end. This is over, this has been over. Before we even began.

Except maybe that first kiss, deep in the woods. Before the world knew who we were, before I was the daughter of an enemy and he the Duke of Death. Before our mouths went to war, just that brief moment of wanting and of sweetness.

The words *do you love me?* Dance across my mouth and I swallow them whole. It feels like he does, but I am not going to ask. It will cost me more than I have to give.

He places a finger on the side of my face, looping it around my jaw to my chin. Killian tilts it up so I have to look him in the eyes. Fire brands there, a jump of the flame. I can't tell how much of it is him or the evil haunting him.

The one that hates me and the one that wants me.

I swallow.

"Tell me," he commands.

"I am wondering how much of what I see in your eyes is you and how much belongs to the creatures within," I reply truthfully.

He laughs. "They are all me, in a way. The want and the hate and the burning desire, we are all entwined."

"So you hate me?"

He doesn't reply for a time. "Perhaps not. But I care for you, wife," he says after a while. "You are dangerous to me."

"Am I?" I ask, half playful, half serious.

"Your mother–" he nearly spits the word. "Did this. It is hard to know how to trust you. But every time I close my eyes, my dreams tell me I have no choice."

This time, there is no answer. Instead, his hands travel down my hips, spasming there. I'm reminded of our coupling together, of our skin flushed and aroused.

He leans in, whispering. "Stop thinking such thoughts, or I will drag you by the hair to our bed."

Our bed. His fingers burn hot against my palm as his ring ignites. "Oh, promises, promises, husband," I rasp. His hand spasms against my back.

A throat clears. We look up.

Satyr stands there, along with invisible hands that hold aloft a floating platter of goblets. "The guests would prefer to begin dancing, should the Duke and Duchess consent."

My cheeks flush.

Oh gods, everyone knows what we came here to do.

A change comes over Killian as he stares into my eyes. The fire in his burns brighter and brighter until his gaze is entirely hot embers and burning coals. When he gazes at me he smiles and I catch the edge of a wolfish tooth, a canine bright white with a promise of mirth or death.

He dresses himself. As he does, blood blooms out of the white of his cravat. New wounds, new fights from the demons inside of him. Telling him to stop. Telling him to leave me.

But he doesn't. Instead, he helps me dress myself and we go to meet fate together.

CHAPTER 66

The music halts when we enter the ballroom. Disheveled and obviously well-fucked, we both exchange a grin. The Witch King lurks in the corner, but instead of fawning over him, the Wolves seem to encircle him. As if waiting to bite. He doesn't move, but sits there alone. I wonder at the laws of the invitation I sent. Only he was able to enter Killian's territory with the invitation I bestowed. Relief slips through me when I realize I don't see Sir Typhen at all. Still, there's comfort in the fact that my blade is right against my thigh, ready to be used if I need it.

When I need it. Because I know that I will. Soon. I shoot a glance at my husband, choking on the dread that convulses in my throat.

Little fae creatures flit around the room. A pixie snatches at a belt, undoing it. The man's decorative sword clatters to the ground. A goblin-type creature slips out from beneath a table, munching on an ill-begotten pastry.

I grin, despite myself.

"Pledge your fealty, Wolves." Killian's voice rings out and the groan of a violin dies down. "The time has come to welcome our new duchess. House Galibran salutes you, Duchess Briar Galibran." Killian kneels in front of me.

The Wolf kneels for me. In front of everyone.

My chest constricts and I blink back a fog of tears. Warmth aches through me. It doesn't matter that everyone doesn't pledge their loyalty at once. Just for this moment, I belong somewhere. With someone. Finally.

Killian grabs my hand and squeezes. "You did promise to let me hold it in front of everyone," he whispers.

Around us, in a reluctant wave, the lords and ladies that have sworn themselves to House Galibran fall to their knees. A few crowd at the back and slip out the door. But that's to be expected. Killian throws back his head and howls.

The pack takes it up. The Cursed and the non-Cursed all fill the room with their song. As the echo dies down, only my heartbeat thrums in my ears. Killian and I lock gazes. The people around us stumble into a dance as the notes from the quartet awkwardly begin, allowing people to dance. Above us the night sky looms a destitute black, no pinpricks of stars. He steps away from me, but somehow keeps himself anchored at my side. A skim of a knuckle there, a brief touch here, and a shiver of skin against skin as he guides me to the center of the dance floor.

"You've been wanting to know about your father." The way he says it stills the world. "I know you have. I...I have a way. I didn't know if we'd make it this far to be able to do this, though."

Above us, the moon hangs like a soaked rag. White light slips through above, skimming the green of my dress. At the mention of my father, the grimsbane blade I keep at my thigh feels colder than ever.

"I can show you him. But then everyone will know you belong to me."

Don't they know that already?

He gestures around us and the young men of House Wolf step out from the crowd. Some wear the uniforms of those on duty, some wear the garb of a nobleman. All of them are at least of age with Killian or younger.

The Cursed.

He flicks a glance around at them before throwing his head back and howling once more. The sound takes on an ethereal quality as the others join him. The notes grow, pulling from the air the ephemeral something that lives inside every living thing. The chorus of the Cursed pierces through the crowd. I can imagine that the moon herself hears their cry.

Satyr slips just behind me. His hand touches my elbow and I flinch. He takes a swig of a large bottle of wine. "They call the ancestors," he says. "'Tis named the Dance of Ghosts."

"What is it?" All the hairs on my arms hold themselves aloft.

"A call to the living and the dead. Of those who are here and who have come before. It is a call that a wolf may make only once in his lifetime. It is the only opportunity he has for his lineage to meet his mate."

His mate. Killian's or Ghost's?

Regardless, Satyr means one thing when he says it.

Me.

CHAPTER 67

*E*verything dims, like a gray film nets over the room. The lights never go out, but they fade as if I've blurred my eyes and look at them from a far off distance. The air chills.

A song that has nothing to do with the cry of the Cursed hums beneath the floor. The Witch King's eyes widen, as if he hasn't seen something like this. And I wonder how often anyone does as hundreds of translucent figures, limned in spritelight, step down from the ceiling.

Their skin is the color of thin rainbows, see-through and shining. People carrying various expressions of surprise and joy slip into the room and they hover about two inches from the ground.

The dead whose blood runs through my veins, or that has loved me as a family member, is there. Agatha waves a cheeky greeting. So many others from House Berrat. Our respective lineages file out in lines around us, encircling us.

I look for my mother but can't find her. Bitter bile coats my throat. She couldn't even come for this. I wonder if I ever had a mother at all.

"I don't see her," I say. "My mother."

I look for someone like me, a woman with Orvellan heritage and tall like mountains. With white hair and angry eyes. All I see is the lineage depicted by the portraits I've seen all my life, and those I've seen since coming to Wolf Hall.

Killian's brow furrows. "I'm not sure what that means, Briar." The way he says it feels like the ground wants to swallow me.

"What do you mean?"

He shakes his head. "I'm not sure. But it could mean that she's not dead."

That's impossible. I bite back the denial as I see Killian's father. He nods at his son before joining the rest of the spirits.

Killian holds out a hand. "The custom is that we dance with them, wife."

The rough calluses of his palm scrape against the ones on mine. His hand is warm. I inhale. Killian slips his other hand around my waist and my free one goes up to his shoulder. The little shadow that dangles from my wrist, that never left me, jitters in silence as we begin to move.

Killian tucks his chin on my head and I burrow into his chest. He smells the way I think home does. Mint and spice.

"Every dream I've had has led to this moment." Killian's words whirl the tendrils of my hair.

"I think mine have to," I say. A rageful sadness cracks through my contentment. My hand spasms in his. The hand on my hip strokes me there, tender and comforting. No fever lights up my blood, no sweat curdles against my skin. The truth is, I don't regret anything except for what I have to do if it doesn't work.

Kill the Wolf.

The spirits around us swirl. For a moment, I see Papa and I gasp. His face is ravaged by the illness. Even his ghost-form holds the erratic energy leftover from the Reezin drug. I gasp. "What?" Killian asks, turning.

"I hate to interrupt this happy moment, but it seems like your dead have left and the living have things to attend to. Duchess," King Thaddeus says. "It's time to kill the Wolf. Let's see if you can do your part."

CHAPTER 68

I pull myself away from my husband. His face takes on a blank look. For a moment, I watch him. The scar across his eyebrow, the little mark beneath his eye. I wait for him to show me a feeling, but he keeps his expression impassive.

"I'm sorry, Killian."

I pull the grimsbane blade from the holster at my thigh. A hiss slithers through the room. The Wolves around us surge, but Killian holds up a hand, halting them. I remember trying to stab my husband back at Gray Hall, how it didn't work. That through the throat, the chest, nothing could kill this man. The crack of bone beneath my blade meant nothing. Unkillable.

But everything can die. It has to.

I slide the blade down Killian's tunic. It parts beneath the metal. Shadows along the walls still, waiting. He doesn't try to hurt me. I don't think he has it in him.

Erebos, is perhaps another story.

The fabric shushes and falls away, revealing his naked chest. The scars are still there, fresh wounds from new inner turmoil. The swirling tattoo moves across his abdomen as the wolf there rises. Ghost depicted across my husband's skin.

The creature who was willing to accept me as Killian's mate. *Kill the Wolf.*

I look at Killian and lean forward, pressing a kiss to his mouth. My blade sits between us, a cold reminder. And my husband waits for me to try to kill him.

Papa's words sing in my head, because the grimsbane is made of something more than metal. It contains magic. If I kill something he cares about, that's the surest way to murder someone. The best way to stab someone in the heart is to slide the blade through the chest of someone they love.

A clever girl with the right stories can do things she never imagined possible.

Kill the Wolf.

The girls in the stories must not only be clever, but they must be sure. And now I have to be sure. It would be better to be kind because perhaps I'd still be back at Gray Hall and wouldn't have been pulled into this mess by the gods at all. Too much violence burns in my blood to be called kind.

"I really am sorry that you have to see this."

At that moment, Killian's eyes widen as he takes in the angle of my blade. Pointed directly at my own chest, right where the tattoo of Ghost sits on Killian's. I abruptly turn. His hand snags at me and the shadows around the room move to grab at me–at something–but it's too late.

The grimsbane blade pierces my chest, breaking bone as I fall onto the floor. A wave of darkness cocoons me. Pain sharpens at my chest and warmth chokes out of my body. My gaze shifts to Killian, who falls to the floor. Blood pools around him. A howl calls again, this time distantly.

I glimpse the thrashing tail of a wolf, bedecked in spriteight, slip up to the sky before disappearing.

"I did say I'm sorry," I murmur.

The world fades around me. I wonder what stories will be told about the witch who went into the woods when she should not, who broke a curse, only to die on her own blade.

I go to join the dead.

CHAPTER 69

*I*t's too bright.

Too much light for death.

My head beats a thick drum on my skull and my throat keens in pain. I smack my lips, sitting up.

"Thank you," King Thaddeus says. My gaze focuses on him. His smile curls in sinister cunning. He reminds me of Killian, around the mouth and at the corners of his eyes.

I should be dead. My hand goes to my heart, pulling at the edge of my gown. Blood smears across my chest, but beneath it is a healed scar. A last gift from Ghost.

A bizarre devastation fills me. The creature only hurt Killian, but he kept Erebos in check. And at the end of it all, he saved me from myself even as he died.

"For what?" I rasp. King Thaddeus looks toward Killian.

"For all you've done for me." His eyes flicker and that's when I see it. Staring back at me.

Erebos.

I'm certain of it. Somehow, this dark creature infects both my husband and the king. If that's the case, who else does he control?

Killian leans against me, blood soaking his tunic. A wooziness grips me from my own blood loss, but I stand up as straight as I can, laying him on the floor. My husband gasps. Little bits of white light—not quite spritelight, but something fuzzier around the edges—evaporate from his body.

"Your mother tried to save him, you know. From us. A favor to our wife."

King Thaddeus throws an ugly look toward Killian. Us, our. The king grins at me, but that's not what stops me.

His wife was...the late Duchess of Wolves?

"She left, ran to this blighted place that the fae won't let us into without invitation or without bloodshed." He throws back his head, laughing. "You've been the perfect weapon, my dear, and have somewhat made up for the ills of your mother."

"Don't speak about her," I hiss.

"Why? Afraid she'll hear me?" He smiles. "Though you still think she's dead. What a child you are."

She's not dead.

The floor itself isn't enough to grip me, but I widen my stance to keep from collapsing as I lower Killian and myself to the floor. Everything I've ever known isn't true. The trail of ghosts that danced around us, that welcomed me to House Galibran. Remarkably absent were two people.

My mother and Killian's.

"You both are but children, bartering with forces you don't understand to save parents that never loved you enough to keep you. Pretending to die, lying, lying." King Thaddeus barks a laugh. "She stole our wife from me, our son—"my eyes widen as I look down at Killian. "—our legacy." King Thaddeus spits. His eyes glow like shining onyx. "And for Erobos here, she betrayed him. So I stole pieces of your memories. And some of hers."

My mother betrayed Erobos. And now—

—she doesn't remember. She might not remember me.

The memory magic the king possesses stole from me. Things I'll never know. The feeling of a slimy violation slips through my lower belly and I hug myself. How did he do it? It would have been when I was young.

The spaces of time that are gone from me. Even the dreams that Killian speaks of, I wonder if they've all been eaten by this monster. Rage fizzles through my bones. I grit my teeth.

"She's been hiding ever since she pretended to die. A clever move, to keep the Wolves and Bears fighting. To keep the line of fate between you and Killian separate. But not clever enough. The mountains won't hide her forever." When the king leans in, it's not him speaking at all. It's the creature. But the words sound far away.

My mother isn't dead after all. And neither is Killian's.

Gods, this will change everything. Hope, unlike anything I've ever felt, cracks through my chest. All I've ever wanted—more than Killian's love—is my mother's. And now, I want the memories this creature stole.

"I'm far more clever than a weak witch. A line of fate to him has been drawn since before you were born, and now you'll pay the price for it. Not all endings are happy, though."

The dagger feels slick against my skin. Clever girls, brave girls. All the stories I'd read growing up rise inside of me. Killian groans next to me.

Ghost has left his eyes. "Gone," Killian answers for me, as I look at the ragged gape in his tunic. Beneath the hole and around the bleeding wound, there's no swirling tattoo to mark the presence of Ghost. "Only one left to go." His voice sounds faint.

Only one demon left to defeat. The one in front of us.

I launch myself at the king. I know what he cares about. Himself.

A few running strides and I slam into him. His eyes widen in surprise. A wave of dizziness slips through me and I stumble, waving the blade toward him.

I slice his forearm. King Thaddeus hisses and a black sludge leaks from his wound. The ravens roosted above free themselves from their perches and dive straight down. A beak pecks at me, talons scratch my skin. And still, I whip the dagger out. This time, I strike the king in the leg. Another burst of black ichor streams from his body.

Darkness surges, but it's weak because Killian is injured. They slice toward the king, but snap into one of his raven familiars instead. Both the bird and the shadow dissipate into nothing.

The flock shifts its attention. Half of them fly at me while the others swirl around the Witch King. The ravens encircle him, faster and faster. As they increase in speed, King Thaddeus floats inch by inch above the ground.

"The other hand will fall." His last words clang to the floor like a stream of gilded coins and he disappears.

CHAPTER 70

*L*ords and ladies swarm the hallway. Half of them are contorted into Wolves, as if a battle is about to take place. I hope not. My hands shiver, blood caking into my nails. I rush to Killian. His chest is less healed than mine, but he's alive.

Sometimes, all you can celebrate is that someone isn't dead.

"You shouldn't have risked yourself like that, Briar," Killian says, sitting up. He winces.

I shrug. I need to see my father. Saving Killian by killing his wolf was worth the risk of it all. I did as the Witch King asked, but Erebos isn't a creature for keeping his promises. Trepidation hangs low in my belly. Soon. I will deal with the rest soon.

Revelation after revelation jerks through me. My sternum feels sore. I rub it. "Our mothers are alive."

"I knew mine wasn't dead. It was perhaps one of the only agreements the Witch King could get me to make to force my hand for a mystery bride. He has her and...I think it's the truth."

"We'll find her. Both of them." I lay a hand on his arm. "If they were dead, it would be terribly rude to not show up with the rest of the ghosts."

"Aye, witch. But then again, I was on the verge of doing something very untoward watching you." He grins. The little beauty mark beneath his left eye creases with his wide smile.

I raise an eyebrow at him. "In front of the spirit of your grandmother?"

"I wasn't going to fuck you in front of my grandmother," he says with a laugh. I look at him. His brow pinches. "Or the Witch King. Just some people. Again, if you like–I mean—"

"*No*," I snap. "Though I wouldn't mind if we were..." I blush. I can kill a man with an ax, but actually use words to talk about sex? That was harder than murder. "Near people again...and we..."

"We...?" He grins, wolfishly, despite the lack of Ghost to haunt him. I wonder what that will do to him. If he'll be the same man as before.

I smack his arm. "I'm happy to fuck you anywhere, you toad, as long as your grandmother or anyone else we *know* doesn't find out!"

"Is it okay if they find out later?"

"Just shut up, Killian," I say with a laugh. "I'll toss another bag of dog shit at your feet."

Right after my comment about the excrement, he pauses a beat. Then asks with a solemn look coming over him, "What do you think we will do this time?"

"This time what?"

"To renew our vows." He turns to me. A dark intensity enters his eyes. Need and fear live there. He doesn't ask me, but there's a question there. And a worry I won't say yes.

I swallow. Summer. Our marriage bond will either dissolve or be renewed. A year and a day were the terms. Though we're not even in winter, I can't help but be warmed by the thought that he'd want to renew them at all.

"I think you might still get dog shit," I say lightly. Not saying yes, but also not saying no. Falling in love is as easy as it is stupid. Killian is the worst choice I could make. My enemy, my undoing.

He grins.

I smile back. But my father's flickering spirit, his pale sunken image oscillating from a man in his prime to the ill creature he is now.

If the Witch King wasn't keeping his vow, he definitely wouldn't be now. The consequences for the king's untruths will not be like the fae have for lying, but surely there will be one. For now, I am the only one with the fallout. Me and Papa.

My pulse kicks up speed. *Run now*, it demands. *Go to Papa.*

I can't stay here.

The realization hits me like an avalanche of stone. My breath stalls in my chest.

"What is it, Briar?"

"I—" I swallow. "I'll need to go back to Gray Hall."

"Come with me." Killian holds my hand in a way that feels like it might be our last. "I have something to show you. We will see what happens between us after all of this is done."

CHAPTER 71

Finally, after all this time, Killian invites me to his study, to what's behind the doors.

I gaze up at the image of my mother on the clawed, ragged canvas. I swallow the feeling, the impulse to tell him who that is. I want to ask him why a spirit wouldn't join the Dance of Wolves if they were truly dead, but the words sit like a jagged plane of glass in my throat. Half hope, half devastation. But I know better than to plan for a future based on a dream.

Whatever is between Killian and me is so real and fragile. And I can't break it. Not yet.

And yet, if asking about my mother will break it, it's something I must do.

He walks to below the portraits, something between half a smile and half a snarl stretched on his mouth. "Ah yes, the two women that have defined my life." He flicks a glance to me. "I suppose, two out of the three."

He inhales, the air ripping through his throat like a blade carves it free.

"Your mother, I suppose. I hope you'll be okay if I hate her. Dead or not, she ruined me." He runs a hand down his arm, which sports a collection of the scars from the years of being torn up from the inside. "They say she hated us back, but I've also heard it was a fucked up way of trying to help. It hardly matters anymore. We are only left with the dust of choices that have come before us."

"What did he say about your mother?"

Killian shivers, eyes flickering. "Thaddeus said he knew where she was. Or Erebos did." His nostrils flair, as if he's trying to control himself. "No matter. You don't need to worry about that. Not anymore."

Beneath the portraits is a domed glass, set atop a simple stand of burnished wood. Floating, suspended mid air without any support, is a single purple rose.

"There is only one Fex's flower," he says. My stomach squeezes. The flower. "Apologies, I did not know who you wanted it for before, but it is not a thing I would give to a stranger." The image of my father, my near-dead Papa, rises up between us. "I had thought to save it, as all the Dukes of House Galibran have done, but I think I have found a better purpose for it."

The glass hums as he slides it off of its stool. The flower floats there, held aloft by something potent, something magic. The petals curl a bright scarlet mixed with plum, little dark dots of black dapple the edges of the petals. The stem, a garish green, is spiked with thorns along every bit of the surface.

"There's only one?" I ask. I think back to that night, all the things that happened to me. Blame and self-hatred soaks me like a wet cloak. Holding me down. I want to drown in it.

He doesn't answer my question, instead, he holds the flower in his hands. As soon as it touches his skin, his hands begin to bleed. "They say so many things about this rose." His voice is the softest I've ever heard it.. He speaks as if words leave bruises on the air, as if a harsh word here will break whatever slips between us. I feel it too. "My father said that a family curse now broken bestowed this gift to us, to pass along from duke to duke until there was cause to use it. That Fex himself broke into our gardens and Amara gave us this as an apology for her lover's callousness. That she once brought him back from dead with it and now it is ours to guard until she has need again." He shivers, holding back pieces of blasphemy. "None of that matters, though, not in the end. Be it from the gods, from the banished fae, from a cursed line—" Killian takes a ragged breath. "Take it. It does what you believed it to—heals what is impossible. All your father will need to do is eat all the petals. And make a wish."

I jerk my head up.

He shrugs. He doesn't look at me, but his manner is such that it's as if he's tossed me a bone he never wanted in the first place.

"You'll stay here," I say. The words are out of my mouth before I can snatch them back. But Killian doesn't blink, doesn't waver. The Dance of Ghosts, the claiming of me as mate–was that for my husband or the demon that haunted him? Who's mate was I really? Killian's or Ghosts?

Killian shivers, as if the one evil that is left to him is just beneath the surface of his skin. Erebos. My mother cursed him with Ghost, evil to keep evil in check. And for all his life, they fought each other and fought him. It shows in the tiny scars on his skin and the deep grooved wounds of Killian's soul. Who will he become with just Erebos inside of him?

"All I ask is that you remember what it was like." *With me.* The words go unspoken. For me to remember what he's claimed I've forgotten.

It's at that moment, I realize he's telling me goodbye. Whatever future could have been between us dies in the air and its ghost will haunt me for the rest of my life. Fine. I'm no stranger to disappointment, to half-alive hope strangled into a grave.

He needs to be here. To take care of the fallout from the Witch King's departure. Everything I am probably represents pain. Perhaps it would be better to take some time away from each other. To see if this is real. Or to see if part of it was a strange spirit trying to claim what wasn't his.

"The vows, then?" I rasp.

Killian shrugs. "Another time, another life. Perhaps one less cursed with villains and witches and kings and evil."

I stand up, holding the flower. It's mine, as Killian never was.

When I use it to help Papa, the rest of its lifespan will be just as fleeting as this love story.

CHAPTER 72

The door shuts behind me with cold finality. Everything I've ever wanted lives right here in my hands. My Papa's health, retribution, a means to end this all. I've killed the Wolf, as I promised, escaped killing the man I'm falling for. And yet, all that I hear is the sound of my own heart cracking like it's as pitiful as a dropped glass slipper.

Erebos looked out of Killian's eyes.

I should be relieved he wasn't coming. Relieved that all I need to do is go bring this to my father—what I wanted all along—and live out the rest of my days in peace. Perhaps our people would fight, but perhaps I'd just leave. I could go to live in the forest, a lonely old witch, and the world would whisper about the wicked one that lived there and her bitter heartbreak.

Because at the end of it all, despite all the pretty words, we're not strong enough to stay together.

"Fuck this." I wipe a harsh tear away from my face and stride to my room.

When I get to our shared room, I see a trunk moving on its own. I only catch snatches of translucent, veined wings and grotesque, thick tails as a fae creature packs my things. Fur turned to something like spiked glass brushes against the cedar wood trunks. *My* trunks. The sigil of the Bears, two axes underneath a roaring, rabid bear, peek out green and silver.

I stare, frozen, as the trunk seemingly heaves itself down the stairs. Little thuds of invisible feet scurry down the carpeted stairway and into the receiving room.

I take a slow step. Then another. Another. My stomach leans into the bannister, but I push it in harder to feel like I've been punched in the gut. Part of me would just like to throw myself over onto the floor.

No one would even care.

Nisha is gone, my friends lost.

Stay in the woods, I don't care. I say through the bond to Nisha. I can barely feel her now, wherever she is. Betrayal ices my core. A heavy feeling that ravages every warm curl of love I could have into nothing but a wasteland.

I am completely alone.

I run to my old rooms—grabbing the last few things that were there. There isn't much, but I don't want to leave a trace of myself behind. A trace of myself for him. He may have given me this flower, but that wasn't what I wanted, not even close. It's not enough. I grasp the thing lightly, piling the odds and ends into my other arm as the thorns bite into my palm like an angry hound. Blood drips between my fingers.

"Your Grace," Asha says, her voice brittle.

I give a sharp shake of my head.

"It's Lady Briar now. The vows will dissolve at this point. Close to a little over half a year left, but I won't be here. Might as well call me that."

She swallows. "It-it's been a pleasure."

Pleasure. Pain. Ecstasy. Desolation. My time with Killian has been the entire world contained in a single teardrop. Everything but love.

Lying about how one feels to oneself, as long as it's not spoken aloud, doesn't count.

"I'm happy to have known you, Asha."

"Likewise, Lady Briar."

I give a last sweep of my rooms and Killian's, taking in the smell of clove and cedar and summer that seemed to never cease. The dark red silk of his bed looks like a river of blood, still mussed from our last coupling.

A small line of servants follow me, as well as a crowd of pixies. The portraits Killian once claimed were not as gossip-minded as the ones in Gray Hall clump just the way the ones back when we first met. Their lips burrow into one another's ears to spread rumors only they can hear. I step onto the cobbled drive looping in front of the manor to the slicked onyx carriage. Midnight-hued horses, coats so dark containing multitudes of violets and melancholy indigoes, twitch in anxious hurry. I alight the stairs, waiting until I'm cushioned in the plush interior and my conveyance moves forward to look behind me. The ring on my finger flares and I take it off, putting it in my pocket.

I don't need it anymore.

Wolf Hall narrows in my wake, the trees of the woods scraping their bones together to hide the home was mine for the past couple of months. A figure paces across the widow's walk jutting out toward the forest. Killian stands there like a specter, half shadow half spritelight. Even from here, his eyes glint the glare of dark shadows. Erebos looks back at me, not really Killian.

My husband didn't really come to say goodbye. Just his demons.

I grit my teeth and turn forward in the carriage. Alone, like I've always been.

PART IV
HALF MADE OF SHADOWS

Between the sun and the moon, a Witch will be born burning.
The light of truth shall be her mantle, though she will walk with lies.
Vindicator, villain, victor, she shall be crowned with all titles three.
When the Witch raises her final weapon,
blood will spill into the great Salt beneath the Mist of Sea
and twist the tides of men. Her fist will fell kings and raise them up. So mote
it be.
But beware the evil carried inside–
[the Priestess died before speaking further]
–Priestess Winnera's last prophecy, the Witch Rises, 600 years prior before
she was slaughtered for speaking it

CHAPTER 73

KILLIAN

He wakes with her name on his lips. Briar, Briar, Briar. *Benediction, prayer, curse. As soon as he saw her in the flesh, he saw witchcraft in her eyes. The turn of her lips spiked a wicked flare through his entire body and lit up his soul.*

The words wicked witch were out of his mouth before he even learned the name of this woman made of thorns.

But life loves to lavish cruel blades on supple hearts and Killian has made a bargain of his own.

A year and a day with his bride. A year and a day of ceasefire. A strange pause on all the lives he's sent north with questions on lips. Where are they? Killian doesn't know, but he's the Duke and is supposed to know everything. He even sends his own uncle, who does not return. Dead, probably. But that's not the life he's asked for in exchange for his side of the bargain.

A woman he thought dead, once imprisoned, and to be returned to him. A year and a day passes all too slow and too fast at once.

He never thought his heart was too tender, but he believes it now. And still. He waits for the Witch King to go back on his word. Magic works its wiles in bargains, but the Witch King brokers like the fae. He speaks the truth but finds a way to make his promises into lies. And still, he has too much power for those he barters with to have any other option than to say yes.

Killian has never trusted gods, especially not since he learned of the cruelty of Lumar's divine sovereign. He doesn't trust what passes from the man's lips because the Witch King has killed his father, stolen his mother, and wants to kill him too.

Just because someone claims to be godly, does not mean they are good.

There are few paths to take when a near-god pulls at the strands of one's fate.

So Killian picks at the corners of each day, like a miser reluctant to spend his coin. Briar, Briar. Her name tastes sweet and spicy on his tongue. His wicked witch. When he can, he snatches kisses that do not belong to him and he wonders if she'll ever remember they once dreamed together.

She never does.

But it's enough to watch the hatred drain from her face, just as much as it will never be enough time together. Still, he lights a candle every night. Eventually, she stumbles into his bed. He makes love to her, worshiping her—body and soul—as if he is an entire congregation devoted entirely to her radiance. Killian is a man who finally has it all.

The little hole in the bottom of his heart says otherwise. As much happiness as he collects, always a small amount leaks out the bottom.

A man half made of shadows is always waiting for the light to die out.

CHAPTER 74

*N*ight has completely blanketed the world by the time I arrive at Gray Hall. The carriage wound its way through a path slicked by the fae. Pixies tittered, but greased the way as I left, as if they were eager to have me leave. My shortest trip yet through the woods.

Winter creeps in through the dying cracks autumn leaves behind. Air slices my cheeks, cutting at my face like it wants to flay the skin from my skull. I pull the furs around me tighter.

He let me go.

Killian let me go.

A year and a day has not passed, but whatever time we have left is forever broken by my departure. What we'd built slips through my fingers, proving that the base of our relationship was flawed to begin with. Killian didn't love me. He lusted for me.

But he let Lukas and Remmy come, likely to protect his own hide. Though what danger there is to him now that the Witch King got what he wanted–Ghost's death–I doubt there is any. The king clearly has plans for my husband and there's nothing to do but wait until time marks our marriage completed. Anyone on his side wouldn't dare touch him physically and, by extension, me.

Still, it's something that Killian let me go at all. An aching part of me holds onto that. If I die, he could still be killed. And yet he let me go anyway. Perhaps, he's just waiting to die.

I can't help but think of the darkness in his eyes. Ghost gone, I wonder now what happens to Erebos inside of him? The demon creature that haunts not only Killian, but the Witch King? Will my husband become just as corrupted as his father is?

Confusion rattles my lungs. But the world hasn't made sense, not since I kissed him until our lips were swollen and bloody those months ago in the Shadow Wood.

The doors to the hall open with an ominous groan. Lukas stands just behind me, to my left. There's something unsettling to Lukas, a shifting weight as if he can't decide if he should run now. The curve of his mouth, the twitch in his eye–something is fragile about Lukas tonight. I think back to the tin coins. The little lies. Remmy flanks my other side. Ready to defend me and solid as oak.

I shake the thought.

I don't need defending here. Not in my–*my father's*–home. A jitter flinches through my spine and up through my neck. My teeth chatter together and I pull the stole around my shoulders tighter. Dead leaves wisp in front of me. A titter sounds in my ear and a spritelight rides the wind. I bite the inside of my cheek, looking closer.

Not a spritelight at all.

Bright curling hair, she's so tiny. The pixie gives a cheeky wave before flying off. I wonder if the spritelights are spirits at all, or if they're only mischievous fae flocking near violent death sites like flies to blood. Perhaps many of the spritelights I've seen in my life have been fae after all. I just didn't look close enough to see the magic. Attracted to blood, to lust, and the Lord Protector of the wood that contains all the banished fair folk.

Why is there one here then? The question sends another convulsion down my spine. They tend to follow Killian. But he's back there, far away.

The hall is silent, but not empty. Lords and Ladies I've known all my life watch me with mouths drawn into thin lines and eyes that dart after my every move. I'd forgotten what it was like, to be watched like an enemy Selvan. The Wolves–the few I'd seen–hadn't seemed to care.

My time away wasn't long, but there's a new hate in their eyes as these people track me. Distrust tightens fists and jaws tick. But it's not just me they watch. The Wolves around me serve as my entourage and earn longer stares. I clench my nails against the meat of my palms. This isn't new. And, what's more, this is to be expected.

Especially given the way things were left last time.

So far, this doesn't look like a friendly greeting. But I have to see my father. I have to know–I have to know something. If anything, I need to be able to say goodbye if this flower doesn't work. But it must.

Flames blaze high on the walls. Arcane lanterns bob with magic mid air above, reminding me of stars if it had been dim enough to warrant a comparison to night. As it is, I miss the shadows.

I miss Killian.

A spasm of grief that has nothing–and everything–to do with my father squeezes me from stomach to chest. I blink back a wave of tears that fog my vision. If Killian were here, I could take comfort in his presence. The shadows would protect me. As it is, I only have this one little strand of him on my wrist–the shadow that I've grown so accustomed to I forget it's there–and a ring that feels cold in my pocket. As if Killian feels nothing. And perhaps that's the truth of it.

As I approach the dais, the memories of all those weeks ago flood me, alongside the outrage to see who is atop, presiding over all of this pomp.

Galinda sits in Papa's chair.

Elegant robes spread around her. Velvet the color of the greenest fields, bedecked with jewels the color of daisies waterfall halfway down the stairs to the dais. Her mouth is painted purple-black and a raven sits at the edge of her high back chair. Its head cocks like it's expecting an answer to an unasked question.

Fucker.

The raven cocks a head, watching. No doubt, looking with his master's eyes.

The Witch King. My bargainer. He isn't here, but it feels like he is.

Little things have changed at Gray Hall— added glimmers of gold. Our bannermen and women peer back at me as if I'm a stranger, and pinned to their breasts—right over their hearts—is a raven set on a circle of gold with a ruby eye. King Thaddeus' symbol. It's not that it is treasonous—far from it—but that used to be where a bear pin rested, the symbol of House Berrat.

An undercurrent of violence shushes beneath the room. My blood sings the same song. Each footfall that brings me closer to Galinda feels like the floor may crack and water will pull me beneath to drown me in the icy depths of the hatred curling around me.

Hurt me. I dare you. I grit my teeth. The grimsbane blade burns on my thigh. I've never let it go and perhaps I'll use it again. The thought sends a zap of shock through my joints.

"Shall we kill her?" My stepbrother, Ewan, asks. His voice seems bodiless, but comes from somewhere behind his mother. The dim light hides him. I wish I could peel back the shadows to see cowardice jitter his body.

"Not yet," Galinda replies, her voice sounds bored, but there's a keenness to her gaze. Galinda cocks her head to the side, assessing me. That's when I notice her stomach. Rounded, she's creased the fabric beneath her stomach to show off her pregnancy. A mixture of feelings swirl through me. Rage, joy, frustration, caution. And an idea.

"Why are you here...daughter?"

The word slaps against me. But it hurts less than before. If my mother is well and truly alive, Galinda doesn't know she's an illegitimate duchess. And whatever child she carries...well, my sibling, but certainly not the heir. Not if Galinda's marriage to my father is deemed false. Whether my stepmother graces me with rage or kindness, I'll not speak a word of that secret to her. Not today, anyways.

"I'm here to see Papa," I reply instead.

CHAPTER 75

Not a breath moves.

I'm here for my father, but the news of a sibling causes my heart to skip a beat.

A brother or sister. It's a thought I haven't had since I was a child, but a wish I'd always desperately craved to be gifted to me. But one by Galinda? I have my reservations.

Her firstborn stands next to her, just behind her chair. He leans forward, enough that a shadow peels away to reveal his face and his upper torso. Ewan scowls at me, face creasing with disgust. Another raven sits on his tasseled shoulder. It ticks something in his ear before flying off.

"Please, Galinda," I say, my voice nearly breaking. I put my hand in my pocket, feeling the silken petals there.

At first I think she'll say no. Then, she cocks her head to the side.

"Mother–" Ewan begins, but she holds up a hand, stalling his words.

Without a word, she stands.

The raven on Galinda's shoulder screeches.

* * *

THE BIRD STALKS US, following us out of the room. The large doors swing shut. Abruptly, there's more air in my lungs and I drag in a breath. Galinda sweeps two steps ahead of me, despite her smaller size and pregnancy, I hurry to keep up. There's a small collection of men around us, bearing swords. Waiting to kill one of us.

I hope to appeal to her goodness. If there is a little inside of her.

"I don't think you're evil, Galinda," I say as we walk. *I just think you're kind of an asshole.*

"Likewise," she replies with haughty starchiness. I half wonder if she has the same thoughts as I do.

We walk with slow steps toward the arbory. Remmy and Lukas follow close behind, alongside a couple of guards dedicated to Galinda. There's a stiffness in the air. Everyone is waiting for someone to try to kill the other.

Half a dozen trees bend inward toward a bench centered there.

Papa sits beneath the foliage, which cracks off. Leaves flake through the air.

A shiver thrills through my nerves. I can feel the eyes of the gods on me. A burst of anger coils inside my stomach, churning amongst a deep grief that wants to ravage everything in my sight. The world is full of terrible stories that the gods would love to see play out. A happily ever after to them will mean only one thing. And I'm not ready–not yet–to be plastered with a happy smile and a half dozen children. Maybe one day. But not today. And if this story were to end, that would most likely be the only way they'd let it.

The raven soars above in a tight circle. Watching. I've no doubt that the Witch King knows exactly what this is–that I'm thwarting a failed promise of his. I take joy in that, beyond saving my father. After everything, all I want to do is shove a finger in the king's face in an unsubtle *fuck you.*

A chill flecks my skin. Leaves–crackled, wretched half dead things–swirl around Galinda and I, enveloping the two of us in a hurricane of brown, red, and yellow foliage.

A blanket of hushed light falls over Galinda, myself, and Papa. I blink, looking around. I can't see Lukas or Remmy. The guards. Nothing except us.

The raven dives, ruffling Lukas' hair. He doesn't flinch, but stares steely eyed at me. He nods. His father at the border is likely dead. He, if anyone, knows what it means—and the cost I'm willing to pay—to bring my own back to me. Lukas continues to gaze toward me, but then his eyes widen. Remmy gasps.

Above, the creature dives again. The raven screams, wind whipping through its feathers straight down toward—

—a figure made of a thousand leaves and hollow wind. The raven meets a wave of wind with a hollow whooshing sound. Another demon? Another spirit? A scream of wretchedness courses up through my throat. I can't do this now, *not now*. The figure of leaves watches me, unblinking with eyes made of the shadow between dead twigs.

"Who-who are you?" Galinda asks.

The voice that replies reminds me of the ocean, of caverns, of ages long past. Of something dead that speaks from somewhere our ghosts don't tread until all life has ceased. *"She who was love that is now vengeance. She who was vengeance who is now love."*

The goddess Amara.

"The tales are older than time, dear. Whoever decreed that such things as love and hatred, life and death, should be put down to a simple thing like *time?* There is never enough. Sometimes all too much." The goddess' voice shifts, this time made of birds and dry leaves. She sounds soft, but everywhere, and the curl of each syllable rasped like she'd smoked a pipe for an eon. "Such old stories have always decreed that one's survival means the other's death."

The leaves surge, one winds itself into a tightly rolled cylinder to form the shape of a finger. The goddess points from me then back to Galinda.

"A stepmother must kill the stepdaughter so the man will not discard her. The daughter must hate the woman that replaces her mother, because she fears that her stepmother will replace her. It does not always need to be such." Amara pauses. She's a goddess, she has to know that my mother is alive. And what that could mean for Galinda. For her unborn child. For the fate of House Berrat. And yet, she says nothing. Sickness squelches through my stomach. Gods, I am a monster.

Not a decision for today. But the thick slime coats my insides lets me know what I will do in the future…well, I might very well become a villain myself. While I might not do everything in the name of power, I will do anything in the name of love.

Sweat lines my palms. I slide them against the cloth of my dress, dispelling the wetness. My fingers catch on the grimsbane blade. A reminder that I'm capable of bloodshed.

"I'm a creature of change, though. Love, vengeance, back to love. And again and again. I'd take my hand out of this one, for a moment, but Erebos won't. He means to win. So my hand is here, because I will not lose." Her face shifts, rustling as she looks at me. No eyes stare back–not really–but something about the way the leaves left a depth in her face makes me feel like I'm staring into the void of what awaits me after this life. Somewhere where the Frost Giants live and die and the gods play their games themselves and don't need mere mortals for their petty frustrations. Little spritelights poke out of the holes gaping through her face, giving the appearance of white pupils. She looks at Galinda. "See that you do what is right, dear one. And you–" Amara pauses, taking me in. "You remind me so much of her. But…for what is to come…I truly am sorry."

A pause. There's only the sound of Galinda's heavy breathing and the rustling leaves.

"Good luck, girl," the goddess says. "I'll be curious if you do what they think you will."

The bits of foliage that make up her body begin to molt, one by one and then all at once. A sigh sifts through the air, like a soft groan of death. Then she's nothing more than a large pile of leaves, as if someone raked them there to discard.

Galinda and I watch the remains of the goddess, staring, as if she'll come back in just another moment. I count the heartbeats that thrum in my ears. One. Two. Three. Four–

"Do it."

The word is quiet. I jerk my head up.

"You came here to help him." Galinda's jaw ticks. Her perfect visage is in disarray. An errant leaf sits askew in her coiffure. Her hand cups the side of her protruding stomach beneath her gown. "Do it. Whatever ill thing you thought would help. Do it."

I grab the flower from my pocket, finally looking at Papa. I wonder what it will be like to have a father who isn't dying. It's been so long since I didn't worry he'd leave me forever.

The purple petals come apart easily in my hand. As they depart from the stem, they take on an afterglow, the way one's vision looks after staring into the sun. Along the tender plum color, swirls of silver vein through it. I ball up several of the petals, squeezing them until they're small.

Papa looks back at me with deadened eyes. My throat aches with hope and fear of failure.

I shove the bits of Fex's flower into his mouth, snapping his jaw shut.

Papa's eyes widen. Choking. Silver foam flecks at the corners of his lips. Spittle mists against my skin as his mouth contorts open again and he gags. His teeth clack shut when I shove his mouth closed once more. Papa's pupils contract, squeezing into pinpricks and his head snaps straight back.

Crack.

Oh gods, is it killing him?

Crack.

Galinda screams. The strange bubble around us that Amara formed thins, enough that the figures we came with are barely visible through the haze. They pound against nothing, their attempts to get to us echoing like they knock against hollow stone.

Crack.

Then Papa's head snaps forward and his gaze snaps to me. "Poppet," he says, smiling. "And my lovely wife. Where have you been?" His voice sounds years younger. Deep divots in his face, furrows frowned into trenches by illness, smooth over in a slow massage of health.

Papa blinks incessantly.

"Why are we out here?"

"You-you've been ill, dear," Galinda says, her eyes tracking him as if his head will snap back once more.

"Aye," he sighs. "And I feel so much better now."

My heart slams up to my throat. I can't blink back the tears as they fall, rolling down my face. I move forward, tucking my face into his chest and I sob.

"What is it, poppet? What's got you so upset?"

"I've just been so afraid," I whisper. "All I ever wanted is that you live. I'd do it all again."

His hand strokes the back of my hair. The pain and joy from seeing him like this wraps around my ribs, expanding inside of me and pushing until I feel full of a twisted happiness. "I love you, Poppet." His voice sounds tired.

I tuck my face back into his thin chest, letting myself ride out the sobs and not caring that Galinda is there to witness my tears. Finally. I have almost everything I want, but this will have to be enough.

This time, the relief mixes with another type of grief and I say goodbye to a different man as I cry in my father's arms.

* * *

PAPA SLEEPS, but color slips back into his cheeks. He looks alive in a way I haven't seen in so long. Galinda sits next to him, his head curls in her lap. His hand–a thin thing that feels made more of paper than flesh–holds mine. We sit like that for a long time. Not speaking.

Our guards haven't gone, but they stand back. One of Galinda's stalks the edge of the arbory. At that moment, I wish for Nisha to be here. For Killian. But there's only one I can call with my mind.

Nisha?

I wait. And wait.

She doesn't answer.

I inhale, pulling on the threads that make up the Sight as I look at

Galinda. "Tell me, do you love him?" My voice snaps halfway through, like a dry stick in winter.

"Of course I do. Sometimes," She whispers. A spew of silver purges from her mouth. The invisible coins dissipate into nothing. One last silver coin thrums from her lips, vibrating the very air and the hairs along the nape of my neck raise. My fist clenches at my side, but I back away. This isn't the fight I'm here for–not anymore. "You cause nothing but despair wherever you go." Her eyes turn hard. "We are not friends. Despite what Amara wants, I have nothing to offer you but this. You may stay in your old rooms for the night, but then begone."

Begone. The word rattles through my mind and I tuck it away. Another day to grieve this relationship with Papa, to think on it, to churn it over for years and years. I won't have time with him, I'm not sure he'll even realize I was here. Whatever his recovery will be like... it won't include me. Not for some time. A hollow feeling coils through my stomach.

Grief isn't something that ever ends. Every moment, it can fit inside and poison it or sweeten it from the inside out. It shifts and coils and snaps and whispers and roars.

I have a lifetime ahead of me for sadness.

"Duchess."

"Yes?" Galinda says, her voice sharp.

"I mean," the voice clears his throat. I look toward the speaker. "The other one," the courtier nods at me. My heart jumps to my throat. Killian. "The Duke of Death is here. Shall I...let him in?"

Galinda's eyes narrow. Her mouth takes on that familiar tightness. "This truce does not last long, stepdaughter. Don't outstay your welcome here at Gray Hall."

"Just the night," I whisper. It's not safe here, not for long. But if Erebos is a danger here, he's a danger wherever Killian is. A fight is on its way. One that is going to splinter Lumar. Perhaps the continent itself. Still, if Killian is here, it's not over. Not yet.

I inhale a shaking breath, exhaling the rising tide of fear and hope as I stand up. An ache cramps in my back, but the walk eases a little of the pain from the spasming muscle. I leave Galinda there, Papa curled safely on her lap. I'm not dead today, not by miles yet.

But waiting for me is a man possessed by the same evil as the Witch King and the Dark One himself. Without Ghost, Killian has no creature willing to fight Erebos on his behalf.

Except me.

CHAPTER 76

*formal reception is skipped. Likely, because with one night ahead of us, the Bears and Wolves will see less violence if Galinda closets us away. Remmy and Lukas trail after me once more. Around the three of us, arcs a team of Bears. Some of them I recognize. They shoot glares at me, despite the familiarity. A boy of about seventeen, named Tona, scowls when he meets my gaze.

If I was an enemy before, I'm certainly something worse now.

The group guides us up the stairs, toward my old rooms. The portraits along the halls fall into each other. Some shake so much, they rattle their frames off the walls. One of the guards curses, pausing as if to pick up the fallen art, before abandoning it on the floor for someone else to pick up.

"I feel like your dog," Remmy remarks, stepping quickly behind me.

I snort. "Some might argue you *are* a dog."

I raise an eyebrow, turning my head toward Lukas. For once, he says nothing. His shoulders hunch up to his earlobes and he steps in silence with a stiff gait.

"What's wrong with you, Lukas?" Remmy asks.

Lukas frowns, gaze still unfocused. "It's just the end. That's all."

"The end of what?" I ask. A knot forms in the pit of my belly. There's more to come, so much more. But the way Lukas speaks, it seems like we're about to die now.

"What was, I suppose." Lukas waves a hand as we round a bend. Up ahead is my doorway to my room. A shadow flickers beneath it. My heart crawls up into my mouth. Killian. Killian is there. "There's beginnings and then the world burns and changes. And then it's a new beginning. *Once upon a time* and *happily ever after*. The phrases don't do much for the reality that nothing really ends. We just turn the wheel again after we pretend something is over. It's never over."

My legs shake as I near the door. It's never over. I turn the words over in my mind. My lips dry. "Are you okay, Lukas?" I ask. A spasm twists my stomach.

"Lukas," Remmy snorts. "You are a nut. Or a bard."

"I'm nothing," Lukas says, his voice soft. It's rare to hear him so serious. "Just a man after his own happily ever after."

* * *

Lukas and Remmy shut the door behind me. The walls are black as pitch, with the exception of one lone, flickering candle.

My husband lounges there, shrouded in shadow at the edge of the bed. The white tunic beams in the darkness. A wisp of his power tendrils out, snaking around my back like a long arm and tugs me to him. Relief slams into me. If Killian is here, that means that it isn't over.

The cool touch of shadow is brief, because the next moment I'm in his arms. My mouth finds his and I press a kiss of every feeling into him, as if I can convey everything that has happened without words. The grief, the joy, the despair, the questions for tomorrow. I give him everything.

And he takes it. Some of the loneliness that plagues my every breath eases. I've never fit in anywhere, but when I'm with Killian, I feel as if I could be anywhere and it wouldn't matter if others don't accept me. As long as I have him.

"Briar," he whispers into my hair. "I've dreamed of you my entire life. Will you finally be mine made flesh?"

I feel as if I've dreamed of him, too, but perhaps not the way he means. I skim my teeth up his neck, fiddling with his earlobe. He growls, pulling away.

"I need you to hear this, wicked witch. Because I will only offer this once. Once, and I'll leave. But accept me..." He shudders. His eyes darken. I can't help the spike of fear in my stomach, but instead of giving into it, I settle onto his lap. I wonder if Erebos will look out with his eyes in a moment. Will this creature that seems to hate me finally kill me? I wait. Killian's breath hisses against my exposed throat.

Killian breathes hard, shuddering, before his eyes return to their normal color.

"Is he...?"

"He's there. He's contained. For now." He pauses, gulping in another bout of air. "This is why we must speak."

"What do you mean?"

"I think you are safe—at least for now. Until we are no longer bound by this." Killian holds up his hand and his wedding band glints there. "Our marriage is the connection that keeps you alive. I don't know why he hates you, but it must mean you're a threat—" Killian bites off his last words. He pauses, breathing hard, as his hand goes to his head. "Fuck."

"I...I think I know what you mean, Killian." I whisper. Erebos is held at bay. For now. For now Killian will not hurt me. But not forever.

"I am not good enough *not* to ask this of you. I am not selfless enough to keep the fact that I need you more than I need to breathe to myself. I tried to stay away, to let you come here alone, but I have to lay out all my cards for you." I cup my palm to his cheek. Killian closes his eyes, rasping his next words."There are a lot of good men out there. Heroes who know that the right thing to do is sacrifice what is most important to them for the greater good. I have never been one of those men. I'm a selfish bastard."

"But—"

He holds up a hand and I cut myself off. "No, my darling witch. My wicked witch. I have never been a hero. I've only ever been a haunted man, hounded by his demons." His hand rakes across his chest and fresh blood stains his tunic, newly clawed wounds from an inner battle he can never seem to win with a darkness that cannot be defeated."But I've dreamed of you for so long."

My throat hardens into a dry ache.

"For years, you were my anchor, the only thing that made any sense. And you weren't real. And then even mirage that you were, you left. Gone." His voice breaks on the last word. Agony rips through my heart and it feels like the organ there expands into my ribcage. Everything in my chest aches. "Then, one day, you came back. But you didn't remember me– you still don't." He breathes heavily. I don't remember, but I believe him. I have since he told me. And even if he hadn't, the uncanny feeling of us being forced together by something greater than ourselves has fit over our every interaction. But Killian doesn't believe in the way the gods work, not the way I do. Their petty plays and sly games. We are at the center of something larger than any of that– a war between gods. Between Amara herself and Erebos.

We are the players for this tale.

The line of fate has been a through line from my heart to his since the beginning. Since before my memories were lost to me. I still don't understand why they're gone.

Witch or villain, player or not. It doesn't matter. Perhaps fate exists, but this feels like mine. The simple fact is I'm falling in love with this man.

That perhaps I've loved him before. Somewhere deep in the space of my mind where all the forgotten pieces of my life dwell.

But the details don't matter, not really. "You smelled of mountains and secrets. And one day you became mine." Killian stops, lashing a hand through his hair, streaking the fresh blood through his black mane. Another scratch, this one shallow, bleeds out from his palm. "All I have ever wanted is the peace you bring, and even then, I had to pretend you didn't belong to me. I had to agree with only a year and a day. I have lit a candle for you every night for years, hoping that the light would bring you back home."

A chill pimples my skin, but warmth flares through my belly. Killian closes his eyes, as if he needs to gather his strength.

"If you want a hero, tell me to leave. Because I'll never be him." This he says with self-hatred dripping from every syllable he utters. "A villain is all I am, all I will ever be—*but I'll always be yours*. And if you're *mine*, I'll never give you up. I don't care what the world asks for. It can beg at my feet for my heart. It can rip the air from my lungs. I'll never give you up because I am a selfish bastard. For what I want, I'll set fires at every front. I'll level kingdoms—I'll break vows. New mountains made of ash will form under my fists and with what I have left. I'll fell all gods that try to take what is mine to care for. I'll slaughter anyone who comes close to harming what is mine. I will fight what's inside me every day—for you. No matter what you choose, for the rest of my life, I will leave the light on for you. My heart is not my own." He inhales a ragged breath, as if he's taking a drag from a spiced cigar.

And I hear what he's not saying. The thrum of the heart that he speaks of is mine.

"We have at least half a year to figure out what we can do about—" He cuts himself off. But he doesn't need to say it. We have to defeat not only King Thaddeus, but also Erebos. And if we don't overcome Erebos in time, it is possible Killian will end me.

"Killian." I throw my arms around him, ignoring my looming death. I can't think on it right now. In a way, it doesn't feel as important as the unsaid words inside of me. I don't know how to say the words *I love you* yet. They thicken my throat.

Fear claws up through my ribcage as I wonder about the evil inside of Killian. If I tell Killian that I love him, will Erebos look out at me the moment I say the words and steal them for himself? That something so sacred from my mouth should be snatched by this evil creature, when the words would be for Killian alone. An ache burgeons in my esophagus as I hold back the words. Perhaps it is better to be sure anyways. "I will follow you to the end," I whisper instead. The eyes that look back at me are warm brown.

"Briar," Killian rasps into the shell of my ear. "My wicked witch, my woman of thorns." I shiver, holding him close. The warmth of his body pressed into the curves of mine and he grips me tighter. A villain, then. Well, if we are villains, I do not know what to make of the Witch King.

"We're going to kill him," I promise into Killian's ear. A vow I can't break. Erebos, whoever he is–I will kill him. I hope he hears me through my husband, wherever he dwells from within Killian.

Killian leans back, looking at me. "I am sorry for all the secrets, my love. For all the things that went unsaid for so long, but…" He swallows. "Gods, I love you. Until I die, my darling. And even then, I will love you beyond the grave."

I quirk a smile. Warmth suffuses my stomach and I ignore the grief that thrums inside of me that I can't return his declaration of love with my own. "You mean you'll love me to the grave and back?"

He barks a laugh. "I will love you to the grave and back, again and again. Beyond darkness, beyond doubt, beyond death. From this life and into the next. As many times as it takes, I'll find you until our souls are but tired tatters left to the wind."

"That seems even longer than a trip around the moon," I say. The quip sticks there and I lean in. This man. How did we come to this point? My lips find his. Our mouths press together. Minty sweetness gives me a heady feeling of falling, of dizziness. I can't help but smile. The edge of his fang dips into my lip and I shiver.

I love you. Soon, I'll tell him. The words feel like they sit just under my throat. Waiting. Waiting until I kill the thing that haunts this man.

"Witch," he says, grinning. That damned eyebrow spikes upward.

"Wolf," I reply, mimicking his raised brow.

"I wonder at that. Without Ghost…" Killian shrugs. His smile disappears, leaving behind only a look that is as tender as it is serious. "I love you, Briar." He shifts down until he's kneeling. He pulls my hand toward him, that should have my ring on it. He looks at my naked finger, eyebrows crashing down.

I pull my hand away, digging into the pocket of my dress and pulling out the wedding ring. Killian glowers at me and I shrug. "You made me angry, so I took it off."

Killian snorts, shaking his head. "I should have come with you, but...I really didn't know if I could control Erebos for any amount of time without Ghost there. But I couldn't stay away from you. It hurts to be without you, after all these years of loving you from afar." Killian takes my now-ringed hand and places it against his heart. Beneath my palm, I feel the steady beat of the organ beneath his flesh. "I've loved you for longer than you can remember." He smiles when he says this, but I can see the little twist of bitterness at the corner of his mouth. "My heart has been yours before we met. I want to ask you now. Here. Will you marry me?"

"Killian..." I pause. "I know you say that I'm the one who doesn't remember, but you do realize we are already married, don't you?"

"Briar." He rolls his eyes. "Will you marry me–properly? Forever?"

Warmth leaks into my chest, burgeoning through my ribcage. My fingers tingle.

"Yes." Gods, yes, a thousand times, yes.

"Bedtime then, wife." The look in his eyes suggests he means more than going to sleep.

"We only have the night here." Unease drifts through me at the thought of staying in this place. Papa is healing, but unable to control the duchy as a whole right now. The last time we were here, it didn't go well. Not at all.

"It'll be enough. We'll post the guards, but Galinda and your father seem...different."

"They do," I say. Galinda still barely tolerates me, but hearing her care for my father feels...not like she's an ally. But something close enough not to kill us in our sleep. For now, anyway.

CHAPTER 77

*W*hen I wake, Killian's side of the bed is cold. I groan, wondering why the air freezes in front of my breath. The dying season is nearly over. Officially, the dead season will arrive and in its wake leave a thousand tombstones littered with snow.

I jolt up in the bed. The sheet falls off my naked chest. "Killian?" I call.

I'm so used to having Nisha around, but she's not here. Not that I forgive her for her betrayal, not yet, but it's a start. Finding her, Daria, Valor, and…maybe Barro. But he's most likely dead. But his spirit needs to be put to rest. After that…we'll look for our mothers. Both Killian and I.

Lukas was right. Every ending is also a beginning.

"Killian?" I call again.

No answer wheezes from the silence, no groaning call. No whispered endearment. No *'wicked witch'* to cause me to shiver.

No light is on.

Nothing.

My husband left me in the dark.

My heart pounds and I slip out of bed, pulling on the onyx silk of my robe that remains slipped against the back of the velvet cushioned chair. The robe's fabric pools in liquid smoothness across my skin and dapples the floor with each step. "Killian?" I call again.

Something cold clenches in my stomach. Dread.

I clutch my robe to my chest and walk to the door, cracking it.

The guard on the other side, Remmy, quirks a boyish smile.

"Have you come to flirt with your dear guard, mildly, while your husband prowls about?" Remmy asks, a brow jolting up.

"Remmy," I say, biting the inside of my lip uneasily. "Where's Killian?"

"He uh—" Remmy pauses, brow furrowing. The boyish look on his face goes distant. For a moment, his face is completely slack. "He said he—"

Silence drops between us. I wait. My breath catches in my lungs. No. Don't say it. Don't–

"I can't remember."

"You don't–" I cut myself off.

Remember.

Remember, remember, *remember.*

I fly back into the room. The door slams behind me, not latching and it wheezes on its hinges. Footsteps follow me. But I'm only distantly aware of them.

Heedless of anything else, I grab the dagger and slice my palm wide open. There's no time for more subtle offerings. Blood drips from the flesh, slipping onto the floor and I call up a light as bright as a miniature sun. It costs me, leaving my lungs dragging in deep breaths and never quite filling. "LIGHT!" I command, my voice rips through the silence. "LIGHT!"

I fling my hand up. The light bursts upwards, shining with white energy in the center of the room and droplets of blood patter into the ceiling.

That's when I see what's by the window.

A phantom stretches there, like a grotesque ghost. It hangs there, the wretched husk of my husband. Next to him is Lukas.

I leap to them.

"NO!" Remmy yells, bolting after me.

I launch myself toward Killian. It's like hitting a sack of bones. Killian's face blanches, husking and sucking like he's melting beneath my arm. Horror cascades through me. No, no, NO. The sound of shushing sand fills my ears as Killian simply *fades. NO.*

I don't realize I'm speaking out loud until Lukas says, *"Shhh."*

My gaze snaps up. He looks back at me, his expression unconcerned except for a faint twitch beneath his left eye. It flickers like an old rag left in the wind.

"WHAT DID YOU DO?" Hot betrayal winds its way through me, igniting beneath my ribs and ripping through my lungs. I gasp, a cry of rage riddling my throat. "HOW COULD YOU?"

"How could I?" he laughs. "How could *you?*"

Lukas steps away, expression smoothing over, but instead holds out something in his hand. A squirming raven. He presses it to my palm.

"You know nothing...*witch.*"

"Why?" The single word curls up from Killian. Lukas shifts a look to him, regret creasing his mouth.

"I'm sorry, Kill. But you must go back to your true father. And you would not have come any other way."

I flick on the Sight, in enough time to see a spittle of gold coins cascading from Lukas' mouth. The bird in my palm turns, silken leaves brushing and tickling. Its beady eyes stare right through me. The creature screeches.

"What did you do to Killian?"

"It's a phantom curse. A bit of body and spirit and you can take someone anywhere. It's painful, though." Lukas' voice drips with regret and silver lashes out from his tongue.

The bird in my palm squirms. The waxy texture of the raven slips against my skin as I grasp it, the feathers turn sharp. Then it burns. The creature screams as it ignites, feathers melt away to reveal the ivory skeleton beneath it. Ember-red, pieces of the bones burn a reddened hue to reveal two words in violent lettering.

HE'S MINE.

"Regards from the Witch King," Lukas says.

Ash falls to the ground and then the rest of my husband disintegrates at the edges of his body. I clutch at the rags of Killian's clothing as ash begins spilling out of the holes as his phantom-torso gives up. The dust slips through my fingers, the way time falls through an hourglass and nothing remains in my hands at all. A sob condenses in my throat, sticking there and part of me hopes it chokes me until I die.

Killian's face crumbles, slipping to ash and carried away by wind. A shining rock of moonstone, and the eye of a raven carved into it, falls out of the now-slack sleeve. A word hangs in the air, the taste of his voice more death rattle than breath.

"North."

On the rasp of wind, the ghost of him slips through.

"Do not yield," the ghost of his voice whispers. "Find me, love."

Something worse than devastation rips through me. The screams ricochet and the room crowds with the Wolves. My father's people will be coming, but I can't stop screaming. Remmy looks at me like I'm a ghost, like he doesn't know me at all. I can't say I blame him.

I look up at Lukas. Haloed by darkness in the window, the breeze from the curtain flutters around him. "Sorry, sweetling," he shrugs. "You're a fool though, wanting a shadow when you could have so much more." A mixture of tin and silver slips from his lips. Why, why? And How? How was he able to betray me? I remember the little bits of tin slipping from his mouth, all the tiny lies that were part of one big lie. Lukas has been working with the Witch King. "I'll take this."

He leans down and plucks Killian's wedding band from the ground just beneath the ledge.

"Why?" I rasp.

Lukas looks at me, a ghost of his good natured grin evident in the curl of his mouth. But it's something else. Bitterness, hurt, longing. A cocktail of a thousand feelings pass over his face. "Perhaps it is because I'm a terrible man." He muses. "But even you should understand doing what is necessary to save one's father. I've done nothing different than you have."

The call of a thousand birds echoes from just beyond the window and they swarm, covering Lukas. The once-good natured man teems with ravens as they latch onto him. They pull at his skin. It stretches, yanking. Lukas takes it silently as they tear apart his flesh.

And then there's nothing but air and a lonely breeze, as if Lukas never existed at all.

Arms wrap around me. Thick, corded muscles squeeze in comfort. Remmy. My rage, my grief, wraps around us both in return.

Killian, Killian.

Where has he been taken?

"Hi-his soul," I stutter, looking up at Remmy. "What did he do to his soul? His body?"

There's no need to define which *he* I mean. The Witch King has dogged our every step since before this even began. And Lukas. His secret weapon. Remmy swallows. "I don't understand this foul magic either, your Grace." He puts a subtle emphasis on this, but I swallow the shuddering grief pooling out of every pore.

I am the Duchess of Wolves. Duchess of Death.

I stand up, even though the effort feels like more than I can manage.

My ax is in the corner of the room. I pick it up, feeling only a little better with it in my hand. I cut my finger on the edge of it, gripping the wood. It hums underneath my touch as the scarlet soaks into the woods. Hungry. More. It's starving for blood.

And so am I.

I stand in the ashes of my husband's phantom-wraith. I grip the small bit of moonstone atop my wedding band, the little piece I have left of Killian. It feels cold, as if he's dead. But he can't be. He can't.

I'll find him. And then I'll bring the Witch King to his knees for what he's done. And Lukas. To him, I'll do something worse.

"This means war," I tell the Wolves.

The End.

. . .

The story will continue in...
LADY OF WOLVES AND WRATH.

LADY OF ROSES AND RUIN
PLAYLIST

- Soul Tie by Deore
- We Have It All by Pim Stones
- How Villains Are Made by Madalen Duke
- Empire by Neon
- I Will Follow You into the Dark by Death Cab for Cutie
- cinderella's dead by EMELINE
- Goodbye by Ramsey
- Bad by Royal Deluxe
- Far From Home (The Raven) by Sam Tinnesz
- Arsonist's Lullabye by Hozier
- Start a War by Clergy and Valerie Broussard
- Morally Gray by April Jai

ACKNOWLEDGMENTS

Every time I read a book, this is the part I flip to first. I love seeing what it takes to bring a novel into the world, because it is no easy feat. And truly, without the support of the people here, this book would not be what it is.

To my Street Team and Cover Coven, thank you. The following folks agreed to have their name acknowledged here, but truly there have been many more that have supported this project. To all that have lent a hand to Lady of Roses and Ruin—thank you each for your time, energy, and excitement. I'd like to honor, in no particular order, the following people: Diana Rosado, LiteratureLacey, Courtney M, Nina Harris, Jessalyn Flint, Breanne Rogge, Elisa Haggy, Hannah Norwood, Cristina Torres, Joanna Westmoreland, Shelbe H., Megan Morales, Elly Grimme, Caitlin Nelson, Chantel Van Dyk, Reagan Burnett, Hannah Campbell, Payton McDonald, Nashi, Devon Unruh, Montana Feighery, Jenn Quinn, Emily Blakeslee, Lynn Davies Brown, Addison Bradshaw, Casey Hayes, Crystal Bean House, Dreama Michele, Bay, Hannah, Heather Beal, V. M., Ayn McKellar, Nicole Ackman, Gabby Woodruff, R.M. Gray, Brooke Gillcrist, Maddie, Rachel Sockwell, Phyllica, Jordan Chatellier, Joanna Westmoreland, Katharina Cahill, Marianne Antonichuk, and Jeanette. Thank you to everyone—named and unnamed—who have supported *Lady of Roses and Ruin.*

For some folks that assisted with different parts of my book: thank you so much to Virginia, my Birdie, Mallory, Kristina, Lacey, and Logan. The insights you provided have been invaluable. Thank you for grabbing so many typos and adding commas.

Maya, thank you for leaning in when I needed you. You always do.

Nadine Flint, you are always there to hold my heart. Thank you for believing in me even when I didn't. I can't wait to meet you sometime (lol).

Ghabiba Weston. Ah, what to even say about you? This book would not exist without your friendship. Full stop. Thank you for seeing my soul and my voice. I think I'll say this here because I know how uncomfortable it will make you for everyone to read it: I love you so deeply and I can't believe I am so lucky to have met you. Thanks for being my word wife.

For my friends and family—thank you for putting up with me and letting me dream. Mom, don't look at the last part of the book. There's stuff in there you can't unread.

For Sweet P, thank you for sitting in my lap and knocking your butt into the computer. Sometimes, it's good to be told to take a break.

And for my life partner, my love. Thank you for dealing with all the dirty dishes, the laundry piling up, and my scattered brain. The amount of support you've given me is something I never could have imagined. I love you and choose you every day. Thank you for being weird with me. Thank you for believing in this and in us.

And for you, reader, thank you so much for taking the time to read Lady of Roses and Ruin. If you loved this book, please take a moment to review it. You're holding a piece of a big dream of mine in your hands, it means the world that you are part of this journey.

ABOUT THE AUTHOR

Courtney Shack is a lover of fantasy and romance. When she is not reading those genres, she's writing them. She lives in Richmond, Virginia with her partner and beloved dog. Courtney co-hosts a podcast, Storybeast, where she talks about her love of story and snacks. *Lady of Roses and Ruin* is her first novel. Follow her on socials to get updates on her next book or check out her website, www.court neyshack.com.

Made in United States
Troutdale, OR
10/31/2023

14185022R00289